Fierce Rivals

Jacqueline Bell

PublishAmerica
Baltimore

© 2006 by Jacqueline Bell.
All rights reserved. No part of this book may be reproduced, stored in a retrieval system or transmitted in any form or by any means without the prior written permission of the publishers, except by a reviewer who may quote brief passages in a review to be printed in a newspaper, magazine or journal.

First printing

All characters appearing in this work are fictitious. Any resemblance to real persons, living or dead, is purely coincidental.

ISBN: 1-4241-2899-4
PUBLISHED BY PUBLISHAMERICA, LLLP
www.publishamerica.com
Baltimore

Printed in the United States of America

*I'd like to dedicate this book to my father, Bruno Leclercq,
and to my husband, Andre Bell*

Chapter 1

It all started when Jane was five years old. She could still remember that evening so clearly. Her grandmother was due. She was coming down for the weekend, a rare treat that left her mother in a nervous flutter. Everything had to be perfect for her arrival. All the bed linen was carefully washed and ironed and new white fluffy towels, bought from John Lewis.

Jane could still remember how beside herself, her mother was trying to arrange exciting and interesting things that they could do together as a family. Things that would keep grandmother happy and entertained. My mother wanted my grandmother to enjoy her stay.

"How on earth do you entertain a sixty-year-old woman?" my mother questioned my father. She knew full well that no answer would be forthcoming. My father was still unsure of what all the fuss was about.

And then, after weeks of careful preparation, it came to her. They would go to the theatre. All older generations, she marvelled, loved the theatre. My mother pondered hard over this new idea, and the more she thought about it, the more she liked it. "She *will* like that, won't she?" my mother asked my father worriedly, eager for a second opinion and some reassurance.

My father, knowing, but not quite understanding, nodded in approval. "Yes, she would love that. Just love it. The theatre is a perfect evening out."

Content that she had finally managed to think of *something*, my mother turned back toward the kitchen and dinner.

"We'll have to arrange a babysitter for Joe," she stated, as she looked at me sitting quietly on the sofa, my doll nestled in my arm. "I think it's okay if Jane comes. She's old enough now." With that last sentence, she had blown me a kiss, and then returned back to the kitchen happily. I watched her go and then looked at my father. He was nodding in agreement, a smile on his lips.

Jane was so proud, as she was considered old enough to go with the adults. Poor Joe, he was only one year old, so did not know any different. She was five. A big girl. She went to big school and everything. She knew that the evening was going to be special, confirmed as soon as her mum took out one of her best dresses. She could still remember the little pink roses embroidered on the collar. She felt so grown up, all prettily dressed, with her dark hair held back neatly with a pink ribbon.

That was the evening that changed Jane's life. She was so excited. It was her first real theatre show. She did not know what to expect, but she was sure it would be grand. Both her parents and her grandmother were excited. They had been discussing it excitedly all day. She was only five, but even she could see that they were eager for the evening to approach. And finally, at long last, it did.

The heavy velvet curtain was drawn back and there stood the ballerina, perfectly still, in the middle of the stage. She was so pretty. Jane could still remember her gown. It was white and silver, and sparkled in the array of lights when she moved. It was the prettiest thing Jane had ever seen. And even now, that memory had remained with her.

The music began and slowly the ballerina started to move. First, only using one delicate arm. Then the other. Jane was enthralled. She seemed to flow like liquid. The movements all seemed to pour into one. She watched as the ballerina slowly raised her leg high up into the air. Higher and higher, until her toe was held perfectly erect, next to her small head. It was impossible to believe that anyone could kick so high and so perfectly neat. Jane was mesmerized by the tall beautiful lady in the white dress. "She's so beautiful," Jane mumbled to her grandmother, barely taking her eyes off the ballerina. Her grandmother nodded in agreement and patted her knee as she held onto a small, white lace handkerchief. Jane was sure she saw a small tear escape, but ignored it. A grownup crying? No, she must be mistaken.

The music changed, and soon the whole stage was a haze of colour. Jane watched all the dancers in the group in perfect sequence. They all seemed to move together as if they were one. Not one foot, not one arm out of place. Everyone moving together at exactly the same time. It was as if they were moving in front of a mirror. And in front of them all was the beautiful lady in white, a smile on her face as she danced in tune to the music.

The music seemed to get faster and faster, and soon the ballerina was spinning. Arms held gently at her sides. Perfectly neat and controlled. Around and around the stage she went, her dress making a perfect circle around her waist, glittering fiercely under the millions of twinkle lights.

And then dramatically, the music stopped and she fell gracefully to the floor. It was the saddest thing Jane had ever seen.

It was way past her bedtime, even she knew that. But coming home that evening, she remembered feeling not one bit tired. All she felt was excitement. Excitement at having discovered something new. It was like finding a lost treasure. One, she never knew she had in the first place. Later, when she was all dressed and ready for bed and everyone had given her a goodnight kiss, she lay under the covers, but sleep would not come. All she could think of was that ballerina. How beautifully she had danced to the soft music. And how everyone had clapped and blown her kisses at the end.

Unable to help herself, Jane jumped out of the covers and stood in front of her mirror. She moved her arm from side to side, hoping to achieve the same graceful look as those dancers, but it looked nothing like their delicate movements. How did they make it look so graceful and so easy?

Jane also remembered looking down her favourite "Winnie the Poo" pajamas that night, at her small feet hidden in her pink Barbie socks. Without a sound, she sat down on the floor and took off her socks. Then, once her feet were free, she wiggled her toes, smiling. She stood up and concentrated hard before trying to kick her leg into the air as she had seen the ballerina do with such perfect ease. It looked nothing like how the ballerina had kicked and not nearly as graceful. Concentrating even harder now, Jane tried again. This time she managed to keep her leg straight, but it still did not look anything like what she had seen performed that evening.

And that was when Jane decided, actually decided that one day she was going to be like that ballerina. On stage, beautiful and elegant.

Chapter 2

"Zara, point your toes!" her mum called sharply. Zara looked at her pink slippered feet, her toes pointing as hard as they could toward the opposite wall. "Zara, hold your hands up. Third position," her mother called again. Zara lifted her arms even higher above her head. "No, honey, not like that," her mother scolded as she left her seat and walked over. She bent elegantly before taking Zara's arms and positioned them in the correct position. "That's it. Yes. Now hold that position and bounce to the music." Zara continued to point then flex her toes, holding her arms in the correct position as her mother had just shown her, trying to count at the same time. It was too difficult she thought as she lost count again. There were just too many things to remember. Her mother must have noticed her falter and stopped counting herself. "Honey," she stressed, "listen to the music. Count! One, two, three! That's it, one, two, and three! Just keep counting."

Zara could not help noticing the clock above her mother's head. She had just started to learn how to tell the time. The big hand was on the three when she had first started, and now it was way past the four. That meant she had been practising for over an hour. It felt so much longer than that. She was tired. Her arms felt heavy and her feet were sore. Zara lost count again, her mind distracted by the little black stick on the clock. Tick, tick it went. Her mother looked on disapprovingly from the elegant silk couch she was sitting on. Zara tried counting again as her mother had shown her. One, Two, Three. One Two Three. Five minutes later, Zara was no longer counting to herself in her head. This is so boring, she thought to herself, as she bounced yet again, watching her mum, watch her.

She had only just turned five years old, and already she knew that her mother was the most elegant lady she knew. She looked like a queen sitting there elegantly dressed in her cream brocade trouser suit, not a hair out of place, her natural blond curls sitting perfectly on-top of her head. The pearls on her neck gleamed brightly in the sunlight. Zara knew they were expensive. Father had bought them for her on her last birthday. It had been a wonderful surprise and Zara remembered how happy they had made her mum.

"Zara, you're losing count again," her mum tutted, shaking her head, annoyed, as the blond curls swung elegantly from side to side.

Zara stopped bouncing. Her arms were tired, so she let them drop to the floor. Her toes were so sore from pointing, they felt stiff into position. If she continued to point as hard as she had been, her toes were bound to fall right off... "Mum, I'm tired," Zara offered in way of an explanation, as the music continued to play on in the background.

Her mum did not move. Did not even smile. All she had now was a dark, frosty look. The silence between them was thick. Eventually, she spoke. "Zara, do you not you want to be a beautiful and graceful dancer?" her mum asked incredibly. "Don't you want to be like that lovely ballerina in the show we watched last week?"

Her mum's voice sounded gentle to anyone that might be listening, but Zara was not fooled. She knew that tone. Her mother was angry, very, very angry, but trying not to let it show to anyone who might be in hearing distance. Her mum never shouted, but Zara always knew when she was cross. And she was cross now. Zara looked at her feet, guiltily. She felt her cheeks blush red. She hated getting scolded. "Yes," she answered softly.

"Well then, you have to practice. And one day you'll be a beautiful and talented dancer. And all this will be worth it. But that does not happen on its own. No!" she stated emphatically. "You must practice." Zara had no choice but to nod in agreement.

Zara was angry. This was all Sally's fault. Sally's mother was so proud that her Sally was taking ballet lessons, and now because of her she had to take ballet lessons too. Not only ballet! Oh no! Her mother had to go one better than everyone else. Her mother had enrolled her in three *different* kinds of dance. She had been forced to take tap and modern dance classes too. Zara could have screamed. Now after school from Monday through to Wednesday, she did some variety of dancing class, and then on a Thursday, she had swimming trials, and lastly, on Friday, she had gymnastics. She had only just started this dancing, but already she hated it. Especially when her mother insisted she practice every waking moment.

And here she was now, on a Saturday, and while all the other girls were out playing in the park, enjoying themselves, she was here inside, practising under her mother's watchful eye. She was thoroughly bored and wished she too, could go outside and play with the others.

"Okay, now start again," her mother encouraged. "Remember to count. One, two three…"

Zara promised herself she would try harder. She *would* concentrate. She began to count again in her head as she bounced. Somehow, the clock was again calling for her attention, and before long she was concentrating on the little black tick again. Slowly, she began to watch the hours fade away.

Lost in thought, it did not take long before Zara had lost count again. Her mothers crisp, clear voice broke sharply through into her day dreaming. "Zara! What is the matter with you?" she asked, exasperated. "You're not going out to play until you get this right. Your class is on Monday and you must, absolutely must, have this right by then. I refuse to have you unprepared and embarrass me."

With a sigh, Zara began her counting again. There was no chance she would be able to play with the others now. She would be stuck inside with her mother for some time yet.

Chapter 3

When Jane's mum walked into the kitchen, she was standing at the kitchen bench, poised in position, ready to do yet another plié. She knew she must look a sight. She could feel her hair falling out in great wisps from the bun on her head, made so perfectly earlier that morning and her face felt red and hot from hours of practising. She was beginning to get tired and her feet were beginning to ache from all the pointing and swivelling. Her dancing exam was in less that two weeks and she were spending very spare minute practising the sequence of steps required. Each movement *had* to be technically correct. There was no room for errors. Not if she wanted to do well. And to Jane, that was the most important thing of all. She wanted to do better than well. She wanted to be the best.

The exams were held once a year. And each year Jane found herself practising, sometimes until late into the evenings. She did not mean to, but she would completely lose track of time and only when she began to feel stiff or hungry would she look at her watch. Hours would have passed. But, she knew her hours of hard work would eventually pay off. She would always receive the Second Highest mark possible. "Honours." Only about five percent of the girls actually managed to get that achievement. And along with the "Honours" title came a small gold trophy. But this year was different. Jane did not want the second highest mark possible, she wanted the highest. It was a difficult barrier to break. Only the very, very best received "Honours with Distinction." No one at their dance studio had *ever* achieved it. And along with that prized gold certificate, came the prize that Jane wanted the most. That was when you received the largest of the trophies. The golden cup.

There were very few dancers that actually had this cup in the whole province. The only person that she did know that had that specific trophy, was Mrs. Stone, her dancing teacher. It was proudly displayed in the glass cabinet at the studio along with all her certificates and numerous qualifications. Jane often admired it when she went to the studio, and wished that she had it too. Now, with the exams looming closer, she hoped she could finally add that trophy to her collection.

Jane liked using the kitchen counter as a makeshift bar. It was exactly the right height and offered more space than her bedroom. Doing her last few pliés, she bent her legs again, taking note that her knees were in the correct angle and her feet positioned correctly.

Her mum walked in then and flipped on the kettle, used to seeing her daughter dancing at the kitchen bench, while Jane continued with her last few bends. Happy that she was doing it correctly, Jane straightened up and kicked her legs loosely. She could feel her tense muscles begin to loosen as she did so. She had to be careful. The last thing she needed was to hurt herself or to start feeling stiff. The exam was too close for anything like that to happen.

"So," her mum asked, "how is it going with the practising?" She asked the question while pouring milk into her tea.

"Good," Jane answered, as she sat at the kitchen table and slowly took off her dancing shoes. Rubbing her feet gently, she noticed they were red and swollen again. She had hoped that by wearing thick plasters it would help, but they had little effect with the constant rubbing and friction. She had long ago decided that if she wanted to be a serious dancer, she would never have nice feet. They would always be scarred, red and full of blisters, but in her books, it was a small price to pay.

Her mother knew what she was like when her exams approached. She could think of nothing else. Sometimes, she had to be reminded even to eat. She was completely obsessed with achieving, being the best that she could be. From that very first dance show she had been taken to, she knew it was all she ever wanted to do.

"You'll be fine," her mum answered back. "You've been practising for hours and hours each day. All that practising will count when the time comes. Don't worry so much."

Jane nodded, she knew her mother was right, that sometimes she got carried away with it all. She knew it and acknowledged it, but there was just nothing she could do about it. "I know," she replied, "but this year it's different."

Her mother raised her eyebrow. "Different? How so? What's different about this year compared to all the other previous years?"

Jane replied immediately. "This year I'm after the cup," she stated without presumption.

Her mother let the words sink in. Then stopped and turned, slowly. "*The* cup?" Jane nodded. Her mum sighed, knowing and understanding, "Honey, just do your best, okay? You *will* get that cup eventually."

Jane could not help laughing. Her mum always had a way of making her see things in the right light. If there was anyone whom she could confide in, it would be her mum. Filling up a glass with water, she made her way up the stairs to her bedroom. Once again she found herself in front of the mirror.

Sometimes, when she was not dancing, her long dark hair was brushed loosely around her face, giving her brown eyes a dark, mysterious look. Her skin was a light olive colour, making her completion a complete contrast to her friend Sarah. Whereas Sarah went bright red in the sun, Jane seemed to soak in the rays and develop a deep, golden tan. But all that was when she was not busy dancing, which was always. Right now, she looked anything like she had just described. Instead, her long brown hair was held in a not so neat bun on her head, her hair looked greasy and dishevelled and her face seemed red and blotchy. Still, she could not help smiling to herself. Yes, she looked a sight, and, yes, her feet were aching, but this was what she enjoyed the most. She would not trade it for the world.

* * * * *

Zara headed for her red sports car, unlocking the boot quickly before placing her designer bags inside. She'd bought some great stuff, she thought, as she dismissed all the admiring glances thrown her way. For any who saw Zara, it was hard not to admire her elegant looks. Long blond hair and striking blue eyes were hard to miss and people found themselves stopping to stare. That, coupled with her parents' wealth, made it hard for any girl not to wish they were Zara. Everyone wanted to be her. Beautiful and elegant with a string of boys tripping over themselves waiting to take her out and with parents that gave her anything her heart desired. It was every girl's ultimate dream.

Her phone rang. Zara reached for her small designer bag, whipping out the silver mobile. "Hello," she purred sweetly into the phone.

She listened for a few minutes, rolling her eyes, before answering. "No I cannot do it now," she answered, aggravated, before flipping the phone shut. Zara threw a quick irritated glance at the thin, gold watch on her wrist. She had exactly half

an hour. Switching on the engine, she hurriedly left the car park and headed toward home. She was only dimly aware that she was speeding as she approached the entrance to her house.

Zara barely glanced up as she approached the elegant wrought iron gates that led to their home. Whereas most people would be impressed with the drive up toward the beautiful, triple story architectural feat, Zara barely noticed the perfectly manicured lawns and large water features carefully designed with such expert precision.

Pulling up abruptly at the entrance of the house, Zara quickly retrieved her designer bags and let herself into the white marble hallway. Dropping her bags carelessly in the corner, she ran hurriedly up the stairs toward her bedroom.

It took her less that ten minutes to change into her black leotard and tights. Sauntering over to her mirror, she brushed her long blond hair hurriedly before tying it neatly into an elegant bun. She quickly added a dash of glitter gel to ensure it all stayed in place. That and a quick dab of lip gloss and she was ready. Zara grabbed her tog bag from the corner of her large room, realizing that she was running out of time. Where were her dance pumps? She threw another quick glance at her watch. She had to get going. She was going to be late for her dance exam. Help. She needed help.

"Rose," Zara yelled at the top of her voice. "Roseeeee." Rose appeared as if by magic at the entrance of Zara's bedroom.

"Yes, miss, you called?" Rose asked in her customary polite tone. Zara threw Rose an irritated look. The maid had been with their household for over ten years, and although her mother felt that she was part of the family, Zara just could not accept it. She was there to help with the housework, and that was it. She was not a member of their family, just an extremely overpaid servant.

"Where are my dance pumps?" she demanded, while looking under her bed, throwing out whatever was in the way, leaving a large dishevelled pile of designer clothes on the floor beside her.

"Miss, I think I last saw them in the cupboard. At the end," Rose replied, as she swept past Zara, still sprawled out on the floor, searching in vain. One quick look inside the wardrobes that ran the full length of the bedroom, and Rose produced the leather pumps. Without even a thank you, Zara grabbed the shoes and ran out the room, taking the stairs two at a time. She jumped into her car and made for the studio as fast as could.

She was hardly surprised when she arrived at the studio to see all the other dancers frantically practising. She struggled to contain her self-satisfied smirk. *She* did not have to do that! Practising was only for those with no talent, and luckily for her, she had bundles of it.

Parking the car, she aimed straight for inside the studio where she headed directly for Mrs. Noel.

"Zara, where have you been?" Mrs. Noel scolded lightly. "You're late. We've had to send in another group ahead of you." Zara knew her dance instructor was irritated, but it really did not matter. She ignored the question and stood still as she waited for her number to be pinned onto her back. She was number three. Probably because she was the tallest.

She knew they would wait for her. She just knew it. Since the other group had only just entered, Zara joined some of the other girls in stretching. She knew she would have to warm up so as to avoid any sort of injury. She was not stupid. Her muscles had to be stretched. Especially before a good workout. As she kicked her legs back and forth, warming her muscles, Zara took in the other dancers. She knew that some of them had been there for hours. Hours and hours, practising the same steps. They did it every year without fail. It never changed. She could not quite understand it herself. She supposed she was lucky. She had talent and she used it to its fullest degree. But hours and hours of practising the same silly steps was really not for her. Exam or not. Zara could not contain the sniggering smile that seemed to take over her pretty face. There was no way she would spend that kind of time practising for something that she knew she would do well in anyway. She knew that she could not fail. Daddy was too important to upset.

*****

The remaining two weeks came around too quickly, and before Jane knew it, it was time for her dancing exam. She knew she was prepared and completely ready after all the practising she had done, but still she could not help feeling a little nervous. Sarah had been around a few times in the evening, and together they had practised for hours. Sarah was just as dedicated as Jane, and together they had rehearsed the steps over and over again. Sarah was different to most dancers. Whereas almost every dancer she knew was small and had a petite build, Sarah was the exact opposite. She was tall, with long legs. She was slim, and together with her short blond bob, Sarah was striking, being in complete contrast to everyone else she knew. You would think that someone of her height would struggle to achieve suppleness and grace, but Sarah had mastered the art and did the movements with graceful ease. Together with her height, she seemed to bend like an elastic. Sarah had just as strong ambition as Jane to be a successful dancer, so the two had developed a close friendship from a early age.

Jane's thoughts about her friend were interrupted as she arrived at the dancing studio. The place was a hive of activity. Girls were even practising in the car park in small little groups. Jane grabbed her tog bag while taking in the sights around her and hopped out the car. This was it. In less than an hour she would be in the exam room.

"Good luck, honey," mum called from the driver's seat.

Jane smiled and waved, aware that the time had finally come. She could feel the tension as soon as she stepped inside the hall. It was no wonder that some of the other girls had chosen to practice outside. It kept them away from the nervous atmosphere and buzzing excitement clearly evident inside. The halls were packed with dancers in various stages of rehearsal and warm up, and one could clearly hear the music playing in the exam room. Jane found a spot for her tog bag, and noted Sarah, who was already warming up, in the corner. Squeezing into the small space her friend had managed to reserve for her, Jane joined the group in their warm up exercises, using the beat of the exam music as her tempo. She had just settled into her place on the floor when the music from inside stopped suddenly and there was a hushed silence. Then, suddenly, all the dancers outside scrambled eagerly for the big double door that had been covered up with thick brown paper. It was the same kind of brown paper that was used every year. A simple method that was very effective in keeping out any prying eyes during the individual exams. It was a method that worked. And worked well. No matter how hard they tried to peek through the glass, there was no seeing through that brown paper. Instead, with their view completely blocked, the girls did the next best thing. They would try and hear what was going on. They would press their ears against the door and strain their ears to hear what the examiner was saying. It made no difference that all that could be heard were dull mumbles. Occasionally, someone would be lucky enough to hear something of value from inside. It was very seldom that they would share the newfound, golden secret since it was their new secret weapon.

 The music was soon back on, and everyone knew the second part of the exam had begun. All the dancers dispersed from the heavily blocked door; they knew they had no chance of hearing anything now. Instead, they went back to their last minute warming up, desperate to keep their muscles as supple as possible.

 It was almost Jane's turn. She was due to go in with Sarah and Mira. All three of them were stretched out in a line together, doing last minute stretches before they were due to be called in. They all wanted their muscles as loose and relaxed as possible. It would mean less chance of obtaining an unwanted injury, and warm muscles meant that they were more supple. Jane felt both warm and loose. A good sign. There was not going to be any problem with her dancing her best.

The music stopped inside the hall for a second time, and again all the dancers scrambled toward the door. There was some mumbles, then absolute silence. And then, quite suddenly, the door was pushed open and three girls walked out, all hot and breathless. All identical in their black leotards and black tights, hair gelled neatly back.

Each dancer took great care in their appearance now, especially after the last incident. One of the girls had actually been thrown out of the exam room, as she had not adhered to the strict uniform. They were a great uproar by the girls parents, but there was nothing that could be done. She had to repeat her exam, but was only allowed to do so the following year. Jane shook her head. A whole year—wasted. She did not have time to dwell on past events as she noticed the three girls that had just made their exit. They were immediately bombarded with the same questions that were fired every year.

"How did it go?"

"What was the examiner like?"

The room was buzzing with excitement and questions were being fired from all corners of the room.

"Did she appear strict, or did she smile while you danced?" Everyone stopped at this question. And waited. It had been decided long ago that this was a very important question. Examiners who smiled, tended to give better results. Those that did not, well, they tended to be selfish with their grades. Everyone was keen for any answers and tit bits that could be used for their own exam. It was considered that any information, regardless of how small, could be used to one's advantage.

A little lady with a small gray bun on her head walked past pushing a tea trolley laden with small dainty cakes and sugary biscuits. She opened the door to the exam room, shutting it firmly behind her. As she did so, she was aware of all the keen eyes looking past her into the exam room. Jane could just see the exam table, but not much else before the door was abruptly closed. The examiner had a short fifteen-minute tea break, and then Sara, Mira and Jane were due to be called inside.

Jane stood up from her stretched out position on the floor, and holding the makeshift bar, began to practice her kicks. First kicking to the front, then to the side and then backwards. She repeated the process on each side a few times, willing her legs to relax. If she stopped moving, she could actually feel them shaking. Her stomach began to get all fluttery and she could feel her nerves begin to increase as the time to go inside drew closer and closer.

The little tea lady was back from inside the exam room. She was not gone for very long, which was strange. Tea was finished in less time than the allocated fifteen minutes. The tea lady stepped through the door again, shutting it firmly behind her. She was adamant that no one should be allowed to see anything from inside. Jane's stomach seemed to become alight with butterflies. She tried to ignore them, but they would not go away. At about the same time as the butterflies arrived, the waiting girls noticed that the cakes and biscuits had not been touched. They grabbed the tea lady, concerned.

"Did she not enjoy them?" one girl asked worriedly.

"Was she in a bad temper? Why had she not enjoyed her tea break?"

The tea lady smiled and moved on without answering any of their questions. She was not here to answer anything. The room was buzzing again as each dancer assessed what this meant. She had not eaten the cakes, and to them this was a sign. A bad sign.

"Jane, Mira, Sarah. You three are up next," called Mrs. Stone.

Taking a deep breath, Jane slowly slid out of her black sweat pants and sweat top, careful not to mess the tube of gel holding her hair in place. Mrs. Stone pinned a number to each of their backs. Jane saw she was number two. The little bell rang from inside. It could only have been a small jingle, but somehow the sound seemed to vibrate right through into Jane's eardrums. It was time.

And there she was—running as she had been taught, into the exam room, each girl taking their appropriate place, ready to begin.

As taught in their practices each week, each girl took their position, forming a neat line. Jane knew she was number two, so she took the position in the middle. After a quick dainty curtsey, as was customary, they were ready to begin.

Jane smiled at the examiner. She did not smile back. That was not a good start. The room was silent. They waited. Time seemed to tick by slowly. There was no sounds except for the examiner, who was sitting stiffly at her desk shuffling papers. She seemed stern, her glasses propped high on her nose. Jane dared not breathe. The butterflies were fluttering with a vengeance and her stomach felt like a tight knot. She tried to concentrate on relaxing, but it was no use. The butterflies would not go away and she knew that her legs were shaking badly. She hoped the examiner would not notice. It would be most embarrassing.

And then the examiner nodded to the music lady sitting quietly in the corner, and the familiar music they had spent hours practising to began to play. Immediately Jane's legs began to move as if on their own. They seemed to know what to do without her even having to think. She could feel the butterflies begin to disappear, and then all she could think of was the movement she was doing. She seemed to get a jolt of energy from somewhere and could feel her limbs take over. The adrenaline set in, and gone were the nerves. It was a strange feeling. She could feel the adrenaline pumping, pumping fast. With a high kick to the left, each girl crossed their legs neatly to the side. Then, tucking their leg behind them and bending slightly forward, they positioned themselves onto the floor.

The floor sequence began easily, in one fluid motion. Jane concentrated hard, pointing her feet, and stretching her back and neck until she felt like they were going to break. She wanted so desperately to take a peek upward and look at the examiners face. *Was she looking?* Jane thought to herself. But she dared not look. She had to keep her head bent and her movements flowing, just as they had been taught. Any variation from the line and the examiner was bound to notice.

With another kick of adrenaline Jane continued the sequence. Then it was time to slide into the splits. Jane remembered that it had never felt so easy before. Normally, one could feel the muscles tugging gently, but this time she felt nothing. It felt so much easier than usual. Jane could only put it down to the adrenaline that still seemed to be pumping through her veins. And then the music came to a slow ending.

Rising, all the girls stood and waited for a second time. The examiner was back to her shuffling and again she was scribbling fiercely, taking notes on each dancer. They waited in silence. Sarah stole a quick peek at Jane, while the examiner continued to write with what seemed like a vengeance. Jane knew by the look on her face what her friend was trying to ask. Her eyes seemed to ask the question for her, "How did it go?" Jane gave a quick nod. The small movement her answer. "Yes, it had gone okay. Better than okay." She almost wanted to smile, but it was not over yet.

The examiner looked up from her writing. Her face still stern. "Okay, and now for the bar. Ladies, please take your positions." As Jane placed her hand on the bar, she noticed how cold the metal felt. Her hands had begun to sweat, and she hoped that would not be a problem. The last thing she needed was to grab hold on the bar and lose her grip. She made a mental note to take care when turning.

All three girls waited silently, and Jane was pleased to notice that the butterflies had totally disappeared. The music began again. Slowly, in time to the music, they each pointed their feet as they had rehearsed. First to the front, then to the side, and then behind. Then came the kicks. In the same sequence. She remembered her toes, and willed them to point harder. As they had rehearsed so many times, they all placed their slippered feet onto the bar, and holding themselves for support, they each arched their backs in a slow curve. Jane remembered going back. Far, far back. As far back as she had ever been before. Somehow she could feel herself dancing better, better than she had ever danced in an exam. And then she was back to facing the bar, ready to repeat the whole sequence on the second side. It was time to swivel and turn. With her hands held on the bar, aware of her sweaty palms, Jane swivelled, using her body weight as her centre. And then it happened! She could remember it so clearly. As she swivelled, she saw Mira. She seemed to hesitate for a split second, and then she lost her balance. Suddenly, she was clutching onto the bar for support. Her arms and legs everywhere. Gone were the dainty, coordinated movements. Mira seemed unable to comprehend what had happened and just hung there, half-groping and half-supporting herself on the bar. Not moving, just hanging in limbo. Jane's immediate reaction was to rush over and help her friend. Then she remembered the golden rule, as if Mrs. Stone was right there in the room with her, repeating the words she so often used. "Never stop," she was saying, "Always stick to the sequence and complete the movements. No matter what happens. Never, ever stop!" Jane concentrated hard on sticking to the routine. But it was difficult. She found herself repeating the steps to herself in her head, as she willed Mira to move. She still had not registered what had happened, and was still clutching the bar awkwardly. Jane tried not to look, and closed her eyes. "Point left. Point right," she repeated to herself. She knew she had to mentally talk herself through the steps, knowing that if she did not, she too, would lose her place and also be lost. Mira finally seemed to recover and with an effort, found her feet and stood up. She bobbed her head to the music twice and then she was moving with them, in time to the music. It was as if the whole incident had never taken place. Jane breathed a sigh of relief and continued with her steps, the loud beating in her chest still strong. And then, as they did their last plié, Jane saw the tiny tear drop hit the shiny wooden floor in a dull splash.

She knew there was nothing she could do for Mira, but she also knew how she must be feeling. Her chances of getting the highest markets had been dreadfully knocked out of her hand. Jane knew she must have been feeling awful. One small slip and her entire grade for that year had been ruined.

The examiner had not uttered a single word throughout the entire incident. She would have seen Mira. It would have been hard not to since her arms and legs were thrown out of sequence as she had grabbed wildly for the bar. Normally, any sympathetic examiner would stop the music and allow the group to begin again. Not this examiner. Instead, she let the music run and chose to ignore what had occurred. Jane was not sure if this was a good or bad thing. What had just happened was any dancer's worst nightmare!

Chapter 4

The examiner showed no emotion or sympathy over what had occurred. Instead, she busied herself by writing furiously on her sheets once again. She did not look up once, with concern for Mira.

Jane was unable to remain still herself. She was worried about Mira. She threw a quick glance in Mira's direction concerned, relatively sure that the examiner would not look up and mark her down.

Mira was holding up well after her accident, but she seemed to be in a great deal of pain and was leaning ever so slightly onto her left leg. It was barely noticeable, but Jane noticed it. The examiner's voice threw Jane back into the present and she had to force herself to concentrate on what was being said.

"And now ladies, I am going to play you a piece of music. You may listen to it once, and once only. You must then create a dance, whatever movements you choose to this piece. Understood?" she asked them. All three girls nodded.

The music the examiner chose to play was at first slow and rhythmic. Then the beat seemed to get faster before dying down. After the initial introduction, the music continued in a gentle, steady rhythm. Jane closed her eyes and remembered seeing green fields in her head. And big puffy white clouds. The music made her feel like she was floating. Floating high up into the air. And then the music changed once again, dramatically, with a loud bang of drums. It lasted a few seconds before ending completely. It was over.

Sarah was chosen to go first. She took her place on the dance floor. The music began to play and Sarah began to move almost immediately. She started with her arms high in the air, and slowly they began to move in a slow circle in time to the rhythmic beat. And then as the music went faster, she flew in the air, her long legs carrying her like the wind, before she landed softly onto the floor. From then, the dance she was creating seemed to take a new turn, as she slowly rolled herself onto the floor. She rolled and pointed her feet, until the music changed once again into the loud banging of drums. She was then up onto her feet, moving in time to the loud bangs. The music stopped dramatically as before, and Sarah held her position.

Jane almost wanted to clap out loud. Sarah had done an excellent job at creating a beautiful dance. Sarah smiled, out of breath, as she joined her and Mira in the corner of the room. Just as Sarah reached them, the examiner called her own name. She was up next. Jane was once again aware of the loud thudding of her heart.

Jane took a deep breath and then took her position. She had decided to keep her right foot pointed to the side, bent over in a dramatic twist, her arms wrapped around herself. As the music began, she concentrated on slowly unwinding, using her arms and then her feet. She felt the rhythm and moved perfectly in time to the slow beat. As the music seemed to get faster, she left her position and began to dance around the room, using her arms and her legs to create a dramatic contrast. She remembered doing a quick controlled pirouette, and then she was sweeping into the air, her legs elegantly finding themselves into a split, held perfectly in mid air, before landing dramatically, just as the music seemed to end again with the thunderous drums. It was over. She held her end position for a few seconds. It was only once the examiner looked down and began to scribble on her notes that Jane realized she was holding her breath. Taking great gulps of air, she concentrated on breathing deeply. She willed her breath to come back normally instead of the uneven, ragged gasps she was taking. Jane hoped that the examiner was too busy scribbling her notes to notice her rather unladylike gasps for air.

Having returned back to the group, it was then Mira's turn. She walked with her head high and took her position in the far-left corner, her back held proudly against the wall. The music began almost immediately and she let her body flow with the steady rhythm. Remaining in the one spot, she danced using her arms, making use of a variety of movements. And then, as the music changed tempo, she let herself go as she sprang into a small, perfectly neat jump. As she landed, you could literally see the twist of pain that marred her pretty face. Jane knew in that instant that the accident from earlier was much more serious than any of them had originally thought. Her foot injury was affecting her exam, and even the simplest movement was now affecting her dance performance. She was struggling. Not only to perform, but now also with the simple task of just holding her balance. Mira recovered quickly under the circumstances. After the initial shock and pain that had gripped her once she landed, she continued as best she could, refusing to give up. She continued to use her body and her arms, moving elegantly. Only to the trained eye was it noticeable that she was using her right foot very little. And the examiner *was* a trained eye. Only when it became absolutely necessary did she use her feet in the sequence she was dancing. Jane recognized that she was preparing for a turn. Mira stepped and swivelled, using her arms once again held neatly above her head, her fingers held in preparation. As she swivelled, she almost fell from the pain, her foot unable to hold the weight from her body. Her face, once again, seemed to twist into a painful expression. Still, she refused to stop. She continued with a forced smile on her lips, her head held up high and continued.

Jane could not help notice the look of pain on Mira's face. She could see right through that watery smile. Behind it was a thinly veiled look of agony that seemed to deepen with each painful step she took. She was hanging on by a thin thread. By the time the music came to the dramatic holt, Mira was barely holding herself upright. Sweat was dripping down her forehead profusely. Her face was as white as a sheet and it looked like she was about to faint.

Chapter 5

As they stepped outside the exam room, they were immediately bombarded with the customary questions from the remaining girls who were all still nervously waiting for their own turns. Their questions were being fired from all four directions. Each girl left was anxiously waiting and ready to soak up any information that they would offer to them.

Normally, relief would flood over Jane as soon as she stepped outside the brown-papered exam door. The exam was over and she had done her best. Today, however, her concerns were focussed on Mira. Until now, she had been forced to ignore her friend's plight, but now that they were outside the exam room there was nothing stopping her from helping her friend. Jane had to admire Mira, for she had put on a good show, refusing to stop, continuing until the bitter end. Jane ignored the swarm of girls buzzing around them, relentless in their quest for information and question firing. Her main concern was Mira, hobbling pathetically. Now that they had left the confines of the exam room, Mira was finally coming to terms that she had injured her foot. And injured it seriously. No longer holding a pretense, she leaned heavily against the closest wall available, all her weight held on her other, uninjured leg. She closed her eyes, as if trying to shut out the pain. She was afraid to exert any kind of pressure. The pain had increased, and was getting too intense for her to bear.

"Mira, are you okay?" Jane asked, concerned, taking her friend's waist and helping her to balance, as she maneuvered her to the only couch in the room. As she did so, Mira let the full force of her weight ease onto Jane. Jane was taken aback at how little pressure Mira was now able to exert on her injured foot. Mira still had not spoken a single word. Jane sensed that she was unable to, all her attention focussed on the excruciating pain hammering her foot. The tears she had been holding back were flowing freely down her red cheeks as she relied heavily on Jane to assist her onto the couch. Jane knew the tears was partly due to the throbbing pain she must be feeling, but also knew that the main reason had nothing to do with the soreness. Mira was as dedicated as the rest of them; she would be devastated that her exam had been ruined. Her hopes of receiving a high score had been ripped out of her grasp.

"Mrs. Stone! Mrs. Stone!" Sarah shouted above the buzzing conversation from the other girls who were swarming around them. Some were still after information, but others were genuinely concerned for Mira.

Mrs. Stone had only been a few feet away when she heard her name being called. She looked up, wondering who on earth could be making such a racket. She only had to look at Mira and was quickly able to sum up the situation. She was an experienced teacher, and she had seen this kind of accident before. It was awful, but not uncommon.

Mrs. Stone *was* deeply worried when she managed to get a look a closer look at Mira' ankle. She knew as soon as she had seen Mira's slippered foot that the verdict would not be good.

She had not even removed Mira's dance slipper yet and already she could see the red bruising. It seemed to travel from under her dance slipper, right to the top of her ankle. In some places she could already see the dark red swelling beginning to turn blue. It was still light, and barely noticeable now, but she knew that it would be almost black by the time the evening was out.

Mrs. Stone knew that she had to get a proper look at Mira's foot and weigh up the seriousness of the injury. She knew it was bad, but just how bad? To view her injured foot, she would have to remove the dancing shoe. Looking at Mira's face, screwed up in agony and glistening with tears, she knew that was going to be a difficult and painful task.

"Mira," Mrs. Stone said in sympathetic tone, "I need to take a proper look at your ankle." Mira merely nodded meekly. "Okay, honey," she coaxed, gently taking Mira's foot in her hand. "It's going to hurt a little," she added softly. Mira nodded again while clutching a white tissue that one of the girls had bought her from the bathroom. Mrs. Stone slowly unravelled the elastic that kept the shoe in place, and as gently as she possibly could began to remove the shoe.

Mira was unable to stop the wince of pain that escaped her lips. Mrs. Stone continued. She knew it was painful for Mira, but the quicker she released her foot, the better. As the shoe came away, Mira's foot was left visible for everyone to see. It was then that Jane winced visibly. Mira's entire foot, from her toes right up to her ankle was very much swollen and bruised. Her whole ankle must have twisted as she grabbed for the bar trying to prevent herself from falling. And, as Mrs. Stone had accurately guessed, some places were already changing into the dark blue-black colour. Mrs. Stone knew that the pain Mira must be feeling would be acute. The throbbing would be intense and she knew that by now, Mira would also have developed a dull, aching headache. She went and retrieved her first aid box and took out two aspirin, which she coaxed Mira into taking. Then, she took out a tube of repair gel. It was all she could do as a teacher. It was not much, but at least it would help to ease the swelling, and the cool feel of the gel would help the painful throbbing that Mira was bound to be feeling.

Both Sara and Jane watched as Mrs. Stone applied the gel with great care, gently rubbing the ointment into Mira's foot. With each gentle rub, Mira's face screwed up with pain. It was horrible to watch.

Mrs. Stone was quiet throughout the application of the gel. Only when she was finished with the ointment and had began to wrap Mira's ankle with soft white bandages did she speak again. "This injury is not going to heal for at least a few weeks," she said softly. "I'll call your mother to come and fetch you. I think you now need to go straight to bed and maybe take another aspirin or two later tonight. It will help you sleep."

Jane and Sarah sat with Mira until her mother arrived ten minutes later. She came in with a fluster, worried and uncertain what had happened to her daughter. She saw Mira immediately and rushed over, hugging her tightly. Mira's tears started all over again as soon as she found herself in the comforting arms of her mother. Only when her mother was satisfied that her daughter was okay, did she stand. She was eager to have a chat with Mrs. Stone about what had happened.

Mira seemed to be as comfortable as she possibly could be under the circumstances. Her foot was propped up on a chair, and as they watched, it seemed to take on three new colours right before their eyes. First red, then blue and then as time passed, it began to develop into a dark black. Her foot looked terribly painful and sore, doubling in size before their very eyes. Mrs. Stone had done an excellent job with the bandages, but you could still see the colours deepen and change where the bandage had not managed to cover all her skin. Mira still did not speak. Instead, she lay with her head against the pillow that someone had passed to her and closed her eyes. She looked drained.

A little later, both Mira's mum and Mrs. Stone re-appeared, ready to assist Mira to the waiting car. After her chat with Mrs.

Stone, Mira's mum was eager to get her daughter home. It took all four of them working together to get Mira safely into the vehicle. The studio parking was not far away, but with Mira's foot so badly injured, it seemed like miles. The only thing to be done was for Mira to lean heavily onto Jane and Sarah's shoulders so that they took most of her weight. Jane knew her friend did not weigh very much, but was amazed at how heavy she felt. It was slow progress to the car, with little whimpers from Mira, spurring them on.

By the time they reached the vehicle, Jane was breathing hard from the exertion. It was a great relief when Mira was finally settled into the back seat, her foot stretched out in front of her once again.

"Thanks you, guys," Mira said through watery eyes. It was the first time she had spoken since her fall.

Jane bent down and gave her friend a hug, glad that her mum had arrived to take proper care of her. "No problem. You just get better now. We'll see you soon."

Mira attempted to smile, but it was evident that see she was in too much pain and the effort too great for her. She laid her head on the back seat of the car and her eyes closed almost immediately.

Mira's mum came round and closed the car door as softly as she could. She turned around, keys in hand. "Thanks, girls. I don't think I could have done that on my own."

"It's no problem," replied Sarah with a smile. "We just hope she feels better soon."

"Yes, me too," her mum replied, as she watched her daughter through the window. "I'll leave it for tonight, but if it gets any worse than it is now, I'll have to take her to the doctor tomorrow."

The girls nodded, both agreeing.

"Let us know if we can do anything else to help."

Mira's mother nodded as she got into the car herself. With one final wave, Jane and Sarah sat and watched until the car had left the parking lot and had rounded the corner out of sight.

Chapter 6

Jane tossed and turned in bed. She was too thrilled and excited to sleep. How could anyone be expected to sleep after the day she had? It was everything she had ever expected and more. It had all began with the long awaited "Dance Prize Giving." After the yearly exams, it was the second most important function the studio held. It was when all the dancers finally found out their exam results. Every year Jane found she was nervous. She could not help it. She knew she would get a good result, but there was always that tiny flicker of worry lurking just below the surface. Until her results were actually called out, she could not relax. She knew it was stupid, but that's just the way she was.

This year was no different from any other year. Jane had been as nervous as she always was. If she were honest with herself, she would admit that she was even more nervous than she had ever been before. She had worked so hard this year. She really wanted that Cup.

The evening itself was exciting. First, they held the Grand Prize Giving. Dancers would be given their exam results and with it, they collected their certificates and medals. It was a grand affair, with invitations to parents, grandparents and friends. Then, once the results had all been delivered, there was a break for refreshments. That was when all the dancers would disappear and get ready for the dance show they had prepared. It was something they did every year to end the evening. It was a fun event, with the entire dance school being involved, from the youngest girls right through to the older, more experienced dancers. The evening had always turned out to be a great success, with vibrant costumes and colourful lights, and this year was no different.

Unable to stay under the covers another minute longer, Jane slipped out of bed and padded softly to her dressing table. She did not pick it up straight away, content just to stare at it for a short while. She did not switch her light on either, there was no need. She could see her prize clearly. Running her fingers gently over the trophy, Jane smiled to herself. All the stiff muscles and sore, bleeding toes had been worth it.

When Mrs. Stone had called her name, she had been unaware that it was actually her name that was being called. She heard her name being spoken through the loudspeaker, but somehow she had not registered that it was her. "And the winner of this year's Golden Trophy, for achieving the rare, 'Honours with Distinction,' goes to…Jane Brown." There was a roar of clapping. Mrs. Stone stood at the head of the table, trophy in hand, waiting for her to come up onto the stage, eager to present her with the award she had worked so hard for.

She could hear her name being called for the second time, and along with everyone else, looked around. It was only when Sarah nudged her in the arm that she realized that it was her name that Mrs. Stone was calling.

"Jane?" Mrs. Stone said again, looking directly at her and beckoning her to come forward. It was only then that she realized that it was her. Jane felt like it was a dream. On stiff and wobbly legs, she had made her way to the front of the stage, accepting the trophy with pride while the clapping continued. She could see her mum, dad and Jo, in the audience, clapping madly, smiles beaming from their faces. As she stood there in front of the entire studio, friends and family, the realization hit her. She had finally achieved her trophy. It was a dream come true for her. She still had not got over the shock and delight of it all when she had returned to her seat. The large trophy she had worked so hard at achieving was finally sitting comfortably in her hands. She vaguely remembered pats on the back and congratulating smiles, but it was the trophy that really held her attention. The metal bar in the front proudly displaying her name to anyone who wished to see it. This was *"The* Cup." She had finally achieved what she had been working so hard for all these months. It was almost too good to be true. She had to pinch herself to believe it was not a dream.

The clapping finally died down. Then came the second announcement. It was unexpected and aimed at all the dancers present. When Mrs. Stone had delivered the announcement to the eager audience, it had the entire hall in an uproar. Parents and dance students alike began talking at once, taking in the full meaning of what had just been said. Each person had his or her own ideas and visions of what the news represented. Mrs. Stone let the hushed whispers continue for a few minutes, allowing everyone to take in what she had broadcast. Then, when all was quiet once again, she continued to explain and offer further details to the great delight of the audience.

Everyone knew that the World Games were due to take place in Germany in a few months. Six to be precise. It seemed that the organizers were very keen to arrange a dance procession as one of the opening acts. All dancers in the country were invited to attend. All studios, all age groups, across the country. There were no restrictions. Auditions were going to be fierce and the organizers expected thousands of entries. At this news, the hushed whispers began again. Mrs. Stone remained silent, waiting for the audience to simmer down. When they did, she released even more information.

Anyone who wanted to enter had to learn a set sequence of steps set by the organizers themselves. It was to be done this way, Mrs. Stone clarified, so that the judging could be as fair as possible. There was many nodding of heads in the hall. It was agreed by everyone that this was the best way that any audition could be held. Everyone was on equal footing from the onset.

Jane set her new prized trophy back down on her dressing table and then slid back into bed. She yawned. The World Games. What an experience that would be. As soon as Mrs. Stone had announced the news, she knew she would enter the auditions. There was no way that she could keep away. Having decided that she wanted a part of this new adventure, Jane was determined that she would be chosen. She did not care if she had to practice until midnight every night or if her toes practically fell off. She was going to make sure she was chosen and be apart of this exciting adventure. She had discussed it with Sarah, and knew that she also felt the same way. Imagine. Three months away in Germany practising for an International World Event. One was not given that kind of opportunity very often. Practically never. Jane was unable to hide her excitement or her enthusiasm. Mrs. Stone had already seen the requirements and anyone who wanted to enter had to be prepared to practice each and every Saturday. They would begin promptly at 9:00 a.m. and continue right through until 3:00 p.m. Weeks later, they would have to audition for the limited places available. Then, the lucky girls that were chosen, had to be prepared to give up more free time as they continued to practice right up until they flew to Germany. Jane knew that most of the other dancers were excited as she was. It was a great opportunity and a wonderful event to be involved in. It was the last thing she remembered thinking before falling asleep.

*****

Zara was also at home, thinking of the upcoming World Games. When Mrs. Noel had made the announcement at dance class, she did not think all that much of it. So what? A procession at some silly show. Who would care? What she had not been prepared for was the buzz of excitement that took over the whole studio. All the dancers talking at once as the excitement that filled the air became toxic. That was when Zara realized that practically every dancer present in the room *wanted* to be chosen. Had she missed something? Surely it was not that important? She listened more carefully. There must be more to it. A prize maybe?

By the end of the announcement, she still could not fathom out what was so thrilling to everyone. Still, the excitement of the other girls was catching. Well, if they all wanted it that badly, she would have to make sure she got in for herself. Zara loved to have what other people wanted. Normally she would just get Daddy to make a few phone calls and she would be guaranteed what she desired, but this was different. She would have to find out exactly where she stood and what extra help she might be able to pay for. She knew already that every dancer who could point a toe would be entering.

Zara realized that the competition for the games was going to be fierce. Fiercer than anything she had ever encountered before. And, by golly, she was going to be chosen. If this was a challenge, then she was determined to win. Although not normally one to try harder than necessary, Zara knew that if she wanted to stand a chance she would have to put in as much effort as she could possibly spare. Already Mrs. Noel was making arrangements for extra classes, although it had been announced that the organizers had arranged their own instructor also. Extra classes? On a Saturday? Now this was serious.

Apparently there was a set dance for the audition. And to make matters worse, after careful investigations, she found out that Mrs. Noel had no influence at all on who would be and who would not be chosen to go ahead onto Germany. She might have been able to use Mrs. Noel, but now knew that it was impossible. Mrs. Noel was a nobody. Just a simple dance teacher, with no influence whatsoever on the outcome of the chosen girls. Zara knew that if Mrs. Noel had been young enough, she might even have entered herself. Just another point proving that everyone who was anyone in the dancing world wanted to ensure one of those valuable spots. It was like winning the lottery. Everyone wanted to win, but only a few hand-selected tickets ever received the cash. Zara knew that she wanted the cash, and since everyone else wanted the cash too, she was determined to be the one to get it. Zara was aware for the first time that this was something she would have to do on her own. No help from Mrs. Noel and no help from Daddy. Well, not at the beginning anyway. If she wanted to get picked, she would have to do this all on her own. She could not help wondering if it was worth the sacrifices.

Grabbing a pen and paper, Zara weighed up the pros and cons. It sounded like a silly thing to do, but she needed to see it. On paper. In black and white. Somehow, seeing things written down helped her make up her mind. And once she had decided on what she wanted to do, there was no turning back. That was just the way she was.

So, the first and most important question was, what would it be like going to Germany? She knew the answer to that question straight away. It would be a fun adventure. She would make sure that it was. Then, the next and equally important question. What would going to Germany do for her? Now that one was tricky. There were so many possible answers. She lay back on her bed and let her mind wander. Only a handful of very privileged girls would be chosen. And she had always been privileged. That in itself meant she *must* be chosen. She imagined her name being called out. The shock, the surprise. Then, she imagined the look of jealousy on her friend's faces and that of the other dancers. They too desperately wanted to be chosen, but unlike her, they had not been good enough to make it. Zara smiled at the thought. That would show them once and for all that she was better than they were. She let her thoughts take hold. They were valuable points. No negatives so far.

Zara continued to make a list of questions, and for each and every question she found, to her surprise, that she had positive answers. Besides, the fact that actually getting chosen would make her mother's dream for her come true. That, in itself, had to be considered very carefully. Her mother would be thrilled and she knew she would be able to use that to her advantage. And Daddy. Yes, that would also work out to her advantage too. It would give him something to talk about at all those boring meetings he had to attend and push her to the top of, "Daddy's successful daughter list." So, summing up her answers, she knew that she must get picked. A little work now, for much greater rewards later. Yes, she decided, she would do it. There was just too much for her to gain out of this. Being picked would ensure her the status of going off to Germany and being the envy of all the girls she knew, *and* it would also mean having both her parent's approval rolled up into one neat little ball. She was not misled, she knew that for this to work she would have to work hard. Gone were her days of idle shopping with her friends and lunch at the river like she was used to doing. In its place would be hard work. Well, for the next six months anyway. She did not relish the idea. She had a busy social life and all the extra classes were bound to get in the way. For the first time in her life, Zara realized that she could not have both. It was one or the other. Zara did not like that feeling at all. In fact, she decided, she hated it.

Chapter 7

The first Saturday of rehearsals for the World Games seemed to arrive quickly. Both Sarah and Jane were immensely excited. They knew that each catchment area would have their own individual tutor who had been specially chosen by the event organizers. The rehearsals were arranged to take place in the local town hall, conveniently located a short drive away from their houses. It was deemed big enough to accommodate the masses of dancers they were expecting.

When Jane entered the converted town hall that Saturday morning, she was surprised at the number of girls present who were as keen as her to audition for the few parts available. It only confirmed that every dancer within the vicinity also wanted to go to Germany and be involved in the prestigious World Games. Still, the amount of girls that actually turned up on the day was unbelievable, and Jane was taken aback by the large masses of girls present. There were so many! Where there really that many dancers in this area? And, if there were that many dancers here, then how many more were auditioning in the other catchment areas?

Jane was not surprised when she recognized a few familiar faces from various other dance studios nearby. The age range was wide, from young girls to much older, mature dancers. All were excited and eager for what was to come, with the one and same goal in mind.

"There's so many people," Sarah said, looking around in surprise.

"Yes," Jane agreed, "there are. Let's go find a good corner. We're early, we should be able to get a good spot near the front somewhere. Better do it now before it *really* gets full."

The organizers had done an excellent job with the hall. It actually looked like a proper dance studio, complete with bars and mirrors. Only those that had been there before would have known that it was in fact a town hall and not a dance studio. It was often hired out and used for a variety of events. Weddings, musicals, and once, even an indoor hockey match had been played there. Due to the large numbers expected, the organizers had arranged two large flat screen televisions next to either side of the stage so that everyone would be able to see the instructor.

Jane and Sarah took their position to the left of the studio and were lucky enough to find a place close to the front near an open window.

"This looks like a good place," confirmed Sara, as she surveyed the area around her that was filling up with rapid speed.

Jane agreed. They had a perfect view of the stage, but could also see the screens if they chose to. It was an ideal position. And the window would definitely come in handy.

The hall continued to fill with each passing minute. Many of the girls had the same idea of getting there early so they could secure a good position up front. Jane was glad they had arrived as early as they did. There were going to be quite a lot of girls who would have no option but to use the screens supplied. They were good, but actually seeing the instructor was a much better option.

Zara had not been so lucky. She had arrived exactly on time with her friend Pat, a tall, pretty girl with striking black hair and vivid green eyes. She was in the same social class as Zara, with their parents being old friends since school days. Because of this, the two girls spent a lot of time together, whether it be on Pat's parent's yacht or Zara's parent's beach house in Florida.

Pat arrived irritated. She had no intention of trying out for the auditions, but had literally been dragged to the town hall by Zara. She loved to dance herself, but she danced purely for the fun. She was not concerned about how talented she was, as long as she was enjoying herself. Now it seemed that Zara had another bee in her bonnet and she was being dragged along into it, as usual. Zara had been adamant that she must come with her, even through she had no desire to. She had been cajoled and coaxed, and finally bribed with a three-month holiday in Germany. Pat admitted that a holiday did sound tempting, but that was not why she had agreed to accompany Zara. In the end, she had given up protesting and agreed to tag along with Zara, just to get her off her back for awhile. When Zara wined and demanded, she really wined and demanded. Pat could not take another minute of it.

Zara was much more irritated than Pat when they arrived. The hall was already full with a mass of girls, and she had been forced to take a place at the very, very back.

"This *cannot* be the only spot left," Zara wailed to Pat in annoyance as she tried to see above the heads in front of her. One glance around the studio and she had to concede that the spot she was in was all that was left available.

Pat nodded, only half listening to Zara complaining and wailing on, again. She really had not been looking forward to this. She had only come because Zara had practically forced her to, but now that she had arrived, she could not help feeling a little of the excitement that everyone else in the room was experiencing. So what if they were at the back? They could use the screens. That was what they were there for. She knew that for Zara this situation was totally unacceptable. Zara was used to getting her own way. In everything. She always got the best seat in the house, or the best tickets available for a show. Being here, and being forced to stay at the very back would have her very, very angry. She threw a look at Zara, who was still ducking and diving, scanning over heads, trying to locate another spot somewhere closer to the stage. Pat knew it would be useless. Instead, she took in all the other dancers. Everyone seemed to be in high spirits, and there seemed to be a nervous energy floating through the room. Pat could not help feeling infected as the excitement permeated the air. She was actually glad that Zara had begged her to come along. She might just be in for some fun yet. And that was what it was all about.

Zara was not given the opportunity to think of a cunning plan to get to the front, or even to try and inch her way closer, as the instructor arrived and took her place on stage. With a loud clap, gaining everyone's attention, she introduced herself as Helen. She spoke with perfectly pronounced English, Pat noticed. She wore a bright red leotard, with her greying hair held neatly at the back of her head. She was tall and slim, and although not unfriendly looking, you could tell she brooked no nonsense from anyone. It was portrayed in the way she spoke and the way she moved.

Zara took in Helen with interest and tried to weigh her up. So, this was to be the woman that she had to win over. Zara wondered what her chances would be like with her. Only time would tell.

The first day of rehearsals began. They spent most of the morning learning the first of the many new steps. The dance routine they were taught was like nothing Jane had ever experienced before. The movements seemed jagged and irregular, with weird kicks and even weirder landings. The movements did not seem to flow into one another, but were instead staggered. Jane found them unnatural. At first, they learnt only the beginning steps of the sequence. Helen used no music during this stage. They practised these same steps, over and over again, until Helen was sure that everyone was up to speed and knew what they were doing. All that could be heard was the soft shuffle of feet on the wooden floor and her voice carrying throughout the hall.

Once she was confident that everyone had mastered the existing steps, Helen would move on and add a few more steps, to the very end of the sequence. As each new set of steps was added Jane found them increasingly strange. She ignored her personal feelings and continued to follow Helen in the mirror. If she was honest, the steps might feel strange to dance, but, in the mirror, they did not look strange.

It was a long time later, when Helen was finally happy with their progress and allowed the music to play. Everything seemed to improve after that as the music visibly bought the steps together. The sequence that had until now felt awkward and strange seemed to work well with the music that had been chosen. It was a clever tactic that Helen had used to get them started.

Jane concentrated hard. The music played was slightly faster, compared to the speed they had been practising at, so she lost her place and forgot her steps in a few areas. Still, she continued to follow Helen as best she could. After few times running through the entire sequence, Jane felt confident that she had most of it remembered. As time passed, Jane began to feel better about the way she was doing, but there were still numerous other dancers struggling to grasp what they had learnt so far. Helen was not put off by this and they continued to go over and over the same sequence. Slowly, more and more girls began to grasp the steps and remember the sequence without stopping and losing their place.

All the dancers who had shown up were in high spirits, eager to make an impression with their technique and talents. It soon became apparent that a lot more was needed. As the hours ticked by, Jane noticed that some of the girls seemed to lose their energy completely. The excitement was now over and they were getting bored with repeating the same steps over and over again. They did not jump with the same enthusiasm as they had when they had first arrived that morning, while others did not point their toes as hard as they knew they could. Jane did not mind the constant repetition of what they were doing. She used the opportunity to master the steps and improve what she was doing and how she was doing it. In her eyes, it was all practise.

The auditions to be held were open to everyone, young and old. It was clear though that many of the younger girls were quickly losing their energy and could not keep up with Helen's pace. Many stopped frequently and took a seat on the sidelines, while drinking great gulps of water from their bottles.

Others, still eager to make an impression on the first day, performed the required steps, but it was obvious from their movements that they were deflated of energy and tired. As the end of the first half of the day approached, only half of the girls present were actually on the studio floor and dancing the steps.

Helen made no comment. She continued to add new steps and whoever wanted to dance was able to follow her lead. Jane began to feel more comfortable with what they were learning and was enjoying herself immensely.

Helen's announcement surprised everyone. "Okay," she said, beaming, "I'd like to see you run through the dance steps on your own." It was almost as if she had spoken another language. Dancers looked worriedly at each other. Hushed whispers began. Some of the girls were clearly distressed at having to go ahead on their own with no one to follow. They were here to impress Helen, but to do that they needed to follow her. Helen sensed their reluctance, but did not acknowledge it. Brooking no argument, and barely registering the hushed whispers, Helen began the music, then settled herself comfortably on a chair, as she watched the dancers perform below her.

Helen watched the girls closely. She knew that her announcement would get them in a fluster. She did not do it deliberately, but she needed to assess the dancers present. Who was coping with what they were learning, and who was not. It was also a good test to see who was paying attention to her when she spoke. If any of these girls present were lucky enough to get picked, the pace that they would be dancing at later would be much faster than the pace they had adopted today. This was child's play in comparison to what would be expected of them.

Jane danced the steps she had been taught the entire morning as best she could. Helen' eyes where everywhere all at once. Once or twice Jane found she lost her count, but quickly continued, hoping that if anyone had been looking at her, they would not have noticed. Some of the dancers, she knew, were faring much worse than her without someone to follow and copy.

Others still, were stopping completely, watching the dancer in front of them hoping to get a lead and then trying to continue. This did not work however, as the dancer in front was doing the exact same thing. There were a lot of abrupt stops and strange steps taking place. Jane knew that it was better to keep moving rather than stopping completely, especially under Helen's watchful gaze.

Chapter 8

Helen made them run through the dance steps on their own three times. At the end of the last run, she thanked them and then dismissed them all for lunch. They had been given an hour, and she had stressed that she was beginning promptly again at 1:00 p.m. whether they were all there or not. Jane believed her. Helen was clearly not there to cajole and pamper them.

Until lunch was mentioned, Jane had not even thought about food. Her mum had insisted she eat breakfast before she left that morning and at first Jane had declined, feeling too excited in anticipation for the upcoming day, but her mother had insisted, leaving no room for any argument. So, in an effort to keep her mother happy, she had forced down some marmalade toast. Jane was glad she had. Thinking of food now made her realise she was absolutely starving. Her stomach seemed to use that precise moment to groan its hunger. Sarah giggled at the loud sound and said, "I'm famished too." Jane laughed as she grabbed her belly. How embarrassing. "There's a shopping centre around the corner. Should we go there for something to eat?"

Sarah nodded and replied, "Yes. That sounds good to me."

They were just making their way outside the parking lot when Jane saw Zara for the first time. It was impossible to miss the tall, pretty, blond-haired girl leaning on the shiny, red sports car. Jane watched as she threw her head back and laughed sweetly, probably at some joke or something. She was surrounded by a group of admiring fans, and even from this distance Jane could see they were fighting for her attention. At first she mistook the group for a horde of friends heading for the shopping centre.

Sarah too, was watching the group with amusement. "Do you know her?" she asked.

"No. Should I?" Jane answered back, intrigued, as they watched the girl flick back her long hair as she laughed into the wind.

"I don't know. I thought maybe you did."

It was only then that Jane noticed that the group was dressed in the same dancing attire as they were wearing. This was no group of ordinary friends hanging out going to the shopping centre. These girls were here as part of the Saturday rehearsals. Jane took another closer look at the girls. None seemed to stick out more than the tall blond girl leaning comfortably on the hood of the car.

Jane forgot about Zara as soon as they rounded the corner and the shopping mall came into sight. The smell of fresh, hot pies hit them almost instantly. They did not waste time looking around for anything else to eat, but headed straight for the bakery. The fresh smell was enough to make up their minds. It took them a few minutes to purchase their lunch before they sat down on grass outside, ready to enjoy their deserved break.

It was the first time since they had arrived that morning that the girls managed to talk properly between themselves, and Jane was full of questions.

"So what did you think of it all then?" Jane asked curiously, as she took a bite of the hot chicken pie.

Sarah was silent for awhile as she took a drink of her juice, thinking. "It's all a little different, isn't it? The steps feel strange, like they don't fit together. Do you feel like that? That the movements are a little odd?"

Jane nodded in agreement, "I know, what you mean. They do feel bizarre. There seems to be all these weird jumps and landings. It feels really awkward."

Sarah nodded in agreement between bites of her pie, the hot steam preventing her from eating too quickly. She spoke instead, "It is better now though. At least we have some music to dance with. The movements don't feel as static."

"Oh, yes, much better. Before, it was too quiet. Just the shuffle of feet. It felt eerie. All of us girls crammed into the studio and hardly any noise. It just seemed so unnatural."

"Did you see how many girls were just standing about near the end?"

"Yes, I know. I'm sure that's why Helen made us do the steps on our own. She probably wanted to see who had been paying attention. She looks like she can be quite strict."

They were silent again, contemplating Helen and her tactics, as they continued eating.

"So, are you enjoying it then?" Sarah asked.

Jane nodded enthusiastically. "It's different, I'll give you that, but it's nice. A change. A challenge."

On their way back to the makeshift studio, both girls agreed that Helen was not going to be any kind of pushover. It was only the first half of the first morning and that much was clear already. Anyone that did not keep up with the strict schedule would be left behind. There was no room for stragglers.

As they re-entered the hall, they noted that already it was full of eager and well-rested girls, all ready to continue with the second stage of the day. Many had not wanted to be late, especially after Helen's stern warning.

"I don't believe it!" Sarah announced, astonished.

"What?" Jane answered curiously.

"They have only taken *our* place," Sarah replied crossly.

"Who has taken what?" Jane asked, now baffled at what her friend was going on about.

"Them," Sarah replied, "over there! Look!" Jane followed her friends gaze. There, in the place they had been dancing in all morning, was the girl with the long blond hair and her array of friends. They were talking and laughing together, but at the same time clearly claiming the spot as their own. Jane's immediate response was irritation. They had arrived early just so they can could get a good position, and now it had practically been stolen from beneath them. From right under their noses, while they had been at lunch, no less. Jane guessed that they must have known that someone else had been there before them. They had deliberately remained as a big group, knowing that no one would go over and say anything to them. They would be able to slip into the stolen position as if they had always been there. Jane could feel herself getting angry. She was not going to lose her good, secured position because some spoilt girls had no manners. This was too important. Her chance of being chosen depended on her doing well, and the only way she could ensure that, was to be up there in front. That was the whole point of arriving early that morning.

Sarah must have sensed her anger. "Jane, just leave it. Okay?" Sarah said. "We will just get a position next to them, that's all. No problem. We are here to dance, not argue over a silly dance spot. Remember that! Keep your focus."

Jane breathed in deeply. Sarah was right. She was here to dance. She did not feel better though. Positioning themselves next to the group, Jane and Sarah ignored the girls, and concentrated on their stretches, readying themselves for the second session.

They began promptly at 1:00 p.m. as Helen had said they would. It was clear that some of the girls had not taken Helen's warning seriously and were not yet back from lunch. Helen must have known they were missing, but she did not let on if she cared. She began the second phase of the day and continued as if she did not even notice their absence. Even later, when the girls turned up at various stages and times, Helen continued without interrupting her flow. She did not give them even a glimmer of a glance. The girls crept in quietly and took their places at the back of the hall, rejoining the dance session.

Helen seemed unfazed by the hours of dance, and continued her teachings vigorously. She paid no attention to the girls who took frequent breaks, but continued in her teachings to those who were listening. There would be no concessions. Everyone was treated on the same level, regardless of age or stamina. The second half of the day was similar to the first half. Helen may be a no nonsense woman who did not wait around, but when it came to teaching to those that wanted to learn, she left no one behind. Only once she was sure that most of the class had mastered the new steps did she continue onto the next section. Slowly, as the afternoon wore on, she increased the steps. Jane was enjoying the routine. Some of the steps still felt alien and strange, but she knew that with practise, she would not be feeling so awkward and stiff. Already, this afternoon, she felt better performing the steps than she had that morning. Besides, it *was* only the first day. The only thing that did seemed to mar the afternoon was her irritation with the girls next to her.

Jane became increasingly aware that she was getting more and more annoyed with the girls that had stolen their spot from earlier that morning. The tall, blond girl, who she heard being called Zara, kept on getting in her way. Jane was sure it was unintentional, but each time Helen began to play the music, this Zara girl somehow managed to find her way in front of her and blocked Helen completely from view. Jane was finding it increasingly difficult to follow Helen, and was making more use out of the screens as the afternoon wore on, even though she was practicality right in front. At one stage, Zara had kicked to the side, and almost knocked her on the head with her foot. Sarah must have seen it coming, and had pulled her out of the way just in time. Biting her lip in annoyance, Jane found herself moving further and further away from the group, just so he could get some space to move freely, without having to worry about getting knocked out by some wayward foot. She really could not dance all cramped up as they were. She needed to be free, and have some space to move. She made a mental note to ensure she kept away from Zara and her gang in the future. They were a irritation she did not need and were slowly getting in the way of her concentration.

Zara, on the other hand, was elated. She had ditched their horrible position from earlier in the morning, and was now almost right up in the front. She could see Helen clearly from her position, helped by the fact that she was foot taller than any of the other girls present. Her height seemed to scale way past most of the other dancers, who tended to be shorter. The first session, she had to admit, had not been very good at all. She had been forced to watch the screen most of the time, even with her height. They were good, an excellent idea, but she would rather be up front and see the instructor for herself. Now, as she followed Helen, she realised just how much she had missed out on being stuck so far behind everyone else. That would never happen again. She would see to that.

At lunch, she had decided that she would not tolerate another minute being pushed to the back. She was here to win, and she could not do that from so far behind. She decided to make sure she got back earlier from lunch so she could secure a place up front. And that was exactly what she had done. She was clever enough to make sure that the entire group of girls followed her and did the same thing. Zara knew that they must be stealing someone else's place, but with a group of their size dominating the space, no girl, unless she was stupid, would dare make any comments. They would just have to find themselves somewhere else to dance. It really was not her problem. As long as she had her better view, she was happy and that was all she was concerned about. And now, comparing the small distance between her and the stage, she was glad she had stolen this position. The difference was much more noticeable than she would have imagined, and she was much closer to Helen, who she would have to work on to impress.

The second session went much better for Zara than the first session. She now had a perfect view of Helen and of her potential competition, which she watched with a critical eye at every available opportunity. Although the day was turning out to be hard work, she *was* enjoying herself. She knew her goal, and somehow it was turning out to be more fun and easier than she had anticipated. There were a number of reasons for this. Already, she knew she was much, much better than most of the other girls present. That gave her an added boost, and having surveyed as many of the girls as she could, Zara knew she was well ahead of most of them. There were a few, however, that were talented and those where the girls she would have to worry about. In her critical assumptions, she became aware of another dancer to her right. Zara watched her with every turn and every twist possible. She would have liked to stop completely and just watch what was going on around her, but she knew that would have been too obvious. So, she had to settle for second best, which was to watch undetected whenever she could. She had to admit, even if it was only to herself, that this dark haired girl was good. Actually, she was very good. She moved with extreme ease and had natural, raw talent. Her movements seemed confident and self-assured. Amazing since they had only been rehearsing for one day. Zara watched the girl out of the corner of her eye, and was loath to admit that she made the complicated steps look easy. She seemed to flow with the music like liquid. She seemed oblivious to everyone around her, concentrating hard on whatever Helen was doing. Zara was determined that she too, would also look like that. She knew she had talent, everyone told her so, but did she have as much as this mysterious girl next to her? It was a question that weighed heavily on her mind.

And, that led her to her second problem of the day. The mysterious, dark-haired girl's friend. Zara noted with interest that she was also tall and blond, like herself. She too seemed to dance with an experienced ease, in much the same style as her friend. Together, the two of them made a good pair. Both extremely talented and looking like they were enjoying every minute of the class. Zara could not see the entire hall, but she already knew that she had two girls right next to her who posed as serious competition. Zara shook her head, willing herself to concentrate on Helen. No use worrying about anyone else for now. She would first ensure that she was doing her best, had gained Helen's confidence and attention, then she would worry about others that were in the way of what she wanted. It was only the first day, she had more than enough time to formulate a plan and make sure she was at the top of the list.

Chapter 9

When Jane arrived home that evening, she was tired. A full day of dancing had ensured that result. Now, as she made her way up to her bedroom, she rephrased her thoughts. Tired was too tame a word for what she was feeling. Exhausted was more the word she would use. Exhausted and aching. It had been a strenuous, although, eventful day. From the onset, it was clear that Helen was going to be hard teacher to dance for. She was efficient, there was no doubting that, but along with that efficiency came a hard edge. She was there to teach and those that did not want to learn had no place in her class. It was clear that you were welcome to take a break if you needed, or stop for a drink of water, but she would continue, with or without you present. She did not spend any time waiting around. Her main goal was to teach. Actually, thought Jane, it was her only goal. The woman had bounds of energy and did not seem to tire. The only break she took was at lunch, with everyone else. Besides that one hour, she continued as though she was a steam train.

Jane was used to hours and hours of practising, but as the end of the day wore on, she knew she was finally running out of steam herself. Maybe it was all the excitement finally sapping her energy. Or maybe it was the complete newness of the steps and how hard she had to concentrate. Others had given up completely by the middle of the afternoon, some even resting against the far wall until the end of the day, content to sit and watch. Jane knew she could never do that. She would rather kill herself trying than take to the bench and watch. And now, as she took slow painful steps up the stairs, she realized she might just have done exactly that. She was in absolute agony.

Jane could still hear Helen's voice echoing in her head. "Step to the music…that's right, one, two, three. Feel the rhythm." Helen's voice seemed to be a permanent fixture in her head already. And it was only day one.

Jane was dimly aware of the dull aching between her shoulder blades. It seemed to penetrate deep, right into the core of her neck muscles. Bending her head slowly from side to side, she decided that what she need most was a hot, relaxing bath. Warming to the idea the more she thought about it, Jane ventured from her original aim of her bedroom and headed straight for the bathroom instead. Even as she bent to turn on the taps, she knew it was a bad idea. Her back muscles screamed in protest. With each movement now, her body croaked in agony. She let the water run as she slowly slipped out of her smelly and sweat soaked clothes. Then, once the water was halfway, Jane added some Raddox bubble bath. She allowed the water to continue running, making a million tiny bubbles as it did so. She read the bottle. Luxury Bath Soak, for Intense Muscle Relief. She smiled. How did her mum always know what she needed?

The way she was feeling now, even that would only help a very little. With the bath water full, she switched off the taps and concentrated on lowering herself into the bathtub. Her body hurt with each movement. Eventually she was in the tub and the water immediately enveloped her like a think blanket. Warm and cozy.

Twenty minutes later, Jane still lay in the bath, her eyes closed against the warm steam, the small bubbles gently teasing her nostrils. She kept her eyes shut, but could smell the sweet essence of the bubble bath. It smelt like lavender fields. The soft, sweet smelling water *was* helping to ease the ache in her bones. She knew it could not be, but it almost felt like the water was massaging her muscles and gently easing away the tension of the day. After just five minutes in the bath, soaking her tired and weary muscles, she had begun to feel better. Now twenty minutes later, she could feel almost normal. Gone was the tension between her shoulder blades and slowly the stiffness that had begun to take hold seemed to disappear. Even her toes, which were red and swollen from a hard day's work, of swivelling and jumping, felt better.

Feeling almost completely relaxed, Jane allowed herself to think over the day. It held many unexpected turns. The dancing itself was very different from what she was used to. At first, she had felt awkward, but the more they rehearsed the steps, the more confident she felt. She knew she was not the only one feeling that way. Sarah had also admitted feeling the same. She was glad. It was better not feeling alone. Somehow, having Sarah there at the studio with her was like having a sturdy pillar to lean on. Sturdy and reassuring. She knew she would have gone to the audition on her own anyway, she would not have missed it for the world, but having your best friend turn up with you was by far the better option.

By the end of the second session things had improved even more. The steps began to feel ever so slightly more natural and even felt easier to dance. And naturally, when that happened, she felt more confident. That had only seemed to add to the ease of her movements. She knew she would still have to get used to some of the weird jumps and strange kicks, but she was confident that after a few more lessons she would be just fine. It would just take some more practice. Of that she was sure.

Although she had a positive outlook on today's rehearsal, it was obvious that many of the other girls were not going to make it. Almost everyone there had arrived with such vivacious energy that morning, eager for the day ahead. But, as time wore on, that vivacious energy slowly seemed to seep away from some of the girls until by the end of the afternoon there was nothing left of the girl that had arrived earlier that day. Some of the younger ones just could not keep up, the steps too rigorous and difficult for them. Others seemed to do well, maintaining their energy levels until lunch, only to return back after the hour, wary and lethargic. From then on, it was downhill for many of them, as they never did seem to get back to the same level of energy that they had on arrival that morning.

Numerous problems and difficulties that the girls experienced began to surface as time passed. Jane noticed them, so she was sure that Helen noticed them too. She was after all, a professional. Jane was positive that by now Helen had made a mental note of whom she thought would be cut out for the next few weeks of intense learning and training. She had a keen eye and Jane knew she did not miss a thing, even when she pretended that she did.

Jane had to admit, even to herself, that it had been hard work. This was definitely not like any training she had ever done before. She was no novice to hard, gruelling dancing practices, especially when they were practising for shows, but Helen's sessions seemed to be the most difficult she had ever had to endure. She was relentless. And strict. There was no room for any inexperienced or undedicated girls in her class. It would be interesting to see how some of the girls would cope with these new teaching methods and steps.

All in all, even with the hard work and aching muscles, she was unable to deny she had enjoyed herself. She was learning all sorts of new steps, and although somewhat alien to her now, she knew that soon she would be able to dance the sequence with ease. To Jane, the whole experience was a challenge. One she relished taking part in. And then, if it all turned out as she hoped, she would be off to Germany soon. The ultimate goal.

Just thinking about the prospect made her giddy. Things had been going so well for her, it was hard to believe it was true. Last week she was just another dancer trying to make it as best she could until she could decide in what direction she wanted to go in. Then she had won the trophy she had been working her entire life for. That changed things dramatically from her perspective. Then, things just seemed to develop for the better, from then on. This world event had given her the perfect opportunity, not just to make it her chosen career, but a good, solid, sturdy career. She could go in any number of avenues if she could just ensure she got chosen. The possibilities this presented were endless.

*****

Zara, too, was reluctant to admit that she also had enjoyed the day, more than she had ever thought possible. It wasn't the best way to spend a Saturday, but she had expected much worse. Pat too had been happy and excited when they had left that afternoon, even though she had to bribe the girl to come along. Zara was not so enthusiastic about Helen or her teachings though. She was beyond strict. It was almost military the way she had pushed everyone. And Zara had felt that any kind of weakness, no matter how small and insignificant, would be noticed by Helen's keen eye for detail. That woman was all smiles, but Helen knew she was a hawk. Her eyes taking in everything. Storing it up for later use. And now that she was right up in front, she only wanted to be noticed for her good, positive attributes. Like her talent. Her willingness to learn. With Helen's keen eye for detail, she knew she would be noticed. So, she had worked herself past endurance during Helen's session. At one stage, she even thought she had pulled a leg muscle. Still, she refused to give in, continuing to dance through her cramp as best she could. If some of the other dancers could do it, then dammit, she could to. And having the girls she knew to be Jane and Sarah next to her only seemed to add to her determination. They looked so perfectly at ease, enjoying every minute of the day. Zara would have thought it impossible that anyone could enjoy Helen's teachings as much as they were, but there was no denying the smile on their lips. They were genuine smiles. Nothing fake or put on about them. Those two really were enjoying every second. She wished she too could feel the same way. Well, she would, she tried to convince herself. When she was in Germany and she had everyone's approval and envy. Then she too would have a smile. The biggest of the lot.

She did notice that a few of the dancers took frequent breaks. It made her feel better when they did, because it meant that those that did not succumb would be more noticeable under Helen's watchful eye. Pat was trying hard too, but she did not get the steps as quickly as the others did. To her this was all fun, a nice way to keep fit. She did not have anything hanging on the outcome. Pat's parents would be thrilled with her just for trying. They seemed so completely different from her parents. Easy going and content. They supported Pat 101% in whatever she chose to do. No pressure. Zara wished, not for the first time, that her parents were more like Pat's. Pat had taken one of those forbidden breaks too, unconcerned if Helen saw her or not. Zara knew she was hoping like everyone else to be chosen for Germany, but her life was not dependent on it. And that was where Zara disagreed. For her, a lot depended on her getting chosen. So, while Pat had sat down on the floor resting her legs, Zara had continued, even though the cramp was killing her. She was not going to be one of the girls looked down upon. To Zara this was like a weakness. And weak was something she was not. She would continue until Helen called for a break, even if it killed her. And it almost did. She refused to be beaten by either Helen or the two sidekicks next to her.

By the time Zara slipped into her car to drive home, she was exhausted. Her toes felt like they were sown into her leather pumps and her arms felt so heavy she wondered how she was going to hold the steering wheel to drive. She was very tired and her leg was aching. Normally, after a class, she would swap her dancing shoes for her sneakers. Tonight, however, she did not have the energy. Besides, she just knew it was going to be too painful and take too much energy. Energy that she just did not have. In all her years of dancing, she had never felt this tired or this exhausted before. She just hoped that it would all be worth it in the end. Even thinking of the final result was unable to bring a smile to her lips, which it normally did. She was sure that even that small movement would be too much for her. All she wanted to do was get home and have a hot shower and fall straight into bed. She hoped that an early night would sort her out.

The drive home felt so much longer than it had ever felt before. As Zara approached the high gates to the entrance of her house, she almost slumped with relief. She had never been this happy to get home before. She headed straight for her bedroom, calling for Rose on the top of her voice as she dragged herself up the stairs. Her leg aching with each step as she did so.

Rose had appeared as soon as her name had been called. She had heard Zara's parents discuss the World Games and knew that Zara wanted to be involved in it. She also knew what Zara was like after just one hour's dance session. All the moaning and groaning. She could just imagine what she would be like after a full day. She had not been looking forward to Zara's return home at all. She was prepared though. She knew exactly what had to be done. She left Zara lying sprawled out on her bed and returned a few minutes later with a foot spa. It was another one of her Zara's mother's attempts at home beauty therapy.

Zara watched Rose bring over the foot spa. She had always thought this idea of her mother's was a total waste of time. Just go to the salon for that sort of thing. Quick, easy and simple. No mess and no fuss. Now, as she watched Rose fill the foot spa with hot water, she was eternally grateful her mother had one. This was exactly what she needed. With great care she began to peel off the leather pumps she was still wearing. She was horrified at what her feet looked like once her shoes were off. Gone were the soft, manicured feet and delicately painted toenails she had this morning. Instead, her feet were now bright red and swollen. They looked like they had been continually punched and then dipped in scalding hot water. All puffed up and peeling. They looked horrid. If they had been anyone else's feet, she would have turned away in disgust. With great care, Zara moved over to the couch and slipped her unsightly feet into the water. The cry of pain and relief that escaped her lips was unintentional, but was out before she could stop herself. She sat like that, feet in the spa, and head resting on the sofa, eyes closed. In the far away distance she could hear music. Maybe her mother in the drawing room, she was not sure.

It was a long time after when she woke. Her feet were still soaking in the foot spa, but the hot water had turned ice cold. She had no idea how long she must have been sleeping. She felt drained of all energy and would have been content to stay as she was, was it not for the fact that her wet feet were now making her cold. Zara knew she would have to make a move and stand up. She could not stay in the foot spa all night. She had just about enough energy to dry her feet with the soft white towel Rose had left.

Somehow the spa had worked its magic, and although her feet still looked red, they were not nearly as bad as they had been when she had first taken her shoes off. Having seen the results, she knew she needed the same kind of treatment on the rest of her body. A long hot shower would be perfect for the way she was feeling. She would have liked a bath, but if she could not stay awake in a foot spa, she knew for certain that she would be unable to stay awake in a hot bath. No, a brisk shower was best. She would be able to stand and keep awake.

Ten minutes later, wrapped up in her dressing gown, Zara felt better. The hot shower had worked wonders. She now felt clean and refreshed, although still exhausted. Another wave of tiredness came over her, and she yawned yet again. All she wanted now was to creep into her bed. She was just about to do exactly that, when she remembered. She had a date with Raymond. Handsome, incredibly keen, Raymond. She had met him at one of her father's dinner parties about two years earlier. He worked at her father's office as a lawyer. He had only just started when she met him for the first time, but it was not long before Raymond had won her father's approval. Daddy said he was smart and on his way up in the world. Two words he liked to hear. Especially in his staff. They had been dating on and off for over a year now. Nothing serious at first, although they were spending an increasingly large amount of time together. Things were becoming more official, if you like. The setup suited Zara perfectly. She always had a date if she needed one and, besides, Raymond was handsome, with excellent taste. He knew exactly were to take her for dinner, what theatre shows she enjoyed and events she would be most interested in. It amazed her that she could actually have so much in common with someone else. Besides Pat, he was the only other person that was so tuned in with her. And Daddy loved him. Something she used quite often, to her advantage. If it had been anyone else, her father would not be nearly as accommodating as he was. So, from that aspect Raymond also had his uses. It suited her, for now, to continue dating him. Now she was left with a predicament. If she missed dinner with Raymond, she knew she would be missing out on a special evening. They always were when Raymond took her out. She allowed her mind to wander over what he had planned. Still, even as tempting as a nice evening sounded, the look of her warm, soft bed was far more appealing. Her mind was made up. She would call Raymond, apologize, and then climb into bed. Normally she liked to read a book or listen to music, but tonight she wanted to draw her curtains closed, slip into bed, and let sleep claim her.

    Zara called Raymond. He had been disappointed and slightly irritated that Zara was cancelling on their date, but she was too tired to care. She was still sore, and her leg felt stiff and tender. As she slipped under the covers, Zara reviewed her plans. Was this really worth it she kept asking herself? It was only the first day and already she had unbearably ugly looking feet, a sore, battered and bruised body, and now she had also done something she would *never* normally do. She had cancelled a date. And not just any date, a date with tall, dark, good looking Raymond. And to make matters worse, it was only the first class. Would it get any better? She was not sure if her plan was worth another three months of this kind of intense training. And then another three months when they finally arrived in Germany. Was she ready for all that? If classes continued as they had today, Zara was convinced she would have feet that looked like they belonged to a woman of eighty. It began to appear as if the sacrifices for this Germany thing were going to be too big. Zara was not sure she wanted it anymore. Or did she? It was too difficult. She let her mind wander again, and imagined what it would be like. Germany. The prestige. The status. And her parents. Already they had been making such a big fuss. Her father was proud, gently egging her on. Her mother convinced that this was somehow a reflection on her work as a good mother, after all the coaching in dancing she had given her when she was young. Both her parents wanted her to succeed for their own private reasons. When she got through this, she knew she would have them both wrapped around her finger. It would be the ultimate reward. It felt horrible now, but deep down she knew that, yes, it was all going to be worth it in the long run. There was no denying that fact. She must keep reminding herself this, no matter how hard it was now.

Chapter 10

Raymond was in a good mood. Things had been going very well for him lately. Firstly, he had landed the role at Bill Maddox Law firm. It was not a hugely successful position to begin with. He knew that, but he also knew what the possibilities could be given the opportunity. So, he had worked hard and been clever enough to make sure he attained Maddox Bill's eye by always volunteering his services when he knew Bill would be around. He also ensured that what work he did do was noticed by the bosses higher up. Some of his tricks had been a little unsavoury, but in the end he achieved the results he wanted. Now, after only a few short months, he was helping to run things. Maddox was just the kind of man he wanted to be. Smart, powerful and rich. Very, very rich.

His next move had fallen into his lap quite by accident. When he first laid eyes on Zara, they had been at a business cocktail party, slash dinner. Zara captivated the room with her beautiful smile and dazzling looks. She seemed to float elegantly around the room, helped by her short, rather striking, red dress. Her audience of admirers were captivated as she glided across the room. Raymond could not take his eyes of her as she talked and laughed with other guests. She was the prefect hostess, one that every man in the room was aware of. Raymond knew that she was just the kind of girl he was looking for. Strikingly beautiful and smart, and above all, someone like himself. He was able to identify that as soon as he saw her and it seemed to be confirmed as he watched her work her way through the crowds gathering around her.

Raymond could not keep his distance for long, and went over to introduce himself and ask for her hand in a dance. Up close, she was even more dazzling than he had originally thought and was momentarily lost for words as he gazed into her blue eyes. He was used to his share of beautiful women, but Zara far surpassed any that he had ever met before. She smiled as he offered her his hand, waiting to lead her onto the dance floor. "That would be lovely, thank you," she replied in her soft, sweet voice. That dance had been the first of many.

The whispers that flew around the room were noticeable. Raymond picked up on it almost instantly, and he was sure Zara had picked up on it too. This was exactly the kind of situation that would help him get noticed more. They made a handsome couple. Her with her long blond hair, and him, with his dark looks. Raymond was enjoying the attention from around the room, and after some conversation with Zara established her to be a smart, intelligent girl. It could be worse. She could be beautiful, but also dumb. He had met so many girls like that before. Even dated some of them. But, he was too intelligent for them, so things never worked out. But here, right before him was a beautiful, and on first impressions, smart girl. The combination created many possibilities. Someone like her would be a great asset in his leap to the top, looking beautiful on his arm at any function. It was an excellent way to get noticed. Especially by the older, more influential members of the company. She was someone who could not be ignored. And that meant, he in turn, could not be ignored either.

When he had discovered that the woman he had been dancing with for better part of the evening was actually Bill Maddox's daughter, he could not believe his luck. That piece of information had been an added bonus for him. A big, huge, massive, incredible bonus. One he had not expected. He had hit the jackpot and it had been an unintentional move on his part. He had already decided that he wanted Zara, but knowing that she was Bill's daughter, made it all the more so. Many things had raced though his mind that evening. And they all concerned Zara. If he dated her, which he was sure he would have done anyway, it would help to ensure his position in the company, and introduce him to a new world. A world which he wanted to be very much apart of. The world of the "Super Rich." And Zara unknowingly, was going to help him.

From that very first night, he had been using Zara in a subtle way. Using her to get what he wanted, personally and professionally. He could do it the long way, though hard work and dedication, but that would take way too long and this was by far more fun and exciting. And, as an extra concession, Zara was possibly the most beautiful, captivating woman in the world. All of these pieces fit to make a perfect picture. And he was the centerpiece. He could not believe his luck!

Raymond picked up the photo he had on his desk of Zara. She was amazingly beautiful, there was just no denying that. A blind person would have been able to feel her beauty had she been in the room. It was just sometimes, after getting to know her, that he found she could be hard work. She always wanted her own way in everything. It was something he tolerated for now, only because it was to his benefit. But he did not like it. Coming from the influential family that she came from, he knew he should expect her to be a little spoilt. For now it was bearable but he hoped to put a stop to it soon. Another difficulty he found since their dating, was always trying to keep her entertained.

She always had to be doing something exciting. Going to the latest theatre show or out for expensive dinners. He was constantly looking for new places to take her, places that would keep her interested and amused. He had no doubt that everything filtered back through to her father, so it was a must in their relationship. He had to keep her happy. Even so, it would be nice if they could have some quiet moments in their lives together. Sometimes he just wished they could sit at his home and watch a movie and eat popcorn. Just chat and laze around together. In all the time he had known and dated Zara, they had never done that. Not once. But he knew that was not his wild, tantalizing Zara. She was used to excitement. Constant excitement. And that meant theatres and dinners. Places where she could be seen. He did, however, agree with himself that it was a small price to pay for what he wanted in the long term, and slowly, Zara was helping him achieve his goals.

Since they started dating seriously, he had been given two promotions at Bills Maddox's Law Firm. Raymond knew he was a hard worker and deserved the positions, but at the same time, knew that Zara's influence also had something to do with it. She had been a good asset to have. Invaluable. What Zara wanted, Daddy got for her. And he had to make sure that Zara knew what he wanted so she could get it for him. He was constantly giving her hints. It was the perfect circle. He dropped it into conversation with Zara and she went running to tell daddy. Daddy hated to refuse his one and only daughter and somehow he managed to get what he wanted. It was the prefect plan with no visible flaws.

Raymond took a walk around his new spacious flat, then went back into his office, taking in the large oak desk with the expensive leather recliner seat. The handmade bookshelves that adorned one side of the wall, contained all his books and work files. It was almost like his office at the office. Except this was home. His home. And everything in it had been carefully selected. He had spent a fortune having the place expertly decorated. Expensive. All of it expensive. Only the very best. He left the office again and headed toward the sitting room. He had been thrilled with the work and overall look the interior decorator had achieved. Leather sofas adorned the thick pile carpets; large pieces of artwork hung on the walls, and all of it done to his exact taste. It was perfect. And he knew without a doubt that without Zara, some of these things would not have been possible. She opened the gateway to the life he wanted.

His thoughts were disrupted when the phone rang. He headed back toward the study and picked up the screaming handset.

"Hello?" Raymond answered.

"Hi, honey," Zara drawled into the phone.

"Hi, you," Raymond replied. "I'm on my way to pick you up, running a little late…will be there in a jiffy…"

Zara interrupted him in mid sentence, "Actually, Ray, that is why I am calling. I have to cancel tonight I'm afraid. Feeling terribly stiff and sore again after my class, and have an unbelievable headache. I won't be good company."

Raymond stopped short, thought for a moment, then replied, "Uhhh, you poor thing."

"I know, I feel horrible. Think I might just go to bed. Sleep it off, if that's okay?"

Raymond smiled at the words. "That's fine. You take a hot shower and get into bed. I'll see you during the week. Okay?"

"Yes, okay. I'm sorry to do this again. I'll make it up to you, I promise."

They ended the conversation, and when Raymond got off the phone, he felt relieved. This had happened for the last two weeks. At first he had been irritated that she kept cancelling their dates, but then it dawned on him that he was actually being let off the hook. He knew that the Saturdays she spent rehearsing were tough on her, and that she would be curled up in bed as soon as she arrived home. As long as he knew that she was there, safe and alone, he felt he could go out and enjoy himself. So, here he was now. Another whole Saturday evening to himself. What should he do? The possibilities were endless. He opened the black book he had on the desk, ran his finger down the list, then called a few numbers.

Hours later, while Zara was tucked up in bed, Raymond found himself at the Reef Bar with some of his old university buddies. They had all ventured into different fields, but still kept in contact. Friends like them were hard to find. The music was on full blast and he was having a great time. Pint in hand, he knew he should be guilty about Zara, but he also knew that she would not like this kind of place. A place where you could eat sloppy chips and drink lager on tap. A place where you did not have to put on any airs. He knew that Zara liked her food served to her in an elegant restaurant, not like here where you had to order it yourself from the bar. A place where she could drink champagne in a crystal-stemmed flute. Here she would be lucky if she could get a glass. He looked around. Most of the girls were enjoying their drinks from a bottle with a straw. It was totally different to what she was used to. He loved the upper-crust lifestyle, loved it a whole lot, but sometimes it was nice to just slip into a dark pub and let your hair down. Not have to worry about what you said and what you did. He had never been in this kind of place with Zara before. And that was why he was enjoying these rare Saturday evenings. He could meet up with old friends and have a laugh. There were no airs and graces and manners did not exist.

The DJ returned back from his half-hour break. Minutes later the bar was filled with pop music. Guys and girls took to the dance floor in large groups. Raymond tried to keep away for as long as possible, but the music was too enticing. Jumping off his seat, he joined his buddies, and took to the dance floor too.

Chapter 11

Zara wanted to be prepared for her class that day. It was only the third Saturday session, but she knew she had to make an impression, and early on in the game. She had sacrificed a great deal over the last few weeks. Firstly, she had cancelled two Saturday evening dates. She still could not believe she had been succumbed to that kind of behaviour. And to make matters worse, she had done it again during the week. She had been so keen on impressing Helen she had spent hours in her room practising. Something she had never done in her life before. But then again, nothing in her life had been this important before. So each and every day she had practised for as many hours as she could. Naturally, her mother had been beyond pleased. Bragged about it to all their friends at her tea parties. She knew that she had already scored big points where her mum was concerned. Still, she knew she could not keep doing this. Cancelling dates because she was too tired? It was ridiculous! Her private life was going to dwindle down to nothing if she was not careful, and that she would not allow to happen.

But now, as she entered the hall, she was glad she had spent all her time practising and was a few steps ahead. One look at Helen and that reconfirmed her original thoughts. She was one tough woman. Making herself noticed might be harder that she had thought, but she was prepared in more ways than one. Not only was she confident with the steps she knew they would be doing that day, but she had also ensured she had the right kind of sustenance with her. Bottles of Lucazade were in her tog bag, along with energy bars and glucose sweets. She did not normally believe in those kind of things, but she had been surprised at how quickly her energy levels seemed to return when she did use them, so was happy to continue to do so. Whatever would help in her cause she would use. They were only two people who were not happy in her newfound goal. One was her friend Pat. Zara knew that this sudden change of direction in herself left Pat without much of a friend. Before, they would do everything together and days were spent shopping, lunching and going to exciting places. They were both enjoying their gap year to the fullest, while deciding what they were going to do with themselves for the rest of their lives. Now, since her World Games agenda, all her spare time was spent practising. She still could not believe herself, that she was being this dedicated to her cause. Zara knew that Pat resented this new found challenge, and although she was enjoying the Saturday classes, she did not understand why Zara was being so adamant in succeeding.

The second person who was being effected by her new interest was poor Raymond. She knew that he must be irritated with her. Cancelling all these dates at the last minute. A part of her thought what the hell, he had to deal with it, and the other part wanted to make it up to him. It was a strange double feeling. She knew she would have to rectify that situation as soon as she could.

Zara scanned the room as she entered the studio. She had been happy with the new spot she had chosen the second half of the previous week, so she headed for the same position again as soon as she arrived. She could see Helen clearly, and also had the added advantage of the screens, should she need. It had been ideal viewing point last week, so she was making sure she had the same advantages from now on.

Zara was just putting down her tog bag, and slipping into her leather pumps, when she noticed Jane and Sarah enter the hall. She saw them stop and scan the room as she had done herself. She was not sure if she was imagining it, but once Jane noticed Zara, she deliberately headed for the opposite direction. Zara thought it strange, but was not particularly bothered. Let them stand where they wanted. The previous two weeks she had been seriously bothered by those two. They seemed to distract her concentration in more ways than one. It was better that they were on the other side of the hall. For both their sakes.

"What was that all about?" Sara asked as she dropped her tog bag onto the floor.

"What?" Jane asked innocently as she rummaged for the small towel she had bought with her. Sara knew her friend too well.

"You know what!" she answered back.

Jane knew that there was no skirting around the subject. Sarah had been her friend for many years. She could read her like a book. "There's just something about her that I don't like."

Sarah nodded her head in agreement. "I know what you mean. I cannot quite place my finger on it either. Just something about her screams, be careful!"

Jane was quiet as she found her towel. "For the last two classes, she has kept getting in my way. I don't know if it has been on purpose or not, but I cannot concentrate when she's around. I'd rather just keep away from her." Sarah agreed it was the best thing to do. They were there to dance and get chosen for Germany. Not to squabble with another dancer. That would only hinder their development and slow them down in the long run. Ignoring Zara would be for the best.

Pat arrived shortly after Jane and Sarah. She too scanned the room and spotting Zara, made her way over. "Good, they've not started yet. Thought I might be late," Pat exclaimed in relief.

"Nope. You're not late. Not yet anyway," replied Zara. Pat quickly set about changing her shoes from her trainers to her dance slippers.

Just as she finished, Helen took the stage. "Okay, girls," Helen said, clapping her hands loudly into the mike, "welcome back." Zara noted that this week Helen had chosen to wear a bright green leotard. The colour made her look even stricter than she had looked the previous two weeks. Her hair was still the same though. Neatly gelled back, held in place in a stern bun. Nothing about her looked different, including the gaze she ran across the room. Zara had already decided that Helen was tough. Now she could confirm it.

The day took on the same procedures as the previous two weeks. Helen first began by rehearsing what they had learnt the previous Saturday. Some of the girls, and it was obvious to see who, had practised the steps due for this lesson and knew what they were doing. They were the ones that looked confident. They were the ones eager to progress and continue with the new phase. Surprisingly, there were a large number of girls that had not practised at all. They had left the previous Saturday's rehearsal and not given the routine another thought until today's class. It was painfully obvious which girls these were, as they were hopelessly lost, having forgotten all that they had learnt the previous week. As Zara watched yet another girl stop and look blank, she was thrilled that she was not one of them. She knew exactly what she was doing and she was confident that Helen would know that too.

The music began for the second time that week, and they danced the set sequence from the week before. Jane knew that compared to most girls, both her and Sarah were doing well. Jane knew it was not because they were any better, but because they had gone home and practised the steps. It made a huge difference to their performance. Jane still could not get over the fact that some of the girls had completely forgotten what they had learnt the week before. It was amazing to think they had even turned up at all today, knowing that they would be unable to remember anything they had learnt. They must have thought that Helen would spend another full day going over it all again with them. They were sadly mistaken. Helen spent the first hour rehearsing, giving some advice to those that required it, but then she moved onto the new phase. Jane was excited to do so. She wanted to learn more. She was feeling much more relaxed with the kind of movements Helen was wanting them to dance now. She had spent ages in front of the mirror perfecting the steps until she had mastered them. It had taken awhile, but she could say that she had finally managed to do it. She knew it required some practice, so that is what she had done. Practised diligently throughout the week.

The next phase was just as exciting as the first phase, although the steps became more complicated, requiring more movements. Some of the girls were visibly struggling. It was not with the new steps, but with what they had failed to practice from the week before. Grasping the second phase, when you had not yet grasped the first phase was what led to their problems. These girls soon flaked out, and spent a lot of time standing around, watching and talking. Helen soon moved those girls to the back of the class. From then on, the talking seemed to cease, but they never did seem to catch up.

By lunchtime, many of the girls felt tired and it was time for a much deserved break. Jane felt tired herself, she had pushed much harder than she had intended to, but she felt exhilarated at the same time. They had covered a lot of ground and had progressed well after only three lessons. Lunch seemed to pass too quickly and soon they were back in the hall, in their same positions, ready to continue with the afternoon session.

The second session was just as exciting as the first, although Helen took the class to the next level, which made things more difficult. The sequence they had learnt over the past few Saturday's contained numerous kicks, both in front of them and to the side. Helen now felt the need to correct odd styles and techniques that she had noticed in some of the girls. For most of the afternoon they listened and watched Helen show them how to kick correctly. They then tried to correct themselves in the mirrors, knowing where they were going wrong. Jane thought it was strange that the kicks did not feel any different when she was actually doing them, but they looked so different in the mirrors. More controlled, but at the same time allowing them to achieve more height and gracefulness. It was a neat trick.

Class was almost over for the day. Helen made them run through the sequence one last time. She sat on her chair and watched them all. Her eyes were taking in the dancers before her, analysing their every movement. Once they had finished, she made them all sit down on the floor. She had an announcement. What she announced was the equivalent to a bombshell.

Chapter 12

Jane sat at the kitchen counter peeling the potatoes for lunch. On Sundays they always had a roast dinner. It was tradition in their household. Her mother would roast a pork leg or a lamb joint, and they would enjoy a meal together as a family. Sometimes they invited friends around too. Normally, Jane loved it when they invited other families, but today she was glad that it would just be the four of them. Jane dropped another peeled potato into the silver dish. She was doing the movements, but her mind was elsewhere. Everything had been going so well until the end of the dancing session. Helen's announcement had sent shock waves throughout the hall, and not just for her. Everyone present had been in shock and disbelief. It was amazing how one small piece of new information could totally change your outlook on a situation.

She had arrived home tired and stiff after her class, just the same as the previous weeks. Her mother had already prepared a thick Irish stew for dinner, which she normally loved. Last night, however, the tender meat stuck in her throat and even four glasses of water would not help it go down. After dinner, she had then tried to watch television with the rest of the family, but she could make no sense of what she was watching. The screen was just a haze of blurs. She had managed to sit through three hours of entertainment and had no idea what she had watched. When she finally made it to bed, she was exhausted, her mind was in overdrive, but as tired as she was, sleep would not come. The question kept playing in her mind. How was she going to tell her parents? The question seemed to loom over her head like a big, dark cloud. It was the last thing she remembered thinking about before she fell asleep.

When she woke up the following morning, it was from a fitful and restless night. At first she did not know why. Then it hit her. The awful news that could bring her life crashing down around her. She had always believed that whatever your problems, they would always look better in the morning. Now with first hand experience, she could honestly say that it did not. Not even a little. Her problem actually seemed bigger than before. Unsolvable. Larger than the world. She knew she would have to tell her parents over lunch today. There was no other option. The sooner they knew the better. But how was she going to tell them? She could barely come to terms with it herself. How was she actually going to put it into words for them to understand?

Jane picked up another potato and began to peel with gusto. How was she going to break the news to her parents that if she was lucky enough to get picked, they then had to worry about the financial implications also?

Jane still could not get over it. When she had found out herself, she had been stunned into silence.

Sarah, also in shock and denial, had dropped her tog bag onto the floor in utter disbelief. Finally, still in shock, she had turned to Jane. "They're not serious are they?" she asked.

Jane did not know what to say in reply. It looked as if they were serious, although it was unbelievable. She had hoped after a few minutes that Helen would break out into a large smile, and burst out laughing. It had all been a joke. Ha ha, funny funny. A tasteless joke she thought, but a joke nevertheless. But as she stood there in disbelief and watched Helen after she broke the news, she knew. This was no joke. She was deadly serious. A number of questions fired into Jane's mind at that precise moment. How could they expect each contestant to pay for their own way on this trip? It was a world event. Surely they had sponsors already lined up for this sort of thing? Three months in Germany at a private boarding school? Without having to be told, Jane knew it was going to be expensive. Jane could not believe the price when they had been given the figure. What were they going to be eating? Gold? Her parents would never agree to pay that kind of money. Who could blame them? It was a small fortune. She knew they would be happy to do so if they could, but the amount they were asking, even she knew, was just too much. Jane had hoped being chosen would help set off her career in the right direction. She already knew there would be scouts present. And everyone knew they were the most important people. You impressed one of them and the possibilities they could offer you would be endless. Besides the scouts, there would also be television and news cameras. Whoever was chosen would be given a whole heap of publicity, that could help any career take off in the right direction. And now it might all flutter away, out of her reach. And all because of Helen's numbing announcement.

Helen's broadcast continued to shock and bewilder. Besides having to pay for their own flights and accommodation in the private hostel, they also had to pay for their own costumes and any outfits in addition, that they might need. Jane could not believe what she was hearing. It was unheard of. If it had been any other event, the organizers would not have got away with it. Being the World Games, they knew that performers would be lined up to take advantage of the tremendous opportunity, regardless of the cost to themselves. Jane was sure the organizers knew this and were using this information to their utmost advantage. It meant less for them to worry about. Any girl picked would know it was a tremendous privilege.

Helen tried unsuccessfully to lessen the blow of her unwelcome news. She assured them that up until today, they had agreed on only one costume per routine, and a two piece track suit, with the team and country colours. Jane knew it was not much in the way of garments for an international event, but she also knew what the price of these costumes could cost. And if her guess was correct, they would have to be specially designed, which meant they would cost a small fortune. The event was slowly beginning to cost more and more, making it more and more unattainable.

What had began as an exciting adventure had now turned out into a financial burden. Jane knew that the total cost of the trip was just far too much for her parents. What they were asking for was a fortune.

Helen must have known that her announcement would cause a shock wave to ripple throughout the hall. Undoubtedly, she had probably seen it happen before, so she had come armed and prepared. For the last half an hour of the class, she had gone through ideas that she had seen work before, that had helped raise funds. She suggested finding large companies to sponsor the event. Fathers, uncles, friends. Anyone who might have an interest could be approached. Many large companies, Helen assured the class, jumped at the chance to have their name spread across billboards as advertisements. She suggested other things too. Raffles, sponsors and donations could all be used to raise money and generate funds.

Jane listed to Helen, but knew with a sinking feeling in her heart that the amount that was needed was too much. There was no way she could generate that kind of money in three months, even with sponsors and donations. It was impossible. The unwelcome news had put a whole new perspective on the trip to Germany. She knew now that there might be a possibility that she would not be able to go. She felt like there was a large knot sitting inside her stomach getting bigger and bigger with each passing moment. She felt completely helpless. There was nothing she could do except face the dreadful situation.

She had finished peeling the potatoes, started and finished all the carrots, and was now setting the table as the food roasted happily in the oven. Keeping busy was good. It gave her something to do. Helped occupy the millions of thoughts running wildly through her mind. She estimated that lunch would be ready in less than half an hour. Jane knew she needed to get a grip. She needed to remain calm and in control. State the facts clearly and in a positive way, then wait her parent's reactions. There was no other way she could break this kind of news to them.

They all came to table at much the same time, just as the bell for the oven rang. Perfect timing. It must have been the warm rich smells coming from the kitchen that beckoned everyone over to their seats. Her mum busied herself with removing the chicken from the oven and brought the large roasting dish to the table for everyone to see. The chicken smelt heavenly, and was wallowing in rich juices and creamy vegetables. It smelt and looked delicious. Her father carved the chicken with ease, and dished everyone a healthy portion while her mother passed along the roasted vegetables. Before long, everyone was served and they were all enjoying the succulent meal.

Jane listened to her parents talking and waited for a gap in the conversation where she could casually bring up her predicament, but no window of opportunity seemed to present itself. Jane knew she would have to do it soon before she lost her nerve. Everyone was dishing themselves second helpings.

Her father reached for some more carrots, and while doing so, he turned toward Jane and asked, "So how was practice yesterday, Jane? You never did mention it."

Jane stopped chewing. Now? Should she bring it up now? Was this the gap she had been waiting for? She swallowed hard and took a deep breath. "It's going well," she managed to get out. "Hard work, but I think it will get easier with each practice. It's only the third Saturday, and already the classes seem to be getting better. Helen seems good, very efficient. Although, I get the impression she's quite strict."

Her father laughed. "That's good. Hard work never hurt anybody."

Jane let the heavy silence sit for a while, wondering what she should say next. And then, without thinking, the words and her problem just tumbled out of her mouth. It was if she had been calmly practising and rehearsing the speech she now delivered for weeks.

Later, when Jane was back in her room, she felt relieved. Relived that the dreaded secret was now out in the open. She hated keeping things from her parents. Now she felt better. They knew. She would just have to wait and see what they would decide. She was pleased by the way they had taken the report. She expected shock, maybe denial. She had been a mixture of both when Helen had broken the news to her. Even now, she could not believe the announcement was actually true. Instead, her parents had taken the news far better than she would have ever thought possible. They had taken the information in their stride. No immediate outbursts and more importantly, no refusals. They had sat calmly at the table and let the news sink in.

"That's a lot of money, Jane," her father replied after some time.

Jane nodded. "I know it is."

There was a long pause while everyone sat and ate in silence.

Finally her father spoke again. "Your mom and I will have to think it over."

It was all he said. It was all she said. They let the matter drop and spoke of other things.

Jane felt relieved, but still nervous. They were thinking it over. It was all she could ask. It was going to be a lot of money.

Still, even so, she could not help wondering what they would decide. They knew how she felt about her dancing. Her soon to be career. They must know what it meant to have this kind of once in a lifetime opportunity. Maybe if they had said "No" straight away, she would have fallen at their feet and begged, but for now, she was content that when they said they would think about it, they meant it.

Besides, she was happy to leave the decision in their hands for a while. It felt good to finally have the burden off her chest. She did not think she could have born it alone for much longer. She knew it would be a tough decision for them to make. It was a lot of money. The amount she needed for this trip could very well be used for a holiday for the whole family to some exotic destination, or it could be used for a new kitchen, or maybe even have been used to build a conservatory onto the house for everyone to enjoy. They would have to give all the other ideas up for a long time. Still, for the first time since she had received the news, Jane felt that there was a tiny glimmer of hope. Her chances were not completely lost, yet.

And that hope got her thinking later that night. If, and it was a big if, her parents agreed to pay the money, there must be some way she could help to contribute. Something she could do to help raise funds. It was, after all, going to be for her benefit. Jane closed her eyes and thought hard. There must be something that she could do that would help. Maybe she should consider doing what Helen had suggested. Speak to her father and her uncles about their companies sponsoring her. She knew it was a long shot, but if she were actually going to Germany, she would do anything to help in its cause. She knew that even if her parents managed to pay for the whole thing themselves, which was unlikely, she was still going to need spending money for herself for while she was there. She knew she had to find a way to make extra money. But how?

It was some time later when her newfound hope allowed an idea to form. The more Jane thought about it, the more the idea seemed to take hold. She went through the motions. Thought it through. Yes, she was sure it could be done. The idea seemed so perfect she could not believe she had not thought of it sooner.

Jane decided that the ideal way to make some cash would be to take on a waiter job. It would allow her a measure of freedom, which she would need if she had to attend dance classes, as well as give her the flexibility to practice when she needed to. She thought about how to make it work. She would make herself available in the evenings. She had college during the day, but as soon as that was finished, she would be free to work a late afternoon or the evening shift. Holidays were coming up soon too, so she knew she could arrange that she worked those full days. Saturday evenings she knew would be a "no go" day for her. After a full day rehearsing with Helen, she was not sure that a work shift would be the best thing for her, especially if the last Saturdays were anything to go by, but she would make it up to them. She would agree to work the full Sunday. Morning, noon and evening, if they required. She was sure that there must be somewhere that would be happy to take her on, for the shifts she could work. Jane tried not to get too excited. If she could pull this off, she would be able help her parents and also make herself some extra cash to take with her. Besides, she thought, it would be fun having a job. For now, it seemed the perfect solution and it gave her almost a full three months where she could save before she had to leave. Jane was excited and thrilled at having come up with a concrete solution. This idea might work very well. She knew her parents said they would think things through, but she was sure that her new plan would help them to make a faster decision. (preferably a yes.) She knew she should probably wait, but was too excited now that an idea had formed and she wanted to share the idea with them immediately.

She skipped down the stairs, in search of her parents. She found her mother first. She was outside, bringing in the dry and clean washing. As her mother unpinned and folded the clean clothes, Jane went through the details of her newfound plan. Step by step she explained her idea and why she thought it would work. Again, the words seemed to flow easily. Her mother listened silently, not interrupting. When Jane had finally finished explaining her plan, her mother was very quiet. Jane could see she was thinking. Thinking hard. She was silent for a while longer. Then she nodded, having made her decision and smiled. "It could work. I'll discuss this with your father later tonight."

Jane was thrilled that her mother also thought it was a good plan. Now that the idea had formed she could not keep still. She wanted to get started as soon as possible. She looked at her watch. It was still fairly early. She was sure that the news agent would still be open. Maybe, if she hurried, she could get the newspaper and begin her search for a suitable restaurant to work in. Jane rushed upstairs, shouted to her mum that she would be gone for ten minutes, then headed toward the news agent. It was only a short walk around the corner, and within a few minutes Jane saw the familiar yellow sign appear in the distance. There was bound to be wanted ads placed by small companies in the area, or even a dedicated employment section. She was sure she could find something that would fit in with her schedule. Normally she liked to look around the shop when she went there. They had a wonderful gift section and every week there seemed to be new things added to the collection. Today however, Jane barely paused. She did not want to waste any time. Instead, she headed straight for the magazine section, chose about five different newspapers before paying and then walked briskly home.

Jane wanted to be comfortable. She made everyone a cup of tea and then settled herself at her desk with a red marker pen. She read the employment section on each paper from start to finish. Any jobs that were suitable, she circled with a bright red ring. When she had finished all her reading, she was pleased to note that she had a few possible options. She read them all again.

There was one job that did seem to jump out at her more than the others. Jane was not entirely sure why that was. It was an advertisement for an Italian restaurant. The placement said. *Waitress required. Flexible hours to cover shifts throughout the week. Please call anytime after 11:00 a.m.* Jane read the advertisement again. Flexible hours. She liked the sound of that. Having picked the job she wanted to apply for, she decided that she would have to give them a ring as soon as their restaurant opened in the morning.

* * * * *

While Jane was surveying the paper at home in the hope of obtaining a new job to help pay for the trip, Zara sat at home wallowing in her glee. The moment Helen had mentioned the price for the trip to Germany, Zara knew her chances of being chosen had increased dramatically. Even with her parents being wealthy, Zara knew it was a heavy price tag. Many of the other dancer's parents would simply not be able to afford the cost of the trip. Zara could not contain her smirk of happiness. That definitely narrowed down the competition. Luckily for her, she had no problems in the financial department. She would simply ask Daddy for the money. She knew he would never say no. Especially for something like this. Zara had heard from Raymond earlier in the week, and he had told her that Daddy was again talking to his colleagues at work about her new goals. It only proved that word was already getting around. Oh yes, Daddy would pay the money and pay it gladly. She was soon to be the favourite and successful daughter of Bill Maddox. Zara could not help laughing out aloud. Everything was all falling into place splendidly.

Zara knew the time had come for her to start making use of her new status. She certainly was not doing this for nothing. She had plans. And one of them was milking this trip for all it was worth. She sat and thought for a while. What else could she ask her parents for? She needed to test them out, to see just how much playing power she had under her belt.

After some careful planning she had decided. She would ask Daddy for the Germany money first, giving him a full rundown of what it was all for. He would like that. Her father loved facts and figures. Then, while she was on the subject, she would try and negotiate a new wardrobe for herself. She would make it sound small and insignificant to his ears, and then if he agreed, she would revamp her whole wardrobe, right down to her belts, shoes and handbags. Just thinking of it made her get excited. She was not sure how he would react to the new wardrobe idea, but if he was willing to go along with it, she could push it even further. Maybe even go a far as negotiating an increase in her weekly allowance. He must know she would need more money for when she was out there. It was all a test to gauge his reactions and then analyse his response. Zara needed to know just how much she could get out of the whole deal.

With the beginnings of her new plan in motion, Zara laughed happily before running down the marble staircase toward her father's office. There was no time like the present.

Chapter 13

The next Saturday came as complete shock when Jane and Sarah entered the studio. They had arrived early again, as was the custom over the past weeks. They wanted to be sure they managed to get a good view of Helen for their upcoming class. The studio was deathly quiet, which was unusual and when they walked into the dancing room, they were greeted with an empty hall. Jane checked her watch. Yes it was correct. Her battery had not run out. There was nothing wrong with it. She checked the clock on the far wall just to make sure. Yes. It was 8:40 a.m. "Where is everybody?" asked Sarah.

Jane shook her head. "I have no idea."

"The venue has not changed or anything, has it?"

"Well, if it has, I am not aware of it. No one has said anything to me." They went to the front of the studio and set their things down before getting ready for the class ahead. Time ticked by and a few more girls entered the studio. They were also surprised at how empty the hall was. Normally, the hall would be a hive of activity already, with dancers loitering around in various stages of warming up. They joined Jane and Sarah. The hall seemed so much bigger now, half empty.

With only ten minutes to go before the class was due to start, Jane knew the reason had to do with Helen's announcement the week before. Undoubtably, many of the girls would have had to tell their parents the news, and ask for their help in funding the trip. No one their age would have that kind of money. The result had been what they were seeing today. More then half the class had not turned up. It was a dramatic contrast to what they had seen the previous weeks. What had began as over two-hundred girls in this area of Shoeing, had now dwindled to less than fifty. If this was happening here, then Jane knew it must be happening in the other areas too. With each dance lesson, the numbers seemed to dwindle. First, because of what was required from each dancer physically. Now it also seemed that the financial burden of the trip was the next factor. Slowly, there were becoming less and less dancers present for each class. It was almost like a process of elimination.

Zara entered the studio. She knew that she could expect less dancers present today, but even she was taken back with just how many had not turned up for the class. She wanted to scream in joy. The more that did not show today the better. Her chances were improving daily.

Helen arrived. She looked unfazed at the number of girls present as she took the stage. It was almost as if she was expecting this sort of outcome. Knew it was going to happen. She looked neither upset nor pleased, only eager to begin the day's class. "Glad to see you have all made it," Helen was saying. "Don't worry about the numbers, it is always like this on the fourth week. For those of you who are serious about doing this, you will notice it's much better with less people in the class. Now, let's get started."

They began the class, and Helen was right. The difference was noticeable almost immediately. The big plus factor was that no one was pushing and shoving for space. There was enough for each dancer to move freely without getting in someone else's way. This made the dancing easier, more enjoyable. The hall itself was also more comfortable. Before, with over two-hundred bodies packed into the hall, it had been hot and stuffy. By the end of the afternoon session, it was hard to breathe, with no fresh air circulating around the room. Now, with fewer dancers present, one could actually feel the air-conditioning and the fresh air blowing inside from the open windows. It made the class and the heat much more bearable.

Helen was keen to get the class started. The first few weeks were always the worst for her. She hated taking the beginning classes because most of the girls present were not dedicated dancers, but chancres. Helen would not have minded if they were prepared to work for their big break, but most did not. Now, at least, after a few classes and her announcements, she had managed to sift out the talented and dedicated girls. The girls remaining were the ones that actually wanted to be there. There was nothing worse than teaching to a bunch of girls who did not want to learn in the first place. Now, looking at the girls present, Helen was pleased to note that she recognized a few faces. The girls she was looking at wanted to learn and make the best of the opportunity given to them. Teaching these girls would now be easier. They would want to learn and would be eager to take any advice and training she offered.

Jane also noticed a remarkable difference in the quality of the class. Gone were the dancers that were unsure of themselves and who kept getting lost. Gone also were those that were guessing the steps and movements because of lack of practice. Instead, all that was left were the dancers that were dedicated and who wanted to succeed. Dancers like herself, who were grabbing this opportunity with both hands. There were still girls present with various degrees of talent. Even so, each and every girl present knew what steps they were doing. These were the girls that had survived.

Helen began the class promptly at 9:00 a.m. She let them run through the dance routine three times. The first time she played the music, she danced along with them as was customary, to help them ease into the upcoming day. The second and third times, she watched and assessed the girls present and their performance. After the music died down for the third time, Helen left her podium, and began to thread her way between the dancers. It was time to correct any mistakes she had noted. She picked various girls in the group and in a firm manner, corrected any mistakes she had noticed. She was patient. She watched them rehearse the same steps over and over again until each dancer had mastered the correction. Then, she would move on to the next girl and start all over again. She did not leave until she was satisfied that the movements were being done correctly. With over fifty pupils in the studio, it was still considered a large class and it took Helen some time to get around to each of the girls present. The girls were like sponges. Whatever she said or suggested, was soaked up eagerly. They were keen to rehearse and correct any areas she commented on, knowing that it would help their performance. While Helen made her way around the class, the other girls listened and practised amongst themselves. They used the mirrors and danced the same steps continuously, going over the steps without pausing. After making her way through all the girls present, Helen played the music for the fourth time.

Helen watched with a critical eye. There were still a few areas that needed working on, but it was far better than before. Once the music finished, she again set about correcting the last remaining problem areas.

Another half and hour later and Helen was pleased that most of the girls had mastered what she had been trying to teach them. The fifth time she played the music, she was silent. It looked much, much better. It was now time to add onto the existing sequence.

Jane was enjoying the new way the class was being run. She found it easier to see Helen and there was a happier vibe in the room from most of the girls present. She was however, finding it increasingly difficult to keep away from Zara. With a large majority of the girls now gone, it was impossible to stay at the other end of the hall from her. She seemed to dance using as much space as she could cover. Jane had watched her a few times as she danced, and had noted a remarkable improvement in her movements. Jane had thought her talented before, but she seemed bored, almost if she was forced to be there. This week, however, Zara was diffcrent. She wanted to be there. Her moves were more defined, and she did not appear as lost as she had on previous occasions. She seemed to have a burst of energy that had been missing before. It was a surprise. She was like a completely different girl. Jane wondered what had gotten into her. Her friend Pat was also still present, which was surprising. She was dancing with the rest of them, but she seemed to be lacking the sparkle. The enthusiasm.

While Jane was watching Zara, Zara was well aware that she was being watched. She was glad again that she had opted missing dinner with Raymond, and instead had spent the evening in her room practising. She had been up for three hours. She had hated it, but she knew it had been worth it. Raymond had seemed to take it in his stride and accepted her reasons without any objections. She was glad that he was not giving her a hard time. It made her decision to stay in and rehearse much easier.

Now, as she danced the steps she had practised so hard on, she was thrilled that it had actually paid off. So, they want to look, she thought. Well, I'll give them a show, one they won't forget. She knew the steps by heart and she was confident in what she was doing. Zara was enjoying this, especially knowing that they were watching her, so she made an extra effort into throwing all her energy into her movements. If they wanted to look at her, then let them look. She kicked as high as she could and made her movements sharp and clear, aware that once she even caught Helen's eye. An extra point for her, she thought. She smiled and danced as if she was loving every minute.

Zara finished her spectacular display and then excused herself, making her way to the bathrooms. Only when she was alone, hidden out of view in one of the cubicles, did she allow herself to breathe properly. The air was not coming quick enough for her lungs to take in. The great gulps did not seem to help, giving her small irritating hiccups instead. She must remember to breathe when she did that again. Even with the hiccups, it had been worth it. At least now they knew she was competition. After a few long minutes, with her head between her legs, her breathing finally seemed to get back to normal. She sat like that for a few moments longer, and waited for her heart to stop racing. Then when she could, she rummaged through her bag. Zara located one of the energy bars she had brought with her, and quickly tore of the wrapper, before biting deeply. She chewed fast and furiously, willing the energy to seep into her body. After a few minutes Zara felt better. Her breathing was back to normal and she had a good energy lift. She threw the wrapper into the bin, and made her way back to the class as if nothing had happened.

The morning session was over and they were due to begin the second session. Zara made a point of breathing. She never knew she would have to concentrate on something as simple as that, but here she was, talking to herself inside her head. She did that through most of Helen's session now. It became harder though as the day progressed. Helen was teaching them all sorts of new steps. Steps she had never danced before and had to concentrate on performing. Somehow today, learning all the new steps, it seemed much harder than the previous sessions.

Jane and Sarah were also both finding the second session in the afternoon complicated. Helen was finally happy with the sequence they had been learning over the last few weeks and had decided that it was time to move on and add some more steps. Jane felt exactly as she had that very first class. Everything seemed weird and strange again. Extra jumps were included in places, and strange kicks were added into the routine. They seemed to take more practice to master. Jane was glad that she was not the only one that was finding the new steps difficult. Others were also struggling as she herself was. Helen continued to walk between the girls, assisting where she could and offering advice and correcting. Jane was annoyed. She had finally thought she had mastered these strange kicks when Helen seemed to add another peculiar kick to the ever increasing long list. Again Jane found herself thinking that the movements were staggered and weird. She felt strange doing them, as if they were not meant to be that way. Still she kicked, kicked as high as could, determined to get the kicks perfect. Jane found that she was pushing herself harder than she had ever pushed herself before. Kicking as high as she could, jumping with all her energies and throwing her entire body into her movements. She always knew when she was dancing hard, as her feet were the first part of her body to scream their protest. Jane knew she could ignore that. For the time being. The second sign that she knew she was pushing harder than she should be, was when she began to feel the deep aching in her muscles. At first, it was just her shoulder blades, a small discomfort. She had ignored it. Then as time passed, the ache in her shoulders became stronger, and she began to feel her leg muscles cramp up. She had ignored that too, determined to continue to dance through it. With Helen watching she was not going to give up.

With fewer girls in the studio, Helen now had an excellent view of all the girls remaining in the class. She watched each and every one carefully. Already she was getting a feel for who was going to make it, narrowing the small class even further. She did not only monitor their dancing skills, she monitored other things too. Things like their energy levels and their discipline. Both were important factors when looking for potentials. She had already began making mental notes on some of the girls present and was happy to admit that there were a few possibilities. She hoped that things did not change as classes became more frequent.

The class came to a slow end as Helen was finally pleased at the progress they had made that day. As the other girls dispersed, hot and tired, Jane instead found herself leaning against a cool wall and sat down for a few minutes. She was exhausted. She had pushed herself hard and knew she would be paying for it later. Sometimes enthusiasm would not allow her to stop when she should. Her leg was cramped up now. She rubbed it gently, willing the pain to go away. She was glad she was sitting on the floor as she did not think she had the energy to stand.

By the time Jane arrived home she could barely move. She had never in her life felt this stiff and sore. Her body ached in places she never knew she could ache in. She was exhausted beyond measure and fell asleep in the car on the way home. She had not meant to, but as soon as she had closed her eyes, she had slipped into a deep sleep, the drive home sapping the last of her remaining energy.

It was only when she felt the gentle nudge of her mother's hand on her arm that she had woken up. They were home. "We're home, honey. Come inside."

Jane was so tired she could have stayed there, in the car, all night. She was content to be left lying on the back seat, sleeping. It was only the fact that she might get cold later that made her drag herself inside the house. With heavy and weary legs, she forced herself to walk to her bedroom. She pushed open the door and fell straight onto her bed. She would just lie there a few minutes and rest before having a shower. She smelt her hot and sweaty hair spread out around her. Yes, she would have to give it a wash too, but later. For now she just wanted to rest a few minutes longer. She was so tired. She ignored her stiff muscles and the burning sensation running through her body and closed her eyes. If she was really still, it almost went away. It felt so good. Just a few minutes rest, that was all she needed, she told herself. Then she would make herself take that hot and revitalizing shower.

When Jane next woke, she was still dressed in the same dancing clothes, her hair still fanned around her, still in need of a wash, but it was morning.

Chapter 14

Jane looked down the little quaint street, known to be the best street in all of Shoeing. It was full of interesting bistros and cafés, right on the water's edge. During the summer people could be seen eating outside, enjoying the shimmering of the lights as they were reflected off the water's edge. To add to the prefect picture, there were a few ducks and swans that had made their home in the shallow water, giving the entire setting a peaceful look. Jane knew that the restaurants themselves were known to cater to the more sophisticated guest, partly because these restaurants were so hard to get into, and partly because they were so expensive. She still could not believe that she had managed to secure an interview at one of these restaurants, and only after one phone call.

Jane took in the street and the hive of activity surrounding it. Music was playing somewhere in the distance and there was a street vendor selling a beautiful array of fresh flowers. It was still early, but already there was a cluster of eager people waiting to be served. Jane just had time to see a girl tie a red ribbon on one bouquet before helping the next customer in line. It was the kind of pleasant street that reeked money and social standing. Not because of the music, or because of the elegant flower shop, but because of the restaurants itself. Each one was painstakingly eager to be better than its neighbour next door and each one was in stiff competition, trying to woo your custom and your wallet in their direction. Competition in this street was stiff.

    Jane squirmed uncomfortably. She was still suffering from her over-exhaustion from the day before. Not even a full night's sleep had managed to allow her body to heal and return back to normal. She had woken up with a start. She had honestly expected to see darkness outside. She could hardly believe it when she had seen the beam of sunlight that had lay across her bed. Had she really slept through the entire night? Only the bright rays of warm sunshine had confirmed it. She had taken the long overdue shower and had washed her hair before she and got ready for her interview. And here she was now. Stiff and sore, but in the market for a job.

    She looked down the street again. Took in the busy movements around her and then, quite suddenly, uncertainty set in. This was the correct street, wasn't it? Jane asked herself. She then dug into her handbag for the advertisement she had cut out. Yes, she confirmed. This was correct. Now which one was is it? She scanned the note again. No 29. Michelangelo's Restaurant. Which one was that?

    Jane began to walk down the street, looking at the names of all the bistros and cafés lined next to each other. She had taken great care when getting dressed that morning, careful to ensure she looked the part of a professional waitress—if you got such a thing. She had changed over five times, not happy with what she had looked like when she stood in front of mirror. Finally she had settled on the most plain, but hopefully the most elegant outfit she could find. Long black trousers and a black frilly shirt.

That, accompanied with a small silver belt, and Jane knew she looked good. A pair of black high heels and a small black bag had completed the outfit. When Jane next looked in the mirror, she had to admit she looked professional. Professional and smart. Like she wanted this job. Knew how to do this job. She also had taken great care with her hair, brushing it until it shone, having decided that she would wear it loose. She felt she might be overdressed for the interview, but she decided she would rather be overdressed, than underdressed.

Now, walking down the smart, lively street, Jane was glad she had dressed as she had. She was not overdressed at all, but fit in perfectly with the settings around her. This small fact seemed to give her a small boost. She had to admit she was nervous. After scanning the papers, she had been left with a number of options, but this one was by far the best one she had seen. And, she hoped it was better paid too. Jane's thoughts were interrupted when she spotted the sign. Dark blue encrusted with gold letters. Michelangelo's. This was it.

The restaurant was on the other side of the street, so Jane had a few moments to survey it from a distance. Huge glass windows ran across from one side to the next. A large door was open to the public in the middle. Jane took in the smart entranceway, delicately decorated with bright flower pots and long elegant ferns. It looked like it all belonged in a book. Tables and chairs had also been laid outside. Jane could see a few ladies having tea, making use of the last of the afternoon sunshine. They seemed relaxed and like they were enjoying themselves. She took a deep breath, crossed the road, and entered the restaurant.

Inside, Jane had to admit she was surprised. She had expected it to be smart, but it was much more elegant than she could ever have imagined. The inside entranceway was small and cozy with bright yellow wallpaper adorning the walls. She could see inside the restaurant to both her left and her right. Each table was elegantly laid with a pale yellow silk tablecloth and matching serviettes. Jane could also not help noticing the long stemmed candles that sat so tall and proud on each table. The whole restaurant looked as if a wedding was due to take place. The flowers alone must have cost a small fortune. The whole restaurant oozed class, and for the second time Jane was glad she had dressed as she had. She was so lost in her thoughts of the decor of the room, that she did not see anyone approaching her from her left. It was only when he spoke, that Jane realized that she was no longer alone. "Can I help you, miss?" a small, balding man asked. Jane could not help noticing his attire, for he was dressed in a smart black suit that fit his small frame perfectly. He seemed totally at ease with his clothes and his surroundings.

Jane gathered her thoughts quickly and focussed on the man before her. "Yes, sir, I am looking for Mr. Ken. I have an arrangement to meet him at 4:00 p.m."

He smiled a jolly wide smile, then replied, "Jane, is it? We've been expecting you. Please come with me."

Jane followed the small man through the left part of the restaurant. She passed the elegant tables that ran the full length of the room, and finally she found herself inside a large, well appointed office at the very back of the restaurant.

"I will let Mr. Ken know you are here. Please make yourself comfortable. He is taking a call at present, but should not be too long." With that, the door was closed and Jane was left alone in the fancy office.

Jane looked around the room. It was a large office, very spacious. She was surprised at how perfectly neat everything was. There seemed to be nothing out of place. The one side of the office was a modern design, as it was made of clear glass and overlooking the river below. The view was spectacular. Jane could make out a couple with young children in the distance, throwing bread to the ducks and other birds. And across the river, was a spectacular view of the other restaurants and bistros. The sight before her made her think of what it must be like in the office at night. It was not difficult to imagine all the lights. It must look beautiful.

When Mr. Ken finally made an entrance, Jane had been waiting in the office for over twenty minutes. Normally she would have been irritated at such a delay, but today she had been lost in thought as she watched the scenes before her through the window, unaware as the time ticked on. When Mr. Ken finally did arrive, Jane was greeted by a tall, dark and handsome man, although in a rugged sort of way, with friendly eyes that creased when he smiled.

The interview itself went well. Jane did notice, more than once, how he surveyed her clothes and her hair. It was almost as if he was assessing what kind of person she was. She saw him look at her nails too, and was glad she had cleaned and painted them that morning. It had all been in an effort for today admittedly, but at least she had done them. He also took particularly interest in her shoes. She had wanted to look and see what he was looking at, but did not dare, thinking it might appear rude. Later, when he received another phone call, Jane had quickly checked to see if she had any scuffs or noticeable marks. No, they were black and shiny. Good. What had he been looking at then? After he had ended his conversation, he returned back to his list of questions, of which he seemed to have many.

An hour later, and she was still in the office answering questions. Mr. Ken seemed very interested in all that she did. There were many varied questions about her family, where she lived, her interests and hobbies. Jane was not sure why he was so interested in her background, as surely her interests and hobbies had no standing for the job she was interviewing for, but she desperately wanted this position, so answered as politely as possible. He then offered her coffee, which she accepted. Then, to her surprise, he proceeded to give her a tour of the restaurant and the kitchens. She did not want to get her hopes up so early on, but surely showing her around had to be a good sign.

Jane was surprised at how large the restaurant actually was. It seemed to twist and turn in all directions, and in each new section, there was an array of tables. Some were partly hidden for privacy. It all looked very cozy, and all splendidly decorated in the same pale yellow she had observed when she had first arrived.

"And this is the kitchen," Mr. Ken was saying.

The kitchen itself was large, with long silver benches running from one end to the other. Although the restaurant was not yet busy, with it only being 5:00 p.m. the chefs were already in full swing, preparing the food for the evening ahead. The kitchen was very busy with all sorts of activities taking place. Some of the chefs were making rich, creamy sauces, others were making little soufflé cakes. Others still, were peeling and preparing an array of fresh vegetables.

While she was taking it all in, Mr. Ken continued talking with gusto. "We pride ourselves in our food and service here at Michelangelo's," Mr. Ken was saying. "Every dish is made to perfection. Nothing leaves this kitchen without first being checked by our head chef," he added. Jane could hear the pride in his voice as he looked around.

She then followed Mr. Ken through the kitchens and back out into the restaurant again before they made their way to his office. "So, you have now seen everything here at Michelangelo's. If you are happy with everything, I would like you to begin tomorrow afternoon—four o'clock. How does that sound? Are you up for the job?"

Jane was so pleased she could barely speak, so she had smiled and nodded instead.

"Okay. Good. I will assign you with Peter for tomorrow. He has been here for over two years and will be able to show you what has to be done during a shift. Don't worry. Peter is an excellent teacher."

Jane smiled and thanked him. She left the restaurant still stiff and sore but elated. She had secured her first job. Things could only improve from here on.

When Jane arrived the next day, there was already a hive of activity inside the restaurant. Customers were still sitting at some of the tables, ordering what must be a very late lunch or maybe even an early dinner. She presented herself at the reception desk as before and was greeted by the same small, balding man. He introduced himself as Pierre Franco. He smiled his hello, took her coat and then showed her to Mr. Ken's Office again. He was expecting her, he had announced. Minutes later, she stood before Mr. Ken.

"Good, good! You're early. I've already called for Peter. He should be here any minute." As he said it, there was a small, soft tap on the door and a young man entered. "Uhh, Peter, we were just talking about you." He said, "May I introduce you to Jane Brown." Peter held out his hand as they were introduced. Jane shook it gently. "Jane will be joining us from today as a waitress. I have assigned her to work with you to begin with. Please, can you show her what has to be done and any other things she may need to know while she is here."

"It will be my pleasure," Peter replied, smiling, gazing down at Jane. Peter was a tall guy, also smartly dressed in a black suite. It seemed to be the normal attire of the men she had met at the restaurant so far. He had fair skin, and friendly blue eyes that deepened when he smiled. Jane liked him immediately.

"Jane, why don't you go with Peter for now. He will show you what needs to be done for this evening. I'll come and check on you a little later."

"Yes. No problem," Jane replied.

"We'll be fine," Peter replied to Mr. Ken, as he smiled back down at Jane again. Jane could not help grinning back. Since Jane had never waitressed before, Peter had to start at the very beginning. He showed her all the basics. Then he spent time showing her how to pour the wine, and where to stack the food orders. How to serve and how to clear away the dirty dishes. He even showed her a few tricks that would ensure she received extra tips. Jane was really enjoying herself and Peter was an excellent teacher. With so much to learn and so many new things to take in, Jane knew that she was making loads of mistakes, but Peter was the perfect trainer. He helped her patiently, joking with her as he did so. She tried even harder. She kept telling herself it had everything to do with her new job, and nothing to do with her handsome teacher.

During her training session, she found out that he was at the local university studying medicine. It was his fourth year, and then he could choose what practice he was to go into. He was keen to make his way in pediatrics. He had another two years to go, one of which was his internship. Jane marvelled as he talked. He was so fueled up with excitement and enthusiasm. He mentioned the down sides too, like the late nights studying and the cost of the tuition, but neither could take away his love for the field he was in. Jane understood perfectly. That *was exactly* how she felt about her dancing career.

They continued working together in an easy, comfortable silence. Time passed quickly. Eventually Peter spoke. "Look," he said as he pointed toward one of her three tables that she had been assigned that evening, "You've got your first customers at table number four." Jane took a quick peek. A man and his wife. Her first table. Everything Peter had told her during the afternoon came flooding back. She knew what she must do. Jane waited for them to seat themselves, and then made her way over, smiling brightly at her first customers.

She took great care when ordering their drinks, and was equally careful when she took their food order. Peter stayed close, in case she needed assistance, but she knew she was doing fine. Her second table had arrived soon after, and she had repeated the process, even reciting some of the specials on the board. Jane was very happy with the progress she was making. She had only been given three tables to start, which was more than enough for her first day. Once she got used to the routine and the way things were done, Peter said she could have as many as twenty tables at any one time. As she served her clients some warm bread from the oven, she was unaware of Mr. Ken watching her in the doorway, taking note of her every move.

As the afternoon turned to evening, the restaurant became more and more full. Jane felt like she had been waitressing for years. She just had to make sure she got the drinks first, and then when she returned with the drinks, took their food orders. She wrote the time on her pad, so she could keep an eye on how long it was taking. So far nothing had gone wrong, and she was really enjoying herself. Peter was around in the background, so she was glad she was not completely alone should she need him. The evening progressed and the restaurant seemed to fill right before her eyes. It was a busy night for everyone on duty. "Here take this to table nine," Peter said as he gave her a bottle of ice cold champagne. "You remember how to do it?" he asked, concerned. Jane thought back to the afternoon lesson on how to open wines and champagnes and how to pour properly. She was confident enough to nod. She was quite taken aback at how many of the tables actually ordered champagne. And it was not the cheap stuff. This was the real thing. She had always thought that champagne was for special occasions only. She was wrong. Here it was as common as water on the table.

As Jane made her way back to the kitchen with another order, she could not help noticing the queue gathering outside the restaurant. There was a line of people actually waiting to get inside. She was surprised. The restaurant was already full. There were no tables available. She was not quite sure where they would all go. She saw Pierre at the entrance, taking details, then coats. He seemed perfectly at ease.

Peter must have noted her interest at the number of people arriving. He nodded toward the line. "Those are the ones hoping to get a table who have not booked," he said.

"What do you do with them? All the tables in here are full."

Peter shrugged. "Most of them have drinks in the cocktail bar. If we get any free tables during the evening, we'll call them. Most of them though, we have to turn away."

Jane looked inside the cocktail bar area and sure enough he was correct. The bar was just as busy as the restaurant itself. Jane soon forgot about the queue waiting outside, or the cocktail bar that was past brimming with people. She had her hands full with refilling champagne glasses and taking desert and cheese orders. Just as she finished with one table, then another table wanted something. She smiled, took orders and tried to remember who was waiting for what. She looked at the gold clock on the wall, it was no longer afternoon, but nine o'clock in the evening.

She forgot the time and continued to wait on her tables. Peter kept a close eye on her throughout, just in case. The night passed in a blur. The next time Jane glanced at the clock, it was almost midnight. She had made it, and without anything drastic going wrong.

She could not believe the evening had flown by so quickly. It was not long after that when the last of her tables had left. She approached the dirty table and cleared away the last of their empty plates and dirty wine glasses. Peter approached her from behind. "Not bad for your first day of work." Peter said as he leaned against the till.

Jane smiled and replied, "No. Not bad at all."

"You did well today. You sure you've not done this before?"

"Nope. Cannot say I have."

"Are you on duty tomorrow? I've not asked Ken yet?" he asked.

Jane nodded. "Doing the night shift again. From 6:00 p.m."

"Uhhh. You'll have my wonderful company again then."

Jane was glad. She did not mind his company in the least. They worked together with the other waiters and waitresses clearing the last dirty tables. They wiped them down, then replaced the plates and cutlery for the following day.

"How are you getting home?" Peter asked, as he laid the wine glasses on the last, unfinished table.

"My father is coming to pick me up," Jane replied. "He did not want me to drive on my own so late at night." She felt foolish saying it, but it was the truth.

"I can take you home, if you like," Peter offered, as he added a salt cellar to the table.

Jane was not quite sure what to say. She would have loved to accept. She almost did. Just looking into those blue eyes and all reason seemed to desert her. But she knew that her father must be outside by now, waiting patiently for her to finish. She declined as best she could, wishing that she could have accepted.

Chapter 15

Zara lay on her bed staring out of her balcony doors. She had her bed positioned in exactly the right spot so she was able to get a perfect view of the hills outside. It was a lovely day, the sun was shining, and there was a soft, gentle breeze blowing inside. It was perfect. She had just gotten out the shower, so she was feeling fresh and relaxed. She had her favorite CD on too and the music floated merrily throughout her room. It was such a nice change to relax and to have the house all to herself. Her parents had gone out to some charity lunch, and she was enjoying the rare solitude. Rose was around somewhere, but she didn't really count.

She had not realized just how badly she had missed some time on her own until now. Time to do absolutely nothing. Not to practice her dance steps, or rehearse yet another sequence they had been learning, but time to enjoy what *she* liked. She just wanted some time on her own alone to do nothing. Before the World Games she had been used to wasting a full day hanging around doing nothing but listening to music and reading the latest magazines like *Vogue* and *Celebrity News*. That now felt like a faraway luxury. Whenever she had a spare minute, she found herself practising Helen's steps or going over another sequence they had learnt. It did not matter if all she had was half an hour or half a day. If she had any spare time she would be hard at work practising.

There were many reasons she was sacrificing her old, pampered life. Her first and main reason had been her parent's reaction to her and her newfound goals. Her mother and father were bending over backwards to help her, giving her everything she needed and also everything she wanted. It was all in the view that it was helping her achieve her goal. And their goals too, if she was truthful. She had not been able to believe her luck when she had bought up the cost of the trip. Her father had written out a check for her immediately as she had watched. He did not question the amount. Did not even raise his eyebrows. She had used that as a good sign and pressed on for more things. She still could not believe what she had received out of the bargain. A new wardrobe for a start. Much bigger than what she had anticipated. Again, he did not question it. Instead, he had given her his Gold Card. To her surprise, she had also received the allowance increase she had wanted. She had not even asked for that herself. Her mother had suggested it and her father had agreed straight away. She had been more than thrilled with the raise, really not expecting that she would receive both things. After that, she had been at a loss for what else to ask for next. She had not thought that far ahead, never expected that she would get as far as she did to begin with. She would not be caught out like that again. Next time she would have to be more prepared. Maybe she should even make a list. She supposed her good fortune and her father's generosity was helped by the fact that twice Daddy had come looking for her and found her hard at work practising in her bedroom. He had been thrilled. His daughter was for once taking things seriously and he, for one, could not be more pleased. Her mother too, could hardly contain herself either, she was over the moon at Zara's new found dedication. "I always knew she would make it as a dancer," she heard her mother bragging to her friends when they came to tea. "It's in her genes. All the good ones, from me!" She knew that secretly her mother had hoped she would advance in ballet, but it was the modern dance that had really taken off for her. Some of the steps were used in both kinds of dance style, but with modern dancing you were able to choose up-to-date, stylish music rather than just being limited to only classical. Zara felt modern dance also offered her more choice in styles of dance. Still, her mother was glad that she had taken an interest in *any* form of dancing. Partly because it proved she had been right all along. Zara would be a dancer. And her mother loved to be right.

Both her mother and father praised her in front of family, friends and colleagues. Zara blushed, but secretly she loved it. Her mother's friends envied her and wished their own daughters were doing something similar. It made Zara popular and gave her mother the edge she craved. Zara adored every minute of it. She was the centre of attention. Everyone wanted to know all about her. She could do no wrong. And with the Germany auditions coming up soon, she was going to use this upper hand she had secured to her advantage.

It had been a hard session the day before at dancing class. Each Saturday had slowly begun to get more difficult than the week before. Zara had at first thought it was her imagination, but when Pat mentioned it on their way home, that she too was finding it more difficult, Zara knew it was not just her that was feeling the harsh new effects of Helen's classes. Come to think of it, it was also evident in the number of girls that showed up for classes each week. Or in this case, did not show up. Zara still remembered her shock when she had arrived at the studio that very first Saturday. There had been over two-hundred girls packed into the hall. All eager and bursting with energy and excitement. She had actually been worried at the amount of competition she would have. Then it had slowly dwindled to fifty girls. Zara knew *that* dramatic drop in attendance was the firsthand result of Helen's fees announcement. After that, the classes seemed to get smaller and smaller with each passing week. Some weeks it was only one or two girls not turning up for class, other times it was more, once as many as five girls not showing. They never did return. Zara was convinced that the money was only a part of the reason, and that was only in the beginning. Now it had more to do with Helen and her vigorous dance routines. As time passed, many of the girls began to find it hard to keep up. Helen pushed and pushed, and it was easy to see that at the end of the afternoon everyone was exhausted. Also, dancing aside, they were missing out on an entire Saturday. While all their friends and family were out enjoying themselves elsewhere, they found themselves working hard under Helen, who was relentless and tireless. It seemed that the combination of hard work and having no social life on the weekends was driving many of girls to give up the idea of trying out for the auditions.

The Saturday just gone, the class, when it began, had felt even smaller than it had ever felt before. Zara had done a quick count on the dwindling number of girls remaining and had managed to count just twenty-five dancers. That was all that was left. Secretly, she was pleased. She had the financial advantages already, and now it seemed the hard work required meant she was well ahead of everyone else. She also had her moments though. She too found it increasingly hard work. The only thing that kept her going was knowing her reward. Three months in Germany, her father's bank account and her mother's constant approval, and that kept her coming faithfully each week. She was not going to jeopardize this. Oh no, it was far too valuable.

Zara was determined to get into Germany at any cost. But she wanted to be sure that there was a place for her and that all the hard work she was doing was not going to be in vain. She wanted to be guaranteed a place. The last thing she needed was to go to the auditions and not get chosen. That would be too humiliating. She could not, would not, let this opportunity slip through her fingers. There must be some way she could guarantee herself a place.

Zara walked to her window and watched as Rose hung out the washing. What she needed was a plan. A plan to ensure she got Helen's attention and was chosen at the upcoming auditions that seemed to be approaching with rapid speed. After all these weeks of rehearsing, the time had finally come.

Helen had explained the procedure to them all in great detail. The girls going to Germany would be hand picked. One by one. All the areas involved had been learning the same dance sequence that they had been rehearsing. It was the one requirement stressed by the organizers that had to be strictly adhered to. All the girls had to be on equal footing. Now the time had come where all the dancers remaining would have to audition for their place in Germany. Only the very best would be chosen.

Helen mentioned that they were looking for a total of thirty dancers. The competition was going to be fierce, and it would be a case of simple elimination. They would begin all together and only the very best would stay on. Zara had no idea if Helen had any swaying power at the upcoming auditions or not, but she did not want to take any chances. After all these weeks of training she would not allow herself to fail now. The most important thing was making sure she was chosen. She did not care how it happened, as long as it happened.

Zara knew that, like before, the competition for the auditions was going to be strong. Except now, it was going to be stronger than before. All the weak dancers had already left long ago. It was only the talented and dedicated dancers that were still showing up each week. She wondered how many would actually turn up at this audition in the city. She knew that the twenty-five girls in her class would definitely be there. She was positive about that. You did not come this far, struggle through weeks and weeks of intense training and then quit when it really counted at the very end. No, they would all be present. Then there was all the other surrounding areas to consider. If there were twenty five girls on average in each class, and there were maybe ten studios around the country, that totaled to a healthy figure of over two-hundred and fifty girls. It was going to be the same as that very first classes in Shoeing. Masses of excited, determined girls, all pushing and shoving the same as before. But now it would be worse. Now only the best dancers would be present.

And that bought her right back to her original problem. How was she going to get and keep Helen's attention? If Helen had any swaying power, any at all, she wanted to know that Helen was right there behind her, supporting her and helping to sway the other judges in her direction so she was picked. She had tried numerous things already, but none seemed to be working, and she was running out of time. She had excelled herself on Saturdays. Kicking as high as she could was one way to get noticed. She also used all her positive energy in her dance movements, hoping to make Helen glance her way. It had worked for a while, but there were others in the class doing the same thing. Helen continued teaching and helping as normal, unfazed by her massive efforts. Everyone was treated the same. Zara hated that. She was not the same. She was better. Now Helen just needed to know that.

She had already scrutinized and summed up the remaining twenty five girls present in the class and knew which girls she could exclude as serious competition to herself. They were all good, but there was a distinct line to be drawn on who were the more talented and more gifted dancers in the class. That girl Jane was very good, as was her friend Sarah. Zara predicted them as being a problem. Actually, they were her biggest problem. Both of them were enthusiastic when they danced and

Zara was loath to admit that they were actually enjoying the intense training. Whereas everyone else had a look of pain on their faces by the end of the session, those two were still smiling, as if pleased by a hard day's work. Like they had accomplished something. She just hoped that they had not managed to secure Helen's attention yet. She wanted Helen's attention all for herself and she would not allow people like Jane and Sarah to steal it from her. This was one of the most important and materially rewarding things she had ever done. No one or nothing was going to get in her way.

Zara was determined to get a place in Germany, no matter what the cost. And after that, once her place was secured for Germany, she would speak to Daddy. Get him to call in a few favors. But for now, she knew it was just too soon for that to be done. She did not want to blow her chances before she had even begun. Zara had no illusions about Germany. She knew that they were supposed to stay in some sort of hostel. Helen had described, in great detail, all about the place. Her in a hostel? It was ridiculous. Once she was chosen, she would see if Daddy could arrange that she stay in a hotel. The Four Seasons maybe, or even the Ritz would do. She was not staying with the others in a hostel. There was no way. She was going to do this her way. At that meant the luxurious way. She could see it now. A big double bed draped in silk, hot, fresh breakfast bought to her every morning, and then some blissful shopping during the day. She knew she would have to spend *some* time rehearing, but she was sure she would have plenty of time to do all the other things she had in mind. Daddy was sure to give her his credit card too. He could not have his little girl running all over Europe without any money. It was going to be the best time she ever had.

Zara knew that Pat would not be chosen. Pat knew the steps, did them well even, but she was one of those people that held no serious competition to herself. If Pat had her own way, she would have stopped coming to classes long ago. But Zara had begged and pleaded with her to continue to attend. She knew how to play Pat. She had made her feel guilty and played on it until she had given in and agreed. Zara smiled. She knew all along that Pat would. Zara was convinced that Pat would not be one of the thirty girls which would make it through the auditions. Even so, Zara would make sure she did come to Germany with her. Maybe not as a contestant, but as her companion. After all, she did not want to go by herself. How boring would that be? No, she needed Pat as company. They would spend time shopping and going to the theatre, or maybe even do some sightseeing. Having Pat with her would mean she would not get bored on her own. The only foreseeable problem was getting Pat's parents to agree. She might have to get Daddy to speak to them for her. Make them see just how badly she needed Pat with her. Zara sat back down on the bed. She did not see it as being a big problem. Pat's parents would agree. She would ensure Daddy stressed the importance.

When Rose strolled into her room a few hours later, Zara was still relaxing on her bed, listening to music. She had whipped out the latest *Vogue* magazine and was flicking through the pages. With her new wardrobe waiting to be purchased, she wanted to see if there were any outfits that caught her eye. She was looking at the pages, but at the same time was concentrating on finding some sort of plan to get and keep Helen's attention for herself.

Then it came to her. Quite suddenly. Helen was a serious dancer. And a serious teacher. Nothing would mean more to her than a pupil who *really* wanted to learn. Okay, so she had a class full of girls, but what she needed was someone who would seek her out directly. Personally. Someone who would ask for her help, her expert advice and opinions. Someone who would make her feel worthwhile as a teacher. *That's it,* Zara said to herself and smiled. *That's it! I'll go an hour early on Saturday. Pretend that I need help with some steps that I am finding hard to perfect. Ask her to help me. We can work together for an hour or so, and*

I can gain her attention. Keep her focussed on me for a while, during which time I'll put on an excellent performance. I'll be right there in the forefront of her mind, and I'll keep myself there. Zara lay back on the bed, pleased. Yes, this would work. Helen was bound to notice her then. They would be working together for a full hour. Zara would befriend her. And when it came to the auditions, Helen might even see it as a personal insult if Zara was not chosen. After all, she had helped her privately. Zara breathed deeply. Finally she had it! A plan to work to.

When the phone rang, Zara jumped out of the bed excitedly. She had it. A plan, and a plan that would work. Why had she not thought of it before? It was prefect. This would definitely get her noticed. All she had to do was play her cards correctly. She picked up the phone and almost sang hello to whoever was on the other end. "Helloooooo?"

"And how is my favourite girlfriend?" the smooth voice asked. Zara smiled into the phone. It was Raymond.

"Doing great. Better than great. And you?"

"Wonderful. I wanted to see if you are free for dinner tonight?"

Zara was in a great mood. Things would now be helped along, thanks to her new plan. She wanted to go out and celebrate, and Raymond was the prefect partner.

"Dinner sounds lovely. Pick me up at 7:00 p.m.?"

"No problem. 7:00 p.m. it is," he replied. With that Raymond hung up.

Zara jumped over her bed and laughed all the way into the bathroom. Tonight she was going to celebrate in true fashion. She took a long slow bath filled with all her favourite smelling bath beads. Then she dressed. Her Christian Dior top threaded with millions of sparkling colours called out to her. It was how she was feeling. All glitzy and happy. Zara could barely concentrate as she put on her makeup. Her thoughts were away with Helen and next Saturday's class. She could barely wait until then. The first stages of her plan would be put into action.

Chapter 16

Zara reflected over the last few days as she drove to the studio. It had been a good week. She had been in high spirits and today was going to be even better. Dinner with Raymond had been as good as it always was. They had gone out for a lovely dinner and then out dancing. She had loved it. She had felt free, willing to take on anything. Raymond was his perfect self, as usual, and it had been an immensely enjoyable date. The rest of the week she had been busy. Busy mastering her plan. She had thought of every possible angle. Whatever Helen did or said she had a counter plan. Something to do, or something to say that would keep Helen's attention focussed on her and work to her advantage. There was no angle that was missed. She was prepared for every situation.

She knew she had to arrive early. That was the first and basic stage of her master plan. Zara knew Helen always arrived before everyone else so she could set up and arrange the music. There was a piece of the dance sequence that a few of the dancers were struggling with. She knew it well, of course, but she would ask Helen for her help on that specific piece. She knew Helen would be only to glad to help her, and it would also show her how serious she was about the Germany auditions. In actual fact, Zara had been practising that specific piece all week. She knew each step and managed to master the technique, but Helen did not know that. It would give her the perfect opportunity to show off her talents and a one on one session was going to help her to no end.

Zara arrived just over an hour early as she had planned and was pleased to see Helen's car already in the drive. Bingo. She was there already. Zara locked her car door and made her way inside. It was time. She was ready for action. Ready to make her mark and dazzle Helen with her talents. As Zara opened the studio entrance door, she heard the same familiar music that they had been rehearsing to, for all these weeks waft into the air. "That's it. Now jump and twist," she heard Helen's voice say. There was a loud thump as someone landed heavily on their feet. "Yes, that's it. You've got it. Now try jumping a little lighter. Like so." There was a slight pause and another thump. This time lighter. More controlled. It must have been Helen. Whoever was in there with Helen tried again. This time the jump was lighter. Not as light as Helen's had been, but still better than before. Who on earth could Helen be talking to, Zara asked herself as she rounded the corner. Then Zara saw her. It was Jane. Zara watched in horror as Helen came round and helped Jane on her twist. Jane tried the twist on her own. Once, then twice, then jumped into the air.

Zara could not look at the two of them any longer. She turned away, furious. Zara knew she was breathing in ragged gasps. She tried to control the fierce anger that gripped her, but she was too furious for any kind of rational thought. She stayed like that, unmoving, for what seemed like ages, unable to believe that her perfect plan had been stolen right from beneath her feet. She felt rooted to the spot, blinded by the red haze of fury.

It was some time later before she could move. She headed for the bathroom. Her anger was continuing to swell, and got bigger and bigger with each passing minute. She could not believe that her plan had been cruelly ripped from her and stood smashed into a thousand unsolvable pieces. Zara felt herself explode with anger. She kicked violently at one of the toilet doors, using the pent up anger she felt. A few more violent kicks later and the door was badly dented. She thought she might feel better, but she did not. It only left her out of breath with a tender foot. She did not care, and continued to kick again and again. She had it all worked out. It was perfect. Foolproof. She smiled sadistically. Except for Jane. She had not thought of Jane as being an obstacle. She had come in, out of the blue, and ruined it. Ruined it all. And while she was stuck here in the toilets, Jane was out there making an impression on Helen. Something that she should be doing herself. Zara could not believe that Jane had stolen her idea. Zara hated her. Hated her with such a passion, she felt like kicking the door again. And then the red haze in her head began to disappear and Zara saw her holiday, her spending money, her father's approval, her mother praises, all disappear into thin air before her very eyes. The red haze returned almost immediately and the fierce anger from before, fuelled up again inside her. Zara could not calm down. It had been a perfect plan. Until now. "How dare she?" she hissed to herself. "How dare she? That no good, devious, sly…" her breathing changed again and she took great gulps of ragged breaths. She must calm down she told herself. "Breathe, Zara, breathe," she coaxed. She sat down on the small bench and concentrated on getting her breath back. Now what? What could she do? She had to salvage this. But how? She had to get in there. Jane was stealing her master plan and getting all the credit that should have been hers. HERS. She sat on the bench for a while and thought. Thought hard, but she was still blinded by her anger and no solutions came. She had known all along that Jane was going to be a problem. She should have stuck to her hunch and dealt with her sooner. She would not let that kind of mistake happen again. No one messed with her and got away with it. Ever.

Ten minutes later, Zara's breathing had returned to normal. She was still furious, but she knew she was now thinking straight. She would deal with this glitch and correct this "out of hand" situation immediately. She would amend the plan, that's all. She would go in as she had meant to, and still ask for Helen's help. Helen would be forced to divide her time between her and Jane. She would ask her questions as she planned and make herself look interested and keen to learn. When it came to the dancing bit, she would make sure she danced better than Jane did. Helen would be forced to notice her. She would make an aim of showing Jane up, at every opportunity she got. She would have to be careful. Helen must not know it was deliberate. Zara leaned back against the bench. Maybe it was a good thing, what had happened. Maybe Jane had done her a favor. Helen now had the prefect opportunity to compare the two of them together. And Zara would make sure she was the better of the two. She had been rehearsing all week. She knew the steps, and had perfected the technique. She would use this opportunity to outshine Jane every step of the way.

Zara smiled for the first time since she entered the studio. She could still salvage this bad situation and turn it to her advantage. She walked over to the wash basin and washed and dried her face before putting on her dazzling smile and headed into the studio. She walked straight in and feigned surprise at seeing Jane already there. "Oh good. You're here. I came early. I was wondering if you could also help me on some steps I'm struggling with?" She smiled enthusiastically at Helen.

The hour flew past quickly, and before long the other dancers began to arrive for the upcoming days class. Zara used the opportunity to have a break and gather her strength before the real class began. She headed for the toilets. She was unable to miss the small hole she had made in the bathroom door earlier and laughed at herself. She had been so furious. Thought it was a complete disaster. When she had walked in and seen Helen helping Jane, she had thought her plan was unsalvageable. Now, after an hour with Helen and ugly Jane, she knew she was in a better position than before.

The practice session had been perfect. Whereas Jane was really asking for help, she was there only to make an impression. She had outdone herself. Used the opportunity to dance her very best. When they had to kick, Zara made sure she kicked higher, when it came to doing a pirouette, she made sure hers was neater and more accurate. All in all Zara knew she looked like the better dancer. It was working out perfectly. It would have been impossible for Helen to not notice that she was the better of the two of them.

While Zara was congratulating herself on her new and improved plan inside the toilets, Jane finished up on the bar and wiped her hands on her small hand towel. The hour she had spent with Helen had been very helpful. She just could not seem to get that jump, kick and twist correct. She had tried it so many times, but still it felt wrong. She could feel it. Helen had been a great help though, showing her how to keep her arms and back, without losing the position and overall style she was trying to create. She had to admit that after an hour with Helen coaching, it did look and feel better. Much better. It was a pity though, that Zara had interrupted them. Jane could not put her finger on it. Whereas she was trying to prefect her technique and iron out her problems, Zara was doing her utmost to outshine her at every turn. Whereas she was trying to master the kick, Zara seemed to think it was all about whom kicked the highest. Jane really was not concerned about her height at the moment. When she had perfected the technique and that was correct, she would worry about the height. Zara also seemed intent on holding Helen's attention. Each time she had opened her mouth to ask a question, Zara had quickly jumped in and taken over, leaving Jane waiting until she was finished, or until the next opportunity. Jane certainly did not want to appear rude, especially if Zara was just as keen on learning, as she herself was. But Jane was not convinced. She was not entirely sure why she felt like that. Maybe because Zara seemed more intent on impressing Helen rather than working on any problem areas. Jane knew it should not bother her, but she could not help it. That girl was getting under her skin. She was sure she was imagining everything, but she could not help the feeling.

Later, when the class was finished, Jane's thoughts were confirmed as Zara jumped into her flashy red car and sped away. It was impossible to ignore the gleeful winning look that Zara threw her way. And no, she had not imagined it, of that she was now certain.

Chapter 17

Jane skipped into Michelangelo's, ready for her shift to begin. It had been a good day. Going to the studio an hour early had been an excellent idea. That extra time with Helen had really helped a lot. She had been struggling all week with that twist and kick. She just could not seem to get it correct. Even as she did it in the mirror, she knew it felt and looked wrong. Now, with Helen's help, she had finally managed to get it correct. It no longer felt as awkward as it had before. She had achieved a lot today and was pleased with her results. "Hi, Peter," Jane called, as she came inside and hung up her coat.

"Hi, Jane," he called back. "How did it go today?"

Jane grabbed her white apron, and tied it around her waist. "It was great. Learnt a few more of the steps. They really seem to be coming together. Not long to go now."

Peter smiled and pushed her playfully in the ribs with his elbow. "Good. You'll be famous yet."

They had been working together for over three months now and Jane still felt weak at the knees every time Peter looked at her. She tried to keep her feelings hidden, but it was not always easy with Peter being so easygoing and with such wonderful blue eyes. When he looked at her, she wanted to melt. She was sure he liked her too, but so far neither of them had said anything, and Jane knew she was not going to be the one to bring it up. They had already gone to the movies together twice, but it was with other work colleagues. Peter had also driven her home on a few occasions. Her father had met him here at the restaurant a few times and trusted him enough to allow him to drive his precious daughter home. Secretly Jane loved it. It meant they could talk more freely. At the restaurant, they had to talk about work, which although fun, was not nearly the same. Working at Michelangelo's did have more than one advantage.

Peter threw a look around the restaurant. It was not yet 6:30 p.m. "We've had loads of reservations for tonight. Looks like it's going to be busy. Be prepared," he said.

Jane just laughed. She would have it no other way. With three months experience behind her now, she had learnt that the busier it was, the better. More customers meant more tips. She had just the other day counted all her tips and was surprised at the amount she had already managed to save. If things continued as they had been, she would have more than enough money for the trip to Germany if she was chosen. The day was looming closer. Only two more weeks left to go. If she was picked, then their flight would be followed close behind. She was so excited. She was also nervous. Nervous and excited rolled up into one ball.

"Look, you've come just in time," Peter said, "Your first table for the evening has arrived."

Jane looked over her shoulder at the table. Her first customers were early. Way too early. "Looks like you're right. It's going to be a busy night." Jane grabbed her pen and paper, and made her way over to the waiting table.

A few hours later and Jane found herself running from table to table. Each table she had so far that evening had been more demanding than the first. Everyone seemed to want something. Another drink, some fresh rolls, a new fork. She was kept very busy ensuring everyone was happy. It was not her worst night, but it was far from her best. All her tables were full and she knew that Pierre had a few more hopefuls waiting in the cocktail bar, eagerly waiting for any tables that might become free.

Jane went over to the bar and placed yet another drink order for the large table she had in the corner. Rico, the bartender for the evening, took the drinks slip and added it to the end of the line. Jane was just turning back when she saw Zara enter the restaurant. She froze.

As Zara entered, she smiled at the young man with her. He took her coat and handed it to Pierre. Jane turned sharply then, hoping that her eyes were deceiving her. She turned and looked again. No such luck. Before her, at the other end of the restaurant, stood Zara. There was no mistaking her. She would know that blond hair and slim figure anywhere.

Jane left the drinks she was supposed to take and ducked into the kitchen to hide. What was she going to do? There was no doubt in her mind that after today Zara was out to get her.

Jane did not want a scene, especially here, at her place of work. She just wanted to get on with her job without any interference. And with Zara here, at her restaurant, there was a possibility that Zara would not allow that to happen. Zara would thrive on this situation, fuelled by the knowledge that she had the upper hand. Jane was, after all, only the waitress and she was the customer. Jane held her fingers crossed. She would ignore Zara and continue as normal. There was no reason why having Zara in the restaurant should effect her.

Jane took another quick look inside the restaurant. Her heart sank as she saw Zara and her date take their seats. A seat at one of *her* tables. Jane could not believe it. Out of all the tables in the restaurant, why did she have to take a seat at a table on her side of the restaurant? Come to think of it why did she have to even be here when there was a street full of other restaurants? What a nightmare. Jane jumped as Peter touched her arm softly.

"What you doing in here?" Peter asked as he retrieved the large pepper mill from one of the counters.

Jane forgot about Zara for a few minutes as Peter's aftershave teased her nostrils. She shook her head. She had a bigger problem at hand. "Nothing," Jane answered absent-mindedly. She knew she needed to get out from looking after that table. She could not put her finger on what was Zara's problem, but she was sure that given half chance Zara was going to make her suffer in some way or another. Zara clearly did not like her.

"You okay?" Peter asked concerned.

Jane snuck another peek outside and watched for a few seconds longer as Zara picked up the elegant gold menu. Ducking back inside, she knew she could not do it. Anyone else, yes she would be fine. But Zara? Spoiled, irritating Zara. No, she decided, she could not do it. That look she had received earlier today had really unnerved her. Zara was in for a fight, of that she was now sure. Zara had an agenda. And somehow Jane had managed to get in the middle of it. She was not sure how or why it had happened, but it had, and she wanted nothing to do with it. The best course of action was to stay out her way.

"Peter, you see that table over there?" Jane asked as she pointed toward Zara.

"The guy and the girl? Yes, I see them. What about it?"

Jane took a deep breath, before answering. *This was going to sound so silly.* "Would you mind looking after that table for me?" she begged. "Please?"

Peter took a second look at the table. Jane knew what he must be seeing. A beautiful, tall blond girl, dressed elegantly in a black velvet dress, a deep split up the one side. Her hair was different to how Jane was used to seeing it. This evening it was loose and cascaded gently down her shoulders. Jane knew that anyone looking at her would agree she was beautiful. Breathtakingly beautiful. Did she really want Peter around someone like Zara? "Okay, no problem," Peter answered before she could say anything else.

Jane breathed a sigh of relief. "Thanks. I owe you one." Jane knew she could not stay inside the kitchen hiding all evening. She had other tables to look after and already two drink orders were lined up and waiting on the bar. She took a deep breath and picked up the tray of drinks before heading back to the large table in the corner.

She served the drinks and headed back toward the bar, ready to take the second order that was waiting to go out. As she picked up the cocktails that Rico had made, she heard Mr. Ken's voice from inside the kitchen. "Peter, can I see you in my office please?"

"Yes, no problem," replied Peter. Peter followed Mr. Ken with a bunch of forms in his hand. As he walked past, he whispered into Jane's ear. "I'll be back in a second. This won't take long. Just a problem with a late delivery from earlier this afternoon."

Jane nodded and set to keeping herself busy. It was difficult, knowing that Zara was in the same room. They had finished with their menus now and were talking. Their heads bent, as if they were sharing some secret. Still, long minutes later, Peter did not appear. Jane became worried. They were bound to start looking around soon for someone to take their drink order. She snuck yet another look at Zara and her companion. They were still talking quietly, but Jane knew it would not be for much longer. She also knew she could not wait for Peter another minute. She would either have to take their drink order herself or risk having them complain about her and the service. Neither option was appealing. She thought for a moment and weighed up the options. Things had been going so well here at the restaurant, she could not risk losing her job. That only left one other option, and that was taking Zara's order.

She gave it a few more minutes, hoping that Peter would show up and save her from having to go over. But the door to the office remained firmly shut and showed no signs of opening any time soon. She would be forced to do this herself. She took a steadying breath and scolded herself. Why was she so nervous, it was only Zara for Pete's sake? What was the worst that could happen? She would simply walk over, say hello, take their order and leave. Simple as that!

When Jane approached the table, Zara barely lifted an eyebrow at her presence. Jane was forced to speak first. "Hello, I'm Jane. I'll be your waitress this evening." Zara's head shot up like a bullet. "Hi, Zara," Jane said politely. Zara stared at her as if she had grown a second head. The silence was uncomfortable. The young man she was with looked from Jane to Zara and back at Jane again. Jane waited for Zara to speak, to say something, anything, but she did neither and just continued to stare. Jane felt compelled to speak yet again and break the awkward silence that seemed to have settled on the group. "Can I get you anything to drink?" she asked politely.

"I'll have a beer please. Fosters. Zara, what would you like honey?" her companion asked as he took her hand across the table. Zara never took her eyes off Jane.

"Martini," she croaked.

"Okay. I'll put that order through now. Just take your time looking at the menu and I'll be back in a while to take your food orders." Jane smiled as she walked off. She could feel Zara's eyes boring into the back of her head as she did so. She headed toward the bar with the drink order and continued as if nothing out of the ordinary had happened. As she moved around the restaurant, she could feel Zara's eyes following her every movement. This was awful. Much worse than she imagined. Why was Zara making this as difficult as possible? What *was* that girl's problem? Jane waited for what she thought was an appropriate time, then went back to her dreaded table with their drinks. She placed the beer and a cold glass in front of Zara's date, and then placed a tall glass with the red Martini in front of Zara. "What is that?" Zara asked accusingly.

"What?" Jane asked, unsure of what Zara was referring to.

"That?" she said pointing toward the offending glass before her.

"It's a Martini. Like you ordered," Jane answered, unsure of what the problem was.

"No," answered Zara belligerently, "I ordered a white Martini. Not a red Martini." Jane looked at the elegant Martini glass. She knew that Zara had not ordered a white anything.

How should she handle this? She asked herself. Jane knew what she had to do, and that was to just get whatever Zara wanted, then leave, pronto. "Okay," Jane answered back, "I'll change it for you. It's no problem." As she walked back to the bar, Jane heard a distinct giggle. So, her hunch had been correct. Zara was going to make this as difficult as possible for her and was enjoying every moment. With a sigh, Jane knew it was only the beginning.

When she next made her way toward the table, she found Zara drumming her perfectly pink nails on the table irritably. "It's about time," she quipped as Jane set the drink in front of her.

Jane ignored the comment and asked instead, "Are you ready to…"

Jane was cut off in mid sentence. "Where is the onion?" she asked accusingly as she peered into the glass.

Jane took a deep, steadying breath. "We don't normally serve Martinis with an onion. They are served with olives." Jane placed the olives, skewered onto a small stick, that were still on her tray, next to the glass. "But if you want an onion, I'll ask the barman," Jane said, trying to sound as polite as she possibly could.

Zara continued, "Everyone knows that a white martini is always served with an onion, not an olive." Jane did not say another word. She picked up the tray and headed for the second time toward the bar. Rico had enough orders to get through without these silly kinds of problems. He was not going to be happy.

The evening did not improve, with Zara being a very demanding customer. She complained about everything she could possibly complain about. She moaned that the food was taking too long, when she had only just placed her order. When the food did arrive, she complained that it was cold and she could not eat it. When Jane had returned with the plate, now warmed, so much so, that Jane had to hold it with a dish towel, she was not at all surprised, to find Mr. Ken talking to both Zara and her date.

She watched in horror for a few seconds as Zara smiled innocently up toward Mr. Ken. She knew she was in for trouble. No man, not even Mr. Ken, would be able to resist the smile that Zara was giving him. He would be taken in. Hook, line and sinker.

Jane knew, without a doubt, that Zara would be complaining about everything. The drinks. The food. The service. She might as well face the fact that she was in for a talk with Mr. Ken. Zara had it in for her. She was not sure what she had done, but whatever it was, it was Zara who had the upper hand here. She was the customer and Jane was nothing but the waitress. She would lose, hands down, against Zara in a situation like this.

Peter had still not returned back from the office, so she was again forced to go back to the dreaded table while Mr. Ken was still there and serve the ordered food before the plate cooled down again. She placed the plate delicately in front of Zara, as all three of them watched and surveyed her every move. She smiled and moved on, feeling like a complete idiot, knowing that they had been in the middle of discussing her. Mr. Ken had left soon after, but he did not approach her to discuss what had happened or what they had said.

As she continued to serve her other tables, Jane noted that Zara barely touched her food. Instead, she toyed with her meal with her fork and sipped her Martini occasionally. Her companion though, seemed unconcerned and was tucking into his meal with relish.

They finished their meals and declined dessert, instead opting for the bill to be brought over. Jane was only to happy to comply. She left the bill on the table, and moved off to assist another table who were eager to order coffees. The next time Jane looked up, they were both gone. She physically felt herself take a deep breath. That had been far too stressful.

They had paid cash. Jane collected the notes and took them to the till. She was a little annoyed when she counted the money they had left. They had left the exact money required, and although the bill included the gratuity, they had scratched it out and paid only for the food. Jane knew she should not be surprised. Typical. The richest girl she knew and she had not even left a tip. Jane knew that it had been done deliberately. To any waitress it was the worst kind of insult.

It was well after midnight when Mr. Ken sought her out and asked to speak with her in his office. She knew that the conversation to follow could only have to do with Zara. Bracing herself for whatever was to come next, Jane followed Mr. Ken into his workplace. She was offered a seat and then waited for the inevitable.

Half an hour later, Jane emerged from the office to find that Peter had kindly cleared all her tables and filled the salt and pepper shakers, for the following day. The old candles had been replaced and new, fresh ones could be seen. He had done everything, leaving nothing for her to do. "Thanks, Peter," Jane said as she went to fetch her coat and handbag.

"You okay?" Peter asked, a worried expression marring his blue eyes.

Jane sighed, "Yes, I'm fine. I knew she was going to be a problem as soon as I saw her enter the restaurant. I just knew it."

Jane knew Peter felt terrible. He had not stopped apologizing. "Who was she?" he asked.

"Someone I dance with. She does not like me very much, although I don't know why. She complained about absolutely everything to Mr. Ken. Said I was incompetent as a waitress and that someone like me should not be working in a restaurant like this."

"What did she mean, someone like you?" Peter asked.

"No idea. Maybe she meant someone that does not come from pots and pots of money like she does."

Peter gave her a quick hug, and Jane was amazed at how much better she felt after he had done that. "Don't worry about it. We all get customers like her. Forget it. She's gone now. The worst is over. What did Mr. Ken say about the whole thing?" he asked.

"Not much really. He was nice enough about the situation. I don't think he believed her, but they were customers after all, so he thought I should know."

Chapter 18

Raymond flew around the corner. The Porsche he was driving took the sharp curves with ease. He had been pleasantly surprised by dinner tonight. He had expected another boring dinner with Zara. He had not really wanted to take her out and waste a complete Saturday evening on her, but he had not taken her out for a while, and he did not want any waves in that department. Especially with his appraisal and pay rise looming close on the horizon. So, a supposedly boring evening with Zara had instead turned out to be a night of first class entertainment. It really had been a front row seat.

Zara had played her hand expertly. He had watched in awe as she took over the upper hand with her friend, or more correctly, her foe. She knew exactly what buttons to push to get results and if Raymond did not know her, he would have thought the entire evening had been rehearsed. She really had played her part to perfection. And Raymond knew that she was enjoying every minute of it. In some ways Zara was just like him, she pulled no punches and went straight in for the kill.

Zara too was overjoyed at the way the evening had turned out. When she had first seen Jane at the restaurant, she had wanted to pick up her things and leave immediately. That girl kept popping up like a bad penny. Then she thought again. She could definitely use this superior position to her advantage. Besides, Jane deserved it. Especially after that stunt she had pulled with Helen that morning.

It had been great fun really. She always drank red Martini, but when Jane brought the drinks, she had insisted that she had ordered a white one. And then it was the scene with the onion. Zara did not even like onions, preferred the olives, but it was a nice touch. Something additional to complain about. Then the meal had come. She had been starving, especially since she had not eaten since breakfast. But she had deliberately played with her food, swirling it with her fork, barely touching the meal. She knew that it would be noticed and it was. It had been the prefect setting for when Mr. Ken, who she found out later was the owner, had came round and asked if the food was to her liking. She had acted the perfectly unhappy customer who was bitterly disappointed with the meal and the service. As she spoke she could see the concern deepen on Mr. Ken's face. He obviously took these sorts of complaints very seriously. So she had gone in for the kill and strung Jane up, good and proper. Plus, as an added bonus, he had given them a complementary bottle of champagne on their next visit. Zara could barely contain her glee when she snuck a peek and saw Jane watching from the sidelines, a worried expression on her face. Jane had to know that they were discussing her. Zara felt triumphant. Served her right. No one crossed her and got away with it.

As Zara reflected on the situation later when she got home, she realized that Jane must be doing the job in order to help pay for the trip to Germany. It was the only situation that made any sense to her. She had been to that restaurant before and she had never seen Jane there before tonight. So this might have been a double success. If she was lucky then she would have gotten

Jane fired. She would certainly deserve it. And then maybe she would not be able to afford to go to Germany anymore. Zara knew that it was hoping for a little too much, but at least she had pushed a sharp spike into Jane's perfect little world. At the very least she had managed to stir up some trouble for her. She hoped that her performance tonight, which she had to admit was better than a professional actor, did some serious damage.

Chapter 19

The time had arrived. Auditions were upon them. It was what they had been working so hard toward all these long months. Jane was more nervous than she had ever been before. She could feel the familiar butterflies buzzing around in her stomach with a vengeance. Both her and Sarah had come by train. It was easier for their parents, and they preferred it that way. It gave them time to muster their strength and prepare themselves.

It had taken over two hours to get to their destination, and for the entire journey they had both been silent, which was unusual. Normally, on any journey they undertook together, they would talk and giggle on every subject imaginable. Today, however, there was no conversation, just both of them staring aimlessly out the train window as the green fields passed them by. To anyone who saw them it was almost as if they were daydreaming, but in actual fact Jane's mind was racing. She was talking herself through each and every step as if her body was actually moving. Even without moving her limbs, she was practising. When she had finished and was satisfied, she looked at Sarah, aware suddenly of the silence between them. It did not seem natural. Jane wondered if maybe Sarah was also mentally going through all the steps as she herself had done. At times like these it helped to ease the nervousness. Neither of them said it out loud, but they were both apprehensive for the day to follow. This was the final stage. Everything depended on today and what would take place. By tonight, on the same journey home, they would know for sure if they had made it or not. A lot of important things were going to happen over the next few hours.

The train arrived at their final destination. Both girls collected their bags and waited for the train to come to a complete halt before disembarking. The map that Helen had given them on their last Saturday class showed that they could walk to the theatre set up for the auditions. It was close, but both girls agreed that they preferred to reserve their energy and catch a cab instead. There was no problem getting a taxi, with a long line ready and waiting to go. The drive was short, and before they knew it they had arrived. Like all theatres, it looked much the same as any other theatre anywhere else. It was big and airy. Mirrors adorned one side of the wall with a long bar running alongside the other, and the floors were highly polished, smelling like wax. This time, there were no television screens in the corners. Today they were here to show the examiners what they already knew and be judged on that knowledge.

They paid the driver and headed inside, following the signs that had been put up for the day. It led them to a large hall where the auditions were going to take place. Already, the hall was buzzing with movement and excitement. It felt very similar to that very first Saturday when they had all arrived for that very first class. Jane glanced at the girls already present. There were so many. Like before. All eagerly waiting and all nervous. Jane knew that each girl present had been through the exact same training as she had been though. She wondered if they had also spent every waking moment practising, rising early in the morning and going to bed late in the evening, all in the aid of perfecting the steps. Jane surveyed the room again in search of any familiar faces and saw Helen through the large crowed. She was up front of what looked like a stage with what must have been the other instructors. Jane saw her laugh at something one of them said. She seemed so relaxed. A very different Helen to the one that she saw every Saturday. Jane hoped that it was a good sign. By the looks of it, Helen and her instructor friends were about the only relaxed people in the entire room.

The auditions were only due to start in another half an hour, so there was nothing much to do except join all the other girls milling around, watching the clock nervously. Time seemed to tick by very slowly. Jane was aware that the one person she did not see was Zara and, of course, Pat. Time was almost up and soon they would begin. Since the episode with Zara and the restaurant, Jane had deliberately kept away from her. It had been hard with Zara going out of her way to seek her out. Peter had told her that she had been back to the restaurant too. She had been so relieved that she had taken that evening off work. Peter had said she had been lovely. A perfect lady. And when they had paid the bill, she had left him a huge tip. Jane was glad for Peter, but could not understand why Zara had this vendetta against her. What had she done? It was now really beginning to bug her. She knew she should not worry about it, but somehow Jane felt that Zara was going to be more trouble. And she did not like for one moment that Peter had said she was lovely. That comment had bugged her to no end.

As if on cue, Jane noticed Zara enter the room. It was difficult not to. She was so dramatic. She walked through the door, stopped and smiled at the instructors. It was as if she knew she would have an audience to watch her dramatic entrance. Jane noticed Helen smile back. Why did it always seem as if Zara had a plan up her sleeve? *Maybe because she always does*, she replied to herself.

"Your favourite friend has just entered," Sarah said softly, as she rummaged in her dance bag for a bottle of water.

"I know. It's hard not to notice her. The whole room has noticed her," Jane replied. She deliberately bent down and tried to ignore Zara, hoping that by avoiding her she would head to the far end of the hall, away from her. Jane did not want to be worrying over Zara. What she wanted was to stay focussed on the important job she had to do today. She did not need any distractions, especially the unnecessary ones that came in the form of Zara Maddox. Today was one of the most important days of her life. A lot depended on the outcome, so Zara should be the very least of her worries right now.

It was almost time to begin. The nervous energy in the room was tangible. The theatre was now full to the brim. Girls from all over the country were present. Jane's journey was over two hours train ride, but for some of the other girls present, the journey was even further. Still, the long distance that had to be travelled, had not deterred any of them. There were easily over three-hundred girls present. Jane knew there was going to be a lot of dancers, but she had no idea that the scale and competition would be so massive. She really had not expected this many dancers present. Competition was going to be stiff. Very stiff indeed.

There was a loud clapping and all the girls whipped round to face the stage. The day had begun. A tall, thin man held a small mike in his hand. He looked around the room twice, before he began to speak in an excited tone. "Welcome, everyone. Welcome," he sang into the mike. "We're now ready to begin the auditions. The first thing we would like you all to do is gather in a neat, straight line." He waited quietly, as the girls before him arranged themselves into the requested lines. There was a lot of scuffling and clamouring about, as they did so. Only when they were all in the lines did the man begin to talk again. "We're now going to divide you into groups. There are to be roughly thirty girls in each group." As he finished speaking, the instructors present came down from the stage. Helen was among them. They began immediately to divide the lines into groups of thirty. When they were finished, there were ten groups. Jane and Sarah found themselves in the same group since they had been standing next to each other. There was no one else in their small gathering that they knew or recognized.

Some of the girls present, Jane noticed, looked very nervous. One girl who was in their group was so nervous she looked an off-white colour, as if she was about to throw up. She seemed unable to stand still, and hopped from one leg to the other in an apprehensive, nervous gesture. Jane tried to ignore it for as long as possible. Then unable to keep quiet any longer, she whispered. "Are you okay?" The girl nodded in between hops, the colour clearly drained from her face. Jane knew she was not alright. She took a step to the side and left a small gap between them. If the girl was sick, she did not want to be anywhere within reach. Jane took a look around at the other groups present. Zara, Jane saw to her relief, was in another group, the group furthest away from her. Good. That was one less thing to worry about.

The man with the mike began to speak again. "Okay, I am sure you are all eager to know how this is going to work today! We have decided that we will watch each group separately. Some of us will be on stage watching from above, while the rest of us will be moving between you. If you get tapped on the shoulder, you must remove yourself from the group. Unfortunately, this is the clue that you have not been chosen to continue with us onto Germany. We will continue this same process until we have a select few girls remaining. This process of elimination will continue to take place until we have only thirty girls left to fill the required positions. These are the girls that shall be joining us for the World Games. We will give you ten minutes to warm up and then we will begin. Good luck to you all." With that he jumped off the stage and joined some of the other examiners that were loitering around, waiting to begin.

The minutes flew past as each dancer frantically crammed in the last session of warming up that they had been granted. Then it was time. The first group was asked to take their position on the main dance floor. The girls complied, ready and eager to begin. They took to the floor and lined up in neat rows as directed, in the centre of the room. There was a large gap between each girl, and Jane supposed it was to allow for each girl to move easily, without any hindrances. This was it.

The music began and the familiar sounds began to pour into the room. The dancers all moved as one. Jane watched from the sidelines as the three judges walked up and down, among them. At first, that was all they did. Just watched and assessed in silence. Jane had to admit the girls were all good. They all kept in time to the music. All perfected, so she thought, with months of training. When the sequence ended, the girls looked around wildly. Out of breath. They had focussed all their energies into the movements, pushing themselves as they had never done before. Jane knew that the adrenaline would have kicked in for most of them, giving them the sharp energetic movements they all desired.

The second time they did the sequence, Jane noted a difference. Almost half the girls seemed to have lost some steam. Not a lot, but just enough that it was noticeable. Adrenaline only lasted for so long. The movements were not as clean and sharp as their first performance had been. Some of the girls even seemed to lose count and lagged behind, ever so slightly. Jane presumed that these were the little things that the judges were looking for. When the first girl was tapped on the shoulder, she looked around shocked. She seemed to be rooted to the spot, not moving, as if she was unable to accept the tap on her shoulder. The judge gave her a little nod, prodding her to leave. She looked bewildered, and then without a word, she left the group in stunned silence. By that stage the tears were rolling freely down her face. She was out. The denial was evident on her face. She grabbed her tog bag and without a backward glance, ran out the room in disgrace and embarrassment. All the girl present watched in silence as she left forever. The first girl was gone.

The music had come to an end and the room was left silent as they watched the first girl leave, with the door swinging silently behind her as she left, never to return. It was sad to watch. Everyone knew it was going to happen, but that did not make it any easier.

The second girl that was tapped on the shoulder did not leave as quietly. She stamped her feet hard in a rage, as if she was about to have a tantrum. She stormed out of the group, her face set in a hard glare, grabbed her stuff roughly and walked purposefully out the door, hitting the wall hard on the way out. Minutes later a loud scream could be heard as she left the theatre. Not the best way to act, but it was hard not to sympathize. All the time and energy spent working so hard over the months, only to be let down at the last, final test. Jane felt the butterflies returning. She hoped, prayed she was not one of the girls chosen.

The instructors played the music four individual times. By the end of the fourth session, the judges had finished walking through the group, and what remained were only four girls out of the original group of thirty. All the others had been tapped lightly on the shoulder had already collected their belongings and left. There was no point hanging around. They were out. The months and months of training for these girls were over. The takings were slim. Very, very slim.

As Jane sat and watched the next group, small things became apparent. Someone who did not land as elegantly as the rest or someone whose twist was slightly off in comparison to the girl next to her. The small irregularities she had never noticed before began to become apparent. The girls seemed to be dropping from the second group like flies. Each dreaded tap leaving the group with one less dancer. By the time the instructors were finished walking between the groups and tapping on shoulders, there were maybe four or five girls remaining. Sometimes even less than that.

It was over two hours later before Jane's group was called to perform. Jane used that time to watch and learn. Just before they were due to be called up, her group began to warm up. No one wanted to obtain any injuries or have stiff muscles that would hinder their chances of a good performance. Both her and Sarah set to doing pliés, being the most useful for warming up their leg muscles. They were long and graceful, with deep bends. Their number was called and Jane froze for an instant. They were up. It was time. They took their places.

"Good luck," Sarah said, as she took her position.

"You, too." Jane replied.

And then, it began. When the music played, Jane danced like she had never danced before. Her body seemed to take over and the movements came naturally after weeks and weeks of training. She felt her adrenaline kick in. It was like a huge burst of energy. Jane did not want to use it all in one go, knowing that it was only the first of four sessions. Deliberately, she stored as much of it as she could, only releasing little bursts at a time. When she jumped, she used all her energy into gaining height. She concentrated on landing softly and neatly, just as she had been taught. She was once again glad that she had asked Helen for help on getting it perfect. The music continued. She turned and leapt again to the left, then kicked as high she could to her right. Jane focussed on her movements as she had never done before. She knew there were other girls in the group, but she completely ignored them by giving herself tunnel vision. She concentrated on herself and herself alone. All that mattered was the music and the steps. Then the music came to an end, as she knew it would. Like before, some of the girls were breathing hard, others sweating profusely. Jane knew that many would have used much of their energy in that one, first dance. The second sequence would separate them all out. The instructor gave them a few minutes to compose themselves and soon round two began. Jane knew that this round they would be scrutinized even further and decisions made on who would remain in the group.

The music began for the second time. Again Jane danced, using a little more of the stored adrenaline. Tunnel vision set in for the second time and Jane became unaware of the other dancers around her. She danced and tried to enjoy each beat of the music, knowing that it would come through into her movements. She knew the importance of what she was doing, but tried to forget of it all. She wanted to focus on enjoying herself and doing her absolute best. Then before she knew it, the music came to an end again. It seemed to have gone so much faster than the first time round. Jane took her first look around herself. More than half the girls had left the group, although the three judges were still milling around between them. Jane quickly looked for Sarah among the girls still left and saw her on the far end. She smiled at her friend in relief. They had both made round one, but it was far from over yet. There was still too many of them in the group and more eliminations had to take place.

When the music began for the third time, Jane knew she had to keep her energies up to the exact same level. She knew she could not let herself slip. She had to repeat the steps just as perfectly and with as much enthusiasm as if it was the first time. She allowed more of the stored adrenaline to pulse through her veins. She went back into the tunnel vision and all she could hear was the steady beat of the music, and feel her body moving to the gentle rhythm. She was almost lost in the whole action of dancing, but then her attention was suddenly broken.

Standing right in front of her, watching her every move, was one of the judges. She did not move. Her eyes were watching every movement that she made. Jane tried to ignore her and focus on what she was doing, but it was a distraction. She knew that at any minute the judge could tap her on the shoulder and it would all be over. The kick was next. When the time came, she kicked high and slightly to the left, as neatly as Helen had coached her. She arched her back ever so slightly, then as the kick ended, she placed her foot back on the ground, and evenly dispersed her weight as she continued to move to the beat of the music. The kick was finished and the examiner was gone.

When the music came to an end for the third time, Jane looked wildly around for Sarah. She saw her friend easily now, as the majority of the other girls had left. In their occupied places were now large, open spaces. Jane was a little awed. She knew what the process was, had been watching it all morning, but it still came as a shock. She had begun in a group of thirty girls, and now there were only three of them left. All those other girls had been tapped. Their hopes and dreams gone. Shattered. Jane knew she could not dwell on it too long. This was a competition and this is what they knew would happen. It was only then that it dawned on her that her and Sarah had both made it. They were through the first stage of the eliminations. They had made round one.

The three remaining girls left their position in the centre of the room and made for their original spot next to the far wall. Neither of them jumped for joy or screamed with happiness, although they desperately wanted to. They had to remain as professional as possible. Jane did, however, sneak a quick wink at her friend and was rewarded with one back. They had made round one! Jane now felt hot, and she also felt sticky. She opened her bag, and like Sarah, they both pulled out their water bottles. Jane drank deeply and felt better as the cold water hit her throat. She retrieved her towel and dried her face and neck. Just those few simple things and she felt better. The music had begun again, and it was the next group's turn.

Zara was in the proceeding group. She stood second in front, next to Pat. As the music began, Jane watched as they repeated the familiar moves. The judges stuck to their procedure and mingled through the group. The first session, only watching, as before. Then, on the second session they began touching the girls on their shoulders. Eliminations had began. One of the judges stopped in front of Pat. Jane could see that Pat was trying hard, but like before, she lacked that special sparkle. The judge watched her dance for a few long seconds, then silently tapped her on her shoulder. Pat still had the courage to smile. She looked around at Zara as she silently left the group. She was not particularly upset, which was strange. She accepted defeat gracefully. No tears, no thumping walls. She collected her bag, opened it and took a sip of water as she watched Zara. Unlike all the girls before her, she did not leave. She drank her water and then sat herself comfortably against the wall and continued to watch. Zara, Jane noted, was doing an excellent job. She danced with a practiced ease and a natural talent. Jane watched as the same instructor that had tapped Pat came and stood in front of her. She scrutinized Zara with a practised eye, and Jane could see why she moved on. Zara was dancing beautifully. When the group had finished all three sessions, Zara was still among them. She too, had been spared the dreaded tap on the shoulder.

It took a few more hours before all the groups had been seen. At the end of each session, only a handful of girls remained. Now, with all the groups having been seen, there was still a healthy handful of around fifty girls remaining. Jane knew that they were only looking for thirty girls, which meant another twenty girls still had to go. The competition had just taken its step up to the next level.

The tall thin man from earlier that morning appeared again with the mike in hand. "Congratulations! You have all passed the first round. You may have noticed that there are still fifty of you remaining. As mentioned before, we only need a maximum of thirty girls for Germany. So, we are going to continue with the same procedure as before, but this time you will all be dancing together as a group. Anyone tapped, you know what to do. This is where it really counts. Good luck again." The girls took their positions in the centre of the hall as before.

Jane stood in the same place as earlier. She took a deep breath, and steadied herself. This was where all her hard work and practice would count. More than it had ever counted before. The music began and the group all began to dance together. This time, Jane noted in between her movements, the judges seemed in less of a hurry. They wound themselves through the group, taking their time, stopping in front of the girls and watching each of them individually for a few minutes. The decision on whom should leave and whom should stay was now harder for them to make. The girls remaining all knew what they were doing. All dedicated. All wanting to be chosen as badly as the girl next to her. Still, twenty had to go. No one was chosen on the first session, or the second, or even the third session. It was obvious on the fourth practice that the judges wanted to see who had the endurance to keep up the pace and not fade. Slowly the sparkle seemed to die in some of the girls. Their adrenaline completely drained away after so many tests and evaluations. It was ever so slight, and to the untrained eye, Jane supposed, it would have been hard to notice. But these were not untrained eyes. These were professionals. Used to making decisions. They knew from years of experience who would make the gruelling regime ahead, and who would not.

When the first girl was tapped on the shoulder from the remaining group, there was a large, loud commotion. Jane continued to dance and feel the music, but it was hard not to hear the screams and protests to her right. The girl stamped her feet and yelled loudly, then pushed another dancer out of rage, out of her way, throwing her flat onto the floor. The judges asked her again, nicely, to leave the floor, apologized even, but she was having none of it. In the end it took two of the judges to physically remove her from the group as she kicked and protested all the way out the big double doors. You could hear her protesting and screaming about the injustices long after she was physically gone. She hurled abuses at how the judges had been paid off and how she had been mistreated. It was a long time later before the screams finally ceased. Jane knew what was happening, but tried to continue as if nothing had happened. She *would not* be distracted. Maybe the judges would use this as another test. A professional dancer should be able to continue under any circumstances. The music came to an end. The remaining group was quiet. Unnerved. That incident had shocked many of the girls. No one had expected such a violent outburst.

The next incident was when the girl in front of Jane kicked her leg so high, that her other leg flew out from underneath her. Jane just had time to see her fly into the air and land on the floor, with a dull, painful thud. She tried to get up as quickly as she could and to continue as if nothing had happened, but she seemed unable to rest her weight on her foot properly. Jane knew she would have a hard time dancing from then on. She tried to pick up the pace for a few long minutes, but she had lost the beat and lagged painfully behind. Jane felt sorry for her. It was one of the most common injuries. And one of the longest to heal. She was the next girl chosen to leave. There was no mercy being shown to anyone.

The next hour proved to be the most gruelling. Each and every remaining girl was studied and scrutinized under the watchful gaze of the five merciless instructors. Jane came to ignore them in the end. Like they were an irritating fly. She focussed on her movements and refused to be sidetracked. One by one the dancers beside her were tapped. Jane ignored them leaving and continued as if nothing had happened. She was far too close now to let anything deter her. She knew she had to hang on for only a little while longer.

When the music finished playing for the final time, Jane automatically looked around for Sarah. She was still present, only a few feet away. Until now, Jane had been on automatic pilot, doing what was required as best she could, concentrating hard on her steps, but not really conscious of what was going on around her. That was irrelevant to her aim. It was only now that she realized she was standing in a group of only twenty-eight girls. Jane looked around in awe. Had so many left already? It was then, half in shock and wonderment, that she realized, her dream had come true. Twenty-eight remaining girls could only mean one thing. She had been one of the lucky ones chosen.

Chapter 20

"And here is to Jane and Sara," her father announced proudly, as he stood at the head of the table and toasted the group. "Congratulations to you both. After all your hard work and dedication, you both deserve it."

Jane lifted her glass along with everyone else. She was brimming with happiness. She looked at Sarah and knew her smile was just as big as her friend's was. She did not think she had ever been this happy. All her dreams looked like they were going to come true. She and Sarah had been chosen for Germany. It was too amazing to believe.

The day had been nothing like they had expected. It had been hard and gruelling, but they had succeeded. And when it had come to the very end, and they had both been left standing in the centre of the studio, they knew. It was still a shock, and only when the tall thin man reappeared and confirmed it on the mike did they actually believe that their dreams had been made. They had gotten through. They had been chosen for Germany.

After his announcement, all decorum went out the window as the girls lunged for each other and hugged hard, whether they knew the girl next to them or not. Laugher was billowing out from all of them in great waves. They were ecstatic. Amazingly, when they had finished hugging and kissing, they noticed a table that had been set up on the stage. Drinks and cakes were made available and a small celebratory party began. They met the instructors and organizers, and the time passed in a haze of excitement of what was to come.

The train journey home had also flown past quickly. Both girls were so excited they could not stop talking about their upcoming trip and what it would be like. Their journey home was a complete contrast to how it had been travelling to the auditions that morning. Now they could not stop talking.

When they arrived back into Shoeing, both sets of parents were waiting on the platform, eager to hear the news. They knew that with the competition being so stiff it was quite possible that their daughters would not been chosen, or worse, that only one of the girls, had succeeded. They had no idea what to expect on their arrival back home, and had to be prepared for the worst. All doubts were cast aside as the girls embarked off the train. Jane and Sarah were unable to hide their success from their faces. Their smiles and laughter giving away the good news immediately. They had barely left the train and their parents had come running. There had been hugs and kisses all over again.

A celebratory dinner had been arranged for if they both managed to get in. Both girls were whisked home and had been given exactly half an hour to shower and change before they were taken off for their celebratory meal. It had all happened so fast. Jane was still trying to take it all in.

As her father's speech ended, Jane was delighted as she took her first sip of champagne and tasted the tiny bubbles as they hit her tongue. She let out a small giggle. The bubbles seemed to trickle all the way down her throat. It was such a nice, queer feeling. She took another sip, savouring and enjoying the sweet taste. Yes, tonight was a night for celebration. There was nothing that could come even close to how she was feeling.

Sarah's dad came around the table, filled everyone's glasses with more of the golden champagne, before taking a position next to Jane's father. They waited until they had everyone's attention again. "And to mark this wonderful occasion, we have something for the both of you. To show you how proud we are as your parents."

Both fathers came around to their daughters and gave them each a small pink box, tied neatly with a white satin ribbon.

"What is it?" Jane asked as she examined the small box before her.

"You'll have to open it and see." came the happy reply from her father. Jane and Sarah exchanged glances and together opened their small delicate packages. Jane stared in awe at the gleaming gold chain that held a tiny gold dancing slipper sitting perfectly on the white, velvet cushion. Jane touched the delicate chain. She loved it. This was the mark of her new career. Good things could only happen from here on. And then, unexpectedly, the tears came. Tears of joy. She turned, hugged her father hard and kissed her mother. Then, after she had composed herself, she took the beautiful chain out of the small box and let her father tie the clasp around her neck. No, there was definitely nothing that could compare to her happiness this evening.

It was a perfect evening. Their parents had chosen a small cozy restaurant, and Sarah's father had insisted on more bottles of champagne to mark the special event. "It's not every day that your daughter achieves something this big." Everyone was thrilled for them and their upcoming journey to Germany. They wanted to share their excitement and be involved in the momentous occasion. It was hard to believe really, that in two-week's time they were off on the plane on their way to take part in an international event. It was everything they had worked so hard to achieve and here it was. The time had finally arrived. Looking at her family, the entire evening seemed surreal.

Chapter 21

The last two weeks before their departure flew by quickly. Both mothers were in a constant state of excited flutter, arranging everything that they deemed necessary, from flights to travellers checks. Jane knew that her mum was enjoying all the hustle and bustle just as much as she was. They had made a list of all that had to be done, and that list never left her mother's handbag for the entire two weeks. Jane could not believe how long that list actually was. There had been so much that had to be done in such a short space of time.

Her mum had taken full advantage of her success and had insisted she get some new clothes and new suitcases for her upcoming journey. "You are going to be away for three months. You have to be prepared," her mother would say. Jane was loving every minute. It was a nice excuse to spend some time with her mother before she left. They had done well with the shopping list, but as expected, with her mother adding more things onto it each day, they had still been trying to complete the list, even yesterday. And now finally, on the day she was due to leave, Jane could say that everything had been done. There was nothing she had left out or forgotten. She was completely prepared. Her new suitcases had already been checked in and her ticket was in her hand, waiting to be used. It was almost time to leave. She had continued to work at Michelangelo's right up to the second last day before she was due to leave. She knew she was going to miss the place. And miss Peter, who she had become increasingly fond off. They had developed a special friendship that Jane hoped would develop into something more. She knew she would miss him terribly. They had all given her a wonderful farewell after her last evening at work, all wishing her luck. Mr. Ken had been a surprise and even given her a small card before she left. She had been touched by the small gesture. She had been even more touched, when she had arrived home and opened the card to find that it contained additional cash in sponsorship for her trip. She knew she was going to miss it all. Her friends, and her family. She was just glad that she had Sarah coming along with her. It would be an adventure they would always share together. One day, when they were old grannies, they could look back on it and laugh about it together.

The time had come for final goodbyes. Jane knew that this was going to be one of the hardest parts of leaving. It was an emotional time, with her mother admitting she was going to be missed and shedding a few tears. Jane was just getting through the last of the goodbyes when there was a light tap on her shoulder. She turned around, surprised, thinking it was her brother Jo, having one last prank before she left. But instead, before her stood Peter, dishevelled, but looking as devilishly handsome as he always did. He smiled down at her.

"You didn't think I would let you leave without saying goodbye, did you?" he asked.

Jane smiled, not trusting her voice. She could not believe he had come to the airport. In the faraway distance, Jane heard their boarding gate being called. She wished she had more time with him. Sarah was tugging her arm. There was so much she wanted to say to him.

"I'll write if you want me to?" she asked, hoping that he *would* want her to.

Peter smiled back. A twinkle in his eyes. "I definitely want you to," he said as he took her hands in his. He played with her fingers gently. "I will miss you, you know." Their boarding gate was called again. Peter heard it this time too and knew his time was up. "You had better go," he said reluctantly. "Good luck. And don't forget to write." He then bent and kissed her lightly on the cheek before hugging her tightly. For an instant, Jane stood frozen to the spot. She could not believe it. Had Peter actually kissed her?

Her brain was slow in taking in what had just happened between them. Then it all kicked in, with a sudden jolt and she felt her heart soar. Her legs seemed to turn to jelly as she hugged him back while she took in his heavenly smell. It was a moment she would never forget. Reluctantly, she pulled back, and smiled at him as she let Sarah pull her away to the entrance of the departure gate.

She handed in her ticket, and then they waved goodbye to everyone one last time before disappearing inside the departure lounge. Peter was the last sight she saw, standing awkwardly with her father, a sad expression on his handsome face.

Jane was soaring as she walked alongside Sarah. Peter had come to say goodbye to her. She kept saying it over and over in her mind, as if she needed to convince herself. And he had held her hand and then kissed her on the cheek. Just thinking about it sent flutters to her stomach. She continued to follow Sarah, who seemed to know where she was headed. They stopped in front of gate six. The aeroplane was already boarding, so they took a place in the queue. It was a matter of minutes before they headed through the last gateway and headed toward the aeroplane.

They stepped onto the aircraft within minutes. Two smartly dressed hostesses were waiting on either side of the entranceway, smiling broadly. "Welcome onboard flight 302," the tall blond one said.

One of the air hostesses took Jane's ticket, looked at it quickly, then passed it back. "You're at the back of the aeroplane. On the left side," she said as she pointed down one of the aisles.

"Thanks," replied Jane, as she made her way down. Jane turned toward Sarah as she walked. "What number are you?"

"Thirty-one. You?"

"Thirty-two. It's at the back somewhere." They continued to walk down the passageway. The aisle was small and narrow.

The first area they passed was First Class. The seating was much more spacious and there was more privacy for each of the seat occupants. Jane knew that the seats could bend so far back that they eventually made a full bed. The space was quite considerable. And so was the price, she guessed. They continued to walk down the middle of the aisle, but progress was slow with people trying to find their seats. They had to stop yet again, as someone in front of them found their place, and packed away their hand luggage.

"Look to your left," Sarah whispered. "Slowly."

Jane turned. At first she was not sure what Sarah was looking at. Then, when she saw what had roused Sarah's interest, a gasp stuck in her throat. There, sitting proudly in First Class, was Zara. An important air hugging her as she smirked at the people walking past her. Jane turned back to concentrating on manoeuvring down the aisle. The last thing she heard was Zara's voice asking the hostess for a glass of wine.

Jane continued to walk down the aisle, past First Class into the Economy section. They waited patiently as other passengers found their seat numbers and got settled in. Finally, when they were almost at the very back of the aircraft, they located their own seat numbers. They unloaded their hand luggage into the overhead compartments and minutes later everything was packed away. Now settled themselves, Jane watched the other passengers as they too readied themselves for the upcoming flight.

"Oh look. There's Lucy." Sarah pointed out. They had met Lucy after the auditions when they were having the celebratory cake and drinks.

Lucy must have heard her name, and looked over. She saw and recognized the two girls immediately. She waved, excitedly, and then took her own seat. As the seats around them filled up, they noticed a few more faces that they recognized from the auditions. The aeroplane continued to fill up, until there were no empty seats left in view. It was a full flight. Twenty minutes later the seat belt sign flashed, and they headed toward the runway.

Jane loved to fly. She was still, however, nervous, always was, until the aeroplane was safely up in the sky. She only felt safe when the clouds showed as small dots out the window. She leaned back and closed her eyes as she felt the aeroplane pick up speed. She felt everything, down to the bumps in her chair as the wheels lifted off the ground. And then they were flying upwards. Jane opened her eyes, and noted that they were still at an angle and still climbing. She dared a sneak look out the window, but all she saw was white puffs as they travelled upwards above the clouds. The bumps she could feel in the chair soon disappeared, and when she next looked out the window it was bright blue. The puffy clouds were now well beneath them in the far away distance. They had reached the correct flying altitude.

Once they had taken off and had been in the air for a sufficient time the seat belt signs went out. The air hostesses left their seats and busied themselves in the kitchen and cabins. They were served drinks first and then directly after that they were served a light meal. Jane was especially hungry. She had been so nervous before that she had not been able to eat anything. Not even at her mother's insistence. The flight itself was only two hours long, so by the time they had eaten their light meal and the empty trays collected, it was almost time to land.

Chapter 22

Zara had enjoyed her flight. Daddy had arranged her a First Class Ticket, and she had soaked up the attention. It had been very satisfying sitting in the luxurious seats, while others from her dance group had to walk right past her, to the Economy section. The air hostess serving her had been very accommodating and had given her everything she asked for. The meal on the flight had been delicious too. Almost as good as one of the fine restaurants she often frequented. Whoever said that aeroplane food was terrible? They obviously did not travel as she did. In style, with every whim catered for. Zara finished her plate and ate another one of the champagne truffles set before her, as she gazed out of the window. She could not help thinking of all she was going to do and see in Germany during her three months of freedom. It was going to be wonderful.

Everything good that had happened came to a sudden halt as soon as she disembarked off the aeroplane, starting with her luggage. It had taken longer than anyone else's to appear on the conveyor belt, and she had become more and more irritated as some of the other girls gathered theirs before her, and still hers did not surface. *Finally,* her bags arrived and she lugged them off the conveyer belt with great difficulty. She then looked around for some luggage trolleys, but none were available. *Great!* Zara thought, her mood darkening even more. In the end, she had to leave her bags on the side of a dirty wall and go in search of one. It had been hard work keeping her eyes partially on her bags and trying to obtaining a trolley at the same time. Eventually, just as she was about to give up hope, she found a deserted, but badly dented one. She heaved her luggage onto it before heading toward the arrivals gate feeling hot and flustered.

A tall man was waiting for her, with her name written on a placard in bold letters. Zara knew that Daddy had made arrangements for her first to be taken to the hostel, to sign in, and then onto the Four Seasons Hotel. She approached him, and was more than a little annoyed when he did not offer to take and push her luggage trolley to the waiting limousine. Zara followed the horrible, rude man to the car in silence, making a mental note that she would have to get his name so she could complain about him later. She was more than a little shocked when he stopped in front of a parked car already filled with screaming, excited girls. It soon became apparent, to Zara's horror, that they were also headed toward the hostel. Zara was now 100% certain that this was not the transportation her daddy had arranged for her. She debated on whether to go back to the arrivals lounge and find her correct chauffeur, but at the same time she did not want to be left at a strange airport all on her own, especially when there was already a cab waiting going that same way. After much debate, she climbed into the car, although unhappily. She would have preferred to be on her own, in an air-conditioned, luxury car. Zara stepped in delicately, and closed the door gently after herself. She immediately regretted her decision to travel with the party when she was pushed hard up against the metal door. The car was very cramped. It was the longest one-hour drive she had ever experienced. This was partially to being squashed the entire journey, and partially because of the other girls, whose excited chatter and giggling was giving her a headache. She wished, for the one-hundredth time, that she had turned back and found her proper escort, but it was far too late now. They were halfway there already. She could not wait until she arrived at the hostel, signed in her name to let them know she had arrived, and had the driver take her onto the hotel and her luxury room where she could enjoy the silence. There, she would take a long luxurious bath and wash away this awful side of the journey. Once she was at the hotel, she would settle in comfortably and that was when the fun would begin. Daddy had already arranged her room and had taken care of all the necessary comforts she might need. All the strenuous work from before had been difficult, but now she was finally going to reap the benefits.

She was excited. She had finally received what she had wanted. Three months away in Germany. Her parents had already spoken with Pat's parents and had arranged that she fly out the following week. Be available as her companion. Pat thought the whole idea was excellent. She managed to get away on a three-month adventure holiday with her friend, and she did not have to work or do anything but go out shopping and enjoy the hotel. Zara had spoken to her the night before, and she already had an array of tourist books, which she had been poring over and had begun to make a list of sights that she wanted to see. She was brimming with excitement. Zara knew that the two of them together would have an amazing time.

Zara was surprised when they arrived at the hostel. It was very pretty really, she had to give it that. An old building set against acres of parks and woodlands. Zara thought it was nice, but knew that the Four Seasons would be much better. Much more to her refined taste. After all, this was only a school. The other girls in the car had all gone silent. Zara knew that it must be the first time they had seen anything so grand. She felt sorry for their underprivileged existence. Still, it was not her problem. All she wanted to do was check in with the organizers as quickly as possible and then head on to the Four Seasons where she belonged. Them staying here was their problem, not hers.

They drove up the winding driveway, passing an array of trees and bushes that curved to make a spectacular arc. After a few minutes the trees gave way, and they found themselves inside manicured lawns as they proceeded up to what led to the old, historic boarding school.

The driver came to a stop in front of the entranceway, and all the girls piled out eagerly. Zara among them. The old building was even more spectacular up close. Intricate mouldings and statues adorned the exterior walls. They looked around for a few minutes in awe, and then made their way inside. The cab driver wasted no time in beginning to unload all the larger pieces of luggage, eager to be on his way.

Zara stopped him. "I'm not staying here. Leave my luggage in the car," Zara said. The cab driver gave her a strange look, but did not say anything in reply. "I'm just going to tell them I have arrived, and then you can take me to the Four Seasons Hotel." Again the cab driver looked at Zara, but made no attempt to reply. He continued to unload the other girl's luggage and left Zara's bags in the car as instructed. "I won't be long," she stated as she too headed inside the hostel. She took care to take along with her, her hand luggage, as it contained all her money, cards and passport. She would rather keep that with her, than leave it with some strange cab driver.

All the girls were crowded around a small table in the front of the huge foyer. "Here, found it. We are in Room Four, on the second floor. We have to follow the red signs on the walls, directing us." Zara edged her way into the group. The table was full of small envelopes, each with a name written on it. She found her name on one of the small envelopes and ripped it open roughly. She was room number Five, also on the second floor. They were to follow the red signs posted on the walls until they found their room numbers. They had the rest of the afternoon to settle in and unpack, then at 6:00 p.m. they were all due to meet in the main hall located on the lower ground floor. They would then receive their formal welcome and introduction to the school before heading toward the dining room at 7:00 p.m. for dinner. Zara watched the other girls retrieve their heavier bags from outside where the cab driver had left them and head upstairs to their new bedrooms. Zara did not want to go to the bedroom that had been allocated to her. All she wanted to do was find one of the organizers and let them know she was here. Then she could be on her way and head to the Four Seasons. After the last horrific hour and a half, she could do with some pampering.

She had been traipsing the halls for over an hour now, and could not find a single judge or anyone else who she could register with. Her handbag was starting to cut through her fingers and her feet were getting sore from all the walking. When there seemed to be no other alternative, she grudgingly made her way to what was supposed to be her bedroom. Room number five. She decided she would leave her handbag there and lock the door for safety until she found one of the organizers. "Where were they all?" she muttered to herself as she found her room. As she opened the door, Zara just stared in horror at the scene before her. The room was tiny. Smaller than her father's study at home. And to make matters worse, there was not one, but four small beds squashed into the tiny space. They look like rats in a cage. Zara walked into the room in shock. The other girls who she was meant to share with were already unpacking and getting comfortable for the next few months ahead. They had been laughing and joking together when Zara entered. Now they stopped, eager to introduce themselves to their last roommate. Zara ignored them completely as she placed her designer bags on the only spare bed left, before heading out again in search of someone, anyone, who could register her. She had to get it over with so she could get out of this Hell hole. She could hear the Four Seasons calling her name and this was wasting valuable time. After seeing the bedroom she was more glad than ever that she was not staying in this place.

By the time Zara returned back to the bedroom some time later, she knew it was hopeless. Completely and utterly hopeless. How had things gone so horribly wrong? She had finally found someone of some authority and had been told that she was not allowed to leave or she would be disqualified and sent home in disgrace. The woman was adamant she was to remain. She had argued feverously and shouted loudly, but it had all fallen onto deaf ears. Nothing she did or said made any difference. She knew she had been a little hysterical, but she just could not believe that she was to be a prisoner here for three whole months. The thought terrified her. She was stuck in this place. The notion made her want to cry and lash out at the same time. In the end, the woman, had walked away, oblivious to her shouts and protests. Zara was not sure what she should do. She did not want to be expelled now; not after all she had been through.

With little other choice, she returned to the empty entranceway and found her suitcases. They had been left on the cold steps. The cab driver was long gone. She lugged her belongings back to the bedroom and dumped them next to the small bed that was supposed to be hers. Going home and leaving this dump of a place was out of the question, although it was what she wished for most of all. Visions of the Four Seasons were slowly drifting out of her grasp. She could not risk losing Mummy and Daddy's approval so late in the game. They had been so excited when she had come home from the auditions and announced proudly that she had been one of the privileged twenty-eight girls out of hundreds chosen. Her mother was beside herself with happiness. Her father had beamed with pride. Now if she returned home, they would be devastated and her plans would fall away into nothing. What could she do?

It was with great reservations that Zara knew she might be at the hostel a bit longer than she had anticipated. She would call Daddy as soon as he was home and explain things to him. He would have to do something. Zara Maddox was NOT staying in some stuffy old boarding school. Her father *would* sort this out. Bill Maddox would not have his little princess share a room with complete strangers.

Another hour later, Zara was back in the small bedroom. She had just phoned her father. Daddy had been in such high spirits about her being in Germany. She had told him about the confusion with the hostel, and he had shrugged it off, thinking it might be better for her anyway, to stay with the other dancers. She had tried to protest and pout loudly into the phone, but he had laughed at her attempts and promised that when all of this was over, he would take her and her mother on holiday. Five Star luxury he had promised, and she could be pampered all she wanted. Zara could not believe she was being forced to stay in this dump, but she knew she must not disappoint her father. Bill Maddox was not a nice man when he was angry.

Zara, though, was mad. She was being forced to stay at the hostel against her will. A prisoner. All her carefully prepared plans pushed to one side. She returned back to her room and looked at the pathetic hard, bed. How on earth was she going to endure three months of sleeping on that? She continued to ignore the other girls completely and refused to acknowledge their introductions. She was still mulling over her colossal problems while she soaked herself in the small enamel bathtub. She really did not want to use the bathroom, but she was desperate for a hot bath, to soak away the day's journey and everything bad that had happened. Besides, it was the only place she could go and be on her own. Her bedroom was crowded with another three bodies, all talking excitedly between themselves. Zara really could not see what they were so excited about. It had been an awful day. She lay in the bath, the hot water steaming the room, and could not help the tears that were cascading down her cheeks. She was stuck. She could not leave and go home. The only thing she could do was stick it out and enjoy the time she had on her own in the evenings. Even that did not sound appealing. She had earlier visions of days enjoying the sunshine, shopping and sightseeing, with nights out enjoying good food and meeting new people. All that of that was now gone. The thought was severely disappointing. What was she going to do for three months cooped up in this hostel? At least Daddy had offered her the holiday as compensation, but that did not come even close to what she knew she would have to endure for the next three months. She thought of Pat jealously. She had not worked one bit for this trip, and she was arriving next week without a care in the world. She would be taken directly to the Four Seasons, and would be able to enjoy the days at her leisure. Zara was fuming, as she, who had made it all possible, was here unhappy and miserable, not enjoying any benefits. None at all. She fumed, and cried even more. It all seemed hopeless. It was going to be a terribly long three months.

She missed dinner that night, but did not care. She had cried so much that she had completely lost her appetite. The other three girls had left without her, so at least she was able to unpack her bags without any interruptions. Finally, she had some quiet time alone. She had been unpacking her things in between the tears that would not stop. She cried even harder when she had finished unpacking only one suitcase out of the three she had bought with her. The one meager cupboard space allocated to her was full. She looked at the rest of her belongings. Knew that she would have to keep them in her suitcases and store them under her bed. There was just no space for them. She knew she was in a hole. A hole that she was not able to surface from for the next three months. It seemed an eternity. She sat on the bed and cried some more. She was alone, so did not care that her mascara was badly smudged and her eyes red rimmed, swollen and puffy. She finished unpacking what she could, washed her face of the tears she had shed and crept into the hard and uncomfortable bed. She knew it was early but did not care. She was exhausted, and all she wanted to do was go to sleep and let this nightmare be over.

Exhausted as she was, sleep would not come as the horrors of the next three months kept her awake. Wiping yet another tear from her cheek, Zara mulled over her desperate situation. It was the last unhappy thought she had before she finally fell into an exhausted, uncomfortable sleep.

* * * * *

When Zara woke, she looked around herself for a few minutes, disorientated. And then it all came flooding back to her. She sat up sharply, aware that her eyes were stinging and her throat red raw. She looked around and saw that the other three girls were all still fast asleep. One girl next to the window snoring softly. Zara looked away in disgust. She still could not believe that she had been forced to share a room with complete strangers. She looked at the gold watch on her thin wrist—5:30 a.m. It was still early. A sharp pang of hunger gripped her. She had not eaten anything since her arrival at this dreaded place, her only meal yesterday being on the aeroplane. She knew that breakfast began being served in a half an hour. She had the option of staying in the hard and lumpy bed or going downstairs for some warm breakfast before anyone else was up. She decided she could not wait. Slipping out the bed, Zara went to the small white wardrobe that she had been allocated and searched for her pink tracksuit. She grabbed it from the first shelf and made her way into the bathroom, dressing quickly. She felt terrible. Her head was pounding, and her throat felt dry. She knew she should have a shower first, but hunger won over. She had to get something to eat before she did anything else. Zara slipped out the room not bothered that she had not brushed her hair or her teeth. In any other circumstances she would never have left the house looking and feeling as she did now. Today, however, she did not care. No one else would even be up at this time, she comforted herself. They would all still be tucked up in bed, fast asleep.

When Zara came back into the bedroom she knew she did not look any better, but she felt better. The coffee was not as good as back home, but it had helped. She had sat on her own in a hidden corner and began to work on a plan. This whole Germany thing was not what she had bargained for, but she knew was not able to leave. She knew she would now have to use the present situation and make the best of it. First thing she had already decided on, was that Daddy was going to pay. Pay dearly for making her stay at this rotten place. She already knew that he was going to take her on a luxury holiday when this was all over. That thought made her only slightly happy. She would make sure it was somewhere exotic and expensive, for a long, long time. She would use these three months to get as much out of him as she could. She may have to suffer now, but it was not going to be without its price tag.

First thing she knew she must do, was get herself organized and back to her old self. She was Zara Maddox, she could not be seen moping around. She knew that a cold invigorating shower was called for. She hoped that no one had seen her downstairs in the state she was in. She had seen a few girls milling around for breakfast, but had tried to keep herself as hidden as possible. Zara knew she looked awful, but she did not realize just how bad she looked. It was only when she was about to hop into the shower that she looked at herself in the mirror for the first time. She took in her puffy red eyes and pale skin. Her eyes were sunken deep into their sockets, surrounded by dark, black rings. Her headache was still a dull thud against her skull, and her nose was still blocked from all the crying. Her usually shiny long blond hair looked bedraggled and greasy. She looked awful. She knew she had to shape up and clean up. She was going to make this all better, by any means possible.

Chapter 23

Jane looked around the terminal. They had collected their luggage with ease and were now through to the arrivals lounge. A small, short man had been waiting at the exit, both her and Sarah's name written on a big board, in huge black letters. They had approached him and were ushered into a waiting car that was to take them and three other girls straight to the hostel. The drive took an hour, in which they managed to see some of the spectacular green countryside. Jane enjoyed the trip and took in as much of her surroundings as she could. When they arrived at the hostel itself, Jane could not believe the size and splendor of it. It was very grand. Very grand indeed, with sweeping views and large grounds. All five of them made their way into the large foyer and found their room numbers almost straight away.

Jane dropped her bags onto the shiny, polished floor. They seemed so heavy after the walk up the old and winding staircase. She took a look around the bedroom that was to be their home for the next three months. Jane was impressed. It was clean and expertly decorated in white. Four beds arranged nearly in a square, all adorned with crisp white covers. Next to each bed was a small table, adorned with a delicate white, silk shaded, lamp. The entire room was light and airy, helped by the light pouring in from the open window. Jane made her way over the stripped wooden floors and took in the scenery below. Their window overlooked a large park full of plants and trees, with wooden tables and chairs dispatched at neat intervals. Jane knew that in the summer months families must come for a picnic and enjoy the weather. In the faraway distance, she could also see a small jungle gym, suitable for younger children. She could imagine it being very busy.

"Not bad," Sarah said, smiling as she disappeared into the attached bathroom. She came out again a few minutes later, smiling even more broadly. "I'll take that bed there, next to the window," Sarah shouted excitedly as she skidded across the room and jumped onto the bed.

Jane laughed as she tried to grab her as she passed. She picked up her bag and claimed the bed opposite, next to the huge window with the wonderful view.

They were halfway through unpacking their clothes into the built in wardrobes when there was a slight knock on the door and another two girls entered. The one girl was tall with bright red hair. Small freckles dotted evenly over her face, showing off bright green eyes.

She walked in confidently. "Hi, I'm Karen. This is Sue. I believe we are sharing the room with you guys." As she said all this, she lowered her bag off her shoulders.

"Hi. Please come in," Sarah replied, standing up. The second girl was also tall, but she had dark hair and piecing blue eyes. Although she was fair, she had a nice glowing tan, as if she had been on holiday recently. She seemed very shy, although she did smile at the group as Karen spoke.

"I'm Jane and this is Sarah," Jane said as she walked over. "Please come in. Grab a bed. Hope you don't mind, but we've taken those two."

An hour later, all introductions and life stories over, the four girls were busy making themselves comfortable in their new home. The room had begun to take a cozier feeling and now had a lived in look. Each girl was adding her own personal touches. Photographs and books soon filled the shelves.

Sue had even brought with her a small portable radio and CD player. "You don't mind do you?" she said as she grabbed a handful of CDs from her suitcase.

"No, of course not," replied Jane. "Go ahead. We love our music."

"You guys okay then if I play a mixed CD?"

Both Jane and Sara nodded and soon cheerful music took over the room as they all continued to unpack and make themselves comfortable.

Sue, they found out, was from the next big town to theirs. Only a half an hour's drive from where they lived. She stayed with her mum and younger brother. Yes, they just come back from a week in Greece. They had gone to see her grandparents, who now lived over there in a small cottage by the coast.

Karen's story was completely different. She was the youngest out of five children and lived in the city with her high flying career parents. Her eldest brother had moved out the year before, and her eldest sister was now also looking for her own flat. It sounded like Karen lived a very exciting life, with parents that travelled all over the world. Sometimes she went along, other times she did not. It all depended on the nature of their business trip and how long they would be away. All four girls were from different backgrounds, but they all still had something in common. They had all been dancing since they were little, and all had great aspirations to become world famous dancers. In that aspect, they were all alike. Stories of the Saturday practices soon become the main topic of conversation as they shared experiences. How hard they had all practised for the auditions, the agony and suspense involved. They all agreed that it had been worth it and being chosen for the World Games was one the best things that had happened to each and every one of them. For all four girls, this was a dream come true.

Reflecting back on the day, after a good meal in the dining hall, Jane had to admire how well thought out and planned the entire operation had been so far. They had all been called into what must have been the main hall, and they were briefed on what the procedures and routines would be for the next three months. Every need had been thought off. The time spent in Germany was going to be fun, although not without its hard work. Most of the days would be spent dancing and exercising. Breakfast was laid out for them each day in the dining hall. They could eat anytime between 6:00 a.m. and 8:00 a.m. Lunch was served as a buffet at 1:00 p.m. and then dinner was a sit-down meal served at 7:00 p.m. In between were the training sessions. The instructors were not without heart and had allocated some spare time during the day. This time, they could spend any way the pleased.

There was a gym on site, they were told, equipped with a pool and a sauna which they had free access to. The school also housed an array of horses in the stables on the grounds, which they were allowed to ride. In addition to these, there were other activities they could take up, from tennis on the six courts, to clay pigeon shooting. Most Saturdays and Sundays, they were informed, they were free to do as they pleased, just like any normal weekend.

These were the only two days that they were permitted to leave the school grounds. On these days, they could go into the local town where they could go out for lunch, or spend time browsing and shopping. If they wanted to remain within the hostel grounds, that was permitted too.

It sounded like every aspect of the three months had been carefully thought out, and every need had been accommodated for. With their timetables in hand, they had been shown around the school, which was very big, and finally into the spacious dining room where they would take their meals. They then had time to roam themselves, before dinner.

Jane was glad that their roommates had turned out to be such easy and fun girls. They were serious about their time here and were eager to begin the dance routines, just as she and Sarah were. The four of them had fallen into an easy relationship with one another almost immediately. As they made their way into the dining hall they were, once again, pleased with what had been provided for them. Unlike most dining halls that were often seen in movies, this dining hall looked like a miniature restaurant. Bright blue curtains adorned the windows, which worked well with the canary yellow walls. It was bright and cheerful, and each table was laid with a checked tablecloth and serviettes. The food that was provided was also of excellent restaurant standard. There were a variety of meats and vegetables, and they had catered for almost every dietary requirement.

Karen, they found out, was a vegetarian. She was apprehensive when they had approached the dining room, well aware that many restaurants and hotels did not cater for her eating habits. She had approached the buffet table cautiously, already resigning herself to being disappointed. She expected to be living on salads and potatoes for her entire stay. One look at the table, and a wide smile crossed her face. There was not one, but an abundance of vegetarian meals, she could choose from. "I cannot believe it," she stated in happiness. She may be a vegetarian, but she loved food. Somehow three months of only salads and potatoes did not make an interesting diet.

They found a small table in the corner and began busying themselves with the buffet. Jane was in awe at the variety of meals that had been provided and did not want to miss out on anything, so she had resigned herself to a small helping of almost everything. She allowed herself only a tablespoon of each amazing dish, but her plate was still full when she had made it back to the table. She felt a little guilty as she sat down, but was pleased that the other girls had done the same thing too. She enjoyed her meal, as much as the other girls did. Karen was especially happy with her tomato and mushroom pasta bake, which she said, was better than even her own mother's. They chatted comfortably throughout their dinner. Jane found that Sue had a funny sense of humour. She was quiet, but when she got going, she was quite a chatter. She had their table in fits of laugher. She was sure she was going to enjoy her stay here in Germany, especially if their first night was anything to go by.

The private hostel had turned out to be much better than expected. Jane could now understand the price they had been asked to pay. The children, who were all now on summer vocation, were wealthy students from wealthy parents. The hostel took care of their every whim and desire. It was obvious that each student was well cared for and a variety of extra classes were provided to entertain them. Jane knew she was going to enjoy the next three months tremendously. She had seen one of the timetables in the hall and the school offered a variety of different courses that could be taken, from fencing, to rowing. There was even a cake-decorating course. It was all there. Everything they could possibly want to do in their spare time was right there on the grounds.

During dessert, Jane yawned. It was still early in the evening, but she could not help herself. They day had finally caught up with her. It was all the practising and running around, then the last minute chores that had to be done before she had left. She tried to stifle the second yawn, but failed. Sarah also yawned, and it seemed to have a ripple effect on their entire table.

As if voicing her views, Sue stretched long and hard. "I think I might turn in after this."

Jane nodded, "Yeah, me too. It's been a long day."

They all finished their desserts and headed happily back to their cozy room. Jane knew that a hot, relaxing bath was just what the doctor ordered before she headed off to bed. That, along with an early night, would do her good. Maybe, she decided, she would read her book a little before getting some rest for their first big day tomorrow.

All four girls were surprised when they made their way back up the staircase and heard shouting coming from one of the offices below. The voice was loud and angry. "I WILL NOT SAY HERE!" came the voice. A girl's voice laced with anger. "NO! Absolutely not!"

There was some hushed mumbling as someone replied, "This is pathetic."

The voice replied again, in a shrill scream, "Why can't I stay in the hotel? Tell me! It's all been booked and everything arranged. This is outrageous!"

All four girls, including Jane, leaned closer, waiting to hear the reply. All they heard was more mumbles, then a silence that lasted a few short seconds. "I said, I won't stay here. I WILL NOT SHARE A BEDROOM!"

More mumbles as someone answered in reply again. "This is not what I came here for. Something MUST be done about this!" The voice was now shrill, a clammy desperation to her words.

"I wonder who that is?" Karen asked questioningly to the three other girls.

"I have no idea," Sarah replied, "but she is certainly angry."

Just then, the office door was flung roughly open and slammed violently shut. A loud bang vibrated throughout the corridor. All four girls instinctively pressed hard against the wall, not wanting to be seen. They could hear the clip clop of heels walking crossly away in the opposite direction. Down the corridor the sound went. Jane ventured having a quick look. There, with her head held high, was Zara Maddox walking furiously away.

If Jane knew anything about Zara, she knew the problem would not be left alone. If Zara wanted to go and stay at a hotel, you could be sure she would do anything to get her own way. Jane did not wish to get caught in the line of fire. As soon as she saw Zara disappear around the bend, she ushered everyone back into their own bedroom. The argument they had all witnessed was the talk of the evening. Jane wondered if any of the other girls on the floor had heard what had taken place. She was sure many would have, with Zara protesting as loudly as was possible, and making such a huge scene.

When Jane emerged from her hot bath, half an hour later, Sarah, Karen and Sue were still talking about what they had witnessed in the corridor. Sue was incredulous that someone could actually shout at someone else that loudly and get away with it.

"What's wrong with this place?" Sue added in protest. "It's really nice here. The food is wonderful and you all heard the list of activities we can take part in. Swimming, horse riding. What on earth does she have to complain about?"

Sue just could not understand what Zara's problem was, and her adverse dislike to the hostel. Over the next hour Sue and Karen were given a detailed summary of Zara. Jane tried to stick to the facts, not let her personal opinion crowd the details and let the other two girls make up their own minds. They included details of her beautiful, flashy red car and the rest of her spoiled existence. Jane could not resist adding in her own piece on the restaurant saga.

Jane had to admit that it did sounded funny now as she told the story, but at the time, she had been really angry. Zara had deliberately set out to ruin things for her. And without that job she would not have been able to make this trip. Now, after the episode in the office, Jane knew that Zara was still going to continue to be a problem. She had only been here one day and already she was making demands on what she did and did not want. Jane knew that all the instructors had thought and planned everything at the hostel very carefully. What they did not bargain for was someone like Zara. Spoilt and rich. Used to always getting her own way, regardless of the cost.

The next morning, all bright and fresh, the four girls made their way into the dining hall for an early breakfast. With going to bed so early the night before, Jane found she was awake at 5:00 a.m. The sun was streaming brightly through the window, making slates of rays on her bed. It was a nice feeling to wake up with the sun warming your face. Five a.m. was much earlier than she usually woke up, but Jane was certain that it was due to the excitement she felt for the upcoming day ahead. She was eager to get to class and begin, but that only began at 9:00 a.m. She still had four free hours to get through, so she snuggled deeper into the covers. She could lie in bed for a little while longer before she would get up and have a good breakfast. Besides, the others were still asleep and she did not want to disturb them just yet. Jane needn't have worried. The other girls were rousing themselves up also, only a little while later.

The breakfast, when they made their way back to the restaurant, was laid out on the buffet table, the same as the evening before and looked just as delicious. All sorts of cereals and fresh fruits were available. There were yogurts, and a variety of hot, delicious smelling dishes. Bacon and eggs, and even fluffy pancakes were arranged on a heated platter. The food looked scrumptious. Jane looked at the food before her and realized with surprise that she was starving.

As she helped herself to bowel of mixed fruit salad, she could not help noticing someone partly hidden in the corner table. Her hair was blond and loose, falling unbrushed down her shoulders. Jane knew immediately that it was Zara. No one else she knew had that colour hair. Although her hair was loose, it did not hide her red and blotchy face. Her eyes were deeply sunken into her forehead, as if she had been crying all night. Jane tried not to stare, but it was difficult. This was not the Zara she was used to seeing. Confident and self-assured, always with an important air clinging to her. But Zara was lost in her own thoughts. Did not even look up as she sipped her coffee. Jane guessed her appearance had something to do with what she had seen and heard the evening before. She continued to serve herself breakfast and when she next looked, the seat Zara had occupied was empty.

The next time Jane saw Zara, they were all in the training room, ready for the first morning's session to begin. All the girls present were eager and excited. Zara blew into the room, her usual air of self-confidence along with her. Jane was surprised at the drastic transformation. Gone were the puffy eyes and red blotchy face. If she had not seen Zara herself earlier that morning, she would have said they were not the same people. Zara looked her normal, self-assured self. It was as if the girl from earlier that morning had completely disappeared. Never existed in fact.

Chapter 24

Raymond smiled as he gazed into the review mirror. The airport quickly disintegrating into a small blob behind him. He knew that Zara's parents had stayed behind, eager to see the aeroplane take off. He knew they would stay there until the very last minute until the airplane was a small dot in the sky, partly hidden by the puffy clouds. He had faked a business deal and left as soon as he could. He had no need to hang around, as he knew they would. He said the necessary goodbyes to Zara, gave the necessary support for what was a suitable time and then legged it out of the airport as fast as he could. Truth be told, he just could not be bothered making idle conversation with Zara's parents. He knew that any business topics would be out the question with Zara's departure, so what would they talk about? Hanging around until the bitter end would not help him in any way. He could just see it now. Idle conversion. Awkward silences as they watched and waited for the aeroplane to take off. No, he could not be handling that. Better to get out of there as soon as he could, so that was exactly what he had done.

Raymond was glad to see Zara go. Three months of freedom. It felt wonderful. He was not fooled by Zara for one minute. A tear here and a tear there, faking a sad face, obviously put on, well to him anyway, saying how sad she was to leave, how she would miss them so. But Raymond knew. Underneath her practised sadness, she could not wait to leave. The entire goodbye had been part of a ritual. One she played very well. For such an intelligent and wealthy man, who had made almost all his money using his brains, her father was a blind old fool when it came to his love for his only daughter. Bill Maddox seemed to succumb to her every whim. How could he not see her for what she was? A very resourceful and cunning woman. This whole affair was the prefect opportunity to get her father eating out of the palm of her hand. Raymond already knew that unlike all the other girls staying at the hostel, her father had arranged a hotel suite for her in the Four Seasons. The entire trip was just a glorified holiday. And she was away for three whole months. A part of him was happy for the personal break, the other part was asking himself how that would affect his position in the company. He needed Zara around to help him reach his goals.

Raymond knew that Zara's father was extremely proud of his daughter. He blew her praises whenever he could. At first Raymond had indulged the man, hoping that all the talk and interest he showed would somehow benefit himself, but now he had discovered Bill Maddox was tireless. He could discuss his daughter at any time of day, on any subject. Everything seemed to stop, regardless if it was an important meeting or closing a deal for a large contract, when she was the topic of conversation. And when she had been chosen at the auditions, Raymond had to admit he was surprised. His first, he had thought that Bill Maddox had something to do with the fact that she was apart of group of girls heading for Germany. Then, after he had talked and talked about the event and what it meant, he had realized that Zara had actually done this on her own. He was surprised. It was the last thing he had expected from her. He knew that

Zara did dancing, but somehow her taking part in an international event that did not benefit herself did not add up. He knew Zara was up to something. She never did anything without it benefiting herself in some way or another.

He had to admit that Zara had surprised him in a few things recently. There was this total unnecessary display of enthusiasm for dancing in Germany, which gave him the conclusion that this was all for some monumental reason and then there was the out of character episode at the restaurant. Even now when he thought of it, he could not help smiling. It had been such a contrast to the Zara he knew. Always controlled and careful, but always planning ahead, preferably without anyone knowing her agenda. She had actually let her feelings be known that evening. Had vented them out loud. He was baffled at the sudden change. This was more like it. He knew she had fire in her, but it was always well hidden from view. Pushed away to the bottom of her core and masked by her cunningness. Her father would have been proud if he had seen her display. Still, even with the latest surprises, which he had found amusing, he was happy to see her go away for a while. He was finding her more and more hard work and it was tiring him out. These three months would give him a well-earned break. With the way that things had been at work, there was no other alternative but to continue seeing her. He could not risk jeopardizing his relationship with Bill, and if he messed up with Zara, he knew that Bill Maddox would be the first to know and interfere. And he also knew that it would be the biggest mistake he could possibly make. It would be career suicide. Gone would be the promotion and the newly acquired luxury and lifestyle he had become accustomed to enjoying. Raymond knew that he had worked far too hard for that all to just disappear. Zara was a pain, but in comparison to the benefits, she was well worth it. A little break would help though. He could recharge his batteries, and after three months, they could take up again where they had left off.

Raymond indicated left and took the corner sharply, enjoying the speed of his car. A Porsche. Brand spanking new. It had been the first large extravagant purchase he had made. In his opinion, it fit the image he was trying to create to perfection. This was him. Fast and Furious. His perfect, flashy vehicle. As he rounded the last corner, he took the next exit, which found him inside the familiar car park. It took him but a few short seconds to find his usual parking bay before he locked up and headed inside the building. Time for a workout at the gym before heading back to the office. Then he would have to sit down seriously and worked out some sort of plan with regard to Zara. He needed to make sure that even with her away, he still had enough swaying power over Bill and in the company. This was going to be a big test. Just how much could he get away with without Zara around?

Later in his office, Raymond had little time to think of anything else but work. His phone was buzzing with a million calls, and his secretary had called in sick. Just what he needed, and there was no replacement as of yet. They had tried to secure him a temp, but somehow he was still waiting for one to arrive. In the meantime he was kept very busy trying to answer all the incoming calls. It was abhorrent that someone of his status should be left to answer the phone. He now also realized just how many calls Sophie screened for him. What did all these people actually want?

He did not have time for this inconvenience. Where was the temp for heaven's sake? As he swapped the telephone to his other ear, Raymond continued to listen to a colleague rambling on, currently out on the field. The problem seemed to have escalated in a few short hours and there was no alternative but for him to get involved. Something he also did not need, but was forced to deal with. "No, that's just not possible," Raymond replied angrily. He was quiet for a few moments longer, listening intently and then replied firmly, "We'll never make that sort of deadline. You have to stall for as much time as possible. I don't care what you have to tell them." Raymond was silent for a few more seconds, then nodded. "You know what will happen if this blows up, don't you?" he asked seriously. "It will be your job on the line, mark my words. And don't for one minute think I will rescue you, because you have gotten yourself into this horrific mess, all on your own. You have called me for help and I am telling you what to do. Now do it! No buts. Just do it." He let the other man say something. Was silent again, as he took in what was said. "Just get it done!" he shouted angrily, as he slammed the phone down.

Raymond smiled to himself. Things could not have been going more according to plan. Stupid Niles. He would do what he had been told and land himself in a little bit of pickle. No doubt his actions would get him fired. And that left him, Raymond, to rush in and salvage the situation. He would be the hero. He already had the prefect plan all prepared. He was now just waiting. And watching. As soon as the mouse took the bait, he would be ready to pounce. And that would leave him, in the spotlight. Perfect. Just perfect. He hoped that Bill appreciated all this effort he was going to. Even without Zara's help, he knew he deserved this promotion. Zara was just a small insurance policy ensuring that he actually got it. And that bought him back to his problem with Zara. What was he going to do about the current situation?

The problem had been with him all day and the next. Now, as he sliced into the thick steak sitting on the plate before him, he reflected on his situation. Somehow he still had not managed to come to any sort of concrete answer to his problem. He had already decided that at some stage, maybe in four or five weeks time, he would fly out to Germany himself and see Zara. Make an appearance. He knew that it would please Zara to see him and that it would eventually filter through to her father. That would keep the old man sweet. Maybe even increase his chances for this promotion, or even better yet, bring it forward. Raymond wanted it so badly he could practically smell it. He cut himself another piece of steak. It was light pink inside. Just as he liked it. He took another mouthful and enjoyed the taste. It was juicy. Cooked to perfection. And that was what money bought. Quality. It was already the second evening, and he was enjoying his newfound freedom immensely. Time was a luxury. And now he had it all to himself. Working so hard, even at home in the evening, he had found that the time he did have for himself had dwindled to almost nothing. Then, when he did have an evening, where he was not burning the midnight oil, he had to incorporate dates here and dinners there with Zara to keep her happy. He had to appear the perfect, willing and eager boyfriend of his boss's daughter. Most of the time he did not mind, as it was good for his image to be seen escorting Zara out, but sometimes, like today, he enjoyed being on his own. As he took yet another mouthful of the steak, he noticed that his phone was ringing again. Raymond already had two missed calls. He was sure that it was Zara. The number did not display, so it had to be international. He had taken one look at the vibrating phone, and ignored it. She would just have to wait. It was only the second day!

*****

Zara rang Raymond's number again. No answer. Where was he, she asked herself for the third time? She had not spoken to him since she had left, which was rather unusual. Right now, he thought she was enjoying a relaxing, fun filled time at the Four Seasons. How wrong could he be? Instead here she was, stuck in this small bedroom again. All the other girls were back in the food hall for lunch. Zara knew she would have to go down soon and get something to eat. She needed to keep her energy levels up, but the food they served was just horrible. She received better food at home, cooked by their chef. How on earth was she expected to eat what they served? She was glad that Pat was arriving on Saturday. She was living for the weekend as she had never lived before. She would be like a prisoner let out of her cage. Freedom. That was what Saturday represented to her. But being only her second day, Saturday felt like miles and miles away. She did not know how she was going to endure it. It was like physical torture.

With a plan underway, she had felt better. She had her shower this morning, put on her happy face, and made her way to the training rooms. Zara was not sure who had heard her the previous evening in the office venting her little disagreement, or who had seen her first thing that morning, all puffy and red-eyed. But she knew she had to salvage the situation. Make everyone forget it ever happened. If she was to be here for another three months, she knew she had to regain control of the situation and start making some friends who would idealize her. That was the only way she could appease herself while she was here. She had deliberately smiled and joked with the other girls, acting as if there was nothing wrong. Her own roommates had even joined her, after some coaxing. To anyone who knew her, the previous night was an fiction of their imagination. That girl did not exist. Zara was lively and fun. One of them. She must have just been tired after the long trip. Everyone gets that way. And now she was back to normal. No harm done.

She had to admit she was happy when class finally started. All that fake smiling was beginning to hurt her cheeks. Now she could concentrate on dancing, and to do that she did not have to talk and pretend to be everyone's friend.

The first class was very different to what she had expected. She had expected to get straight into the dance routines like when they had been practising. It was not so. They were told that one of the main objectives for the first four weeks was to increase their fitness level. A small well-muscled man, obviously a body builder, appeared with pop up punching bags. He placed one bag in front of each girl as Paula, the instructor, explained what they had to do. Zara looked at the bag in front of her, not quite sure what to make of it all. It was very different to what she had expected. Fitness Levels. Oh Great. The music began and so did they. Zara now had a plan, but that did not make her any less angry. In fact, she was still furious at having being forced to stay here at the hostel. Angry too, that Pat would enjoy the benefits of her hard work, staying at the Four Seasons while she was here slaving away. She was angry too, at her father for not helping to get her out of this horrific situation. All it would have taken was one phone call and this whole mess would have been sorted out. Zara was still furious. Nothing was going according to plan. She took her anger out on the little punching bag. She especially enjoyed it when they had to practice their kicks. She kicked high and hard. The bag flew backwards and bounded back sharply. Zara was surprised at how much better it made her feel. She kicked again and again and again. As soon as the bag popped forward, she would repeat kicking it as hard as she could. Repeating the process over and over. At the end of the session, her leg muscles were stiff and sore. Stiff and sore yes, but she felt so much better.

Zara was famished. The kick-boxing had worked up her appetite. She had made her way to the restaurant with her newfound friends, a false smile fixed to her face again, just as before. She laughed at their jokes and joined into their pathetic conversations as if she was really enjoying herself. They headed to a large table in the centre of the room and then headed to the buffet table, plates in hand. Zara took in the food before her and gagged.

"What is that?" she asked in horror, half to herself, half to the girl next to her.

"What?" came the uncertain reply.

"That?" Zara asked as she pointed toward the dishes before her.

"Uh, well, that's lasagna," she offered, "and that's Spaghetti Bolognaise. It's pasta. You know, Italian food."

Zara looked at the food arranged before her and held her breath. Just the smell of it was enough to make her want to hurl. They were not serious. She was NOT going to eat that. Surely not? Zara would not even have offered this food to Rose. A servant. She watched in horror as the other girls helped themselves hungrily to the food. Zara watched in scary fascination. How could they possibly find that food appetizing? With that sweaty horrific smell? She was hungry, starving in fact, but she just could not force herself to eat that slush. At the same time she knew she must eat something. It was a long way until dinner, which she hoped would be an improvement, and all that boxing had worked up her appetite. But what? She continued to look at the dishes spread before her. What could she eat out of all this unappetizing goo? She walked the length of the table. Got to the very end. Then spied a basket of fresh bread. She helped herself to a generous portion. Bread! Was that going to be her main staple food while she was here? And then, as if by magic, one of the kitchen staff appeared with a long tray in her hands. Zara watched as she placed it next to the bread. She almost jumped with joy. The tray held a selection of fresh fruits and a variety of cheeses. She helped herself to an array of what was offered. She disregarded the possibility that there might be others that also wanted. At least bread and cheese was something that the kitchen staff were unable to mess up. She would have liked something warm, but this would have to do for now.

Lunch was finished and they were back in the training rooms. Zara had enjoyed the first session, only because it meant that she could hit that bag as hard as she could and vent all her suppressed anger. The second session of the day was supposed to be more of a fun session. They were to learn their first new steps for the dance routine. Zara listened to the music. It was very similar to what they had been practising to before. Now that she had already been subjected to this kind of training, Zara found she was bored. The whole point of trying so hard in the first place was to get chosen for Germany. Now that she was chosen, there was no real reason she should to kill herself doing these steps. Her original, main plan was to get three months away from her mum and dad on a joyous, unsupervised holiday. Now it had all backfired. She had found herself in Germany, yes, but instead of the luxurious hotel, she was being kept at this stuffy, ancient hostel. She had an awfully small bedroom, with an uncomfortable hard bed, and to top it all, she was being forced to share with three strangers. The food was terrible, so much so, that she just could not force herself to eat no matter how hungry she was. And, as if that was not enough to bring anyone down, she had another three months to wait in agony before she was able to get out of this hellhole.

Zara knew that she was not going to gain anything for now. She was trapped. Callously being held here. When this whole affair ended she would then go on her promised holiday, which she would ensure Daddy extended. She would certainly deserve it. And more. Until then, she would do as little as possible. She was not going to kill herself in these daily-training sessions. She had no interest in being here, none at all. This was all a complete waste of her time. The only comforting thought was the weekend to arrive in a few days. She was sure that things would look up as soon as Pat arrived. They would hire a car and she would be free to come and go as she pleased. The first thing though, on her agenda, was going out for a decent meal. That was her top priority. She had enjoyed the bread and cheese, but she was certain she could not eat it every day for the next three months.

Jane and Sarah sat close to the stage. They were eager and excited to learn the new routine. So it seemed were all the other girls in the class. There was a sense of excitement floating around the studio. The sense was almost tangible as if you could reach out and touch it. Jane was surprised that Zara was at the back of the class. Firsthand experience had always found her at the very front, waiting and ready to steal the best possible view. Jane threw her a curious look, but had no time to dwell on Zara and the way her mind worked, although she was grateful that for the past two days they had managed to avoid each other. She was too busy anyway, concentrating on Paula's steps. Paula had let them listen to the music once, and now she was on stage performing the routine. Jane admired her moves. She was grateful and extremely talented. Jane knew the steps were difficult just by looking at them, but Paula managed them with ease. Falling into each step perfectly. The overall look was dramatic. It worked well with the previous steps they had been taught over the months. As Paula explained, they were going to merge what they had already learnt, with what they still had to learn. By merging the steps, they could cover more ground, much more quickly. With only three months to go, they had a lot to cover and get just right.

"Okay, don't be afraid to count. One. Two. Three," Paula counted aloud for everyone's benefit. "Now move to the left. Skip and Jump." She paused as she helped one of the girls gain the correct position. "And now move to the right. Skip and twist," she continued. They watched and followed, until they had learnt the steps, piece by piece. At first, many of the girls were lost. The sequence was new, and unlike Helen, Paula did not stop very often. They would watch a few minutes lost, then fall back into line. As time passed, they practised the new sequence over and over again. Slowly, the number of girls stopping became fewer. Paula was clever. They went over and over the steps until it was impossible not to know what came next. Then when all the girls knew the steps, she began to work on the technique. She stopped now regularly, explaining each step in detail. She watched and corrected. Watched and corrected, until she was happy with what she saw. It was slow progress. Paula was a perfectionist. They did not stop all afternoon and continued right through until 5:00 p.m. By that time, most of the girls were tired. It had been a full and tiring day.

"Okay. One last time. From the top. And try to add some fire into your movements—please," Paula added. The music began and they danced. All the girls knew it was the last dance of the day so they pushed themselves, using all their remaining energies into the last movements. The music came to an end and everyone relaxed.

"Excellent work girls," Paula praised them as they left the hall. "Tomorrow, we begin the second set."

Zara dragged herself up the winding staircase. They looked so much bigger than she remembered. She was surprised she had never noticed that before. Each step looked like a mountain and her leg muscles seemed to scream in protest. She dragged herself up the last set of steps and barely had enough energy to open her bedroom door and flop onto the bed. She was so tired. She lay there on top of the covers, mentally and physically exhausted. She had planned to get dressed and sneak out for dinner, desperate for something decent to eat. If the food for supper was anything like what they had served at lunch, Zara knew she could not eat it. Just the thought made her throat close and her stomach go into spasms. It was impossible for her to submit to the goo that they served. But as she lay on the bed, she also knew she could not move. If you had paid her, she knew she could not move a muscle. She was glad the other girls had not yet made it to the bedroom. She had heard a few of them say they were going to the canteen for a drink. She could just lay there on her bed and enjoy the silence. She let her eyes close but did not fall asleep. She knew that a shower would probably make her feel better, but she could not summon the energy to move off the bed. Today had really taken it out of her. First had been the kickboxing. That she had enjoyed immensely. She had felt liberated, venting her anger like that. If only she knew that her body would feel like it did now. Battered and bruised. The second session, after lunch, she had found boring. The music was the exact same as what they had practised to all those Saturdays and the movements were in the same tone. No variation. She had no motivation at all in that area. Her goal before had been to get here, but now that she was here, she wished she was back at home in her own comfortable bed. She hated Paula, who had made them do the steps over and over again. She did not try at all, did the very least she could get away with, but by the end of the day, the little bit of movements had still taken their toll. Her muscles were screaming in agony.

Chapter 25

The week had flown by very quickly for Jane and before she knew it, it was Saturday. The first weekend to do as they pleased. Each girl had big plans for the two free days allocated to them. Everyone was excited and eager for a break from the gruelling week. The hostel offered a wide variety of entertainments, but so far they either did not have the time or the energy after the day's training to go out and explore any of them, until now. They had two whole, free days to take in and explore their surroundings. Jane and most of the other girls agreed to spend their first Saturday relaxing around the swimming pool. It was a glorious sunny day and it had been unanimous that they wanted to enjoy some of the facilities offered by the hostel. The facilities that they were paying so much for. Some of the girls opted first for the warm bubbling Jacuzzi, while others went for the hot and humid sauna. Jane knew that both would be very busy so early in the morning, so she was content to enjoy the Olympic sized swimming pool situated on the grounds. She could wait until the afternoon to enjoy the sauna and Jacuzzi when it was quieter. She was quite content to swim some lazy strokes and enjoy the sunshine as she did so. Jane stood on the diving board while Sarah laughed at her.

"It's too cold," she replied, as she dipped her toe into the water.

Sarah, who was already in the water herself, splashed her jokingly. "Just jump in. It's easier than sticking in one toe at time, you big baby," Sarah added, laughingly.

Jane looked at the cold water before her as it simmered in the sunlight. She took a deep breath. This was it. She dove in quickly before she had time to change her mind, and as she hit the water she heard the squeals of delight from the other girls. She immediately felt the icy coolness sweep over her. After lying in the sun for over an hour, the water felt cold and tingly. Jane opened her eyes under the water and breathed out. Large, big bubbles escaped and hit the surface. Still she continued to swim. Long flowing strokes, underneath the surface. It was as if she was in a different world. Still she swam and swam until she saw the edge of the pool come clearly into view. She took one last stroke and headed upwards, toward the surface.

"See, that was not so hard, now was it?" joked Sue as she swam lazily to the other side on her back.

"Nope, not bad at all," Jane replied. Jane had to admit they were right. After lying in the hot sun for so long, the water had at first felt cold. The best thing was to dive straight in. Touching the water, one toe at a time was not the best way to get in. As she lay on her back and paddled, Jane marvelled at how bright and sunny it had turned out that day. None of them had expected it to be so warm, but it just made the day more enjoyable. It was the perfect weather to enjoy relaxing around the pool, especially after how hard they had worked all week. Some of the others, although also opting for staying at the hostel, had preferred to spend the day around the stables and the array of horses offered.

They could be seen in the far away distance, riding the horses in the green hills. Unlike Jane herself, who preferred the pool to cool down in, they were content to let the wind flow through their hair and cool them from the heat of the day as they galloped through the woodlands.

Until today, no one had really had much of an opportunity to see all that the hostel had to offer. Daily life at the hostel had taken on a set routine. Breakfast first, then morning workouts, a snack for lunch, and then practice for the rest of the afternoon in preparation for the upcoming Games. By the time class had finished, the girls usually made their way back to their rooms exhausted. They had just enough energy to have a hot bath or reviving shower and only just made it through dinner without falling asleep from the intense fatigue. Most of the girls fell into bed early and slept soundly. After the hard day's training that they were put through, all they wanted was their beds and a good night's sleep. Going out in the evening was not missed or even thought about. They were all just too tired.

Today was the first day where the routine was broken. No gruelling workouts, no strenuous classes. They were free to do as they pleased. The day had begun warm and sunny and had remained that way. Jane had come down to the pool prepared. She had reserved a corner with her bright red towel, and was armed with her book, her sunglasses and her suntan oil. She was expecting to keep herself occupied for hours. Not moving, unless she had to.

Jane had been surprised that morning as she had gathered her things for the day out in the sun. She had, quite by chance, looked out the open window, eager to take in the sweeping views. She had been mildly interested when she noticed Zara far off in the distance. Jane knew it was Zara, as there was no mistaking the striking blond hair as it caught the morning's sunlight. She had walked quickly to the waiting cab and hopped in without a backward glance. Jane did wonder, briefly, where she was going all alone. Not so much where, but with whom. If she knew Zara, she had something up her sleeve again. She always did.

Jane turned over on the towel and lay with her stomach toward the brilliant sunshine. She had been pleased that until now she had been able to avoid Zara. They always managed to be on the opposite sides of the hall, or rows apart in the training rooms, which suited Jane just perfectly. She wanted no incidents or any problems with Zara. But she had a strange feeling that she could not shake off, that an incident was still to follow. She lay on her towel and soaked up the sun for as long as possible, until finally, she was too hot. She needed to cool down for a while. Jane sat up quickly and laughed as she saw tiny purple spots in her head. Her mother always told her that it was because she sat up too quickly. Thinking of her mother made her homesick. She missed them all. Her family and her friends. They had arranged to go into the town tomorrow, and Jane remembered she must not forget to buy some postcards to send to everybody. Thinking of postcards soon had her thinking of Peter. She was not sure how long she sat on her towel thinking about him, remembering his handsome smile and his deep blue eyes. She knew she would not easily forget to buy him a postcard, of that she was certain. With thoughts of Peter in mind, Jane jumped up, ran to the pool again and dove in to cool off. She swam some rapid lengths, enjoying the rush of water over her body. Swimming, she decided, was the prefect way to relax.

Jane hopped out the pool and grabbed for her towel. As she dried her hair, Sarah came over with a few drinks clattering on a pink tray. "Drink?" she offered, holding the tray upwards.

"Oh, yes, please," Jane replied, as she took one of the glasses filled with lemonade.

Sarah pointed to one of the straps on Jane's costume. "You're quite sunburnt you know. You should get some more sunscreen on those shoulders. You don't want to peel on your first day in the sun."

Jane looked down at her shoulders in surprise. Sarah was right. There was a distinct white line between her skin and her costume where she had begun to go red. Taking Sarah's advice, she looked for her sun-screen and squeezed out a generous helping before rubbing it onto her red skin. She took another dollop and rubbed the cream into her face. The last thing she needed was a red raw nose. But, what she did want was a well-rounded tan.

When the girls made their way inside to their bedrooms it was late afternoon. They had spent a glorious day swimming, reading and frolicking in the sunshine. Jane felt like it had been a perfect day. She had managed to read a great deal of her new novel, and after taking her turn, first in the sauna, and then in the Jacuzzi, she had headed back into the swimming pool. She had remembered to apply sun-screen continuously, but already she could feel the slight tingle of the day's sunshine on her skin. She knew that in a few days she would be showing off a nice healthy tan.

They wasted what was left of the afternoon painting their nails, drying their hair and listening to music. Sarah had produced a deck of cards, and began to shuffle and divide. Shuffle and divide. Seconds later, a game was set up on one of the beds. All four girls were eager to play.

An hour later, giggles and squeals could be heard by anyone passing their door. "Hey, you're cheating," Karen exclaimed, as she grabbed yet another card from Sue's pile.

Sue laughed slightly. "No, I'm not!" she protested, although unconvincingly.

"Yes, you are, you liar!" she joked. All four girls packed out laughing when she grabbed for yet another card.

The game came to an end with Sue well in the lead. This was obviously a game she was used to playing and winning. They finished packing away the deck of cards, slipped into clean jeans and T-shirts, and then headed toward the dining room for much wanted dinner.

Chapter 26

As Jane walked into the training room after the restful weekend, she could not believe that it was Monday already. The weekend had flown by so quickly. Saturday had been an enjoyable day, with most girls spending the day relaxing around the pool, or enjoying the hostel's other facilities, which had been extravagant at the very least. Then, on Sunday, as a group, they had ventured out into the adjourning town. There was a local bus that stopped just outside the hostel, which was perfect, as it took them straight into the town centre. It was only a short ride, but it gave them plenty to see on the journey, from old cathedrals with colourful stained glass windows, to modern art galleries and historic museums. Jane made a mental note that they must try and get back to see some of the sights on one of their next trips to the town. They arrived at the town centre, and were dropped off next to a blue pained bus stop. They all disembarked as noiselessly as they could, considering the size of the group. Almost everyone had come to the town eager to see what it had to offer them. Once they had disembarked the bus, the girls began to pair up and venture off on their own. Some agreeing to meet later, while others preferring to make their own way back to the hostel, unsure of what time they would be finished in the small, quaint town. All the girls disappeared quickly and soon it was only the four of them left standing at the blue bus stop discussing who wanted to do what. It was soon clear that Sue and Karen had similar ideas of what they wanted to do and see, so they decided to stick together. It was agreed that they would all meet again around 2:30 p.m.

"We'll meet you in that tea room, the one over there," Karen said as she pointed to a cozy, neatly decorated pasty shop. Jane nodded. She could see the array of sweet pastries and tarts from where she was standing, and they looked delicious. A nice hot drink and cake might be just the thing they needed once all their errands were finished. Agreeing on the time, everyone dispersed, not wanting to waste a single minute of valuable shopping time.

Jane and Sarah rounded the first corner and headed into the first shop they saw. "So, is there anything particular you want to do today?" Sarah asked.

"I would like to get some postcards. Maybe look for a few presents for my family. And do some well earned shopping, of course," Jane replied.

At the mention of shopping, Sarah let out a whoop of joy. If anyone loved to shop it was Sarah. She spent all her time in shops and boutiques, and spent ages deciding what she could afford on her meager allowance. Jane was amazed at the bargains she could normally get just by keeping her eyes open. She always seemed to come out with so much more than Jane did, and they pretty much got the same amount of money from their parents each month.

The town itself was larger than they had imagined, with a variety of shops and boutiques. At the end of one of the roads they had also come across a small shopping mall, which was fitted out with all sorts of eating and drinking shops, from flavoured fudge to exotic cheeses and vintage ports. During their explorations, they also came across a large modern restaurant. It immediately reminded Jane of Michelangelo's. She was not sure why. Maybe, it was because it also had the flower pots outside, billowing with colourful blossoms as Michelangelo's did, or maybe it was the wide windows with pretty colourful hanging baskets. Whatever it was, it immediately had her thinking of Peter. And thinking of Peter got her thinking of that kiss. Yes, okay, it was only on the cheek, but it *was* still a kiss. She wondered how he was doing and quite suddenly knew she missed him. Missed his smile and his sweet jokes. Was she supposed to be feeling like this? She *had* only been away for one week. She knew that his exams were coming up soon, and he was probably very busy, studying hard. While she was in town, she reminded herself, she must get some postcards and send one on to him, wishing him luck for his exams. She'd sent it to his home address, which he had slipped to her as she had left. She was suddenly aware then of her stomach and the butterflies that had swiftly appeared. Could thinking of Peter really have that kind of dramatic effect on her?

The glorious weekend was only marred by one incident. The four of them had been walking down the old and winding stairs after dinner on the Sunday, laughing at a joke that Sarah had just told them. They had been in fits of laughter when they had walked directly into Zara. Jane saw the instant look of annoyance cross her pretty face, and then almost instantly, it was gone, hidden by her permanent, fake smile. The look was so quick that if you blinked you would have missed it. She smiled at the group sweetly, but did not stop walking. They all turned and watched her make her way back to her own bedroom, her heels clicking loudly on the corridor floor, wondering what she had been up to on her own all weekend.

Jane's thoughts were pushed back to the present, as a new instructor walked into the training room. She smiled her greeting and introduced herself as Jay. She was also tall, although a lot younger than Helen and Paula. She was, however, not dressed in the usual leotard and tights that the instructors favoured, but was instead dressed in a bright pink Nike track suite and sneakers. Jane wondered what was to come next. This was not the normal attire of the instructors that they had so far.

"For today's class, we're going to watch a video," Jay announced to the group. "It's not very long, maybe an hour. It's of a choreography of what we did last year for the Chinese festival. I'd like you to take note of the formations. The steps. This is the kind of look we are trying to achieve for you."

A television was rolled into the room and placed in the front of the studio next to Jane. At the same time, four men appeared holding a large stack of orange chairs. Within a few minutes of Jay's announcement, the chairs were arranged in neat lines and the men had disappeared.

"Ladies, please take a seat and then we can begin."

Everyone did as they were instructed. Then, once they were all seated, Jay began the video. When the video played, and the music began, Jane noted that the routine was completely different to what they had been listening and practising to over the past week. She also noticed all the dancers were very young. Maybe eight or nine years of age. They began to dance as a group, all moving as one, in time to the music. They may have been young, but they were flexible. Jane watched as they all jumped into the air, performed the splits, long and wide, before landing neatly. Yes, young, but extremely flexible. She then also marvelled at the timing. Everyone knew that to get such a large group to perform exactly in perfect time to one another and the music was extremely difficult. But here they were. All dancing as if they were joined together. Not one arm or one leg out of place. And it was a large group, possibly the largest group that Jane had ever seen dancing together. Maybe one-hundred or more girls all dressed identically in brilliant white costumes.

Until then, they had been dancing in a straight line. Forming a perfect square. As the music continued to play; the lines seemed to disintegrate with each new step. Before your very eyes the group transformed. The music changed tempo, and the dancers kicked. Half to the left and half to the right, leaving a large void in the middle. As the landed, they dropped to their hands and knees, heads bent down. Then, out of nowhere, another group emerged, dancing down the centre aisle. They danced until they reached the front of the two groups, bending and flexing their bodies to the music. There was a loud bang and all the dancers jumped up together in unison. Two steps later, there was no sign of the three groups, as they all mingled and joined together, forming one large group again. The whole look was overwhelmingly dramatic. They danced like that for a further twenty minutes, white movements against the dark stadium ground. Then again, before your eyes, the group began to move, some taking small steps, others large steps, until they were back into yet another formation. While doing all of this, they still maintained their neat, straight lines, as before. The first line of girls fell neatly into the splits, frontways, while at the same time, the second line found themselves leaning forward, hands on the floor, back leg held high into the sky, held in perfect position. Lastly, the third line. Each dancer took on their own pose to create a dramatic, unique finish. They held their positions as the music died down, while the audience thundered, clapped and whistled.

The video came to an end, and the screen went blank. The training hall was silent. Jane was unable to speak. She had been very moved by the dancing and by the music. It had been brilliant. Each member of the group had been in perfect time with the next. Then there was the choreography. Jane had never seen anything like it before. It was different and unique and would hold even the most uninterested male audience, who normally hated this kind of thing. Jane's thoughts were interrupted, as Jay pressed rewind on the video. The tape was now the only noise audible in the room.

"Okay, that was the first showing," Jay announced to the group. "That should give you a feel of what we would like to achieve. Obviously, we have our own steps, and our own style of music, which differs to this one we did in China, but this should give you a good visual basic of what we would like to see." Jay looked at her captivated audience. "Any questions, or comments, so far?" she asked.

Someone in the rear spoke up. "Did you choreograph that display yourself?" a voice asked.

Jay nodded. "Yes, myself and a few others. You know Helen, and Paula. We all worked together on this project, and what you just saw was what we came up with. I think it turned out pretty well."

Everyone nodded quickly in agreement. It had been a spectacular display. "We'd like you to do something just as great. We have a few ideas that are unusual, but like the display we have just watched, once you put them together, you create a dramatic effect. I know some of you feel that the steps are strange, but I promise you, once they are all linked together, the effect will be amazing. That is what we want. We want to show you girls off to the best of your abilities. Give the audience something to really get excited about. They will be talking about this show for months to come." All the girls nodded enthusiastically. If anyone had any doubts about the instructors' abilities, then these were all swept away. They knew exactly what they were doing, and what they wanted to achieve for the upcoming show. "I'd like you to watch the video again, but this time, I am going to point out things for you to take note of. Important things. Ideas we are going to incorporate into our own sequence. I want you to note each dancer's individual steps, but also what they look like as a group." Jay then clicked play and tape began to play again.

As everyone watched the video for the second time, Jay pointed out many features that Jane had not noticed before. She took each row separately, dissecting their movements and discussing it in detail. She paused the tape continually as she pointed, and expanded on each set of steps. She went into great detail, explaining how she was going to use a certain idea or what she would like to do. It was then that Jane realized that she was working with the very best professionals in their field. She had always known that the event was important, but sitting there and listening to Jay, she felt her hopes and excitement rising. By the end of the three months, she knew they would have a spectacular show. And she, Jane, was going to be in it. This was by far the biggest event she had ever been involved in.

"Now see this part," Jay said, as she let the video run for a few seconds. "We are going to try and copy this look, using different steps, of course. However," she continued, "unlike these girls here, all in white costumes, we are going to divide you into three different colours. We are going to use the lines and colours to create many varied, vivid images. Keeping each colour separate for some of the sequences, and for others, blending you all in together." Jay let the video play again for a few minutes and paused again. "And this section here, we are going to have someone run and jump high into the air. Something dramatic and complicated looking. We are not sure what yet. Everyone else will be head down on the floor while this takes place. All the attention will be on this one person. She will almost be like the lead."

Jay went through the entire video, pausing as often as she felt necessary to explain what they hoped to achieve. She expanded on the importance of the three colours they would use. How they would use the contrasting colours to try and create a colour wheel effect, sometimes dancing on their own in-groups and other times blending everyone in together. As Jay spoke, Jane tried to imagine what it would look like and had to agree that it sounded like a splendid idea. All sorts of colourful shapes could be formed and manipulated.

They watched the video for a third time, and Jay discussed more ideas. She was happy to explain and answer any questions that arose and there were many. Seeing the video helped each girl to realize just what she had come to do. By the end of the third viewing of the video, each and every girl knew, what was needed to create the perfect dancing show. Everyone was still discussing it during lunch. After a light lunch, the next class was taken by Jay.

"Right. Let's see what you have learnt so far this week," she said. Jay played the music and everyone danced the steps they had been working on all week. Jane knew that there were under strict watch. She danced using all her energy, knowing that Jay was using the time to analyse them all. The music came to an end. "Not bad. A coupe of things I'm not happy with, so this afternoon we are going to correct all these little quirks. By tomorrow you'll be doing this perfectly. No mistakes and definitely no quirks."

They practised and practised and practised again. In a way, Jay was far stricter than Helen had ever been. She was not happy until she had every girl doing each and every step down to perfection. They did the same routine over and over and over again. She refused to have any mistakes present. Jane felt she could do the steps in their sleep if she had to. She pushed herself hard. Now that she had the steps correct, she was concentrating on her technique. When she kicked, she tried to kick higher than before. As she turned; she tried to keep her feet in one position, hold herself neat and tidy. It was difficult. She had not worn her dance slippers today because it had been so hot, and her feet had been sweating terribly in the tightly bound, leather dance pumps. It had been a bad mistake. Each time she turned or swivelled, she could feel the skin on her toes tighten and scrape against the hard floor. The front of her soft toes took most of the pressure and pain. Under Jay's watchful eye, she tried to ignore the increasing soreness.

By the end of the afternoon, she could feel her thigh muscles starting to shake from the overexertion. She knew she was pushing herself too hard and, too fast but was unable to stop herself.

A few more turns, and Jane had to admit that her feet were crying out in agony. She knew, without even looking, that they were red and raw from all the turns and swivels, and she had probably lost a few layers of skin too. Jane looked around at the other girls present. How many of them had also opted to go barefoot like she had? She saw that there was more than half. She knew they all must have been feeling the same pain that she was feeling. Just when she felt she was unable to take it any longer, and had to say something, Jay bought the class to an end.

Jane looked at her watch in surprise. Was it five o'clock already? Where had the day gone? Jay switched off the music, said goodbye to them, and gathered her belongings, ready to leave for the evening. She did not hang around. "Good work, girls. See you all tomorrow. Bright and early."

Now that Jay had left the room, Jane no longer had to pretend all was fine. Her feet were killing her. She limped painfully to one of the chairs propped up against the wall. She slumped down with a great sigh, glad of the rest and the weight taken off her feet.

"You okay?" Sarah asked breathing deeply, stretching herself.

Jane looked at her swollen and peeling feet before nodding. She knew they were going to be sore tonight. Very, very sore. Sarah, though, would probably be fine. She had been one of the sensible ones that had opted to wear her shoes, regardless of the heat. Jane made a new resolve that no matter what, she would always have her dance shoes with her, just in case. She would not go through this senseless pain again.

"I have some cream that will sort that out." Sarah offered as she bent closer to have a proper look at her friend's mangled feet. "They are going to be sore tonight."

"Forget tonight." Jane cried in pain, "They are sore now." Jane rubbed the balls of her feet softly and winced in pain. They were too sensitive to even touch. She was glad the class had finished when it had, as she really could not have continued any longer. Now that she was sitting, small, thin cuts began to appear on the underside of the soles of her feet. Very slowly they began to seep blood. Not a lot, but the lines were now deep red as the blood tried to escape through the broken skin. It was like a million tiny paper cuts, and anyone who had ever had a paper cut knows how sore they could be. The fact that they were tiny meant nothing.

"Come on," Sarah coaxed, "let's get you upstairs. We can soak your feet in the tub. You'll feel better too."

Chapter 27

Zara raced out the class and up the stairs two at a time. She was in a hurry. She had deliberately stayed at the back of the class throughout the lesson so she could be the first one to get out when the time came. She knew that she was not supposed to leave the hostel grounds during the week, but would anyone really care? She highly doubted it.

The class today had been a total bore; she needed something fun to stimulate her mind or she would go mad. Some new teacher had made them watch some boring video of some past performance. Not once, but three times. Zara had literally almost fallen asleep with the boredom. Who cared about some stupid dance show she had done last year anyway?

She had already made her mind up to take things easy anyway. And that was exactly what she had done. She was sure no one was going to notice. Not if she stuck to the back of the class. Zara reached their bedroom door. The room was empty. Good, none of the other girls were back yet. She locked the door, baring them out. She could have a shower and get dressed without any interruptions and explanations to the others. They probably would not even notice she was gone anyway, Zara consoled herself. They'd be too busy discussing the boring video and today's class. They were nerds, all of them.

Things had improved dramatically since the weekend. On Saturday, Pat had arrived. Zara had never been so pleased to see anyone in her life. She had almost wanted to weep with joy. As Pat exited the arrivals lounge, Zara had ran over excitedly and hugged her friend hard. Finally, someone who would understand her predicament. Someone who would understand the torture she was going through. She hugged Pat even harder. "Hi!" she breathed.

"Hi, yourself!" Pat replied, as she pulled away, surprised at the unusually warm welcome. It was not what she had expected, not by someone as cool as her friend Zara.

"Good flight?" Zara asked.

Pat nodded. "Not bad. Food was good, although I'm glad it was not a long a trip."

Zara agreed. She had felt the exact same way after her journey. It was hard to believe that it was exactly a week ago today that she too had arrived. At the very same airport. God, but if felt like a lifetime.

After they exited the airport, Zara hailed one of the black cabs waiting on the sidelines. "Where to?" asked the young, handsome cabby.

"The Four Seasons, please," Zara answered happily, the words rolling off her tongue. She had been dying to say that all week.

Pat watched her friend in amazement. One week in this place and she was a totally different person to the Zara she knew at home. Zara almost seemed excited to see her, and anyone who knew Zara, knew that was one thing that Zara *did not* do. Get excited. She was way too cool for that kind of behaviour. But here she was now, eager to go and talking non-stop as the cab drove silently. Pat rubbed her head. She must be wrong. She could only put it down to the jet lag.

Zara knew she was practically home as soon as they approached the entranceway of the Four Seasons. The hotel had a luxurious air about it, that could be felt as soon as they stepped out of the cab. Zara was sure even the air smelt different, Clean. Invigorating. Maybe her feelings were helped by the large water fountain in the middle of the drive. It was gray marble, shining brightly in the sunlight. Small delicate trees were planted expertly, surrounding the water fountain. Someone had also taken great care in arranging millions of colourful flowers in neat rows. The cab driver had rounded the fountain and parked in the designated area. A bellboy appeared almost immediately and relieved Pat of her luggage. Zara remembered her arrival at the hostel. It was a complete contrast to Pat's arrival. She had been left to lug her heavy luggage around the stuffy hostel herself and then up the old and winding staircase. Her arms had ached by the time she had actually reached her bedroom. Now this was more like the arrival she deserved. A nice peaceful cab ride, without the company of other screaming girls, and a bellboy to whisk away the luggage so you were free to check in without any hindrances or worries. Zara's feelings were only reconfirmed as they entered the hotel foyer held open by a doorman, elegantly dressed in a black morning suit. Everything was just perfect.

Now, as she sat in the soft, fluffy armchair, as she waited for Pat to finish checking in, Zara looked around her. This was exactly what she had wanted. The foyer, like everything about this hotel, was large, with delicate crystal chandeliers hanging elegantly from the ceiling. The floor was light gray marble leading up to gold elevators on the right and a large, wide sweeping staircase was to her left. The effect was dramatic, but then, could you expect anything less at this chain of hotels? This was, after all, why her father always stayed with them.

The checking in counter was an eye catcher on its own and ran the whole breadth of the hotel foyer. It would have looked like any other hotel check-in, except for the massive fish tank behind it, holding every colorful fish imaginable. Zara sat and watched the fish from her comfortable chair, and had already noted a variety of expensive and rare fish in the collection. She had also seen a large eel that swam from side to side, its long body slithering slowly through the blue water. She had also caught sight of a small shoal of brightly colored, orange clown fish. Zara was not aware of what all the species were, but it made for an impressive background. She saw Pat at the far left desk, still checking in. She noted the large array of beautiful white flowers on each desk. White roses, white lilies and white daffodils, all arranged in tall glass vases. Zara closed her eyes, and actually believed she could smell their sweet fragrance from where she was sitting. The arrangements seemed to permeate the air with their sweet perfume. Zara leaned her head back onto the soft cushions and closed her eyes for a second. This was exactly what her arrival, her accommodation, should have been like. She should have come here as soon as she set foot off that aeroplane. If she had, she might have had a more successful case in staying at the hotel. Zara let her mind wander, just for a minute, back to the hostel and the bedroom she shared. Then she opened her eyes. It was a living nightmare. The contrast was indescribable. All at once, Zara knew she missed these luxuries. She had never paid them much attention before, that was just how she had always lived, but now that they were gone, she wanted them back. She deserved them.

Pat sidled over, smiling broadly. "Checked in. Got the bedroom key. Let's go up," she said happily.

Zara jumped out off the chair eagerly, and they left the impressive, large foyer, opting to take the gold elevators up to the room, rather than the winding staircase. They rode up to the fifth floor. The ride to the room was quick and it took only a few seconds before the doors opened onto the grand floor. They walked down the plush corridor, until they came to Pat's room number.

"This is it," Pat said, as she swiped the key card. The front door unlocked open with a soft click. Pat entered first, followed by an excited Zara, and took a look at her friend's new temporary home. Zara entered behind Pat, and was unable to hold the gasp of delight that escaped her lips. The room was exactly as she had pictured it. Better. A huge queen-sized bed sat in the centre of the room. The cream embroidered duvet cover, adorned with various silk cushions, all neatly arranged in the center of the plush bed. It looked like a big, comfortable marshmallow. Next to each bedside was a small table, one side holding a beautiful array of bright, long stemmed, red roses. Zara could not resist walking over and breathing deeply. They smelled heavenly, as only expensive roses could. To the left of the room, she noticed, was a small desk with a matching chair equipped with a full set of of writing utensils. Then, to the right was an open plan sitting room, holding two plush couches that seemed as if they would swallow you if you sat down on them. Zara was unable to hold herself back. She ran and jumped onto the couch. As she predicted, she was swallowed up into the soft covers. She snuggled for a long moment. Now this was Heaven. From her comfortable position, she noticed that in the middle of the sitting room was a solid oak table adorned with yet more flowers. This time, bright pink and purple blossoms surrounded by dark green ferns. There was also a large flat-screen television on one wall, and a small mini bar, complete with drinks and snacks on the opposite side. This section was obviously going to be used the most. It was almost like a perfect, self-contained flat. The room was total and complete luxury with every small luxury imaginable. It was all the small touches that separated the Four Seasons from any other hotel. Zara loved it.

   This was exactly what she had wanted out of her holiday stay. Somewhere luxurious and pampered. Zara left the position on the marshmallow couch for a second and made her way into the bathroom. It was in the same elegant taste as the bedroom. The corner bath was to the left, and a long dressing table adorned the opposite wall. There was an array of Elizabeth

Arden bath salts and Molton Brown bubble baths to chosen from, and thick white fluffy towels hanging on the heated handrail. Zara took in her surroundings and was jealous. This was where she should have been. Surrounded by the luxury she was accustomed to. Not in that stuffy, old, smelly hostel. As she thought of the injustices of it all she could feel herself getting angry. This is where she belonged. She was seething with rage. How could things have gotten so mixed up?

At that moment Pat walked in, smiling happily with the joy of her new bedroom. Zara almost hated her for being subjected to this kind of luxury, luxury that by rights, should have been hers. And while Pat was here enjoying these luxuries, she was holed up miles away in some old, creaky school. It was too unfair for words. And to make matters worse, Pat was only here because of her. She had been the one who had worked hard to ensure she was chosen. What had Pat been doing? Only lunching with *their* friends and whisking them off shopping. And now Pat was here, staying at the hotel of her dreams, while she, Zara, who was responsible for it all, had not one single luxury on offer. Zara stalked out the bathroom, unable to take in Pat's joyous expression any longer.

Pat, having finished examining the bathroom, walked past Zara to the second door in the bedroom. She threw it open, like a child opening a big present. The door opened wide and before them, just waiting to be filled, was a walk in wardrobe. Long sexy mirrors ran the expanse of the wall, with empty hangers waiting to be used. "This is perfect," Pat exclaimed. "Isn't this just perfect?" she asked as she walked inside.

Zara refused to answer, but Pat did not seem to notice, as she continued talking. "I think I am going to be quite comfortable here," she remarked, beaming. Zara was spared having to answer her again, as the doorbell rang. Pat made her way to the door, and opened it to reveal the bellboy from downstairs. In his hands were Pat's suitcases. "In the dressing room please," she sang as she retrieved her handbag. When he had finished with the unloading, she gave him a big tip and arranged with him that someone come and unpack for her.

Zara watched it all silently. This was so unfair! No one had come to unpack her clothes. She had to do it all herself, and even when she had, she still did not have enough room for all her things.

Pat came back into the bedroom and headed straight for the balcony doors, eager to see the view her bedroom held. She unlocked the glass sliding doors and disappeared. Zara knew the view would be breathtaking, giving an excellent view of the town below. She had asked for just that. Pat reappeared and jumped onto the fluffy couch, beaming with pleasure. "So, I'm all checked in. What do you want to do now? Some breakfast maybe?"

At the mention of food, Zara's spirits soared. She had been waiting all week for something better than that slop they served in the canteen. "Yes. I'm starved. Let's go and get something to eat." Zara was famished. She had left for the airport as soon as she had awakened that morning and had not even managed to grab some fruit before she left. At home she did not favour fruit for her breakfast, but since her arrival in Germany, it was all she ate. Cold scrambled eggs and runny porridge were not on her menu. Now, after a week of fruit, she was dying for something different. Something like what Rose would make her at home.

"Let's get some food then. I'm sure I saw a restaurant downstairs. I'm sure the breakfasts here will be delicious."

Zara nodded, in high spirits again. Anything would be better that what she had been subjected to eating the past week.

There were actually two restaurants located in the hotel. One was situated on the ground floor, which served a variety of snacks and meals and was known to be less formal. Then, on the second floor was the elegant, dinner only, restaurant. Zara and Pat studied both menus, liking all that they read. Since it was only breakfast time, they headed to the restaurant on the first floor.

As Zara settled comfortably into her chair next to the window, she noted that she was enjoying every minute away from the hostel. When Pat had suggested getting something to eat, Zara had been delighted. She had practically starved herself since her arrival. At least now she could enjoy a good, healthy meal. It took her ages to decide on what she wanted to eat, and undecided, she ordered everything that sounded delicious. After she had placed the order, and the waiter had gone, she admitted that she would never be able to eat all of the huge selection that she had insisted on getting. Oh well. She would pick and choose the best of it. After her awful week here, she deserved it.

When the waitress bought their breakfast, Zara had been thrilled. Homemade pancakes with blueberry jam, thin and fluffy just as she liked it. Perfectly fried eggs, with crispy bacon and soft sausages, accompanied by a portion of fresh mushrooms, tomatoes and fried potatoes. Fresh orange juice and strong percolated coffee, came on a separate tray. The rich aroma itself almost smelt as good as it tasted. Zara tucked in, aware of her appetite. It was all so delicious. She helped herself to a little bit of this and a little bit of that, piling her plate up high. Pat chatted non-stop as she finished her meal and helped herself to a pancake.

"So how is it going? The training and stuff?" Pat asked interested, as she buttered some toast and added a dollop of the fresh honey.

"Don't even get me started," Zara stated matter of factly, more interested in her pancakes.

Pat looked up from her toast. "So, it's not good then?" she asked.

"Good! Good? It's anything but good. That place is horrible." Pat had not yet taken a bite of her toast and the honey dripped onto her white plate. Zara eyed it hungrily. She had eaten a whole plate of breakfast, was now on her pancakes and was still eyeing Pat's honey toast. What was wrong with her?

"I thought this was some private hostel you were staying in," Pat continued.

"Private, yes, but nothing like what *we* are used to." She sniggered.

As Pat bent over in laughter, Zara could not help join in. Nothing came close to what they were used to. They only ever got the very, very best.

Over the rest of the meal, Zara told Pat all the horrific stories since she had arrived. Everything. She did not leave out a single pathetic piece of information. Pat found the entire thing more than amusing, which infuriated Zara.

"Why don't you just quit and go home?" Pat asked, still laughing.

Zara looked at her friend. She could be so dense sometimes. "You know the answer to that," Zara replied in a deathly, quiet tone.

Pat nodded, saying nothing. So, she had been right all along. Zara did have her own agenda in action. She was here for a reason.

"But Dad *is* going to pay for this. When I get back home," Zara stated, "I will make him pay. And pay dearly." Zara helped herself to another pancake and smothered it with some more homemade jam.

"Well..." Pat began, unsure if she should let her secret out.

"Well, what?" Zara asked eagerly. "What do you know? Tell me!" she demanded.

"Well, Your father was talking to my father last night and he mentioned how unhappy you were. He is very concerned that you are considering leaving and said that after the World Games were finished, he was going to send you away for a while. A holiday somewhere. Just like you want. I think he mentioned Barbados for a month. And then some time on a yacht somewhere. But that's all I know."

Zara dropped her fork in shock. "Barbados?" she asked questionably.

Pat nodded, "Yes, Barbados."

Zara let out a whoop for joy. Strike one for her plan. Now there was absolutely NO question of quitting. She had to get through the next three months, no matter what. She was adamant that she was going to make her father pay for all of this. She was going to milk this entire disaster for all it was worth. And the holiday in Barbados was just the beginning. Only her father did not know it yet.

Zara looked at the empty plate before her. She could not believe she had eaten so many of the pancakes, but they had been so delicious. And the coffee had been a gift from Heaven. Strong and fresh, with a hint of vanilla. Not that half hearted attempt she had to force herself to drink at the canteen each morning. It had been a good meal. No, it had been a splendid meal.

Pat too had polished off all her toast. As she wiped her mouth with her serviette, she asked, "So, what should we do for the rest of the day?"

"Well," Zara said excitedly, "there's supposed to be all sorts of shops and boutiques nearby. We could take a look. How does that grab you?"

If there was anyone who loved to shop, it was Pat. Her eyes automatically took on a bright sparkle. "That grabs me just fine," she replied as she stood up.

Pat was enjoying herself immensely. Zara had been right. Every shop, no matter how small, contained delicate little trinkets. Things that she had never seen before. She wanted almost everything she picked up. In the end, she decided on a small jewel box, hand painted and encrusted with small rubies. It had been expensive, but she just had to have it. It was perfect for her stay here. She would leave it on the dresser and fill it with the jewelry she had bought along with her from home, and maybe, if she saw something nice later on, in one of the other boutiques, she could add that to her collection. She was sure her mum and dad would not mind. The clothes boutiques themselves were also fabulous. Pat tried on a few garments, and with Zara's help, came up with a completely new outfit for dinner that evening. Pat knew it was perfect. It was dark maroon and made of soft velvet, fitting perfectly to her figure. It was formal, but not exceedingly so. In fact, Pat admitted, it was perfect. Like everything else on this trip so far. Pat knew she was going to have a splendid time while she was in Germany. The hotel was fabulous and she had her best friend with her to share most of the joyous times. Pat knew she would be on her own most of the week, but that did not bother her. She was quite content to visit the array of museums and galleries that the town had to offer. She could spend hours and hours in them, and had done so many times before. If there were any that were really good, she could even take Zara and go again. She did not mind. Zara, she knew, was not interested in most cultural activities, but Pat supposed, if she asked really nicely, Zara would go. As Pat pulled out yet another one of her father's credit cards, she knew that she might be going a bit crazy, but it was their first day. She could always say that Zara needed a few things. They had not yet even been to every shop on the street and already her bags were getting a little too heavy to carry.

The day passed in a happy blur, and Pat enjoyed every minute in the small town. It was one of those quaint little villages that was hard to get bored with. Pat had enjoyed the variety of shops on display, and was so excited at seeing all the trinkets and designer shops, that they had completely missed lunch. Food was the furthest thing from their minds after the hearty breakfast they had eaten earlier that morning. They had stopped only once during the day, and that was only for a quick cold drink. At the end of the day, Pat gathered her parcels and bags and they made the short walk back to the hotel. It was early afternoon. They would have enough time to shower and freshen up before they would have to change for dinner and once again, they were starving.

Zara watched her friend go, laden down with designer bags from the day's shopping trip. She had enjoyed the day. It was such a nice change from the last week, but she had to admit, she was more than a little envious. She had spent most of the day wishing she had enough space in her small closet to buy the things she had seen. Normally she would not have hesitated, but now, staying at the hostel, things were different. She could have bought them, she knew, but where would she put them? Already, she had most of her things in suitcases under her bed, unpacked and gathering dust. There was just not enough space for her stuff, so she knew she could not go out and buy more. Maybe before she left, she consoled herself, she could go wild. The thought was a little comfort to her as she watched Pat enjoying herself and buying everything she saw and desired.

It was still bright outside when Pat swiped the bedroom key and they let themselves back inside the bedroom. Again Zara was hit by the splendour of the bedroom and connecting suites. Oh, how she wished she was staying here. She dumped her handbag on the bed and sauntered over to her new favourite position, the massive marshmallow couch. She sunk low into the cushions and watched Pat unpack her new purchases enviously.

It was some time later when Pat disappeared and had a shower. Zara was glad for the time alone. She opened the sliding doors and sat on the balcony, enjoying the view of the town. She could see people milling around and enjoying what was left of the late afternoon. The sun was perfectly positioned, and she had an excellent view of the setting sun. She watched it turn from bright yellow, to a dull red before it completely disappeared. Time ticked by, and soon Pat was out the shower, and joined her on the balcony, just in time to see the last of the setting sun. Lights from all over the town were being switched on, and soon the view was a blaze of lights. "It's beautiful," stated Pat as the lights twinkled before them. Zara nodded. It certainly was.

They came down to dinner soon after the lights in the town went on. Zara looked at the menu hungrily once again and could not decide what she wanted to eat. It all looked so good. And having missed lunch did not seem to help her appetite. She was glad that she had eaten such a hearty breakfast, although it felt like a lifetime away. She could not believe that she was so starving again. She never usually ate this much. "What are you going to have?" Zara asked as she scanned the menu.

"Ummm. Not sure. The seafood sounds good." Zara jumped to the seafood section on the menu.

"Yes," she agreed, it did sound good. Prawns. Scallops. Fish. What to have—what to have? She could not decide. And then she saw it. Lobster. A little extravagant, even for her, considering there was no particular occasion. No birthday. No anniversaries. Maybe she should have something else, she tried to convince herself? The fish looked just as good. Just then, as if to rub her nose into her decision, walking to a table directly opposite them, was one of the smartly dressed waiters, holding a large silver tray. Two large, pink lobsters were hanging delicately off the plate, looking scrumptiously good. Pat turned in her seat, and watched as the waiter laid the tray down, in front of the loving couple. The steam was rising upwards and the smell of lemon wafting past, teasing their nostrils. Zara shifted and looked at Pat questionably. Would she have a partner in crime?

"Oh, yes." Pat nodded, immediately.

"Okay, then. Dinner's settled," Zara confirmed, as she slapped her menu shut. "That's us sorted."

They busied themselves with fresh bread and soft butter until their food arrived. When the food came, Zara could not believe how hungry she was. As the waiter placed the tray in front of her, Zara could actually feel her mouth beginning to water. She knew it was a little too extravagant, but she deserved this. After the hell she had been going through, this was exactly what she deserved. She took a few minutes to squeeze the lemon onto the pink meat and then tucked into the food with relish. As she took her first mouthful, she savoured the taste. Sweet and succulent. For a brief moment she let her mind wander back to the girls at the hostel. She could only imagine what sloppy dishes they had been served that evening. She took another bite of the tender lobster. She was so glad she was here and not there. She hated it there.

When they entered the apartment again, it was late. Much later than they had expected to return. Luckily, they did not have far to go to their room. Not if you considered a two second ride in the elevator to the fifth floor. During the evening, a band had taken up playing some musical instruments. Pat, who played the violin and piano, thoroughly enjoyed the affair. She did not want to leave, not even after their meal was finished. "Please, let's stay a little longer," she pleaded. Zara could see the look on her face, and just did not have the heart to deny her friend. Besides, she was feeling in a good, giving mood. She had to admit though, as she listened to the soft music fill the air, they were good. Very good. Not a bad way to end a thoroughly enjoyable evening. Now as she flopped back down on the couch, Zara felt at home. She kicked off her shoes and snuggled deeper into the sofa as Pat switched on the state of the art television. This was where she belonged. In between the plush cushions and room service. She knew she had to return to the hostel, but she could just not face it. Not now, after being here. In this amazing, prefect place. Zara lay back against the pillows and snuggled deeper into the folds. Maybe she should stay the night? Would she be allowed? Would she be in trouble? She looked out toward the sliding doors to the dark evening beyond. It looked so un-welcoming. So dark and cold. Here she was snug and warm. It took her only a few seconds to make up her mind. Yes, she would stay. Draw out the weekend for as long as possible. If anyone asked about her absence, she could say that she did not know there were such strict rules for the weekends too. Pretend complete innocence. Zara sat up, the idea forming with deceptive clearness. "Do you mind if I spend the night?"

"Good heavens, no," replied Pat, "If it weren't for you, I would not be here myself. Stay, as long as you like. It'll be fun."

Zara smiled, "I'll have to borrow some pajamas," she stated.

"Top drawer, on your right. Help yourself."

Chapter 28

They were sitting comfortably around the table. Breakfast had been eaten, and they were now ready for their second class of the second week. The Saturday and Sunday had flown by quickly as had Monday and now it was Tuesday and they were back to the routine that they had developed over the first week. Jane could not believe that over a full week had passed already. It felt like it was just yesterday that she had been arriving. Karen took the last sip of her orange juice and then asked, "I wonder what kind of routine they have planned for us today?"

"Not sure," Jane replied, "but we'll soon find out. Class starts in less than ten minutes." Since they had arrived, they had been kept busy with a variety of lessons. So far, they had four instructors taking the classes. There was Helen, who they had worked with back home, and then there was Paula, young, vivacious and full of life, and lastly, there was James and Velicity. They tended to take more of the workout classes set for the mornings. Jane was enjoying the different varieties of programs they had set, but she had to admit it was tiring. She did not think she had ever worked so hard at anything in her life. Most evenings, she found herself early in bed, feeling tired—yet fulfilled. Often she would fall into an exhausted sleep as soon as her head touched the pillow. It was hard work, but it was what they had come here to do.

The organizers had gone to great lengths to keep the classes as varied as possible so that none of the girls would become bored and lose interest in the vigorous training that had been planned. Jane enjoyed the kick boxing class, and she also found that she enjoyed the aerobics sessions, that they seemed to have every second day. These were taken mostly by Velicity.

They had found out that Velicity was a gym instructor in her home town, and had even coached a few famous actors and celebrities. The music she used was alive and energetic, so it was hard not to get into the tempo that was set.

Today, Jane was actually looking forward to one of Velicity's aerobics classes. After the weekend of doing no physical exercise she felt ready for another packed week. Today though, as they walked into the training rooms, there were no punching bags or aerobic steps waiting. Just an empty, open space. The girls began to file in one by one, and before long the training room was full. It was time for class to begin, but Velicity was nowhere to be seen. Instead, Helen stood leaning against the far wall. Once all the girls were in the room, she made her announcement.

"Okay, "clapped Helen loudly, the sound echoing in the silence. "Today's morning workout is something a little different from the aerobics you have been doing. Today, we are going to have a class called Callanetics."

Some of the girls looked at each other, a questioning look on their faces. "What's Callanetics?" whispered Sue into Jane's ear.

Jane did not know, but even if she did, she did have time to respond, as Helen began to explain. "Callanetics is a slow, gentle workout. It contains deep movements which helps to build the strength of your muscles, and your endurance," she added as she smiled to the group. "There are mats in the corner. Each girl get one and find a space on the floor." Jane felt slightly disappointed as she got herself a thick yellow mat. She had been looking forward to the aerobics class. She was in the mood for a good, hard workout and wanted to be jumping and hopping to the music. This Calanetics sounded too slow and not that much fun. Jane lay her mat on the floor and waited. Only once all the girls were settled, did Helen positioned herself in the front of the class. She pressed play on the CD player and soft, tranquil music began to waft throughout the room. Slowly, Helen began with the floor exercises. First she lay on her back with her pelvis lifted off the floor and when they were all in position, she began to work on their top thigh muscles. She began with slow bounces of her buttock, up and then down. Stomach pulled in. Jane lay on her back, staring at the ceiling, copying Helen's movements, concentrating on keeping her stomach in place. This was very different to the aerobics she had hoped for. At first, she did not feel anything happening. Just a boring movement of up and down. Jane wondered when Helen would move onto something else. Then as time passed and she continued to bounce, she began to feel the movements taking effect. She could feel her buttocks begin to tighten as she moved. Tense, release. Tense, release. The movement began to hurt, just as she also began to feel the burning in her top thigh muscles. She was not sure which movement felt worse. Her buttocks or her thighs. Jane closed her eyes, trying to ignore the sharp sensations as she continued to bounce and try to enjoy the music which was slow, and rhythmic. It seemed to be making the burning sensation, even more painful. When she turned her head slightly to the left she could see Karen's face. Her pale, freckled cheeks squeezed in pain as she too bounced up and then down. Then, just as she thought she was going to have to stop, or collapse from the sharp pains in her legs and buttocks, Helen let them take a rest.

"Okay, now bottoms on the floor. Legs now stretched out ahead of you, and arms held up over your head, toes pointed. Really stretch those muscles you've just worked."

Jane obliged and stretched hard. The feeling felt wonderful. Helen gave them a few more seconds to stretch and then she continued. "Now, hands behind your head, feet up, knees facing upward."

Jane watched Helen for a few seconds as she began to do stomach crunches. Sometimes in aerobics class they did stomach crunches or situps, but they were always fast. In pace with the music. This felt very different. Instead, Helen was taking her time. Slowly up, and slowly down. Jane began to feel the same sensation that she had in her thighs and buttocks begin to take hold in her stomach. Her muscles felt tense, and with each part of the upward movement, she felt her muscles tighten even further. The pain was incredible. Still, she continued. She concentrated on her breathing. In and up, down and out. Just this small movement of breathing seemed to take all her concentration. And then, when her muscles were screaming out in pain, Helen allowed them to relax for a few seconds. They repeated the same process about five or six times. Jane had lost count. On the last set, Helen made them hold the position. Jane grabbed her legs with her hands, hoping it would take some of the strain of her stomach muscles, but it did not feel as if it was helping. The burning sensation seemed to pass right from her lower stomach muscles, right to her sternum. She collapsed then, unable to hold the position any longer.

"Okay, stretch again. Arms straight above your heads."

The rest of the class was much the same. Small delicate movements that isolated some part of their body, until it burned with excruciating pain. Helen was excellent at managing to find a new body part to torture. By the time the class had come to an end, Jane felt like she could barely walk. Each and every muscle seemed to scream out in protest at the harsh workout they had received. Her body felt hot and her muscles felt stiff from the excursion. It was so unexpected. Slow and graceful movements were not supposed to hurt so deeply.

When they next made it back to the training room after lunch, Jane had to admit that she was going to struggle with the afternoon class that had been set. Her stomach still felt tight and clenched, and her leg and thigh muscles still felt like they had been pulled violently. With each step that she took, she could feel her muscles straining against the pressure. As if it was some compensation, Jane was glad to note that she was not the only one that seemed to have the same aching feeling.

Much, much later, when Jane was bathed and in bed, she knew she had not performed the second part of the day as well as she should have. She was disappointed in herself, but there was nothing she could do about it. Her muscles had just been too sore. The Calenetics class had been much harder than she had expected, and her muscles still ached—even now, hours later.

Jane knew she would have to sort herself out if she wanted to be able to move tomorrow. She scratched around in the first aid box until she had found some "Deep Heat." Jane read the tube. Gel used for sore and aching muscles. This was exactly what she needed. She squeezed and rubbed a healthy dose all over her legs, stomach and thighs. It stunk, but Jane knew she needed the cream to help her muscles recuperate overnight. She was sure she had pulled something. Ever part of her body was sore.

As she lay in bed, some music playing softly in the background, Jane waited for the warm sensation she knew would come. It seemed to start on her one leg muscle and slowly began to spread until her whole body felt on fire. She knew it was working. The other girls had decided they wanted dessert, and Jane had used the opportunity to come back to a quiet, empty room, have a hot bath and then doctor herself. But the time alone was short-lived and half an hour later, she heard the other girls enter their bedroom.

"Ugh, what's that smell?" Sarah shrieked.

Jane was unable to hold the smile. "Deep Heat," she replied.

"Is it working?" she asked. Jane nodded, afraid to move, her body on fire. "Mind if I have some too then?" she asked as she sat on her bed, careful not to wince herself

Jane nodded, "No. Go ahead. It is better to have a bath first though. Are you also sore?"

Sarah nodded in reply. "Aching."

As Sarah booked the bathroom, she noticed that the other girls also seemed to be moving slower, with less energy and although they did not want to say it, they were also feeling the after effects of Helen's workout. It seemed everyone was suffering. By the time the lights were out and everyone was in bed, it was safe to say that the whole bedroom stank of the ointment that had all rubbed into themselves. There had been no victorious pupils in Helen's class that day.

* * * * *

Zara too was in agony. The day had been so different to the wonderful weekend she had enjoyed. She had made it back to the hostel late Sunday night after dinner. Pat had to literally push her into the cab to make her leave, as she had not wanted come back. At that final stage, she knew she would have given up everything just to stay at the Four Seasons a little bit longer. If is had not been for Pat, she knew she would not have come back at all.

The drive back to the hostel did not take long, and before she knew it she was standing outside of the old familiar building, cloaked in darkness. Gone was the lovely water fountain and pretty flowers of the hotel. Gone too was the bellboy and delicious food. She was now back at the dreary smelly hostel, where she had to do everything herself and was surrounded by a bunch of boring girls that she did not even like.

When she stood at the bottom of the staircase looking up toward her bedroom, Zara knew she wanted to cry. It all seemed so hopeless and now after having spent time with Pat, she knew just how much she was missing out on. Her mood did not improve when she opened the door to their bedroom. Clothes and food wrappers were everywhere, but the room was empty. The girls were probably downstairs she thought, watching television after their dinners. Zara plopped herself onto her bed.

There was no bounce to it, like the hotel bed she had spent the previous night in. Instead, hers was stiff and flat. Pat's was lovely and soft and comfortable. She turned and took in the stiff white duvet. Hers seemed to scream hospital. It was too clinical and very unwelcoming. Zara looked around her, and the room had never irritated her as much as it did then. There was no space to even swing a cat. There was nothing to do but change into her pajamas and get into the bed, horribly miserable.

And here she was now, Tuesday evening, still wishing she was away from the hostel and in Pat's big, warm and comfortable bed. It would have been just what she needed, especially after the day's class. It had been very hard and her muscles were throbbing. She had hoped, when she heard the Calenetics music, that the morning session would be easier than the aerobics, which she had decided she did not like. Instead, it had turned out to be the hardest class she had taken yet. She had already decided that she was not going to push and strain herself any more than she had to. She would do what was required, but only the bare minimum. At first she had begun the movements half heartedly. Bounce up, bounce down. But then, quite suddenly, she began to feel the burning. And she was not even trying. She wanted to stop, but knew that she would be the only one not continuing and she was bound to stick out among all the girls. So, she had been forced to carry on, while her legs screamed in pain and her stomach growled in protest at the movements. Even now, Zara was sure that Helen had used the class as some sort of torture for them all. Zara could not believe she was struggling as she was. Even taking a slow, revitalizing shower had proven to be too much for her. She just did not have the energy to stand up without her legs giving in. In the end, she had run herself a bath and soaked for an hour in the tub. She was just closing her eyes and beginning to relax, when there was a loud banging on the door.

"Zara, you finished yet?" Zara opened her eyes lazily. "Zara!" came the voice again; "Can you hear me?" Zara knew she should answer, but she just did not feel like it. "There are other people out here, you know, who also want to use the bathroom?"

Zara used the last of her remaining energy and pulled herself up and out of the bath. If she did not feel so bad, she would have put up some sort of a fight, but as she stood on two weak legs she knew she was just too tired, too drained. It was easier to just get out the bathroom and submit herself to her hard, clinical bed for a restless, fitful night's sleep

Chapter 29

Zara opened her eyes slowly. Her head was in a haze and she felt groggy. "Where are my trainers?" came a voice.

"Look under your bed," came the reply. Zara heard some rustling.

"Got em."

"You know, Sonia, you have this problem every morning. Why don't you just keep all your stuff in the closet like everyone else?"

"I do not have this problem every morning," came the indignant reply.

Another voice popped up, "Yes, Sonia, you do." The girls continued to argue amongst themselves. Zara closed her eyes again, and tried to block out their whiny voices. It was too early for this. Couldn't she just sleep? In peace? Alone?

"You better wake her," came the same voice a few seconds later.

"*You* wake her," came the short reply. There was some more rustling.

"Oh, for goodness sake." Zara felt a gentle tap on her shoulder. "Zara," came the whisper, "Zara. You'd better get up. Class is in half an hour." Zara nodded through closed eyes, hoping they'd leave her alone. There was some more noise as they moved around the room and then the door slammed loudly. Without moving in acknowledgement, Zara could feel her muscles. They were still sore and stiff. She had hoped a good night's sleep would find her recovered this morning. Now, as she moved ever so slightly to her side, she knew she was wrong. Her body still ached. Zara opened one eye and saw that the room was empty. Good, they had all gone to breakfast. She snuggled deeper into her duvet. Five more minutes. That's all she wanted. Five more minutes to lie in bed and enjoy the silence.

Zara heard the bedroom door open in the faraway distance. "You're not up yet?" came the surprised voice. "Zara, wake up!" She felt another nudge on her arm, although this time it was not as gentle as before. "Zara, I said get up!" The voice seemed very loud now. Right above her head. Next thing she knew the covers were yanked violently off her body. Gone was the nice, cozy, warmth. "GET UP! Class is in ten minutes." Came the voice again, somewhat angrily. With great effort Zara rolled over and sat up, before yawning loudly. With all the yelling, there had been little alternative. "Ten minutes," came the reply. "Make a move. NOW!" Then the person was gone. As she made to get out of bed, Zara felt the sharp pull of her muscles from yesterday's Callanetics. Zara groaned. It was going to be another *wonderful* day, she thought sarcastically.

There was no time for a shower, so she walked carefully to the ridiculously small wardrobe, and managed to throw together something to wear. She dressed slowly. Painfully slowly. Her body ached. The door to the bedroom opened again. "You've missed breakfast again," Sonia highlighted, somewhat annoyed. Zara nodded, barely listening to her. She was not interested and far too tired. "Here, I bought you an apple and a yogurt," Sonia said, as she put the items on the dresser. Zara did not say thank you, or even look up as she left the room again. When she finally made it to class, she was the last one to arrive and was bordering on late.

Later, back in her bedroom, Zara was glad that Sonia had bought her the apple and the yogurt. She knew she would have been starving without them. Out of all the girls she had to share the room with, Zara found she liked Sonia the most. Well, not liked, but tolerated. Small, petite Sonia, with long light brown hair and a strange, skew smile. She might be the most untidy girl Zara had ever come across, but she was okay.

Zara had feared finding out what the day's class was going to be. As usual, they had met in the training room. They had Paula this time. All fresh eyed and bushy tailed. Zara watched her in amazement. How did they manage to get through these strenuous days and still be so fresh and ready for anything the next morning? She shifted position and winced as she felt another short stab of pain. She looked around her. Was no one else in agony? No one else suffering like she was? Her muscles were still screaming in complaint from the day before, and Zara knew she could not cope with another strenuous day like the day before. What she really wanted to do was crawl back into bed and give her body a chance to recuperate.

Minutes later, Zara looked up toward the sky and offered a short prayer of thanks. She had been saved. When Paula had announced that the day was to be spent swimming, she had wanted to run up and kiss her, except, running was too sore and would inflict too much pain on her already weak muscles. She had smiled instead, eager to accept this little piece of salvation gracefully.

As they had made their way to the Olympic sized swimming pool, Zara knew this was a good idea. The weather was warm, and it promised to be a hot day, even though it was still early morning.

Zara had not been wrong. As the day progressed, it seemed to get hotter and hotter, so the pool was the perfect place to be.

It allowed everyone to cool down and relax. She knew that if they had been stuck in the training room they would all be hot and sticky within half an hour of their workout. This was a much better option. And her muscles did not seem to mind having to swim. They were still stiff, but the movements in the water did not hurt as much.

They swam the length of the pool. Up and down. First breaststroke and then crawl. For those that could, they even tried butterfly. Zara knew from her years of swimming when she was younger, that butterfly was the most difficult of all the strokes. It required the use of each and every muscle in your body. Zara watched one of the girls try the stroke, arms and legs kicking wildly, her head just barely above the surface. It took a few seconds for Zara to make a decision. If she was asked if she could swim butterfly, she would simply say no. It required the use of too many muscles, and today her body needed to rest. She *was* enjoying being in the pool, but she was not going to strain herself any more than she had to. Zara got out of the pool after completing her last lap and dried herself. She had to admit, only to herself though, that the day had been a good one. The water had provided a nice gentle massage on her muscles and they did not feel nearly as bad as they had earlier that morning. She stopped and then tested her body out. Twisting to the left. Twisting to the right. Okay, so she was still stiff and she could still feel the pull of her muscles, but at least it was not as bad as it had been when she had got out of bed. The day had been a pleasant surprise and different to most. Normally they would stop for lunch, and then continue practising the dancing steps until they were ready to collapse, but today things had been done differently. Today, lunch had been bought out to them at the pool. Then, instead of the dancing lesson, they had come to expect, they had been allowed to continue to swim. They had races, then more laps. They had continued swimming the length of the pool, all the way up and all the way down, right until 4:00 p.m. Paula had insisted that each and every girl reapply a water-based sun-screen every hour, and walked around with a bottle permanently in her hand. Each girl had to be doused in sunscreen, every hour. That was the rule. Zara did not mind as long as it kept them in the sunshine. All in all, it had been a pleasantly enjoyable day, considering that she hated the hostel.

There had only been one incident that had marred the day. And that had been Jane. How she hated that girl. They had been swimming laps and somehow Jane had ended up next to her. She was not sure how it happened. Then, as she was concentrating on her stroke, Jane had bumped into her.

"Watch where you're going," Zara said stiffly, before Jane could apologize for the mistake. "Can't you swim in a straight line like everybody else, or is that too difficult for you?" she asked sarcastically. Then without another word, she swam to the end of the row, as far away from Jane as she could possibly get. Zara could not help laughing out loud now as she remembered the incident. The look on Jane's face had been priceless. And when she swam away, Jane still had that surprised, shocked look on her face, as if she was not sure what had happened. It had been so funny.

Zara was still thinking of the incident and Jane's shocked face as she made her way to the dining room. She was starving. All that sun and swimming had really worked up her appetite. She scanned the buffet table in disgust. How could she possibly eat this mush? She took in the roast lamb before her. That would have been nice, except Zara had decided, the cook did not actually know how to cook. The lamb was roasted to oblivion. Dry and crusty. Lamb should be roasted until it was cooked well, but still tender inside, with a slightly pink middle. Even the vegetables looked suspicious. The carrots looked old and withered, and the peas were the size of watermelons. Accompanied with the lamb was mash potatoes, but Zara could see the huge lumps, without even touching the spoon. She walked away from the lamb, and took another look at the dishes lined up in front of her. She could not eat it that. She just could not. The next dish in the line was chicken enchiladas. A Mexican dish, made of large pancakes filled with chicken and spices. Zara took one smell and decided that too, she could not stomach. Her thought was only reconfirmed when the girl in front of her helped herself to one of the pancakes and a overcooked piece of chicken fell from the soggy pancake onto her plate. Zara blocked her nose and moved on further down the line.

She took her time with each meal she passed, but somehow the chef had managed to mess each and every dish that had been served. Zara was amazed. How on earth had he stayed employed? And to think this was a private hostel. The last meal that Zara came to was the lasagna. Zara looked at the dish critically. It looked okay. Lots of melted cheese. It did smell nice. How bad could that be? And she knew she was starving. She had to eat *something*. She glanced behind her at the other food. Her opinion was still the same as before. She looked at the lasagna for a second time. It would have to be that. It was not her favourite, by far, but that was all that was left. She leaned forward and took a helping of the lasagna and the accompanied garlic bread and fresh salad. It would have to do.

Half an hour later, Zara was still sitting at the table, toying with the meal before her. It was horrid and tasted like cardboard. She had picked off the melted cheese, and that was all she had managed to get down. The mince had been soggy and far too salty. She had eaten the garlic bread and salad, but that had been all. Zara summed up the food and knew she could not survive another two months and three weeks of this kind of assault to her taste buds. She would have to do something. Zara analysed the other girls at her table. They were all eating with gusto. Completely enjoying their meals. "This lasagna is lovely, isn't it?" one of the girl at her table said, as if on cue.

"Yes, absolutely delicious," replied Sofie. "I'm going to get another helping," she said, as she hopped off her seat and waded to the buffet table. Zara watched her go in awe. She was not serious, was she? She watched as Sofia lifted the big silver spoon and dished herself a second healthy portion.

"Have you tried the lamb? It's cooked to perfection," came another voice to her left. Zara was unable to hide the horror on her face. Were they mad? Stark raving mad? Cooked to perfection? What on earth did their mothers feed them at home? Sofie returned to her seat with a second helping of the lasagna and dug into the dish with enthusiasm.

"Delicious," she replied between forkfuls. "Don't you like yours, Zara?" Sofie asked, looking at her still full plate.

"Umm, it's yummy," Zara lied. "I'm just bursting, I've eaten so much today. It's my second helping and my eyes are bigger than my belly."

Sofie nodded. "I know what you mean. The food here is delicious. If it weren't for all the exercises we do every day, I'm sure I'd go home a nice, fat lump." Everyone laughed. Zara smiled too, but she thought they were all mad.

Jane watched Zara talking with the other girls at her table and was furious. She had remained so all day, since the incident. That Zara was really getting on her nerves. Today, there had been another insult to add to the growing list. The girl next to her had stoped suddenly, as she had choked on some water. Jane had stopped to help her and Zara had swum right into them. Then, she had the audacity to say it was *her* fault. Jane did not even have time to reply. Zara had been gone in a flash. Happy with her few vicious words, she swam away. If it had not been for the girl still choking and gasping for air, Jane was sure she would have swam after Zara, and they would have had it out with each other once and for all.

"You're not still thinking about her, are you?" asked Sue questionably. Jane dug into her roast lamb, nodding sheepishly.

"Just forget about her," Sarah joined, "she's obviously got a problem."

Jane nodded and continued eating her meal. They were right. She should not waste any more time worrying about Zara.

Zara came back to the room after dinner and dialled the Four Seasons number. She wanted to see how Pat was enjoying the hotel on her own. She knew that it was stupid and by calling she would only make herself jealous, but she would not help it. The number rang a few times, with no answer. Zara was angry. She wanted Pat to be as unhappy as she was. Alone and miserable. It was not fair. Pat was not allowed to enjoy herself. *Where was she anyway?* Zara asked herself angrily. *Probably enjoying another lovely meal,* she thought. "Some perfect creation in a perfect restaurant," she whispered to herself, answering her own question. She left it another hour before trying to call Pat again. This time Pat answered the phone almost immediately.

"Hello?"

"Hi, Pat, it's Zara." she replied back, in a chilly tone. "Where have you been?"

"Zara, hi. I'm so glad you called. I have had a fab—u—lous day. You know those touring books I bought?" she asked excitedly.

"Yes."

"Well, I went to the museum yesterday and met this really interesting guy." She paused for effect, and then flew into the second part of her sentence. "His name's Mark. He's also here on holiday for a few weeks."

"Oh, wow…" Zara said, trying to act interested. She really was not.

Pat did not detect the tone of her friend's voice, and continued excitedly. "And he's so handsome. The perfect stereotype. Tall, dark and handsome. We went for coffee after seeing the museum yesterday and then today he picked me up and we went to the Feline Gallery. It was amazing. The art was wonderful. We have to go, Zara, we just have to go. I'm sure you would love it there."

"That sounds nice," Zara replied. "Maybe we can try and go on the weekend?" she added, bored.

"Sounds perfect. And you must meet Mark. When are you coming over again?" At the promise of going back to the Four Seasons, Zara was instantly alert.

"I will try and come and see you tomorrow after class. I just cannot bear this food. It's awful. And the worst thing is that all these girls here think the food is wonderful. I really just cannot understand it." It was then Pat's turn to listen in silence, as Zara flew on to tell her, in great detail, what kind of awful food they were being served.

"Ugh, it sounds positively awful," Pat confirmed.

"Yes, it is," wailed Zara in reply. "I hate it here." Zara sat on the phone for another half an hour and complained bitterly until there was nothing more she could say. When Zara finally put down the phone, she felt better. Yes tomorrow night. She could not wait until then.

Chapter 30

Zara had finished class and raced upstairs, eager to get dressed. She had been excited about meeting Pat the entire day. Well, it was not only meeting Pat, it was knowing that tonight she would be getting some of the luxury she was used to. She was really looking forward to a nice meal. She was absolutely starved. After three days of eating the hostel food, Zara thought she was going to wither away and die of starvation. She had tried, really tried to eat the meals they served, but even after the first mouthful she knew she could not do it. The food seemed to stick in her throat and was either too soggy, too salty or not cooked enough. She had only just managed to swallow some of the food she had tried, and that had been because she had drank so much water there had been no other alternative.

So, at the prospect of a decent meal, she had raced upstairs happier than she had felt in days, jumped in the shower, washed her hair, and got dressed into one of her designer outfits. She felt instantly better. Somehow, to her relief, she had managed to do all of this without any interruptions from the other girls. They had still not yet returned from class. She had already ordered the cab, which would be arriving in ten minutes. Zara took one last look at herself in the mirror. Yup, she was all set. Time to go off and enjoy herself. Tonight was going to be fabulous.

Rushing down the stairs, eager to get on her way, Zara made it to the large entrance way. The door that led to her freedom for one night. As she turned the knob, she was startled by a question.

"And where do you think you're going?" came the sharp voice from behind her. Zara spun around. There, in one of the little side rooms, stood Helen.

Helen was still clad in the day's tracksuit. It looked like she had been on her way to her own bedroom when she caught sight of Zara. Zara knew she had to reply. The woman was waiting for an answer. "Out to dinner," Zara replied as nonchalantly as she could.

Helen blinked twice before answering, "I don't think so, young lady."

"What do you mean?" answered Zara.

"No one is allowed to leave the grounds," Helen stated in her usual matter-of-fact tone. "At all."

Zara stared at Helen in shock. Uncomprehending. "What do you mean? I don't understand," Zara replied, "We leave the hostel every weekend to go into town. I'm having dinner tonight with a friend. I did the exact same thing on the weekend."

Helen was not fooled. "That's weekends, and weekends only. During the week, NO ONE is allowed to leave the grounds. That's the hostel rule." With that Helen had turned around and left Zara shocked.

Zara found herself alone in the big empty foyer. The silence seemed to echo loudly. This was ridiculous. She was a prisoner. A prisoner in this place. She knew she could not openly disobey Helen. She was the head of this whole operation. But, Helen had now seen her. Uh, she wished she had known about that stupid rule. She would now have made more of an effort to keep hidden.

Zara knew she could not miss the hostel dinner that evening. Helen was bound to ask the other girls where she was if she did not appear. Knowing Helen, she would now be keeping a special eye open for her, just to check up on her movements. Zara sat on the wooden bench and thought hard for a few minutes. What could she do? She had to get out of here. She had been looking forward to this meal all day.

Then she had an idea. Hoping that it would work, Zara run back up the stairs to her bedroom, her heels clicking loudly on the floor, as she ran. She had been lucky. The other girls still had not made it back to their room. Zara knew it was only a matter of time. They would be back soon, want a hot bath or shower before they headed down for dinner. She jumped into her bed, fully dressed and waited.

She did not have long to lie there waiting before she heard the loud laughing of the girls as they made their way up the stairs and into their shared bedroom. "We were wondering where you were?" Sofie said, as she sat herself down onto her bed.

"I'm not feeling too well," replied Zara, in the most hoarse, scratchy voice she could summon up.

"Oh dear," replied one of the other girls, "what's the matter?"

"Migraine. I get them regularly," Zara replied.

Sofie dug into her handbag. "Here, try these. They are strong headache tablets. They should help a little."

"Thanks," Zara replied, as she took the pills.

"I'll get you some water."

Zara took the tablets and water offered and pretended to swallow the small white pills before sinking back into the covers, groaning loudly. She then closed her eyes and covered her head with her sheets and waited. There was a thick, heavy silence in the room. "We'll just have quick showers and then leave you alone to sleep," Sofie said.

Bingo! "That would be nice," Zara whispered back.

"Do you want us to bring you back anything to eat from downstairs?" *Most definitely no,* she thought to herself. Instead she whispered back, "No, thanks. My head is too sore to eat food." As Zara lay in the bed, she had to admit that they were especially quiet as they took their quick showers and dressed. They talked in whispers and drew the curtains tightly shut so she would not have to suffer any light or disturbance. Then, as quietly as they could, they left the room. Zara waited until she heard them walking down the stairs, then jumping out the bed, she listened at the door to make sure they were truly gone. Minutes later and she was unable to hear any footsteps. Then, as she had planned, she took her pillows and laid them neatly in a straight line, before covering them with her sheets. If she were lucky, they would not turn on the lights when they returned and think she was still fast asleep. If Helen asked anyone where she was, she'd be told. Zara was certain that Helen would think she was sulking alone in her bedroom and she doubted Helen would seek her out.

Zara opened the bedroom door a small crack and looked outside into the corridor. There was no one in sight. She slipped off her heels. She did not want to make any noise. Carefully, she tiptoed her way back to the foyer. She was careful. She hid behind corridors and doors and made certain that she was not seen by anyone. She strained to listen for any sounds of people nearby. Zara knew that most of the girls would be at dinner, but she did not want to take any chances. Tonight was just too important. She had to get out of the hostel without being seen.

When she finally managed to sneak out of the main entrance, the cab was ready and waiting. She quickly slipped on her shoes again and ran across the gravel, jumping into the cab. "Four Seasons please," she said as she breathed a sigh of relief. She had done it. Tonight was still going to be great. She could almost taste her dinner.

Helen sat down at her own reserved table ready for dinner. She was irritated and needed a glass of wine. A large one. Imagine the nerve of that girl, thinking she could come and go as she pleased. Out for dinner! How absurd. Helen was glad she had bumped into Zara when she had, before she had left the building. They could get into so much trouble if she had actually managed to leave, unnoticed. All the parents had signed a letter, and it confirmed that the girls would have excellent care. Weekends were the only time they were allowed to go to the town and leave the hostel, but weekends had been especially agreed with by their parents and permission obtained. And she was certainly not taking responsibility for all the girls going into town on their own, especially after dark. Imagine thirty girls running around as they pleased? It would be complete chaos.

Now as she poured herself a glass of white wine from the bottle left on the table, Helen took in the restaurant. All the girls were seated, enjoying their meals. Helen sought out Zara. After the incident downstairs, she could not help herself. Her thick blond hair was normally easy to spot in a crowed, but somehow Zara was nowhere to be seen. Helen scanned the room again, this time looking into the dark corners and the half hidden tables. No, Zara was not in the restaurant. Disturbed by the feeling that Zara might have disobeyed her, she continued to scan the room for a third time in case she had been mistaken. There was no mistaking it. Zara was definitely not among the girls present.

She did note Susie sitting in the corner booth, laughing at something one of the other girls had said. Knowing that they shared a room together, Helen made her way over. "Good evening, girls."

"Good evening, Helen," they replied in unison.

"I do hope you're enjoying your meals?"

"Oh yes, the food is delicious, thank you."

Helen made a display at gazing at each girl at the table. "Is Zara not joining you for dinner this evening?" she asked innocently.

"Oh," Susie replied, "she had an awful migraine. We left her in bed, asleep."

Helen nodded slowly. "Okay, well enjoy the rest of your meals. The dessert this evening is especially delicious."

Helen made her way back to her seat and took a sip of the cold wine. So, Zara was sulking in her room and having a bolt of rebellion. Helen knew that Zara was not like the other girls they had chosen for Germany. At first, she had not been sure what it was that made that girl so different from everyone else. Then, quite by accident, she had overheard some of the other girls talking. It seemed her father was a very important man and extremely wealthy too. Helen had paid it no attention, but then there was that whole episode about her being refused to stay at the Four Seasons hotel. Helen had never heard anything so ridiculous in her life. A hotel for three months. It was impractical for a start, and she knew they could not allow any of the girls to stay somewhere on their own alone without sufficient supervision. There was no control on ensuring they appeared for classes or if they were even safe. Helen thought the whole thing was finished and that Zara had cooled down. Maybe it was for the best that she did stay inside her bedroom for the night. It would give her time to cool off.

Helen tried to enjoy her starter, but even with the wine, she could not keep herself from thinking of Zara. Then, eager to ease her trepidation and as a way to stop this madness, Helen decided she would check up on the girl. After all, Zara was used to getting her own way, so this kind of refusal would be something she was not accustomed to and Helen did not want bad feelings between them. They still had to work with each other for weeks to come yet.

Helen rounded the corner and went upstairs and walked to what she knew was Zara's shared bedroom. Instantly, she remembered the big commotion when Zara had learnt that no, she was not able to stay at a hotel as she had planned. Then, another screaming match had followed, when she learnt that she had to share her bedroom. Helen found it all a little strange that someone so young could be so spoilt. Her parents had obviously indulged her since she was born, and she was not used to "not getting" what she wanted. This was the best private hostel in the whole of Germany. The parents who sent their children here were very wealthy and "well to do" families, expecting only the very best for their children. Only the most privileged children were accepted into this school. How Zara could find fault with it, she was not sure. Yes, the children had to share a bedroom, but that was to ensure that friendships were developed. Each room slept four, but the rooms were massive in size. Helen had been to other hostels, including private ones, and she knew that these rooms were by far the biggest and most luxurious. And each room also had their own bathroom, which was normally unheard of at a hostel. Yes, these children led a life of privilege. Every need was catered for. And here was Zara, complaining about it all. It was unreal really. How could nothing be to her satisfaction?

Helen looked at the closed door and noticed the silence coming from within. Helen had hoped she would hear Zara from outside, maybe moving around or snoring which would confirm that she was still on the hostel premises. She wanted nothing more than to head back to the restaurant to finish her dinner in peace. No one would ever know that she had actually felt it was necessary to check up on Zara. But, all was silent behind the door. She tiptoed closer to the room and opened the door a tiny peek. There under the covers, was Zara, fast asleep. Helen could just make out her sleeping form in the darkness. Happy that her mind was put to rest, Helen closed the door behind her as quietly as she could and returned to the dining room, glad that Zara had not been stupid enough to disobey her.

*****

Zara was enjoying herself immensely. She had picked up Pat, who had been waiting eagerly in the foyer of the Four

Seasons, and then they had gone to the local town in search of somewhere to eat dinner. At the cab drivers recommendation, they had found themselves at a classic Chinese restaurant. A bit expensive he had said, but worth every penny. They had taken him up on his suggestion. Zara had not eaten a decent meal in three days, so the price of the food was the least of her worries.

After arranging that the same cab driver pick them up later that evening, they made their way inside the restaurant. The smell of the spices teased them as soon as they entered. It smelt delicious. A young woman dressed in a bright red silk traditional Chinese dress approached them. "Good evening. Do you have a reservation with us tonight?" she asked.

"No, I'm afraid we don't," replied Zara.

"That's no problem. How many of you shall be dining with us this evening?" she asked politely

"Just the two of us," replied Zara, again looking around.

"Wait here, please," the waitress replied, "while we arrange a table for you."

Zara took a step forward into the restaurant and was pleased with what she saw. It was exactly what she had hoped for. Big pictures adorned the walls in bright and radiant colours. On closer inspection, Zara recognized that they were all hand painted with scenery from Thailand, Singapore and China. To add to the scenery, there was a huge bronze statue in the middle of the restaurant. Zara guessed it must be a statue of one of the famous Chinese gods. The hostess returned, and they were led to a table next to another statue. This one carved in wood.

As they sat down, Zara enjoyed the feel of the red silk tablecloth. The hostess lit the candle on their table, and proceeded to pour ice water into their water glasses. All the candles that were lit throughout the restaurant sparkled furiously, which made it easy for them to catch the sparkle of the crystal chandelier, hanging in the middle of the room. The waitress left and they were free to talk.

"I'm surprised you were free tonight," Zara said as she lay her serviette across her lap.

"Why's that?" replied Pat, doing the same.

"Well, I thought you might be dining with Matt again this evening."

"No, not tonight. But I am meeting him tomorrow." Zara tried not to show her surprise. Pat had been seeing this Matt guy almost every day since she had met him.

"What are you doing then tomorrow?" she asked.

"Matt wants to go and see the Wildlife Park. It's supposed to be really good. All sorts of birds of prey and an array of predators. Snakes, crocodiles, that kind of thing."

"So, you're going to the zoo," joked Zara.

Pat laughed, taking no offense from her friend's tone. "Yes, I suppose we are."

"So what does this mystery man do for a living?" Zara asked politely, hoping she did not sound like she was probing for information, which was exactly what she was doing.

"He's a vet," Pat replied.

"A vet?"

"Yes, a vet. And a very good one by the sounds of things," Pat replied back, as if to defend him. "That's why he is so interested in going to the zoo. Anyway I have not been to the zoo or anything like that for years so it should be kind of fun."

Zara could just imagine Pat now. All dressed up in her designer outfits for her date to the smelly zoo. The thought made her smile. When the food finally arrived, Zara was unable to hold back taking a deep breath. It smelt heavenly. She eyed the hot steam rising up toward the ceiling, then decided not to waste any time in dishing up and tucking in with gusto. They had a mixed starter that consisted of miniature spring rolls, lightly toasted prawn toast along with a side order of chicken skewers roasted over a low flame, followed by yet another dish of small tender baby back ribs.

The main meal was just as delicious as the varied starter. Red Tai curry and chicken with cashew nuts, all with the normal accompaniments of special fried rice and beef egg noodles. Zara enjoyed her meal immensely and did not want to leave. She ate and ate and ate. It was just wonderful. *Why didn't they serve meals like this at the hostel?* she thought. She would have no problem eating there every night if they served food as good as this.

At the end of the evening, the driver was there as promised, waiting patiently as they settled their bill. They dropped Pat back to the hotel first and then the cab driver drove Zara to the hostel.

Zara knew that she would have to be careful as she made her way back to her bedroom. She got the driver to drop her around the corner of the hostel as she did not want to risk someone hearing the car's engine, prompting them to come outside and investigate. It was a dark night, and there were no lights as she approached the familiar driveway, but Zara was not afraid of the dark. Besides, her eyes had already gotten used to the darkness and there was a full moon giving off plenty of natural light. As she had done previously, Zara slipped out of her heels and entered the foyer as quietly as possible.

There was no one in sight, but she still remained careful as a precaution. It would not do to get caught now. She hid inside a dark corner and kept her ears open for any noise that would tell her someone was wandering the corridors, but she heard nothing. All was silent. She continued to sneak back down the corridors on tiptoes. She supposed that by this time of night, most of the girls would be tucked away in bed anyway. Everywhere was deathly quiet, and when she got to the winding staircase, she realized how noisy and loud the stairs were, squeaking with each step she took. It sounded so loud in the still silence of the night. And then, as she took the last corner, that led almost directly to her bedroom, Zara walked dead bang into someone.

Zara started at the face of the girl she had come to dislike with such a fierce intensity. "Can't you watch where you're going?" Zara hissed angrily into the silence.

Jane had enough. She had been forced to keep quiet and be polite at the restaurant as her job had depended on it. It had not been the time or the place, and she was not going to lose her job over someone like Zara. Then had been the second incident in the pool. A incident that had not even been her fault. And here she was again facing Zara and her bullying ways. Jane had just about enough of Zara. "No!" she shouted. "You watch where you're going! You walked into me!" Her firm reply echoed loudly into the still silence, and seemed to vibrate against the walls. With that Jane turned around and walked off, this time leaving Zara with the look of shock on her face.

Chapter 31

Raymond was irritated. Even now, driving in his Porsche he could not simmer down. He had hoped that driving on the long open road, fast and reckless, it would make him feel better, but now he realized that even this, his most joyous pastime, was not helping. He was furious and he did not know what he could do about the situation.

It had all happened so quickly. He had not even seen it coming. Now, as he reflected back on the past month, he kicked himself for not noticing before. He had been so confident that all was going well. He had been sorely mistaken. Now it looked as if the rug might be pulled right from underneath him. He was furious about it.

It had been a standard interview. They needed someone new in the office. The workload had just been too much for them all. They needed a go-between. Someone who could pick up all the little bits and pieces of work that no one had the time to look into, but work that still needed to be done. They had finally selected Bob Turner who was bright and enthusiastic. He was fresh out of college, although he had worked as an intern for over a year, so he was not completely without experience. Everyone had liked him and he was by far the best person they had seen on the many interviews they had conducted. Bob Turner was offered the position the very next day.

That very first morning everyone had been surprised by Bob. It was obvious that he was extremely capable and very eager. Two good assets to posses in their line of work. Then, on the second day, one of the senior directors unexpectedly needed assistance with an important briefing. Raymond knew they would have normally asked him, but he was already tied up with another equally important case. So naturally, they had asked Bob. He had been the only one available. In a way, it had also been a test. How would the new guy cope? Raymond sat on the sidelines and watched with interest. Bob was going to crash and burn. He was far too inexperienced to know how the company worked and what was to be done. It was going to be fun to watch.

What Bob had not been told was that there was a permanent position open for an assistant, and they had been systematically testing possible candidates. Raymond knew that he was in the running. So far, he had proved the most successful applicant with the best track record, and he knew, that with Bill Maddox's vote, he was guaranteed to get the new position. And now, here he was. Bob Turner. A thorn in his side. Raymond was worried. Bob was beginning to become a problem. A serious problem. He was far too good for someone so new. Raymond did not care for the unexpected competition.

The directors were impressed. Bob really knew his stuff and was extremely eager. He did not care that he had to work late nights and had to come in on Saturdays. After a few weeks in the office, he was considered one of the best newcomers that had been employed. So, as Raymond had first predicated, he had not crashed and burned. Now it looked like the position he had taken so much care in assuring was his was now in jeopardy by this new rookie. Raymond wanted to ensure that when they chose him, they had no doubts. None what so ever. And they would choose him.

Raymond knew he had to squash Bob. And quickly, before he made too much of a name for himself with the big bosses who made the decisions.

Raymond pushed his foot down on the accelerator and the car shot forward. The speed of the car still had no effect on his mood. He was still furious. He needed to take some drastic action.

Raymond knew he had to do something. Something that would ensure his position. Guarantee his status. And unfortunately Zara was not there to help in his plan as she usually was. He thought of Zara. She had been gone for one month now, and he had spoken to her almost twice a week. She was hating it there. Raymond, on the other hand, was still enjoying his newfound freedom. At the office, Raymond barely saw Bill Maddox anymore. He was so much busier now with the company growing steadily as the months passed. Not seeing Bill had never bothered him before. If he was unable to see Bill at work, then no one else was seeing him either. And he had the added bonus. The trump card. He was going out with Zara—his daughter.

Raymond had it all worked out. When he came to pick up Zara, he always ensured that he saw Bill at home, when he was calm and relaxed. Zara was always late, doing her last minute touch ups to her makeup or whatever she did. And that left the prefect opportunity for him and Bill to talk work. They would usually have a drink or two together, and talk shop. Raymond had even thrown in one or two of his unique ideas for the company. Tested the water. Built some confidence in his abilities with the old man. Raymond always practised what he would say before he arrived. He could not afford to mess it up. He knew that Bill was a smart man, and everything he said, or did not say, would be analysed. So far, he had done well.

Raymond knew that if Bill had not liked him, there was no way he would ever been allowed him to see his precious daughter. Raymond knew that Zara was his most priced possession.

But now, with Zara out the country, Raymond had no excuse to go around to the old man's house. No way to see Bill and talk with him over a drink. No way to ensure that he left a lasting impression with his ideas. It was almost as if, out of sight, out of mind. Raymond was irritated. He needed Zara here at home helping him to win the new position. Raymond cursed her yet again.

Then it came to him. He would have to fly out and see Zara. She would be thrilled. And if he knew Zara, she would be talking to her parents every evening. If he went to see her in Germany, then the news would filter through to her father. Raymond decided to coax her a little, get her to talk to her father. Tell her father how hard he had been working. How he had secured some very valuable and important clients. Even though he could not see Bill personally, at least Bill would know he was still around, working hard. That would again force his name to the top of the list. And Bill would be pleased with everything because his daughter was pleased. And when his little Zara was pleased, Bill became a very manageable boss.

Raymond began to feel better. Finally he had come up with a plan that would work. He eased his foot off the accelerator and pulled off to the side of the road as the dust continued to fly haphazardly around his car. He knew that Zara would be free to talk now. It was early evening. Her classes were finished for the day. He flipped out his phone and dialled her number.

* * * * *

Zara was thrilled. Had been since Raymond's phone call and his surprise news that he was coming to visit her for the weekend. He was arriving in a few minutes. She would not be able to meet him at the airport, but she had promised to get out as soon as she could, which meant only after class. Zara looked at her watch for the fifth time that hour. When would they finally be finished? She was so excited; she wanted to finish up here and get out as soon as she was able. She had not seen Raymond for over a month now. They had spoken on the phone, but it was not the same. She had missed him. Missed going out and enjoying the evenings he had planned for her. She wondered if he would bring her a present. Ugh, she hoped so. She loved presents and she wanted to be spoilt. This weekend was going to be good. She just knew it.

Paula broke into her thoughts. "Okay, one last time. From the top." Zara danced the steps as required, but half heartily. She really did not want to be there, especially now. Her mind was far away at the airport. On Raymond. When she managed her last lunge, she knew the end had come. Finally. The class was finished.

They all left the room, and Zara had to stop herself from skipping out the room. As had become the routine, some of the girls opted for a drink before heading to their bedrooms while others took preference to a long, cooling swim before dinner. Zara had no intention of doing either. She wanted to go upstairs, have a quick shower and then get dressed into something extra-special. She was so excited she could barely breath. Tonight was going to be a good night. Raymond was here.

Now as Zara left her bedroom, she knew she had to be careful again. She had become quite an expert at leaving after class and meeting Pat in town for dinner without being detected. Sometimes they stayed at the Four Seasons, enjoying the in-house restaurant, while other times they ventured into the little town. So far, no one had noticed that she was never at dinner herself. She was glad the hostel restaurant was open for two hours, so everyone tended to come and go as they pleased. No one had set hours for dinner. It had been the perfect alibi. No one was really able to keep tabs on her time in the evenings. The only one she had to stay clear of was Helen. With her, she had to be careful. Extra careful. Thankfully, Helen had been very busy with the last bits of organizing so she had been working late almost every night in her office. She had no idea who was at dinner and who was not.

Zara had developed the habit of taking off her shoes once she hit the foyer. She knew that the best way to stay undiscovered, was to be as quiet as possible. She made no noise that could be heard. Now, as she took her shoes off as was the ritual, she tiptoed until she was outside the entrance.

Zara had also arranged with the cab driver, whom she had discovered was named Toby, to meet her every second evening, around the corner of the hostel premises. That way, no one would see the cab or hear its engine and ask any questions as he waited for her to appear. She had thought of everything.

Zara looked to the left and to the right. There was no one in sight. Then, she listened for a few minutes. There were no sounds of anyone being nearby. Only some laugher in the far away distance, but then it stopped. All was quiet again. Zara tiptoed, barefoot down the stairs. She stopped again, as she heard some girls making their way to the restaurant. She knew they would probably not see her, but she did not want to take the chance. Normally, she left much later while most of the girls were eating dinner, so it was easier to slip away, but tonight she could not wait. She had to get to Raymond as soon as possible.

When she finally made it to the waiting cab, she breathed a huge sigh of relief. All had gone according to plan. And now she could look forward to an enjoyable evening ahead. She was surprised at the dull ache in the pit of her stomach. Nerves? It was the only thing she could thing of. No, not nerves, she had nothing to be nervous about. Excitement. That was it! It was excitement for the evening ahead with Raymond.

Zara arrived at the Four Seasons, where Raymond was staying. It was only natural that he would stay there. Pat had arranged yet another date with her friend Matt, who had started becoming much more than a frequent companion. That left Zara free to enjoy a long overdue date with Raymond without feeling guilty about her friend eating alone. She gave herself a quick spray of perfume, checked her lipstick and then headed inside, eager to see Raymond after the month she had been away from home. She saw him immediately, as soon she entered the foyer. Standing tall and handsome next to the fireplace, in the corner. Zara ran over, unable to hold herself back. "Raymond!" she shouted excitedly.

At the sound of his name, Raymond half turned. "Zara," he said, smiling just as she reached him. They hugged for a few minutes.

"I've missed you," Zara breathed into his ear.

Raymond coughed. "Yes me too. And starving after my flight."

"Let's go up and get some dinner, then we can catch up."

Zara couldn't have been more thrilled at his suggestion.

* * * * *

Zara downed some more wine. She knew she shouldn't, but she needed something to occupy her mind as Raymond waffled on about work. Then, unable to take it any longer, she had excused herself from the table.

The evening had not turned out as fun as she had hoped, which was unusual. She always had a good time when Raymond took her out. Tonight though, he just seemed to be talking and talking, boring her to death. All he seemed to want to discuss was his job. And that was the last thing she wanted to discuss. She wanted to talk about their friends. What had they been doing? Who had he seen? Where had they gone? She was dying to get some up to date information, or better yet, some gossip. Instead, all she got was talk of work. Even her blatant and abrupt subject changes had not helped in her efforts to change the conversation. Somehow they managed to come straight back to his job. She had also been a little upset when she had first arrived. She had expected a little more enthusiasm and attention from him. Maybe some flowers or exotic chocolates. She had not seen him in over a month and he should be spoiling her. But no, there had been nothing. Not even a tiny gift to show how much he had missed her. She had thought he might have arranged a little something during dinner. Maybe have the waiter deliver her a gift box, or sing her a song serenade. It was the Four Seasons; they would do anything for a price. As the evening progressed, Zara realized that he had not arranged anything special for her at all. They were just having a normal dinner.

To make matters worse during the evening, Raymond had not asked about anything regarding her awful stay. Instead, he had not stopped talking about himself the entire meal. She was trying hard not to be upset, but it was proving difficult. She wanted more attention.

Zara looked at herself at the mirror of the bathroom once again. All the effort she had gone to for this evening was ruined. The special dress, the expensive perfume. It all meant nothing. All wasted time. He had not even said how lovely she looked that evening. It was so unlike him. The man she saw tonight was not the man she knew. It was so strange. Then she had a thought. Maybe it was the long flight. Maybe he was tired. He probably had a long day at the office and then long uncomfortable flight over here. Yes, that must be it. He was tired. Things would be better tomorrow. After he had some rest. A good night's sleep would work its charm and she would have the old attentive Raymond back. Zara washed and dried her hands. Yes, she decided. That must be it. There was no other possible explanation. Poor Raymond was exhausted. Zara tossed her head to the left, checked her reflection in the mirror one last time, and then headed for the door and back to their table.

"Oh there you are. I was wondering what was taking you so long," Raymond said.

Zara tried to smile. "Yes, here I am."

"I thought you might have drowned in there," he said, laughing at his own joke. "Well, I'm ready for dessert," he stated. "How about you?"

Zara nodded eagerly, as she took another sip of wine. The bottle was almost finished.

Her dessert was only half eaten. She had been enjoying it at first, but the more Raymond droned on, the more she was put off until she was not able to take another bite. She knew he was tired. Exhausted in fact. And she should be excusing his bad behaviour tonight, but Zara had never had a more boring evening. She did not think it was possible with Raymond, but here she was, sipping her water now, acting interested in what he had been saying. All evening the subject had been the same. Work work work. It had not changed. The only break she had received was when he excused himself to go to the bathroom.

*****

Raymond looked at himself in the mirror. Irritably, he splashed his face with water. His plan was not working. He had been trying all evening to talk to Zara about his job, make her understand his position, his situation, but he knew he was not getting through to her. He had not even asked her to speak to her father for him yet. She seemed completely bored as soon as work came up as a subject. He knew she was trying to change the subject at every turn, but he would not allow it. This was too important. Stupid girl. Did she not see? He grabbed a paper towel and wiped his face dry. What could he do to make her understand?

It did not help either that she smelt like a perfume factory. He had almost choked when she had hugged him. He had actually been embarrassed. Then, throughout the entire meal, she had looked over his shoulder at everything and everyone else, paying what he was saying—very little attention. She had not been listening to a word that had come out of his mouth all evening. He was glad that this trip was only for a few short days. He could not take much more of this. He had tomorrow and half the day Sunday, and then he was flying back home. He hoped that he'd manage to get through to her before he left. Raymond smiled wickedly at himself in the mirror. Whether she liked it or not, he *was* going to get through to her.

Chapter 32

Zara listened to the music and danced her steps vigorously. One, two three. One two, three. Hop and jump. Twist and turn. Arms up. Pirouette.

Zara repeated the words of the routine to herself in her head, even though they were now almost automatic. She barely had to think anymore of the movements she had to perform. As soon as the music began to play, her feet seemed to move on their own accord.

With the next kick, Zara used more of the pent up anger she felt brimming. She kicked high. As high as she could. It felt good. The higher she kicked the more it seemed to be helping her red hot temper.

Helen watched Zara intently, in a way that no one would discern she was analysing the girl. She knew that Zara was not happy with her lifestyle here at the hostel. She had made that perfectly clear from the day she had arrived. Everyone knew she had expected a long luxury holiday for the duration of the three months, but life at the hostel was anything but a luxury holiday. It was hard work, and as time progressed, there would be very little time for much else. From the very first class, Helen had noticed a lack of enthusiasm in Zara. She did the steps, but it was obvious to anyone who cared to watch that she had been doing the absolute bare minimum. Helen still could not figure out exactly why Zara had elected to audition for the trip to Germany at all. She obviously did not want to be here.

It had been a very different story when they had been auditioning for the limited places. Then, Helen had seen some fire in the girl. She had really wanted to win then, and at auditions, Zara had excelled. Helen knew she could do it. She just had to *want* to do it. That was the problem. For some reason, Zara no longer *wanted* to be involved.

And now it seemed that the intense fire she had witnessed before had come back into action again. Helen wondered what had triggered it off as she watched Zara kick for a third time, with her leg high and perfectly aimed. The girl was talented. There was no denying that. Now, after over a month of messing around, she could actually see the old Zara coming back out. The Zara that she first knew. She wondered what had bought about the sharp and drastic change.

*****

For the first time since she had arrived in Germany, Zara felt alive and she was sad to see the class end. She still had so much pent up energy that she wanted to rid herself of. She did not know what to do with herself. Everyone had left after class and she was alone in the room. Then she saw the black punching bags. She had an idea. Dragging one over, Zara took position and began to kick. Kick hard. She kicked and kicked and kicked. She was so mad. The entire weekend had been a complete disappointment. She had been so excited about seeing Raymond after a whole month and was thrilled to have the weekend with him. She had so many ideas of what they could do together. Fun things in the little town. They could stroll along to the art gallery, maybe even pick out a painting as a gift for her parents. Then, another one of her ideas had been to drive to the little town only half an hour away. Pat had been there already with Matt and said it was the cutest little village. Zara had hoped that they could spend the day there and maybe have lunch along the river. She had been so positive that it was going to be a excellent fun-filled weekend. She had been bitterly disappointed.

On Friday evening she had her first inkling that things were not going as well as she had imagined, but she had been convinced that it had been due to Raymond feeling tired after his long flight. Then on Saturday, Raymond had surprised her again and threw all her carefully laid plans for the day out the window. No, he did not want to go to the little town nearby. And no, the art gallery did not sound like fun. Zara was at a loss. These were exactly the kind of things that they usually did together. Why was it all of a sudden a massive problem? She really did not understand it and was disappointed. "Well what do you want to do?" Zara asked, completely at a loss for ideas and more than a little annoyed that her plans had been tossed away so callously.

Raymond looked thoughtful for a few minutes then said. "Let's go for a walk."

Zara almost tripped on the pavement. A walk? A walk where? They both hated going for walks. It was a joke they had shared between themselves many times. Zara held her tongue, but it was difficult. Fine. If he wanted to go for walk, then they would go for a walk.

They began by heading downhill on a little cobbled street. It was not long before Raymond began to talk, and very quickly Zara became aware that they were back on the dreaded subject of his job. Work Work Work. It was all that was on his mind. She debated with herself if should she say something? Zara pondered over her dilemma for a few minutes as he waffled on. No, she decided, she would act interested, and eventually he would run out of steam on the subject. After all, there was only so much he could say. She agreed with herself to let him get whatever it was, off his chest. Then they could continue their weekend and forget all this craziness

By lunchtime, Zara still had not managed to stop Raymond talking about his job. She had listened intently, as she had first decided, to all his woes and troubles in the office, but her interest had just fuelled him more. By dinner, the subject was still much the same. Zara was bored. He seemed to have endless tales and stories. All of which were negative. Zara knew he worked hard, but dammit, she was also working hard, and worse, she had to endure living in a hostel for three months The entire day had not been anywhere near to her idea of a fun outing.

When it was time to go back to the hostel, Zara was actually glad. She could use a little peace and quiet. And she knew that was not a good sign as she hated it at the hostel. Sunday had been just the same and by the time Raymond was due to leave for the airport, Zara was ready to pull her hair out. She did not even get a proper goodbye from him. And Raymond, as much as she hated to admit it, looked just as eager to leave. She said a quick goodbye and left the airport before he had even boarded the aeroplane. She was furious. Now kicking and punching the boxing bag, she felt so much better. How dare Raymond ruin her weekend like that?

Zara was concentrating hard on punching and kicking the bag in front of her, and did not hear the back door of the studio open.

Jane slipped into the training room and retrieved her towel which she had forgotten to pick up earlier. She was already inside the room before she heard the heavy knocks to the punch bag. In the middle of the room stood Zara, kicking the punch bag with an intense ferocity. Jane took one look at the force Zara was using, and knew that something was amiss. She slipped out the studio quickly, before she was noticed. The last thing she needed was another unwanted confrontation with Zara.

Jane was not stupid. She had seen how angry Zara had been today, much angrier than usual and that anger seemed to flow into her dance movements. Today, for the first time since arriving in Germany, Zara had used her talents to her fullest degree.

She wondered if Zara's newfound anger had anything to do with the weekend that had just passed. It would make sense. Zara was never around unless it was absolutely necessary. Even at mealtimes, Zara remained strangely absent. She was very rarely *actually* seen in the restaurant, and when she was, she barely ate anything.

Jane knew that she was sneaking out most evenings, even though it was strictly forbidden. How she was doing it or where she was going was anyone's guess. Jane had wondered if she should report it. They had all been given stringent rules, and leaving the premises had been the main one. But then she had decided against it. Whatever Zara did was her own business. Jane was not going to get herself involved. Besides, she was here to dance. That was her love. She was not here to keep tabs on some spoilt, little rich girl who was determined to do things her own way. As long as whatever Zara got up to did not affect her, Jane would turn a blind eye and let her get on with it. It was none of her business and she could not afford to let herself get sidetracked. She had to keep her eye on her goal and that was to be the very best she could possibly be. She had to keep focussed, keep concentrating and practising hard. Her parents had gone through a heap of sacrifices to get her here, and she would not let them down. Nothing was going to distract her from her goal.

Zara was the first to appear in the training room the following morning. She had worked herself past endurance the evening before, but today, she still felt like she had loads of extra energy. She was not quite sure what or how this had happened. She supposed she had Raymond to thank. Just thinking of the wasted weekend made her angry and see bright red spots. Determined not to get worked up again, Zara turned her attention to the other girls that were arriving.

Slowly, the hall began to fill and then Helen also arrived, clad in one of her usual bright tracksuits. Her expression was strange, set with a determined look. Helen entered and took to the front of the room before clapping loudly. "Okay ladies. Attention please."

Talking ceased immediately and all the girls looked up expectantly. Helen had something to say and it looked important. Helen paused until the room was silent, then said, "Today we have an announcement to make." She paused after the first sentence, for effect. "We've decided that there needs to be a main dancer in the group. Someone who will lead the procession onto the field." There was a gasp of surprise from all the girls. Everyone automatically would be after that lead. Helen waited a few more minutes, and then held up her hand to cease the chattering that had developed among the girls. "The girl chosen to be in the lead, will dance a solo sequence on the field, before the main group joins her. She will also do another solo piece at the end of the precession. I do not need to tell you that whoever gets this role will be very privileged, and will receive a great deal of individual focus." Everyone nodded and again the chatter began, as the excitement buzzed wildly around the hall. "Any questions so far?" Helen asked, knowing in advance that she would see an array of hands go up. She was not wrong. Immediately hands flew into the air.

"How are you choosing the main lead?" someone asked.

"Good question," Helen responded. "From today, everyone is going to be monitored. You all know the set sequences, so now it's a case of perfecting your technique. We will use this opportunity to watch all of you individually and assess your capabilities. From today, everyone has a clean slate, but be warned. The person lucky enough to be picked will have a lot of extra work to do. This is a prestigious part, but it also requires dedication. If everything goes smoothly, we should have a decision made in roughly two weeks. We will announce who the lead is then. Good luck."

Jane was excited. Things just seemed to get better and better. Wonderful opportunities were popping up at every turn. Coming to Germany, was helping her in more ways than one and she would love to be the one chosen. It would be perfect. Her Jane Brown, chosen to lead the procession onto the field. She already knew that she wanted this. She was determined. She would practice every spare second she got. She *would* get that lead.

Chapter 33

"You just have to meet him. He's gorgeous," purred Pat, as she took a sip of her coffee.

Zara nodded. "Okay. That'll be fun. It's about time I meet this guy anyway. You've been practically spending every spare second with him."

"I know, he's wonderful. I'm so glad I've met him. We've just clicked. He loves all the things I love to do and we've had a fabulous time visiting all the sights together. He's amazing. You'll just love him. Just wait and see."

That was a few days ago and now Zara was finally going to meet this Matt. Dressed in a red silk dress that she had carefully picked, she was raring to go. Sneaking out every night was now becoming an easy habit. She found the hostel far too boring and the Four Seasons so much better in every aspect. Sneaking out was now a nightly ritual she looked forward to. She had it timed down to perfection and knew exactly when the halls would be the most deserted. Helen was no longer a problem. She was extremely busy with the event looming, so Zara almost never saw her.

She was curious to see what this guy Matt was like. She had heard Pat's version, but she wanted to see for herself. The real man, behind Pat's rose tinted glasses. He must be some specimen of a guy to keep Pat's attention for more than a few days, and it had now been over a month. Pat was not the kind of girl to stick to one man and one date. She liked the attention too much. So this was a surprise. A guy who actually had Pat spellbound, and Zara had to admit, Pat was spellbound. She was very much taken by this new man in her life. Zara knew it was going to be an interesting evening. She adjusted her red dress one last time and then sneaked her way to the waiting cab which was ready to take her to meet this famous Matt.

*****

Pat had been worried all day about this evening. She was so stupid. Why on earth would she want Matt to meet Zara? Perfect Zara, in her size ten dresses with perfect long blond hair and flawless skin. No man was able to resist her. She knew that. It had never bothered her before, but now it bothered her. Would Matt be taken with Zara? She was nervous. She had practically pushed Zara and Matt to meet each other. She wanted to kick herself for being so stupid. Why had she not thought of this before? Matt would take one look at Zara and he would be instantly spellbound. Who could blame any guy for giving into her perfectly girlish looks? Pat knew she had created competition for herself. It was so silly. Things had been perfect since she had met Matt. And now she had sabotaged her own happiness. So she did the only thing she knew she could do. She dressed to kill.

*****

Zara made her way into the hotel foyer. Finally, she was home. "Uh, there you are," exclaimed Pat; "We were just wondering how much longer you were going to be." Pat gave her friend a quick hug. "Matt has just gone to get some drinks. He'll be back in a second." Zara was still trying to take in her friend's appearance. Gone was the old Pat she knew. Instead, looking back at her was a woman who looked stunning in a long black diamond studded dress that hugged every curve of her slim figure and makeup done to perfection. Zara hardly recognized her. In that instant she was glad she had worn her new red dress. So this was interesting. Pat dolled up to the nines. He must be worth it then, this Matt, for her to go to all this trouble.

"How do I look?" Pat asked as she smoothed her hair one last time.

"Wonderful," Zara replied, and meant it. Pat looked good. Very good.

"Here he comes now," Pat said as she beamed in the opposite direction. Zara turned slowly, unable to get over the complete transformation in Pat.

And then came her second shock. Her tongue stuck to the roof of her mouth. She felt like she could hardly breath. She noticed that she was automatically and unwillingly holding her breath. Slowly, Zara exhaled as the man of Pat's numerous phone calls sauntered over. Zara knew she must be staring at him, open mouthed, but she just could not help it. Okay, yes, Pat had said he was tall, dark and handsome, but she had not taken the words literally. She knew she had been wrong. Oh, so dead wrong. The man, who seemed to be gliding over as if on a cloud, was exactly as Pat had described. Tall, dark and handsome. Very, very handsome. In very aspect possible. As he got closer, Zara noted his shiny dark hair, and his dark, piercing eyes. They were a dark deep blue, like the ocean. It was hard to describe them. *No,* thought Zara. *There was nothing closer. They were definitely the same deep blue of the ocean.* By the time he had made it to their little group, Zara was still fighting for some sort of control over her breathing.

Pat introduced them, smiling from ear to ear, and all Zara could do was smile in return. And smile some more. It was hard to even think with him so near. As he smiled back at her, Zara felt her knees go weak. He had a perfect smile, showing his even faultless white teeth. She knew she was acting like an idiot. *Get yourself together,* Zara reprimanded herself. Throwing a quick glance at Pat, she smiled at her friend. Maybe they had not noticed. It all happened so fast. One minute she was a gawking teenager, and the next minute she found herself seated at the dinner table. What had happened to the time in between? Zara could not remember. Then Matt spoke again and she was lost in his smooth voice.

"So, any idea what you want to eat?" Matt asked as he scanned the menu before him. Zara shook her head and tried to concentrate. She had barely looked at the menu. She was too busy peeking at Matt over the rim. He was gorgeous. She watched him for a few more seconds and then turned to Pat, on her left. Pat, she could see, was deep in thought as she read her menu, trying to decide on what to eat. *How on earth can she concentrate on anything besides Matt?* Zara asked herself.

"I can't decide," replied Pat, smiling up at Matt in adoration. Matt smiled back, and again Zara got lost in his lovely blue eyes.

"What is the choice between?" he asked laughingly. A rich throaty laugh that seemed to reach his eyes.

Zara listed intently. Good, she would have whatever Pat ordered. That would save her from actually having to make a decision. She could then use the remaining time to observe Matt from behind her menu without being noticed.

"Mmmm, the fish in cream and garlic sounds nice, or, the other option, which is the grilled lamb in red current sauce."

Zara's head popped up sharply. Who on earth would consider eating garlic or even fish on a dinner date? Especially with someone like Matt around. Was Pat losing her senses? Zara decided she would have the lamb. It was the safe option. There, her decision was made for her. Lamb it was.

"The fish with cream and garlic sound good," Matt stated. "Why don't you have that?"

Pat smiled at him over the table. "Okay, the fish it is," she announced. "Zara, have you decided what you're having?"

Zara looked from Pat to Matt, although she saved the most alluring look for Matt.

"I think I'll have the lamb," she replied in the sweetest voice she could muster.

Pat smiled again, but underneath she was furious. She had brought Zara here to meet Matt and here she was openly flirting with him. She should have known. And with her sitting right there at the table. How could she do that? Pat was not stupid. She had seen the sly looks Zara had been throwing Matt's way since she had arrived. And now, *pretending* to look at the menu, but Pat knew Zara had barely glanced at the menu since they had sat down. She was too busy sassing him out over the rim. Oh yes, she was trying to be discreet, but Zara seemed to forget they had been friends for years. She knew Zara's tactics. And that sweet little laugh she made whenever he said something, that was also beginning to irritate her. Unable to take it any longer, Pat raised from her seat abruptly. "I'm going to the ladies," she said.

Matt stood up, as he waited for her to leave, always the perfect gentleman. Pat looked at Zara, who remained firmly in her seat. She had expected Zara to come with her to the bathroom. They always went to the bathroom together. It was the golden rule. One they had lived by since they were little girls. Instead, here was Zara, nodding in her direction, but with no intention of actually joining her.

Pat walked to the bathroom with a fake smiled plastered onto her face. She would not let it show, she told herself. Zara was acting just as she should have known Zara would act. Pat looked at herself in the mirror and she knew she looked good.

Every effort had gone into getting dressed that evening. She knew that she had to shine one-hundred percent and shine brighter than Zara. She did not want Matt's attention anywhere but on her. Luckily, to Matt's credit, he had been the perfect gentleman, as he usually was, and was paying no attention to Zara's outlandish and obvious flirting attempts. For that, at least, she was grateful. She did not have any problem with Matt, but she did have a problem with Zara's behaviour. And knowing Zara, it was only going to get worse as the evening progressed.

She applied a dash of lipstick to her lips and smoothed her dress. She was set. She would go back to the table and pretend as if she was having a fabulous time.

As she opened her door leading back into the restaurant, Pat stopped short. Her eyes seemed to be rooted to their table. Zara was leaning slightly forward toward Matt, her arms resting delicately in front of her. She was all smiles and gazed adoringly into Mart eyes as if she had known him her entire life. Pat was unable to move. Unable to do anything but stand and stare as her friend tried to make a move on her new man. Pat took in Matt and his handsome smile. She looked at Zara through his eyes. Any man's eyes. Before him was one of the most beautiful girl he would ever meet. Long blond hair draped gently on her shoulders. The glow of the candlelight giving her eyes an extra sparkle. And then there was the dress she was wearing. It seemed to fit snugly against every inch of curve she possessed.

For an instant Pat hated Zara. She had everything. And, as if that was not enough, she now wanted Matt too. It was all there, you just had to read the signs.

As she approached the table, Pat was sure that Matt himself leaned a little closer toward Zara. She saw the smile and the little dimple on his cheek she had come to adore. As she got nearer, she made a firm resolve. She would not let them know she had observed their little moment. She would act completely oblivious and try her best to woo Matt as she had before.

* * * * *

Zara knew she was just around the corner from the hostel. The cab drive back seemed very short tonight. She lifted the small red rose in her hand and sniffed it deeply. It had a sweet delicate smell that enveloped her immediately. It had been the prefect evening. She had no idea that Pat's friend would prove so charming. Or so handsome. She had been barely able to taste the lamb she was eating. She had trouble swallowing, so she was glad for the bottle of water that was on the table. She knew she should not stare as she did, but she was unable not to. Matt was the most handsome, sweet man she had ever met. And she loved it when she was able to make him laugh. It was one of the nicest sounds she had ever heard.

A florist had come around with roses halfway through dinner and Matt had pleased them both by buying them each one. Zara sniffed it again and it immediately bought her back to her memories of the previous week with Raymond. She had hoped that he was going to bring her flowers or a present of some kind. Just a small token to show that he had missed her. But no, there had been nothing. She knew she should be feeling a little guilty for liking Matt so much, but she did not. Matt was a dream. One she could very easily get used to.

* * * * *

The good feeling had continued until she finally made it to bed and right into the morning. She woke up early and felt alive and full of energy. Each time she looked at the red rose, the good feeling came flooding back. Bigger and bigger, until she thought she might explode.

Unable to hide her happiness and stay in bed, Zara dressed quickly and made her way to the cafeteria. Even the weak coffee was not able to bring down her good spirits. It was then that she decided to ring her parents. She looked at her wristwatch, the diamonds beaming proudly. Seven a.m. at home. Yes, her father would be up and about, probably downstairs eating his breakfast.

Half an hour later, Zara took another sip of her coffee, surprised to find it cold. How long had she been on the phone with her parents? She looked at her watch again. Half an hour. She let out a small giggle. She had been unable to stop herself from talking. She had spoken to her father about the dance routine, dinner with Pat, her weekend with Raymond, and all the while aware of the deep glow she felt inside the pit of her stomach. She had even mentioned the news that Helen had announced the day before. One main dancer in a solo piece. Someone to lead the procession. Her father had been ecstatic. Had yelled for her mother to come to the phone. It was only after she put down the phone that she realized why they had been so thrilled. They actually thought she might get it. Zara rose to get herself another coffee. As she stirred in a sugar, she thought about this. If she were chosen, her father would be even happier with her. She could use that. Later on. She would have to think of more things she wanted out of this. Bigger, better and more expensive. Even with her father's new aspirations for her, she had not managed to lose her high, emphatic feeling. Today everything would be wonderful. She only had to look at the red rose and knew it would be so.

Chapter 34

Jane knew she only had a few hours. But she wanted to rehearse the steps a few more times before she had to leave. She pushed play on the button of the small radio, and the familiar music floated up into the air. She stood in front of the mirror and watched each step that she danced. She surveyed her kicks. Maybe she should kick slightly to the left a little more she thought. Twist and turn. She must remember to hold her arms more loosely too. Turn and leap. Okay, that looked good, she told herself. That was how the last few remaining hours flew by, with her analysing each movement she made.

She continued to watch her reflection in the mirror each time she did a step. It helped to see what she needed to work on. She had the correct posture and she had the turns mastered to perfection. She knew that everything looked much better. And the more she practised, the better she would become. Jane looked at the big white clock on the wall. She had time to run through it all one last time, and then really she had to be going.

Now as she sat in the car, on her way to the airport, Jane continued to go over the steps from that morning in her mind. She was only going home for the weekend, but knew that even those two days could find her behind if she did not continue her practices. As they rounded the last corner, Jane noticed how strange it felt to be leaving the hostel. After living there for over a month, they had adjusted to the routine and had gotten used to the workouts that they were put through each day. Jane knew it sounded unrealistic, but she could actually feel her endurance levels lasting longer. Things just seemed to get better and better with all the training they were given. She had also been thrilled to learn that there was that main lead position open. She had gone to bed that night and it was all she had thought off. To her, that would be the ultimate dream. Imagine her, chosen to lead the procession at the World Games. And with hard work and practice, it might be within her grasp.

The flight had been non eventful, the same as before. She had enjoyed her lunch, although the excitement of seeing her parents again had prevented her from eating very much. Now, as she made her way through the arrival gates, she saw them straight away. They were standing in a line to her left. She had barely made it out the barriers and they had come running. Her mother was the first to grab her in a big bear hug as her father ruffled her hair affectionately.

"I'm so glad you're back," breathed her mother, hugging her even harder. Jane knew she was crying. Crying and laughing at the same time.

"Me too," she whispered back. She had missed them terribly. Even Jo her brother was there for the homecoming. She received a hug from him too, much to her surprise.

They gave her an hour to settle back into her old room, and then the questions began. "What was it like?" they asked. "Was Helen there also? Did she like the food and was she eating her vegetables?" asked her mother.

Jane answered all their questions and painted them a wonderful picture of what life was like inside the hostel.

*****

Zara, too, was enjoying a festive welcome from her parents. They had met her at the airport in the family limousine and had been fussing over her ever since her arrival. Zara was enjoying every minute of being the centre of attention. She could not wait to get back home and enjoy some of the luxury she had been missing out on. There'd be no lumpy hostel bed, and no sharing of her bedroom. She was going to lap it all up. It was going to be a wonderful weekend.

Zara brushed her hair one last time knowing they were due to leave for the restaurant shortly. Her father had arranged a cozy dinner for them that evening at one of her favourite restaurants. She already knew what she would have since they had been going there since she was a little girl. She loved the place. Zara retrieved her handbag, and headed downstairs, eagerly.

As she descended the stairs, she heard her father's voice. He was talking to someone. "Yes, sir, just closed the deal."

Zara entered the room and her first sight was of Raymond seated comfortably in one of their large comfortable sofas. She was shocked. Why on earth had her parents invited Raymond along to their cozy family dinner? Irritated, although not wanting it to show it, Zara walked up to her father and kissed him on the cheek, while he beamed up toward her. "Hello, Raymond," she said evenly.

Raymond smiled back and leaped up to give her a kiss on her other cheek. Zara could not help comparing him to Matt and was annoyed that he had been asked to join them. "I've got something for you," he replied as he winked at her father. From behind the chair, he produced a huge bouquet of rare blue roses. Zara smiled and accepted them, although aware that this display of affection was for her father's benefit and not hers. She was even more annoyed.

"They're beautiful," she replied, knowing that it was the right response. "I'll just get Rose to put them in a vase for me." Zara disappeared into the kitchen, dragging the flowers upside down behind her. A few days ago, these flowers, she knew, would have thrilled her. Today, all she could think of was a single red rose laying out to dry upstairs in her bedroom.

As soon as she left the lounge she heard Raymond continue with the conversation that he had been having with her father. It was as if she had never entered the room.

Rose was nowhere to be seen, so Zara left the flowers in the sink with some tap water. When she reentered the lounge, her mother was present and everyone was ready to leave for the restaurant.

Zara sat at the beautifully dressed table next to Raymond, as was appropriate. Since she was a little girl she had loved coming to this restaurant. The food was excellent, and she always had a good time when she came. It was clear as they ate their starters that tonight's dinner would be an exception. From the moment they had sat down Raymond had monopolized the conversation. Zara was annoyed. This was her homecoming dinner and Raymond could talk of nothing else besides profits and losses and the new deal he had just closed. Her father looked mildly interested, but her mother looked as bored as she herself felt. She stared hard at Raymond. Why had she never noticed how boring he was before? She let her mind wander, and slowly Matt's handsome face began to drift into focus. Gorgeous, sweet Matt with his dreamy blue eyes. She still got that deep warm glow inside her stomach whenever she thought of him. She stared at Raymond again, but did not see him. She saw Mark. He smiled at her, and she smiled back. That one simple movement and her heart seemed to do flip-flops. Then he took her hand and held it across the table. His touch was electrifying. Zara felt like she was in Heaven. It was impossible to ignore that devoutly handsome face. And then, just as suddenly, she was jolted back to reality as Raymond began to speak. She looked down at her hand then, appalled to see it was Raymond's. The shock made her jump. She excused herself hastily and went to the bathroom to recover.

She came back to the dinner table and sat down as if nothing had happened. As she expected, Raymond was still gabbling about work. She was now very annoyed. She waited for her opportunity. When Raymond next took a sip of his red wine, she jumped in and changed the subject. It was abrupt, but it worked. Her mother soon joined into the conversation and finally they began to talk of other, more interesting things. Raymond, however, did not join into the new conversation. He sat quietly in his seat and acted as if he was sulking. Zara completely ignored him.

*****

Jane had been gone for a few weeks and she could not believe all the news she had to catch up on when she arrived back home. They ate an early dinner, and by eight o'clock she found she was exhausted. She excused herself, took a quick hot shower and crept back into her comfortable bed. Her head had barely hit the pillow and she was fast asleep.

When she woke, the old familiar feeling was there. The sun was shining brightly onto her bed and it promised to be a beautiful day. She was glad she had an early night because now she felt fresh and alive and excited for the day ahead. She opened her window and breathed in the fresh air. As she turned back toward her bed, she sniffed. The familiar smell of warm croissants filling the air. Fresh out the oven. It was a comforting smell, one she had grown up with. She jumped back onto her bed and dove back under the covers. A few more minutes to lie in and then she would make her way downstairs. She rolled over onto her side and looked out the window as she went over all she had to do that day. The minutes seemed to tick by and she was unable to ignore the heavenly breakfast smells wafting up to her room. Giving in, she yawned. She'd better get up, there was a lot to do today.

The kitchen was a hive of activity. The fact that it was only eight o'clock in the morning made no difference. Jane pushed open the kitchen door and there sat her father in his usual chair, coffee cup in hand, paper spread on the table. Mum in her usual position behind the stove, retrieving the croissants. Jo, as expected, with his face in the fridge. She wandered over and gave both her parents a peck on the cheek.

"Morning," her mother said brightly.

"Morning, precious," replied her father as he took another sip of his coffee. "You sleep well?"

"Like a dream," Jane replied.

A car tooted from somewhere outside. Her mum jumped. "That's Sam! Jo, are you ready?" as asked as she retrieved a coat and rucksack from the chair next to her.

"Yes, I'm ready," he replied as he stuffed a bag of crisps and an apple juice into his rucksack. "Bye!" he shouted as he ran out the back door.

"Playing football today," said her mother, as if in explanation.

That morning she enjoyed a relaxed breakfast with her parents. Over her second glass of orange juice, she told them more details of her life at the hostel and how much she was enjoying the unique experience. Once breakfast was finished, she went upstairs to get dressed. She wanted to go to Michelangelo's. She wanted to drop by and see Mr. Ken, who had been so kind to her, and more importantly, she wanted to see Peter. But she was nervous. She could not help it. Would things be different between them? She had missed him so much, and hoped he felt the same. They had been writing to each other, but that was not quite the same and she hoped that when she saw him their feelings for each other would not have changed.

Chapter 35

Zara woke up lazily and yawned. It was so nice to wake up in her own bed. The familiar feeling swept over her like a thick snug, blanket. She had never before noticed how fluffy her duvet was or how cozy her bedroom. It was so nice to be back home. She would never have thought she would miss it this much. She turned inside the warm covers. The clock on her night stand proudly displaying that it was in fact nine o'clock. Zara closed her eyes again and enjoyed her rare lie in. At the hostel she was up and dressed by nine o'clock, breakfast had already been eaten and she was ready to begin her first session for the day. She did not miss it one bit.

She made a point of deliberately not getting out of bed, and just laying under her covers, looking out the window at the leaves on the trees, almost ready to fall to the ground. Then she sat and listened to the variety of birds singing in the morning sunshine. Finally at ten o'clock, when she could no longer deny that she was awake, she sat up and stretched deeply. Ten o'clock was a decent time to make her way downstairs. It felt nice to enjoy the small treasure of finally doing nothing and breaking the set routine she had been forced into. Zara breathed in deeply and sighed as the rich aroma of strong coffee wafted upstairs. It was almost as if the aroma was deliberately teasing her nostrils. Unable to resist the smell, she pulled back her covers and stepped into her dressing gown before heading down the marble steps and into the dining room.

It was such a comforting, familiar scene. Again, one she had not realized she would miss. There was Rose, glad in her familiar black and white uniform, serving a cup of coffee for her father. Her father sitting in his favorite chair, ready to begin a full meal of bacon and eggs.

"Morning, sweetness," her father said as he added some salt to his eggs.

Zara walked over and planted a delicate kiss on his cheek. "Morning, Dad."

"Good morning, miss. Nice to have you back. May I get you anything to eat or drink?" Rose asked in her usual polite manner.

Zara nodded lazily, "Just coffee please." While Rose poured the strong liquid into her cup, Zara slid into one of the seats next to her father. "Where's Mom?" she asked, as Rose placed the cup before her.

Her father was about to answer, when her mother swept through the doorway. "I'm here," she sang. She walked delicately over to the table and hugged her daughter. "You sleep okay?"

Zara nodded between sips of steaming coffee, "Like a dream," she replied. And she meant it. She really had no idea she would miss home so much.

Breakfast had always been a grand affair at their house. "You must start the day on a good meal," she would hear her mother say every morning. "You cannot expect to function properly without good brain food." Since she was little it had become a family habit to meet in the dining room for the much needed nourishment required to face the day ahead.

Rose had surprised her and made her favourite meal. Pancakes. That, accompanied with more strong coffee, had made her feel like she had given the day the good start that it deserved.

By the time breakfast was over, Zara was stuffed. She had eaten one too many of the delicious pancakes. They had just been so delectable that she could not help herself. She walked slowly up the staircase to her bedroom and pushed open her door. She stood at the entrance and took it all in. It was now clean and tidy. Her bed had also been neatly made by one of the maids while she had been downstairs enjoying her breakfast. It was one of the many luxuries she had taken for granted and forgotten. The room had been sprayed with something too. Rose oil maybe? She wished for the millionth time that she did not have to go back to the hostel. Life over there in Germany was a million miles away from what she enjoyed here at home. Silly little things that she had never noticed before became apparent. Things like decent coffee. She had gotten so used to the weak instant coffee they had served in the canteen every morning, that she had actually begun to get used to it. Now, back in the comfort of her own home, she had been reminded exactly how proper coffee should be made and how it should taste. Smooth and rich.

Zara walked inside her bedroom and headed straight for her cupboard. She threw open the doors, and before her, hung an array of clothes, the mixed blend of colours jumping out at her as each outfit begged to be worn. Zara laughed. It was so nice to actually see all her clothes on hangers. Until today, she had been practically living out of her suitcases, which were still stuck under her hostel bed.

Thirty minutes later, when her mother popped her head around the door, Zara could be seen tapping her foot to the music that pumped joyfully out of her stereo. She had dressed casually, already having decided that she wanted a casual, relaxing weekend. Nothing too serious. She just wanted to stay indoors and enjoy being pampered at home. Zara contemplated this. Never before had she realized that living at home was being pampered. She relished the thought. Life at the hostel had really opened her eyes. For the first time in her life she was glad her father was rich. Very, very rich. It could only be used for good. Her good.

She skipped down the staircase and headed for the garage and her little red sports car. She had missed driving it over the last few weeks. It was time to take it out for a much needed spin. Zara heard her father's voice booming in the quiet foyer. She rounded the corner, but did not see him. *He must be in his office,* she thought. The door was closed but in the silence, she could hear everything he was saying. *Business, all business* she thought uninterested as she turned away, in the direction of her car.

"Zara MUST get the lead," he stressed. At the mention of her name, Zara stopped short and her ears pricked up. What on earth was he talking about? "I don't care," came his strong reply. "She must get that lead role being offered. She has been working so hard. I would hate for her to get this close and not get it. She would be devastated." There was more silence for a while as her father listened to the voice on the other end. Zara did not move.

"We could sponsor them with more money. Money always has a way of helping decisions," he suggested. More silence followed. Zara knew she should not be listening, but she was unable to draw herself away. She was rooted to the spot, eager to hear as much as possible. "Okay then. I'll leave it with you to arrange. And Louise, be generous. This is my Zara we are talking about. Do whatever it takes," came her father's confident reply.

Chapter 36

Jane and Sarah had eaten breakfast and were making their way to the training rooms. The weekend had been great, but now it was over and they were back to their usual routine. Jane had not forgotten her promise to herself. She had practised whenever she could over the weekend, determined to better her movements. She had faith that, with practice and hard work, she would have a good chance in getting the lead role. Just thinking about it made her excited. Her parents had been very understanding when she locked herself away in her room for a few hours in the morning, and then a few more, later in the evening. They knew there was no break for those who wanted to succeed.

As they pushed open the door that led to the training rooms, Jane was not surprised to find that the entrance to the training room was already buzzing with excitement. All the girls were eager to hear what everyone else had gotten up to over the weekend. There was loads of news to be caught up on, as they stood in the large hall. Jane headed straight for the door and tried to open it. Unlike before, the training room was locked. That was strange, but everyone was far too busy chatting to pay it any further notice, including her.

They also waited longer than usual for any of the instructors to turn up for the class due. This was also highly irregular, but again, the girls were far too busy catching up with one another and were not in the least bit worried over the wait.

They were all surprised when much later, all four instructors arrived together. That had never happened before. Now, the girls started paying more attention. Things were not happening in their usual manner. Helen, as usual, was taking the lead, followed by Paula and Velicity, and lastly, there was James. Helen unlocked the door in solemn silence, and everyone filed in behind them.

There was an weird silence hanging over the room. The buzz and excitement of the weekend quickly died down. The previous banter that had been present only minutes before disappeared amazingly fast. Something was definitely up.

Jane followed the crowd of girls into the familiar training room. Immediately everyone noticed the twenty-eight hangers neatly displayed on hooks at the far side of the room. All the hangers were covered in thin, black sheets, hiding something. They were not given time to guess what lay hidden.

Helen spoke almost straight away, "As some of you may have noticed we have some hangers at the front of the hall." Some of the girls nodded in answer, their eyes never leaving the hangers on display. Everyone in the room was dying to know what they contained. "Well," she prompted, "these are your costumes for the show. They were flown in from India yesterday."

At first, the hall was deadly silent as Helen's news sank in. No one had expected the costumes to arrive this early. Normally, costumes only arrived a few days before a show. As the news began to sink into the girls, the hall changed from a stony silence into a happy thunder.

Helen let the excited buzzing continue for a few seconds, then strove for everyone's attention again. When she spoke, she was unable to hide her own excitement. This was an extraordinary surprise and meant they were well ahead of schedule.

"Each hanger has a name. As you may remember, when you first arrived we took all your measurements and sizes. All the costumes should fit perfectly, but for any of you who do have a problem, we will be getting a seamstress in tomorrow morning. She can help with any small glitches, although we don't foresee any major problems." Helen knew the girls were itching to get a closer look at their costumes, so continued quickly. "This is what we are going to do. I will be calling out each of your names and with it a number. That will be the number of your hanger. Do not, I repeat, Do not, get your numbers mixed up with anyone else. Each costume has been made exactly to your measurements. If you swap numbers, you will end up with the incorrect costume." All the girls nodded.

One by one Helen called the names on her list.

Jane's name was called almost immediately. She was number nine. She approached her hanger eagerly and tried to look inside the thin, black sheet. All she could see was blackness within.

Without waiting for anyone else, she gently took off the black protective cover, aware that she had to be gentle. It took great restraint though for her not to rip the covers off wildly. She was desperate to see what the package held. Jane compared it to Christmas, when she was desperate to get into the colourful wrapping paper and see what the present was. She was always wary, just in case it was something delicate or breakable. Each year she was crossed with the same dilemma and ended up patiently peeling the wrapping paper, being far more careful than necessary. Jane felt just like she did on Christmas day and knew she had to be careful.

She peeled the sheet back carefully until the plastic fell away. Piece by piece it come off, until finally, she was delivered her first real look at her costume. There before her, was the most beautiful costume she had ever seen.

Helen had decided that she was to be red. The red costume was a deep, rich colour and perfect for her skin colouring. Jane held the costume up against her body. Helen had been correct. The costume looked exactly the correct size. She checked the length too and it seemed a perfect fit. She was not sure how long she twisted and turned in front of the mirror admiring her new costume, but all of a sudden, Jane was aware of the others around her. Everyone else also had their costumes at the ready. "Okay, now that you all have your costumes, you will be allowed thirty minutes to go back to your bedrooms to try them on." Helen had not even been allowed to finish her sentence, as some of the girls were already darting for the door. "Make sure you come back wearing them," Helen sang behind them. "I need to take a look for myself."

Jane looked at the red costume in her hand and was thrilled with it. She had been so taken with her own costume, that she had only just noticed that not everyone's was red like hers. Some of the girls were holding canary yellow outfits and others had a dark ocean blue. Jane had no idea that three such dramatic, varied colours could look so contrasting next to each other.

In the excitement of uncovering their sheets, Jane had lost sight of Sarah. Now she was dying to find her friend and see what colour she was. She looked over the heads of the other girls, but Sarah was nowhere to be seen. The stairs were busy. Everyone was trying to get back to their bedrooms to try on their costume. It was then that she saw Sarah a few feet ahead of her. She squeezed through the other girls, calling, "Excuse me. Coming through." She came up along side Sarah, breathless from her running.

"What colour did you get?" Sarah asked excitedly. Jane held up her hanger in answer. The blazing red color, beaming proudly. "That's gorgeous," Sarah responded. "Mine's blue. Isn't it beautiful?" she asked. Sarah was right. The blue costume was also amazing.

When they pushed open their bedroom door they were greeted by Karen who was already inside. She must have been the first to arrive as she was already dressed in her new outfit. Her costume was also blue, the same as Sarah's and she looked incredible in it. "You look lovely," they both gushed at the same time. Karen smiled, pleased at the compliment. She had liked her colour immediately and it was a perfect fit, just as Helen had predicted. Karen surveyed herself in the mirror, turning first left and then right. Yes, it was prefect, in every way.

"Where's Sue?" asked Jane, as she looked around, noticing their other friend was missing. No one knew where she had disappeared to.

Jane and Sarah both slipped into their outfits and were pleased. They were a perfect fit. Not too long at the ankles and not too tight either. Jane loved the red colour even more than before. It suited her perfectly and brought out the brightness of her eyes. She eyed her legs and her bottom. Sometimes costumes had the tendency to make you look fatter than you actually were, as they hugged every curve of the body, but in this case, it did not. She looked trim, so she was pleased.

Sue only appeared some time later and it was immediately obvious that something was wrong. "This is awful!" she croaked in despair as she came inside.

"What is it?" Sarah asked, concerned.

Sue held up her costume in answer and it all became clear. She had been one of the unlucky girls who had been chosen to wear the canary yellow outfits. Jane looked at it and tried not to cringe. It was bright. Not a bad colour when next to the red and blue, but on its own it was not attractive at all. There was no denying that fact.

"It's not that bad," sympathized Sarah as she tried to make light of the situation.

"Not that bad! Not that bad!" Sue shouted almost hysterically. "Can't you see it's yellow?" she moaned, now almost close to tears. "Not even a nice yellow. A horrible ugly canary yellow. It's disgusting. I DO NOT want to be seen wearing that on television," she cried out, then crumpled onto her bed, her head in her hands.

Everyone forgot about their own costumes and tried to make Sue feel better. Nothing anyone said had any effect. She was devastated. She knew she had been chosen to wear yellow, so yellow she would have to stay.

They were all dressed in their new outfits, waiting for Sue to change herself, but she made no attempt to move off her bed. Instead she clutched the yellow garment tightly, an unhappy look fixed firmly on her face. "I don't want to put it on," she moaned. "It's awful. I hate it."

It was only after gentle coaxing by all three of them, that Sue finally agreed to give the costume a try. It took awhile, but finally she relented. They all watched in apprehension, as Sue went into the bathroom and closed the door behind her.

Jane, Sarah and Karen all sat on the edge of the bed waiting for Sue to emerge from the bathroom. It had been a tense few minutes and they were overdue downstairs in the studio. Helen was bound to be waiting and wondering what the hold up was. "What's taking her so long?" asked Karen, looking at her watch for the third time in the last five minutes.

"I don't know," Jane replied.

Sarah walked over to the bathroom, and knocked gently on the door. "Sue. You okay in there?" she asked gently. There was silence on the other end. They all waited a few more seconds. No response. When it was clear that Sue still had no intention of answering, Sarah knocked again. "Sue, are you all right?" she asked more forcefully.

The bathroom door was yanked open. Sarah jumped back. There stood Sue, still dressed in her same clothes as before. The yellow unitard was nowhere in sight. "No, I'm not okay!" she shouted in response.

"What's wrong?" Karen asked, as she jumped off the bed.

Sue was silent for a long while. Then she answered. "It's see-thru," explained Sue in almost a whisper.

"See-thru?"

"YES!" They were all silent again as they let the horrific words sink in. "I am NOT going downstairs in that," Sue said with more venom.

Karen walked into the bathroom and grabbed the offending yellow costume lying on the floor. "How see-thru?" she asked lifting it up and studying it in the light.

Sue gave her a hard stare. "VERY see-thru," she replied in a flat tone. All four girls stared at the costume. True enough, they could see right through the garment. Finally, Jane spoke, "You'll just have to tell Helen. She *will* understand," Jane said, patting her friend on the shoulder. "It'll be okay. You'll see." Sue nodded as they headed for the door, but she did not feel any better. Not only was she given the ugliest colour around, she was also given something that was totally impractical and totally unwearable.

When they headed downstairs, almost all the girls present were dressed in either the red or the blue outfits. A few of the girls had attempted to wear the yellow unitards, but they had opted to cover up with T-shirts and shorts. The rest had come down refusing to change. Like Sue, they had refused to wear the yellow outfit as it was far too revealing. They were the ones who looked worried and unhappy. What was Helen going to say? And more importantly, what was she going to do about this massive problem? Their colour was a disaster.

It took Helen only a few seconds to notice that hardly any yellow costumes found their way downstairs, then even less seconds to find out what the problem was. "Girls. Girls. It's okay. We will get the yellow unitards lined. It will be fine, don't worry. All of you with yellow costumes, please hang them back on your numbered hangers and leave them on that chair over there," Helen replied, taking charge of the situation and smiling reassuringly at the worried girls "It's going to be fine," she repeated. Her soft words seemed to calm the near hysterical girls. There were even a few smiles as they breathed a sigh in relief. Helen would solve this problem. "Now, let us take a look at the rest of you." Each girl was surveyed in detail by the instructors. By the end of the inspection, they all agreed that the costumes fit well, and there was no need for the seamstress the following morning. Helen then spent the next hour talking to the girls, reassuring them that they looked great and that for those in yellow, all was going to be fine. She would make a few phone calls, and the problem was going to be sorted out. She then urged the girls to change, have some lunch and then meet Velicity in the hall, ready for their afternoon practice.

By the time Helen found herself back in her office, she was exhausted. This cannot be happening, she told herself as she slumped into the chair next to her desk. What on earth would they do now? Yes, she had suggested getting the costumes lined, but would that actually work? She had no idea.

Helen sat at her desk and thought hard. If that was not successful, then there would be no other choice but to change the yellow costumes to some other colour. Maybe green, or lilac. Helen knew that meant more valuable time would be wasted as the new costumes were prepared. And time was something they did not have. It was a luxury. She had been thrilled to learn that they were ahead of schedule, but now it seemed that this knock back would render them behind. She was annoyed. Why had no one thought of this potential problem before? she asked herself, irritated. It must be a very common problem in the dancing world. Taking a deep breath, Helen made her way back to the training rooms for round two. She knew she had to appear as normal as possible. If the girls knew she was in a panic, then they would also be in a panic. And that she knew, was the worst thing that could possibly happen. People did all sorts of silly things when they were in panic.

Over the course of the next two weeks, Helen was very busy and had many difficult tasks to deal with and then resolve. All sorts of problems were popping up as the deadline loomed closer and closer. She was mighty glad that she had vast experience in this kind of event coordination, so was able to deal with each problem head on. So far, so good. Her first major problem had been the yellow costumes. It had taken some persuasion on her part to get the design company to double up on the lining in less than two weeks. She had originally wanted the costumes back in one week, but they had refused and wanted another whole month to complete the task. For Helen that just would not do. After many hours of negotiation, and a large cheque in the post, they had finally agreed on a two-week deadline. That had now almost ended, tomorrow in fact, and all the lined costumes were due back at the hostel again. The shop had telephoned and confirmed that the manager himself would be dropping off the revised costumes. She hoped and prayed that when the costumes arrived, they would be fixed and it would be the end of this messy problem—it would be one less thing to worry about.

Then, there was the other urgent matter of who should be chosen to lead the dance procession on the big night. That was going to be one of the most difficult tasks at hand. She had been watching the girls over the last few weeks, and after much deliberation, she had made up her mind. She needed someone who was dedicated. Someone who really wanted this position. Someone who would welcome the extra work. And it was going to be hard. There would be many late classes running well into the night. And extra workouts too, sometimes interrupting the weekends. It would mean that while the others were enjoying their weekends in town, the chosen candidate would be hard at work, on her own, in the studio, practising. It was going to be tough. With only a few weeks to go, they needed someone who was totally dedicated to the cause. And no one's name seemed to pop into her mind more often than Jane Brown's did.

Helen had been watching all the girls like a hawk and she was confident that Jane was the best choice for the entire group. She was a strong dancer, but she also worked hard and was happy to exploit herself and use her talents to the utmost. She was good, better than most, but still she practised and practised until she had mastered the steps to their fullest degree. Helen had noticed her determination and admired her dedication. Yes, Jane was by far the best choice and Helen knew she could be counted on to perform to the best of her ability. All the girls chosen were dedicated dancers, but there were a select few in the class that had the unique hunger and drive that set them apart. She was pleased to say that Jane was one of those girls. She would make an excellent lead. Tomorrow, she decided, she would announce her decision to the girls.

With two major problems resolved Helen felt better and got to work on the list of smaller, less urgent problems, but which still needed her attention.

After three hours of even more phone calls, she had managed to resolve almost every issue at hand. She laid her pen down and stretched. That was it for today. She had done well and was pleased with what she had accomplished. All she now needed was to have the costumes delivered and make her announcement to the girls and everything would be up to date. It was a good feeling. She walked around her office doing the last of the filing, with a light spring in her step. She packed away all her important documents, and was just about to leave her office when the telephone rang. *Who could that be?* she asked herself, as she headed back toward her desk and answered the ringing telephone.

An full hour later, Helen made her way warily up the stairs to her quarters. She unlocked her bedroom door and went straight to the mini-bar. She poured herself a stiff vodka, and sat down on her comfortable sofa. She was still registering shock over the phone conversation she had just finished with Bob, the superintendent and main organizer for the World Games. They had been working together for years now and shared an easygoing relationship. This was mainly due to them both understanding the demands of each other's position. The conversation that had followed had been a complete surprise and an unwelcome shock. She took another sip of her drink. Never, in all her career, had she ever been forced to go back on a decision she had already made.

In no uncertain terms, she had been told that Zara Maddox *had* to be chosen for the lead role. No buts, ands, or maybes. Zara had to be chosen.

When she had asked why, Bob had told her that if they did not, then they would cease to continue receiving their sponsorship funds. Helen knew that they depended heavily on these funds and without them, there was no chance of being involved in the games. Their involvement would fizzle out as soon as the funds were pulled. She had seen the figures once before and it had been thousands and thousands of Euros. All the fuss could only mean that the person involved was their biggest sponsor. And for the Bob to actually have to ring her, could only mean that the men involved were very important.

Helen was not happy at having her arm forced and an important decision being made for her. She made this known, but there seemed to be no other alternative. For a brief second, she allowed herself to think of poor Jane. Poor Jane, who would never ever know just how close she had came. Helen felt guilty. Zara was not her first choice, and for Jane this was an unfair decision. Jane deserved this lead role more that anyone else in that class.

Helen finished her vodka and poured herself a second glass. She took another sip. Her first choice had been shoved under the carpet and the decision made for her. She had no other alternative. She had to announce that Zara was the lead, which annoyed her. Helen thought back to all the classes during the last few weeks. Zara was okay, certainly a talented dancer, she would not be here otherwise, but she lacked that extra zoom and power that Jane seemed to posses in bundles. Jane would have been SO much better for the role. Helen supposed it could have been worse. She could have been forced to take someone with completely no talent at all. At least Zara could dance and they had enough time to train her thoroughly. She just hoped that Zara was fully prepared for this. The next few weeks were going to be very tough and she did not want to hear any of the nagging and moaning that she was always hearing from Zara. She was not as good as Jane, so she would just have to work doubly hard.

* * * * *

Helen stood before the class. They all knew why she was there. Making this announcement was going to be hard. She looked around the room before her and saw Jane, and not for the first time, felt a stab of guilt. Then, she looked at Zara. Zara who was going to get exactly what she wanted out of default. She sat in her chair, beaming from ear to ear. Helen was suspicious. *Did she know already?* Helen shook her head in answer. *No. There was no way she could possibly know! Her father gave strict instructions that Zara was never to find out.* It was a secret that she would have to take with her, to the grave. She had been surprised when Bob had said to her, "Zara must think that she was chosen on her own. Over and above everyone else." Helen wondered what it must be like to live that kind of a life. Where you did not have to work for anything. It was all given to you on a silver platter. Whether you knew about it or not. And then, there were those that really *did* deserve it and who really *did* work for it. They were the poor ones that were always pushed one person behind, in the ever increasing queue. In this case, Jane would be that unlucky person. She was the one who would miss out, and there were no second places.

Helen pushed the guilt as far away as she could. She was here to do a job. This had never happened in her career before, but she knew she had to deal with it and continue. She had no other choice. She would announce Zara's name as if it had always been her first choice, and then they would work together on giving the most brilliant performance anyone had ever seen.

Helen held up her hand, and as if by magic, the hall quieted. "As you know, I have been watching all of you over the last two weeks. I have now made my decision on who will lead the procession." The hall was silent. "I would like to make it clear that this was a very difficult task. You have all improved so much during the last few a weeks, and I can see a remarkable improvement in all your dancing. By choosing this person, it does not in any way mean we have not noticed you." There were some nods. No one spoke. No one dared breathe. The silence seemed to last for an age and Jane actually had to force herself to breathe. Helen made her announcement. "I have chosen Zara Maddox for the role."

Zara dropped her dancing shoes onto the floor in pretend shock. YES! Finally! Finally, she had been chosen. It had been confirmed in front of everyone. She, Zara, had won. And over and above all the other girls present. She was then taken into an armful of hugs and kisses, as the girls around her proceeded to congratulate her. She smiled proudly at them all. Yes! She had done it! She was the chosen one!

"Well done," cried one girl.

"Congratulations!" shouted another. She hugged and kissed everyone as if her life depended on it. It all seemed too good to be true. She had hoped that Daddy's phone call would swing things in her favour, but until this very minute it had not been a certainty. And she dared not ask anyone who might actually know the answer. This was her secret and she was not going to tell anyone. So, when her name was announced, she acted as surprised as possible. She knew she had done a good job of acting shocked, as she had been practising it in front of the mirror. No one knew that she knew what was going on. It was a perfect weapon. She wondered who Helen really would have chosen, if Daddy had not stepped in and come through trumps. She only let herself dwell on this for a second and then continued to bask in everyone's kisses and well wishes. Who cared anyway? All that mattered was that she was chosen. She was going to be the lead.

Jane had also almost dropped her shoes, not in happiness, but in complete shock. As soon as Zara's name had been called, she had been rooted to the spot in absolute dismay. Zara? Zara Maddox? The same Zara who complained about absolutely everything? The Zara who did not want to stay at the hostel with the other girls and who made life a misery for all those who did? The same Zara who was continuously breaking the rules and who sneaked out almost every night? It was impossible to believe. Jane looked on at the other girls swarming around her, bestowing hugs and kisses in way of congratulations. Some of those girls were so much better than Zara. How on earth had *she* gotten chosen? It was hard to believe, e*specially* after the last few weeks, where she quite plainly, didn't even try in class. It was all too strange and Jane could not take it in. This surely could not be the right decision. It made no sense. No sense at all. And then she saw Helen looking at her from across the room. Her face a thinly veiled mask. Jane felt a great surge of disappointment. It was like a physical blow to her stomach.

She knew she had to go over and congratulate Zara. It was the right thing to do. She really did not want to, but it would look as if she was a bad sport if she did not. Sarah too, she could see, was also having great difficulties coming to terms with this surprising announcement. "We have to go over there," Sarah said.

"I know," replied Jane, "but I really don't want to."

"We have to, now come on." Sarah took the lead and Jane followed as she took a deep breath. It was now or never.

Just then, Zara saw them approaching her. Jane spoke first. "Congratulations, Zara."

Sarah offered her congratulations right after Jane. "Well done." Neither of them said she deserved it. Zara offered them both a sweet, victorious smile, and without a word, turned sharply away. She made it crystal clear that she was dismissing them and their congratulations. Jane could have cared less. She had done the right thing in coming over and offering congratulations but now that she had done that, she just wanted to get out of there.

Helen watched from the sidelines unobserved. She had witnessed the entire scene.

Chapter 37

Pat had hardly seen Zara over the last few weeks. And she was glad. After the disaster of introducing her to Matt, Zara had flown home for the weekend. Then, since her return, she had been hard at work practising, so most of her time was already scheduled. There were only a few weeks left before it would finally be the World Games.

All the free time allowed Pat some time to reflect on their friendship. Zara's behaviour had left many doubts in that area. She had come over, as promised, and acted as a companion to her friend. But now, with Zara settled in and practising almost every day, she knew she could fly back home at any time. She had done her duty. Pat knew she could do this, but she did not want to. She was having too much fun. There was so much to do and see, and of course there was Matt. She found she was enjoying his company more and more. He was intriguing, and had a wonderful sense of humour. Matt was still his usual self and had not said anything about Zara since *that* awful evening when she had introduced them, so she felt pretty secure that all the flirting had all come from Zara's side. That fact really bothered her. Zara was supposed to be her friend. Why would she do that? Especially since she already had a boyfriend. Pat promised herself that she would not make *that* mistake twice. She knew she would have to keep Zara well away from Matt.

Pat had made up her mind. She could not allow Zara to destroy her relationship with Matt. They were seeing each other, but they were still not a couple, and until they were, Zara was not to be allowed to jeopardize anything.

Zara's phone call half an hour later was a surprise. She wanted to meet up for dinner. Pat was not sure. She was still cross and hurt that her friend could flirt so openly with a guy she liked. Wasn't that one of the unspoken rules?

Zara went on and on, and eventually Pat had agreed, although reluctantly. They spoke for a few more minutes, then Zara changed the subject completely and asked her to bring Matt along. Warning bells started to ring.

Pat put the receiver down. Even at Zara's insistence, she knew she would not invite Matt to join them. She had no intention of having another dreadful evening. Pat was still finding the whole incident upsetting and now this. Her friend, her best friend. Why was she being so persistent? She already had Raymond.

She dressed nervously that night. If she knew Zara at all, which she did, then she knew Zara was quite capable of making a scene that evening. Especially if she did not get her own way. She was not looking forward to it.

* * * * *

Zara's disappointment was all too obvious when they met in the foyer for the long awaited dinner. "Where's Matt?" she asked almost immediately. She had not even said hello to Pat, and was looking around the room, trying to spot his wide frame.

Pat took a deep breath. "He's not coming tonight," she replied and left it at that.

"Oh!"

Pat ignored the look of disappointment on Zara's face and changed the subject, "I'm starving. Shall we go up? We can have drinks at the table." They both remained silent for a few minutes as they made their way up the stairs to the dining room. Pat was lost in her own thoughts. If she had any doubts about Zara's interest in Matt before, she did not have any now.

"Why not?" asked Zara.

Pat looked up. What was Zara talking about now? "Why not, what?" she asked.

"*Why* is Matt not joining us tonight?"

Pat looked at Zara and felt herself getting angry. "He had a meeting with some other friends. Is that *okay* with you?"

Zara ignored the barb as they followed the waiter to their table and took their seats. Pat tried to keep herself under control, but she was seething with anger. So, it looked like she had been correct all along and this just confirmed her suspicions. It was Zara who had the hots for Matt. Which led to another question. What should she, Pat, do about it? Pat pondered the question, over and over. Nothing. She would do absolutely nothing. Just never let the two of them meet ever again.

*****

Zara made her way back up the stairs, barefoot, so as not to make any noise. She had been bitterly disappointed that Matt had not joined them for dinner. She wondered if Pat had actually invited Matt, as she had asked. She had looked so forward to the evening and toward seeing him. She had not seen him now in two weeks. Was it that long? She just had to think of his devilishly handsome face and his gorgeous smile and her knees seemed to weaken. Zara pushed open the bedroom door. Everyone was asleep, as she knew they would be. She tiptoed into the bathroom, undressed and slipped into her pajamas. As she switched off the light, she noticed the small red rose. It had finally died and since she did not have the heart to throw it out, she had dried it. It was now a permanent fixture next to her bed. She slipped silently under the covers and reached up for the rose. If she closed her eyes, and thought really hard, she could almost still smell the sweet delicate fragrance. It was the last thing she remembered before she fell asleep.

* * * * *

The next morning, Zara woke up and found she was still clutching the little red rose. It was now a dull, maroon colour, but even so, it still made her think of Matt. She smiled. The rose had become her good luck charm and always seemed to give her extra energy now when she needed it. She would have to call Pat again. She just had to see Matt, and soon. She decided she would call Pat that evening and arrange another dinner date for tomorrow night.

Her thoughts were interrupted as Sophia walked out the bathroom. "You better get up," she sang toward Zara.

"Yes, I'm up. I'm up." While the other girls continued to ready themselves, Zara had a scalding hot shower. She had received a new level of status ever since Helen had announced her name as being the lead. Now all the girls wanted to be with her, sit with her and talk to her. It was nice. And, she had the added bonus the other day of watching Jane come over and congratulate her. That had been a heap of fun.

Her classes were not *that* much more difficult. She had two extra dances to learn, but she had almost finished learning them already. This all gave her the status she wanted. It proved that she was the best and more special and more talented than the rest them. She smiled to herself and her little secret.

Zara was excited about the day's class. They were to learn something new with ribbons. The instructor was someone new too. A small petite girl who danced like the wind and who used the ribbon as if it were an extension of her body. She moved with great grace and ease. The satin ribbon would twirl neatly in front to her, while she danced in and out of the circle she created. Her body seemed to twine and interlope as if it was a part of the ribbon itself. She was excellent.

Jane had also watched the new ribbon instructor and agreed that she was amazing. Then, annoyed, she picked at the knot she had managed to entwine in her own satin ribbon. It looked so much easier that it actually was. She had watched the instructor's every movements and she looked very graceful and elegant.

Jane struggled with the ribbons, and each time she approached the instructor for help Zara was there, doing a great job of manipulating almost all of her time.

She had now gotten over the fact that Zara had been chosen ahead of her for the lead role. It had been such a great shock and she could still remember how numb she had felt when she finally made it to her bedroom. She had wanted to be alone, but in a hostel, there was nowhere to go, so she had opted for a bath. A long, quiet hot bath with lots of bubbles. A place where she could be alone for an hour at the longest, left with her thoughts. As she lay there, she could not forget the look on Helen's face. Or that of Zara's.

When the tears came, she had been unable to stop them. And she had not wanted to. They flowed hard and fast, and came pouring out the corners of her eyes. She had wanted it so badly, and had worked so hard. She knew it was pointless crying, it solved nothing, but when she had finally emerged from the bath she had felt better. Now, as before, she would continue to practice as hard as she had always practised. She was in the World Games. That in itself was a great achievement. She thought about all the girls that had not made it. Coming to the very first audition and being rejected right from the very beginning. This was just how they must have felt, she thought to herself. At least she was here, and still taking part. She twirled the ribbon again, determined to do her best, even if she was not the lead.

The next week passed in a haze of excitement. They had received the yellow unitards back and Helen had been relieved when she had been told that they were no longer see-thru. The shop had done an excellent job with the lining and they looked great. No one would ever have suspected the near disaster. It was one less thing to worry about. Then she had set about arranging a bus that would take all the girls to the stadium. With less than a month to go they had finally been given permission to practice at the actual grounds. Helen had been thrilled. She wanted the girls to feel as comfortable as possible in the big open space, so they needed as much practice time on the field as they could get. In response to her many phone calls, they were finally given permission for half of the following day. She had already called and checked ahead of schedule and the music and speakers had all been set up. All they now needed was their dance music and the girls. Helen knew that it was imperative that they all be comfortable individually and as a group. They needed to familiarize themselves with the settings. This was completely new to these girls and unlike any place they had ever danced before. They needed to be prepared.

Helen looked at her watch again. Where was the coach, she asked herself? They could not be late. She had exactly half the day booked at their disposal, and she wanted to make sure they used every second. There was another group also rehearsing, so they could not run late.

As if in answer, the yellow coach made its appearance, and could be seen turning the corner and heading toward the school.

The girls were all excited and jostled and joked as the bus came to a stop. This was their first real look at the stadium where they were to perform. The jostling continued as they embarked on the bus. As was the normal rule, it was best to sit at the back of the bus, so everyone was clamouring and climbing over one another, hoping to book one of the valued seats. Jane knew they were the best seats, but was not bothered if she did not get one; as long as she could see out the window as they drove, she would be happy. She heard her name being called and looked up.

"Jane. Jane! I've booked you a seat!" shouted Sarah. Jane squeezed past the line of girls and made her way to the very rear of the bus where Sarah had booked her a seat with her tog bag. They had an exciting day ahead of them. After all these weeks of training, they were going to see the stadium. Finally see where all the magic was all going to happen.

The bus journey did not feel long. Partially because they were all so excited, and partially because all the girls were too busy looking out the window taking in the scenery around them. It was beautiful. No wonder they had decided that the World Games would be here, thought Sarah. Everything seemed very lush and green. And very clean. No rubbish laying anywhere. All the gardens and parks, neatly pruned. Before they knew it, they had arrived. Large iron gates blocked their entrance, and only after a guard had checked the bus did he unlock the gates for them to enter. They drove inside, following the long entranceway and eventually they came to a massive gray building. The bus driver parked in one of the special parking bays saved for them right at the very entrance of the stadium. The girls all jumped up and began to exit as soon as the driver opened the doors. As Jane and Sara had managed to get the best seats at the back of the bus, they were the last to exit, but the line moved quickly and before they knew it they were outside.

When Jane took the last step off the bus, she was surprised to see how big the stadium actually was. To the left was parking that stretched on and on for the many buses and coaches that were expected. Then, in the faraway distance, Jane could see a massive open-air car park. It was empty now, but she knew that it could hold thousands of cars. And soon it would.

The group all followed Helen inside the grounds and then they found themselves inside the massive gray building. All was deserted and it had an eerie feeling about it. You knew the building could hold tens of thousands of people, and here it stood, empty. It felt very unnatural. When you spoke, it was almost as if your voice echoed through the empty corridors. The lights were on, but it still had a empty, dark feel to it, and shadows could be seen climbing up the gray walls. The eerie feeling only increased as they walked deeper and deeper into the building. Jane wondered if the wind howling through the gates had anything to do with it.

The guard who had met them at the gate had now joined them. He took great delight in giving them the grand tour of the building and its facilities. You could hear he was proud to be working there. They were shown where they would arrive on the day, which was not too far from where they had arrived that morning. They were also shown where their dressing rooms were, and then where they would exit onto the field for the show. They walked the length of a long dark tunnel, and soon they the found themselves on soft grass. Surrounding them was the entire stadium. Jane turned around in awe. It was massive. She had been to see a football match with her father and brother before, but it was nothing as large as this. Then, as she took in the millions of seats, she suddenly started to feel excited. She, Jane Brown, would be standing here in less than four weeks time, ready to do the most important dance of her life. Her parents had already booked flights and they were determined that they would be there to see and support her. Helen had already told them that the TV crew had been booked and Jane knew that on the day, they were to have a group photo taken first and then a live interview was to be held. This interview was to be broadcast worldwide. Jane suspected that Zara would probably be the one to take the interview, as she was the lead and representative for the entire group. Jane had already arranged that her grandparents tape everything, just in case she did manage to get some live coverage for herself. She always knew that this was her master plan, but to actually be here, see the massive stadium somehow, put everything into perspective. She could just imagine it. All those people. Watching and clapping. It was going to be amazing. For now though, she was content to see the empty seats. They would all be full soon enough.

"It's huge," whispered Sarah as she came up alongside Jane, still taking in her surroundings with awe. Jane nodded in agreement. It was much bigger than even she had anticipated. "You cannot even see the top of the stadium it's so big," continued Sarah. Jane looked. And nodded. The chairs at the top of the stadium, looked like tiny dots melting into each other.

All the girls began to drift off in their own directions, eager to take a look around the stadium and explore the grounds. Helen checked on a few last minute details with the technical crew and then called everyone back to the dressing room. It was time for their first proper rehearsal. Jane was excited. This was it. From today, it was the last final steps, and in four weeks time, when they appeared from the tunnel, the stadium would be full. Full of watching and expecting spectators. She felt the shiver run down her spine. Yes, it was exciting. Very, very exciting.

Ten minutes later they were changed and back onto the field, ready for the first rehearsal. They took their formations and waited. Jane knew it was only a rehearsal, but still, her heart hammered in her chest. The music began. At first it was soft and cracking, but Helen was quick to rectify that as they continued to dance.

It was strange dancing in the middle of an open field. There were no mirrors, so you were not able to watch yourself. Instead, you found yourself surrounded by millions and millions of empty seats. It was the strangest sensation. Helen had also been given a little radio and she used that to communicate with the music room. When she gave her go ahead, the familiar music would pour onto the field. After the first few adjustments, it became louder and clearer, just as if they were in a dance studio. They set to practising the steps over and over again. Then, halfway through the morning, someone announced that Helen was now able to use the lights. At her command, large, beams pounced onto the centre of the field.

In between all the adjustments, the girls continued to practice. While Helen and James busied themselves with lighting and music, Velocity kept an eye on who was losing formation. Who was out of sequence and who was losing form. She walked around between the group and helped anyone who lost their configuration. Being it was the first practice, it was almost everyone. Each girl had their landmark in the training rooms. Here on the field, there was nothing. All the landmarks were gone. Jane knew she would have to make new ones for herself, as would the rest of the girls. It was the only way to make sure they all stayed in their exact formations and did not mess up on the big night.

They had been rehearsing for over two hours. The music was now perfect and there was no longer any distortion or static. Helen was also happy with the improvements to the lighting, although she was keen to play around with some ideas the lighting technicians had given her. After running through the full dance a few times, the girls began to get more familiar with their surroundings and began to locate some essential landmarks. At one stage, a group of older girls emerged from one of the open doors at the very top of the stadium. They sat and watched them dance for a while as they ate their lunches. The only reason they had been noticed was because one of the girls wore a bright red pullover and it illuminated against the dull gray of the stadium chairs. Otherwise, they all looked like small, faraway dots. "Check the lighting is pointing directly onto them as a group," Helen said as she spoke into the loudspeaker in her hand. The light seemed to move, first to the left and then to the right. "Yes, that's it. Keep it there. That's the exact position," Helen confirmed Still, during all the conversations and adjustments being made, the music continued to play and they continued to dance. Someone was constantly fiddling and adjusting the beams. One minute, they had blue lights pointed toward them, the next red.

Still Velicty seemed to take no notice and continued to stop and start the music, pointing out any errors she could see taking place. "Nancy, when you kick, try and stay between Jane and Paula," she would say. Nancy nodded. "Susan, when you turn, make sure you don't pass behind Jay. You have to be seen at all times." They continued with the steps again. Velicity giving guidelines and instructions as they did so. The lighting crew seemed to have calmed down, and the lights seemed to be working now in time to their movements. Jane also noticed that the lighting colours seemed to change at exactly the right moment. Then the lights altered again, giving them all a surprise, as it took on the form of millions of little small dots floating on the field. It was hard not to stop and enjoy the moment. It looked amazing. And that was on the field. During the day. Jane knew that at night, wearing their costumes, it would look amazing.

Jane had no doubt that everything would be amazing. Anyone in the stands, no matter how low or how high they were, would be able to view the lights on display. It was going to be spectacular.

They were just practising one last dance when another group emerged from the tunnel. Their time was almost up. Jane watched as they approached and their instructor spoke to Helen. He was a thin, small man, deeply tanned. Helen threw her head back at something he said, and laughed deeply. Then they were called to leave.

Back in the dressing room, everyone seemed to be in high spirits, chatting excitedly among themselves. Just as they were ready to make their way back onto the bus, Jane snuck back out through the long dark tunnel and made her way to the stadium entrance. The new group that had arrived, had set up and were ready to continue with their own practice. One small, petite girl ran and then rolled into a neat flick flack. Jane watched as she repeated about six of them at once. Just as she completed the last one, she ended, in a perfect stance. Feet together, hands up. The gymnast group, Jane thought to herself, as she was about to make her way back to her own group, now heading for the bus. Then quite suddenly a boy, of similar height and age ran and joined the girl. The two of them began to flick flack around the stadium grounds together as a pair. It was mesmerizing to watch. Jane had to drag herself away before she missed her bus.

She arrived back at the dressing room and everyone was already gone, so she headed back to the entrance. The driver was already inside, with the engine running. Most of the girls had boarded.

The journey home was filled with excitement and laugher. All the girls had felt the energy of the day and realized what they would be a part off. All the hard work and gruelling hours had been worth it.

Chapter 38

Zara had expected to be tired after a day dancing at the stadium, but she was anything but tired, even after doing her additional entrance and exit dances. After everything was finished, she was still rearing to go. She felt alive and energetic. Everything had been working out perfectly. She thought of Pat. She would ring her tonight and make that invitation for dinner. If she were lucky, Matt would be available. It would be the prefect end to a perfect day. She picked up her mobile and rang the familiar number, as she sniffed the dried red rose.

A few minutes later, she had spoken to Pat, and then hung up. She could not help but smile. She had called Pat, who incidentally was with Matt at the time. It could not have been better planned. She had asked if they should meet for dinner again that evening and gave Pat no room for refusal. "Let's go somewhere nice. Get Matt to pick a place," she added, as a way of confirming that this time, he would be there.

She listened to Pat stumble into the phone, then heard Matt say something in the background. She was not sure what he had said, but Pat had gone silent and then replied. "Okay fine." Then, abruptly, she had rang off. Zara had looked at the phone, mildly irritated at first. No one hung up on her. Then she realized that she would be seeing Matt again and everything was once again perfect.

An hour later, Zara found herself in the familiar cab and on the way to the Four Seasons. Sneaking out was now second nature. She knew exactly what to do and how to do it. She had it all worked out and she could come and go as she pleased. As the cab pulled up to the entrance of the hotel, Zara had to admit that she actually felt excited. Tonight was going to be full of happy surprises. She sprayed herself again with her Elizabeth Arden perfume, popped a mint in her mouth and headed confidently inside.

She headed straight toward the hotel bar and noticed Matt immediately. His profile was unmistakable, even from behind. She sauntered over, and made a great display in saying hello to Pat, hugging her fiercely and kissing her on both cheeks. Then, she turned her attention onto Matt. Zara took in every inch of him. Yes, he was just as good looking as he had been when she had last seen him. Her stomach did a little flutter. Then she hugged and kissed him on both cheeks too, acting if it was the most natural thing in the world to do, even to a person she had only ever met once.

She was momentarily lost in his smell. Clean shaven and masculine. What was that after-shave he was wearing? It smelt like Heaven. She pulled away and tried to recover from her reeling senses. "Nice to see you again, Matt," she replied in her most alluring voice.

Pat listened to Zara's put-on, sexy voice and tried not to gag. She really did not want to be there. She would have ditched her way out of dinner with Zara if Matt had not been so close and heard the conversation. She had wanted to keep the two of them as far apart as possible. She knew that Matt would not be able to resist Zara's charms for too long. But here she was again, in the same position as before, dreading the evening to come. She knew Zara would have something up her sleeve. She just knew it.

Matt had chosen a small Italian restaurant for them to dine at. They had discovered it together one afternoon while shopping for gifts for their families and had been there a few times for dinner. It was perfect for the two of them, but with Zara there, she knew it was going to feel too intimate and too cozy. The last thing she wanted either Zara or Matt to feel that evening.

Zara had arrived and dressed perfectly in a soft, light-blue cashmere sweater and black molten skirt, which hugged every curve perfectly. As usual, she looked stunning with her hair swept up into an elegant twist.

Pat had opted for something subtler herself, but just as sexy. She knew she had to make a lasting impression on Matt without it being too noticeable. She also knew that Zara was giving her a serious run for her money. She watched as Zara lingered in the hello hug for a little bit too much longer than was necessary. Pat tried to keep the annoyance from showing in her eyes.

Zara acted exactly as she was expected to act. She gazed lovingly into Matt's eyes during dinner and laughed at everything he said. Pat had to physically stop herself from being sick every time she leaned forward and touched his arm. She had wanted to rip away those perfectly painted nails and push her away. If Matt gave any sign that he noticed her needless, unnecessary touching, then he did not let it show. Instead, he acted as relaxed and easygoing as ever. She watched in numb fascination as her friend tried to woo Matt and openly flirted with him. It was no wonder that no man could resist her. She was practically oozing sexy confidence. Pat leaned back in her chair as Zara told him all about her father's company. *Yes— great! Rub in Daddy's money as an extra bonus.* Pat thought. *There. She's done it again,* reflected Pat. *Can she not stop touching him every second?* Pat knew she had to leave. Now! For the bathroom, before she was sick. She knew that she could not expect Zara to accompany her, so she stood up abruptly, excused herself, and headed to the ladies on her own. It felt like deja vu. Her, in front of the mirror, the same as before. While outside, at their table, her best friend flirted with the first man she had liked in ages. *Get a grip,* she scolded herself. *Act normal. If Zara has any idea you've noticed, then things will only get worse.*

When she got back to the table, Pat noticed that Zara's chair had inched ever so slightly closer toward Matt's. She was in the middle of telling him all about the games, and how she was chosen to take the lead. "I've never wanted anything so much in my life," Zara said dramatically. "It was really hard. Hours and hours of practising." She moaned in just the right way, as if she had been through a horrific ordeal.

"It must have been tough," Matt agreed politely.

Zara continued. "And the worst was my feet. They used to actually bleed. Sometimes I could not take off my dancing shoes because of the pain."

Pat sat in silence. Watching the pair of them silently. Had they even noticed that she was back from the bathroom? She was trying really hard not to let her disgust show, but it was hard. Matt was hanging onto Zara's every word, in awe. Pat felt the dread in her stomach deepen. *Was Matt taken with Zara? Was that it? Was she just being blind?*

"Pat dances too," chirped in Zara.

Pat was all ears. Why was she now graced with being included in this conversation?

Matt looked up at her, and smiled. As he did so, Pat just wanted to melt inside his lovely blue eyes. "Oh, is that so?" he asked interested. "You never mentioned that to me before."

Pat debated on her reply. She could just blush silently, or she could tell the truth, that unlike Zara, she had nothing to gain by lying and cheating. That she did not want to take advantage and use her parents for holidays and cash and anything else they would give her.

She had time for neither, as Zara responded. "Of course she wouldn't tell *you!*" Zara smiled in way of explanation.

Matt ignored Zara, his attention focused on Pat. "Do you still go to classes? Did you audition for the Games too?" he asked, interested.

Pat opened her mouth to reply, but Zara was too quick again and jumped in, answering for her. "No silly." Zara laughed maliciously. "Pat was not chosen. She went to the auditions, but the organizers did not think she was good enough."

Chapter 39

Pat stared in open mouth wonder at the girl she thought was her friend. How could she say that? To Matt of all people. Pat moved her lips to say something in her defense, but no words seemed to form. She looked at Matt, then Zara, and back at Matt again. She did not have to put up with this. If they wanted to be together, then fine. She was not going to stand in their way. But she would not be bashed around by Zara, and made to look like a complete idiot in front of Matt. Oh no. She had some dignity. Better to leave now, while she still had some tact, then to wait until they had sapped the last of it. If she stayed, things would only get worse, of that she was certain. Enough was enough. Pat rose from her seat. "Thanks for a lovely evening, Matt. Zara," she said with a dismissive nod. With that, she picked up her bag and headed for the entrance without looking back. At least she could say that she had remained polite, although it had taken every ounce of her strength to do so. With her head held up high, she left the restaurant, and was relieved to see a cab already waiting on the curb. Without a backward glance, she opened the door and got in. "The Four Seasons," she said to the cab driver as he sped off.

For the whole drive back to the Four Seasons she wondered if she had she done the right thing. Should she have left like that? Matt and Zara alone? Things were bound to escalate between them now that she was not there to interfere. Then she decided. Yes, she had done the right thing. Whatever happens, happens. Matt was his own person. He had a voice. If he liked Zara, too, then it was better that she found that out now.

When she next looked up, they had arrived at the hotel. Pat paid the driver and left an extra large tip, then made her way to her bedroom. She was exhausted. What had began as a lovely day with her and Matt had now turned out to be a complete nightmare. And she had no one to thank but her own stupidity and her so called "best" friend.

*****

Zara stumbled inside the cab. It had all been going so well. What had happened? She had been making such progress with Matt and then, all of sudden, Pat had jumped up and left. It was so typical of something that Pat would do. Ruining everyone's evening like that. Matt had not been pleased, and Zara knew that he blamed her.

"What did you say that for?" he asked angrily.

"Say what?" asked Zara in the most innocent voice she could muster. She knew that if she feigned innocence, almost all men would forgive her. She loved to play on the, "Poor Zara. She did not mean it," role.

Matt gave her a hard stare, not buying her practised pout. It was the first time that anyone had directly voiced their anger toward her. Over anything. Ever. "I think you know what!" he said, rising from his seat. "And you call yourself her friend? What kind of friend makes comments like that?"

Zara was about to say something in her defence, and then realized he was right. Okay, maybe she had been a little too forceful this time, but damn him, no one ever spoke to her like that. Regardless of what she had done.

Matt was now standing at their table and ready to leave. She watched as he paid the check, left a tip and ran outside, not glancing in her direction once. All this, in a desperate hope to catch Pat before she was gone. Zara was devastated. Never in her life had anyone left her at a table alone. Alone and angry with her. No one was ever angry with her. It just did not happen. She looked out the glass window. Surely he would come back. Realize how irrational he was being. Apologize and then finish his meal with her. She knew that she needed some time to be able to work on him—alone. Without Pat around to interfere. But then she noticed him still outside with no signs forthcoming that he was going to return back to their cozy table. It was the perfect opportunity for them to be alone, but he seemed oblivious, determined to wait outside in the cold for the next available cab. She knew then that he had no intention of coming back inside the restaurant to her. Zara grabbed her jacket and handbag and followed him outside. She still had time. She *would* win him over. Pat was gone, out of the way, and finally she could now really make her move on him.

Matt paid her no attention when she slipped outside the restaurant door and stood next to him. He kept staring down the street, as if a cab would magically appear if he stared hard enough. "Oh, Matt, it was only a joke," she coaxed, as she lay her hand on his arm. "It's not my fault if Pat's so sensitive at times. It is a problem with her, you know," she said, as if confiding a little secret.

Matt stared hard at his arm, then moved slightly to the left, just out of her reach. "You don't get it, do you?" he said. Zara knew she had a baffled look on her face. "The problem is not Pat, or her being over sensitive. The problem is you. You are rude. Rude *and* arrogant. And not a very good friend from what I have seen."

Zara was in shock. No one had *ever* spoken to her like that before. It had happened too many times that evening and she did not like it—one bit. "I am NOT rude," she almost shouted back.

Matt turned slowly. "Yes, you are. And, add selfish to that list. You are a person who does not care about anyone except herself."

"That's not true," Zara defended herself.

"Yes, it is. Look at how you treat your friends."

A big silence developed. Zara tried to think of something to say, but nothing seemed to come to her mind fast enough.

"You say you are Pat's friend," he asked softly.

"Yes, of course I am. We have been friends since we were little."

"Then why would you flirt with me? If you were such a good friend, why would you do that? In front of her. While she's at the table?"

Zara did not know what to say. She did not think she had been *that* obvious.

"You were enjoying every minute of it," Zara replied back triumphantly.

Matt laughed. "No. I was trying to spare your feelings so *you* wouldn't be embarrassed. And, I didn't want Pat to know that I think her choice in friends—is rather weak." A cab appeared then from around the corner, followed by a second cab right behind it. Matt held up his hand, let Zara have the first one, and then hopped into the second one himself. "The Four Seasons please," he said without another backward glance toward Zara.

Zara watched the cab as it drove away. He had left her. Actually left her. Alone and standing on some pavement. She was furious. No one had EVER had the nerve to do that to her before. Matt was unique in every way and she liked it. And she knew, deep down, he had liked all the flirting. And that he liked her. There was no way she would believe that he did not find her attractive. All men did. That was just the way it was. Still, she was upset. He had left her and gone to see if Pat was okay. How could any man choose Pat over her? Even if it was only for one night and because Pat had run off, making a huge scene of being upset. Matt was probably filled with guilt. He was too special not to be. Stupid Pat. She had ruined everything.

"You getting in or what?" asked the cab driver impatiently.

Zara watched the departing cab, Matt's head clearly seen in the back window. She nodded and opened the door.

And here she was now. Not quite sure what had happened. At first she had been cross that he would even think such a thing. Her rude. No, it was *him* that was rude. Then once the anger disappeared, which took the whole of five minutes, Zara felt devastated. Matt, he thought she was rude. It was too much to bear. She felt like her legs had turned to lead. And he thought she was a bad friend. She wanted to cry. Why had that happened? What had she done wrong? It had all been going so perfectly. Then she was unable to stop herself. Big tears began to slide down her face. Not because she had probably ruined her friendship with Pat, but because Matt had chosen Pat over her. Even if it was only for one evening. Nothing like this had ever happened to her before. All she kept thinking was she had lost. Lost it all. The perfect man. She could feel her mascara clogging in the corner of her eyes, but she did not care. Mascara seemed to be the smallest, irrelevant thing right now. All she cared for was Matt. She would make it up to him. She would. Matt did like her, she was positive he did. He was just too nice and felt bad when Pat had run off. It was, after all, Pat that had introduced them. Zara vowed to make it all better. Not once did she even consider Pat and her feelings.

Chapter 40

Back at the hostel, things were not going as smoothly as Zara would have liked to think. She had been sneaking out more regularly and become comfortable in the knowledge that no one would ever notice. Tonight, however, her absence was noticed. Helen had been at her dinner table all evening working on some reports and had not yet seen Zara appear for supper. The last of the girls had left their table and still Zara had not materialized. Helen ate her own meal and waited while she worked. Zara was bound to show up for something to eat sooner or latter. Helen finished her dessert and continued working on her reports over a cup of coffee. As time wore on, she found she could not relax. Not having seen Zara kept playing on her mind. She had a bad feeling. She packed up her files and took them back to her office, then headed up to Zara's room. Maybe she was feeling ill, or fancied an early night, like sometimes the girls did after a hard day. One of her roommates could easily have brought her some food up. Either way, Helen had to check, if only to ease her own mind.

She knocked loudly on the door and when it opened, she questioned all the girls present. No one had seen or heard from Zara since they arrived back from the stadium. Her phone was also still there next to her bed, so she had to be around somewhere. "She likes to kick box!" one of the girls offered. "Sometimes, at night. On her own. She does that quite often. She might be down there now." Helen thanked the girl, and headed straight for the training rooms. She opened the door. It was dark, with the only slither of light coming from the moon shining through the open window. All was silent and nothing had been disturbed. The punch bags were leaning against one of the walls where they had been left the day before. Zara had not been in there. Helen began to feel uneasy. Something was not right.

She made her way back to the girls' quarters. She knew she had to keep looking. An hour later, almost every girl had been informally quizzed. All the places she could have been were searched but still there was no Zara. Helen began to feel increasingly uneasy. Where could she be?

Helen sat in her office and thought, what else she could do? She could call for Zara over the loudspeaker. Everyone in the entire school would hear it, so if she were on the grounds, no matter where, she would know she was being looked for. Helen thought it through. No, she decided, she could not do that. If Zara was still somewhere on the premises, it would raise all sorts of questions and embarrass them both. It could get totally out of hand. With her father being such a major sponsor, she really did not want to create any waves unnecessarily. Helen revised her plans. She would have to call for *all* the girls over the loud speaker. Ask everyone to gather in the large, communal television room. She would use tomorrow's rehearsal as an excuse to get them all together. That way, Zara would have to appear too and would not know that she was the one that was specifically being looked for.

Ten minutes later all the girls were crammed into the television room as requested. Some were in their pajamas, others in their swimming costumes, while others still came rushing in with tennis rackets in hand. Everyone was present, except for the one girl Helen really wanted to see. "Does anyone know where Zara is?" she asked innocently. Everyone looked around then and shook their heads. "No one knows?" Helen asked. Again, they all nodded. No. No one knew where Zara had gone off to on her own. It was time to get serious. "Does this happen often?" Helen asked. No one knew. No one knew anything. Or, if they did, they were not saying anything. "If anyone knows anything, I'll be in my office for the next half an hour. Whatever is said to me will be kept confidential. You girls are excused." Helen finished her announcement and then dismissed them.

She left the room and headed straight for her office. She was beginning to panic. What if she had been mugged? She might have been kidnapped from the hostel and no one had noticed until it was too late? Someone must have found out how wealthy her parents were and were planning on using her as a hostage. Hold her for ransom. She would wait another half an hour, as she had promised the girls, then she would have no other alternative. She would have to call her Zara's parents. It was the last thing she wanted to do. Call a parent and have to admit that a child had gone missing in her care. Her career would be over. Finished. But she had no other alternative. Zara's safety had to be the main concern.

Helen tried to think calmly. She had two options. She could call Zara's parents first or she could call the police. What to do? What to do? She sat down. Think rationally, she said to herself. After much debate, she decided to call Zara's parents first. She may have spoken to them, and although unlikely, they might know where she was and informing the police could be avoided.

She braced herself for the phone call she knew she had to make when she was interrupted by a soft knock on her door. She looked up surprised. Half an hour had long since passed and she had not expected anyone to come forward with any information anyway. "Come in," she said. Jane opened the door and stepped inside. "Oh, it's you Jane. Can I help you with something?" Helen asked. Helen knew that Jane and Zara did not like each other. In fact, they barely tolerated each other, so the chances that Jane knew anything were almost non-existent.

Jane was still unsure if she should say something. She had debated the whole half an hour, then finally made up her mind. She really did not want to be a tattletale, but it looked as if Helen was taking Zara's disappearance very seriously. She would speak to Helen first and see what she planned to do. Maybe, if she was lucky, Helen would wait it out and she would not be forced to say what she knew. Helen looked at her expectantly. "What is it my dear?"

"What will happen if Zara cannot be found?" Jane asked.

Helen sighed. "I was just about to call her parents. They have to be the first to know. Then, if that is unsuccessful, I will be forced to call the police. There is no other alternative. With her father's wealth, it is quite possible that she may have been abducted. We have to consider all possibilities at this stage."

"I don't think she has been abducted," Jane contradicted before she could stop herself.

Helen looked up sharply. "What makes you say that?"

Jane really did not want to squeal. But if Helen thought she had been abducted and was going to call her parents, and then the police, she had no choice but to speak up. "Zara sometimes goes out in the evenings," confessed Jane quietly.

"What?" Helen replied shocked. "Where?"

"I don't know."

"How do you know she sneaks out then?"

"I caught her once. And I know she misses dinner a lot. I think she goes into the town and meets people. Friends," Jane added.

Helen was not sure if she should be pleased or even more worried. Out there, in the dark, was Zara on her own. Anything could happen. "When you last caught her sneaking back inside, what time was it?" Helen asked.

"Around 10:00 p.m., 10:30 p.m. something like that. She saw me, so she knows that I know."

Helen breathed a sigh of relief. There was still plenty of time for Zara to reappear, especially if this was something that she did on a regular basis. "Okay, Jane. Thank you very much for letting me know. I'll keep your name out of this. I promise. I will deal with Zara and please don't mention a word of this to any of the other girls."

Jane nodded. No problem there. The last thing she wanted was to be known as a squealer. Jane left soon after, but did not feel any better about what she had just confessed. She knew she had saved Zara's skin, but if Zara ever found out, well, she did not want to think what would happen then. Zara would be furious and not the least thankful that she had managed to stop Helen from calling her parents or the police.

An hour later, Helen had worked out that Zara must have been sneaking off around 6:00 p.m. each evening, returning just after 10:00 p.m. The doors to the hostel would still be open at that time. The caretaker only locked them after 11:00 p.m., as he often did odd jobs late in the evening when all was quiet and he had no interruptions. Helen sat in the dark angrily. She could have lost her job. Everything she had worked for all these years could have been lost because of one stupid, rich girl. She should have known there was something not right from that very first evening Zara had come in and tried to change all the rules and bend them to her satisfaction. She was still furious about the hotel situation. This was a good school, an expensive school that many of the girls felt honoured to stay in, and Zara had ripped it to shreds on the very first day. And then there had been the constant incidents. Like when she had caught Zara trying to leave the grounds. Helen was not amused. Zara had deliberately disobeyed her. She seemed do whatever she pleased and always got away with it. It was proved again this week. She, Helen, a professional in this business for years, had been forced to choose Zara as her lead when she had actually already decided to choose Jane, a far more talented, dedicated dancer. All of this because of her father's money. Would Zara ever achieve anything on her own? Helen was furious. That girl got what she wanted *all* the time. She had no manners and was spoilt and rude. Until now, Helen had tolerated her behaviour, but that had just come to an end. She would not be made to bend for the likes of Zara Maddox any longer. She had been made to look like a complete fool. But she knew what she had to do. She would rectify this immediately.

The foyer was dark and deathly silent. Then, in the far away distance Helen heard a low hum of a car engine followed by a soft slam as a door was shut. Helen sat up in her seat and knew that it was Zara arriving back at the hostel. She waited, listening to the low rustling just behind the great foyer door. The door opened gently, and she heard Zara slip inside and take off her shoes. She then began to creep, hunched over, toward the staircase. Helen sat very still, amazed at the nerve of the girl. She had it all planned out. Knew exactly what she must do. Helen switched on the small lamp and light immediately flooded the foyer. Zara turned, shocked. Helen continued to sit in the small chair. Unmoving. "The door will be locked early on in the evening from now on. You are not to leave again. If you do, you will be asked to leave permanently and your parents will be called to come and collect you. You will not be allowed to participate in the games, and nothing your father does or how much he pays will alter than fact. You will be out. For good." With that, Helen stood up and walked back to her bedroom, leaving a gaping Zara behind her.

Zara stood in the hallway with her shoes in her hand and was at a loss on what to do. Things had escalated further from bad to extremely worse. Helen was not the kind of person to disobey and that was exactly what she had been doing for weeks. What would happen now? She knew she was a mess too. Her eyes were swollen from all the crying and she could feel her mascara blotched and clogged up on her face and cheeks. And now this had happened to top off her brilliant evening. How on earth had Helen found out about her disappearances anyway after all these weeks? She stood in the foyer for ages, unable to move. This evening everything had gone horribly wrong, nothing was as she had planned. The tears kept streaming down her face until she was unable to cry anymore, leaving her face stiff and crusty. Eventually, she forced her legs to carry her back to her shared bedroom, indifferent that she was making a noise. It did not matter who heard her now. She had been caught red-handed. And worst of all, Matt still hated her.

Zara walked into her bedroom, unconcerned for the girls sleeping in their beds. Normally she tiptoed around the room and slipped into bed as quietly as she could so no one would know she had been out. Tonight, she did not care who heard her. It made no difference. She switched on the bathroom light and slammed the door behind her, then ran herself a shower. Within a few minutes, she was under the hot spray, washing the horrible evening down the drain.

She played the evening over and over in her mind. Each time she recalled Matt and the way he had spoken to her, the tears seemed to flow uncontrollably and she was unable to stop them. And then there was Pat. How could Matt possibly choose Pat over her? She contemplated this, unbelieving, over and over in her mind. It made no sense at all. After she had washed her hair and cleaned the make-up off her face, she felt better. She thought of Helen too, waiting for her in the darkened foyer. How on earth had she found out? No one had any idea about her second life away from the hostel.

Then it came to her. Quite suddenly she knew. *Jane.* Zara sniggered. Jane was the *only* person who knew she snuck out in the evenings. There was no one else who knew her secret. Zara was furious. She was more livid than she had ever been in her entire life. Jane was jealous of her. Jealous that she had not been chosen as the lead, so had tried to sabotage her success. Zara *knew* she was right. Jane had let the cat out the bag on purpose. She had done it deliberately, in a hope that she would be tossed out and expelled. That would have left the lead role open for someone else. Zara gritted her hands and teeth in incensed rage. Jane would pay for this.

Zara dressed quickly, opened her door and walked purposely toward Jane's bedroom. With each step she took she felt herself get more and more angry. Who did Jane think she was? She was a stupid nobody. Zara refused to let her get away with it.

Zara came to Jane's closed door and opened it roughly. She flipped on the light mercilessly, uncaring toward the four girls who lay curled up in bed fast asleep. Dazzling light flooded the room and the bodies began to stir. Disorientated from the bright light, they covered their faces with their blankets turning away from the bright beam that flooded the once darkened and peaceful room.

Sarah, still half covering her face, was the first to sit up, "What's going on?" she asked, as she blinked against the strong light.

Zara ignored her question, fueled with a mighty rage. She walked over to the first bed and ripped the covers off cruelly. Underneath lay Karen, who was not yet used to the sudden light. She sat up quickly, highly annoyed, pulling the covers back over herself.

"What is going on?" she demanded angrily. "What are you *doing?*" she asked Zara in astonishment.

Zara continued to ignore the questions being fired her way as she walked over to the next bed and did the same thing. She ripped the covers off, showing no mercy for the poor girl who lay sleeping underneath.

Jane sat up in the third bed next to the window, watching Zara go from bed to bed. "Zara, what on earth are you doing?" she asked.

At the sound of Jane's voice, Zara whipped around. The anger she felt bubbled over. "YOU!" she screamed. "IT WAS YOU!" She marched over and stopped dangerously a few feet in front of Jane.

Jane took in her pink face, red from rage and her eyes that were glazed over with anger. She said nothing else. "I should have known!" she shouted. "You! You are so JEALOUS of me, you just could not mind your own business, could you?" she shouted accusingly.

Jane kept her voice as calm as possible, before she answered. She knew why Zara was angry, so there was no use in pretending that she did not. "It was not like that Zara, I…"

Zara would not let her finish. She did not want to hear. Instead, she pointed her finger again at Jane, this time jabbing her hard in the chest. "Why don't you just STAY OUT of other people's business?"

"She was going to call the police," Jane replied in her defence, trying to make her see reason. Zara was too furious to acknowledge what Jane was telling her. She was like a woman possessed and there was no calming her.

Sue, now also wide awake spoke up, eager to defuse the fraught situation. "Zara, it's late. Why don't you go to bed? We can talk about this in the morning."

Zara threw her a mean, filthy look. Before anyone could take in what she was planning, Zara lunged wildly for Jane. The room flew into immediate chaos.

Zara grabbed purposely for Jane as her target. Her long blond hair was still wet from the shower and was like a fierce whip. As she lunged, her hair whipped brutally against Jane's cheeks as she tried to grab her nightshirt and drag her closer. Jane jumped back out of reach, but only just in time. Zara, not deterred, somehow still managed to grab a large chunk of Jane's hair and once she had that hold, she refused to let go. Karen and Sue saw it happen and immediately tried to pry Zara's fist off of Jane's hair. Zara held on fast with a vice-like grip, refusing to release her. Jane grabbed her own head too and tried to pry Zara's fingers off her hold, or at the very least, loosen the grip. In between all this chaos, Sue tried to keep hold of Zara's other hand, which she was using to scratch and grab whatever she came into contact with. It was a terrible sight to see Zara kicking and screaming, pulling and scratching, like a madwoman.

The three girls tried with all their might to keep Zara away from Jane. With a great force, they all tumbled over the bed, head first, onto the other side of the floor. Sue staggered and was forced to release the grip she had on Zara's free hand. Zara immediately used the opportunity and slapped Jane hard across the cheek. Jane's head flew back from the force. The noise from tumbling over the bed had awakened many of the other girls and then had come the high-pitched screaming. Naturally, they had come to investigate.

It was immediately evident that a fight was taking place and many were shocked at what they were witnessing. It took only a few minutes for the initial astonishment to wear off before they jumped into the squabble, trying to assist in keeping Zara off Jane.

Zara was undeterred by the increase in rivals and was still kicking and screaming at anyone she could lay her hands on. She wanted to hurt someone, anyone. "Let me go!" she screamed in frustration, as she noticed Jane getting helped further and further out of her reach. Zara continued to kick and it was difficult for the girls to still her wild legs. She saw Sue nearby, helping Jane and with one powerful kick, she shoved Sue back by kicking her in the stomach. Sue flew backwards and hit hard against the wall, winding herself. She slumped to the floor, holding her stomach, struggling to breathe.

It then became even more clear that if Zara got a proper hold of Jane, there would be worse to follow.

Eventually, with six girls pulling and tugging Zara away, they eventually managed to pry her hands off from Jane's hair. She was dragged, kicking and screaming to the other end of the room, still holding onto a large clump of Jane's hair inside her balled fists. Still, she screamed wildly and the other girls had to physically drag her from the bedroom.

Her screams and protests could be heard echoing through the halls for a long time after.

Jane was sure that Helen was going to appear at any moment. It was impossible to believe that she had not heard the loud and disrupting commotion that Zara had caused.

It was ten minutes later before the other girls returned back to their bedrooms. Sarah was among them and the last to enter. She closed the door behind her and turned the lock. The small sound seemed so much louder than it actually was. They were all silent. Zara's screams had finally died down. They listened further until all that could be heard was their own ragged breathing. Eventually, they began to relax, feeling safer behind the locked door.

"Are you okay?" asked Karen, coming round the bed toward Jane. Jane nodded, holding her head.

She had developed an intense headache. It did not surprise her, after she had seen the great clump of hair that Zara had managed to grab. Now that the shock had passed, her head was reeling. "I'm fine. What about you?"

"Fine," they replied in unison, looking worriedly at their friend.

Sarah left her position on the bed, "Here, Karen, let me take a look at that." Karen lifted her arm. It seemed that Zara was also good with scratching. She had managed to dig her long nails deep into Karen's wrist, leaving four large, deep scratches. The cuts had already begun to ooze blood from the four narrow slits.

Sarah set to cleaning and disinfecting the scratches before dressing them. Karen tried not to wince, but the gashes were deep. Once the wound was cleaned and bandaged; Karen asked the question everyone wanted to hear the answer to. "What was that all about, Jane?"

Jane knew she had to tell them the truth. She had hoped it would all just die down, but with Zara's outburst tonight, she could not keep quiet. They had all been involved. She had to tell them. And so she did.

"So, she blames me," Jane concluded.

"That is ridiculous," Sarah said in Jane's defence. "She's the one who has been sneaking out. And now that she has been caught she wants to blame it on you? That's absurd."

Jane nodded and replied, "I had no choice. I had to tell Helen the truth." They all nodded in agreement, understanding. "I think it's best we sleep with our door locked from now on. We don't want any more of these kinds of outbursts." Everyone nodded again but no one felt tired after the evening's events. It was well after midnight before they all crept back into their beds and switched the light off.

Jane lay awake for a long time. She would have to be careful from now on. For someone, anyone, to get that mad, was dangerous. She was just glad that Zara had not managed to get her when she had been on her own. At least tonight she had all the others to help her. She reached up and touched her tender head. It was extremely sore and very tender. She could also feel the bald spot where Zara had managed to rip out the tuft of her hair. Zara was tipped over the edge, and Jane considered her dangerous. Very dangerous.

Chapter 41

The following day, everything seemed to be back to normal. The fight from the previous evening had been like a bad dream. Zara was acting as she normally did, and could be seen laughing and joking with some of other girls that had not been involved in the scuffle. None of her deluded, deranged anger seemed to be present any longer, and if it was, she kept it well hidden. To anyone who observed her, it was like the incident never happened.

Jane was not fooled and knew that Zara was only bidding her time. The incident was far from over. Zara had not forgotten and certainly not forgiven. Jane had to ensure that she kept a safe distance from her. No one, not even the girls that had come in later to help, had mentioned the incident from the previous evening. Jane was not sure anything like that would happen again, but she did not want to take any chances. It was agreed that locking their bedroom door at the end of each evening was a good idea. One they were going to stick to.

Although the incident was not mentioned again, no one could dismiss the evil looks that Zara would throw Jane's way. Jane was aware of it, but pretended she did not notice. Although there had been a lot of noise from all the kicking and screaming, Helen had not managed to hear about the incident, and no one thought to tell her. If she *did* know what had happened, she kept it to herself, and did not say anything.

They went back to the stadium for rehearsals every day now. The music came out loud and clear on the speakers, and they practised for a few hours every day, without fail. By the second week of practices at the stadium, the girls found that their movements were back in perfect time and sequences were running smoothly. With everything proceeding on schedule, all the dancers began to get more and more excited.

With the Word Games in only a few weeks, they soon had to share the grounds with other groups that also wanted to practice. Each day the yellow bus would appear, and they would be taken to the stadium grounds. Jane was not sure how Helen managed it, but somehow, they always seemed to have the stadium to themselves for a few hours in the morning. They would dance under Velicity's watchful gaze, while Helen continued to instruct the lighting and music men. The lights had to be perfectly timed, and with the number and array of coloured costumes being used, it was hard work to ensure that everything was perfectly synchronized. Helen had also developed a strange obsession with her radio. It went with her everywhere, and she could be seen roaming the grounds and talking in earnest.

Their costumes had been sent off for a second time to the hired seamstress and her task had been to sow millions of beads and sparkles onto each costume. It had taken her a week to get the costumes returned, but when they did came back, each girl gasped at the difference. Tiny little beads had been sown in various patterns, so that every slant of light would have them shimmering brightly. Even the yellow costumes looked much better. The beads had a dramatic effect and the colour no longer looked like canary yellow but more like a shimmering gold. Even Sue could not contain her amazement at the difference. In fact, her costume was the best out of all of theirs.

*****

After the first week, they began to wear their new and improved costumes during practice on the grounds. It became clear why three colours had been chosen, and that, with the sparkles and the array of lights, made for a spectacular show. Helen made a few more adjustments to the many lights and soon it was exactly as she wanted. When the girls in blue costumes danced together, she used an array of diverse blue lights for the lighting effects. Some were royal blue while others were light sky blue. Then, when the red costumes danced together, she had the lights change to different shades of reds and maroons. The effect was dramatic. All the different lighting was used to help compliment the beads on their costumes, which could be seen sparking and glittering from a faraway distance.

Then, as the big day drew closer, it was time to start a full dress rehearsal. The organizers wanted to get all the acts to fit in together, on schedule, one after another, so that changeovers were as fluid and easy as possible on the night. They did not want everyone knowing only their individual piece, and when the final show came, no one knowing what to do as a group. So it was also arranged that every day there would be a full group practice for all those that would participate. It included everyone, from music and lighting men, to the actual performers.

The first day of full rehearsal was exciting. They arrived at 8:00 a.m., as usual, in their faithful yellow bus. Normally, when they arrived, they were the only ones there and would drive right into to the closest parking bay situated at the very front of the entrance. Today, things were different as numerous other busses had already arrived before them. The driver parked as close as he could get, but they still had a short walk. When Jane stepped out onto the gravel, she noticed that the clouds were light and fluffy and the sun was streaming down. It promised to be perfect weather for the day ahead.

They made their way to their dressing room, eager and excited. The stadium, when they entered was a hive of activity, with people everywhere. All the designated dressing rooms were full. Suddenly, the stadium walls did not seem so cold and hollow as they had felt before.

They dressed into their new, sparkling costumes, knowing they looked good, and soon the first proper dress rehearsal began. A soft, gentle music began to play. Gymnasts came running onto the field in bright white costumes. They took their places in the centre of the field, and then the music changed to their own chosen piece. It was fast and had a steady, dramatic beat. They began to move, all at once, in all directions. The display they had worked on was spectacular. And as expected, they moved in perfect time with each other. Some girls then began bending and kicking as others were running and jumping into neat displays. The small girl and boy that Jane had seen weeks before were there too, and ended their routine with the same flick flacks around the grounds. It was all perfectly sequenced and again, with the lighting they had chosen, it was an excellent performance. They were all extremely talented. Their brilliant white costumes were also spectacular, dazzling under the array of multi-coloured lights they had chosen to complement them. Someone had even mentioned that they were actually glow in the dark costumes and that on the night, the effect would be completely different. The group finished up in the centre of the field as they had began. Then they bowed quickly before running off the field.

The second procession appeared about five minutes later. Five minutes did not sound like a long time, but when you are eagerly waiting for something to appear, five minutes seems and age and ticks by at an agonizingly slow pace. Their lateness was mentioned over the tanoid. Everything had to run directly after each other, with no gaps in between. It turned out that the next group had not realized they were second to appear and that was exactly why the organizers wanted a joint practice. To iron out any small incidents like this before the big night.

When the second group did finally appear, it was a bunch of young girls, all dressed in pastel coloured costumes. They took to the field with an array of hula-hoops in their hands. Jane watched fascinated as their music started and they began to move. The hoops were first swung high above their heads and then they would twist in a circle, before catching the hula-hoop as it fell. It was a clever trick of which they performed many more. Jane had not realized that there was so much that could be done with a single hoop. Then, just before they were due to exit, a very young boy, who could have only been about four years old, appeared. He had many small multi-coloured hoops around his waist. Maybe twenty or so. As the music drummed into the speakers, he began to move. Around and around his hips went, and along with it, the hoops. They spun around at a furious speed, so that all the colors began to melt into one. When he finished, their was loud applause, which bought on a beaming smile from him.

The morning flew past quickly. It was the first time anyone had seen the full procession and each act was a new, wonderful surprise. Jane marvelled at the imagination used for some of the shows. The ideas the organizers had come up with were unique. It was like nothing she had ever seen before.

One group that Jane particularly liked was the group that came onto the field with big, powerful black stallions. Together, rider and horse performed intricate and delicate tricks. The horses were amazing and gleamed powerfully under the lights, while the gymnasts danced expertly on their backs. They would jump from one horse to the next with ease. The horses had been finely dressed in dark red coats and adorned with long colourful feathers that gleamed like hot wax in the sunlight. It was almost like watching a mini circus, although the tricks they performed were much better than any circus Jane had been to see. These performers were professionals and much more skilled. Then, as an additional extra, they had a small brown Shetland pony bought onto the field. This horse was adorned in a yellow silk coat and upon her back was a small girl. Together they rode around the field, waving a small flag, performing some more unusual tricks. The little girl then jumped off the horse and took a bow. Jane clapped and clapped.

Finally, just after the drum majorettes, it was their turn and they were called. Helen almost dropped her radio from the excitement of it all. "You're up next, girls. Go back to the dressing rooms and start from the top. You have to run though the tunnel and take up your places, just as we have practised." She clapped her hands to get everyone moving. They all nodded. The time had come.

Jane knew it was only other performers outside on the field, but she still felt nervous. Butterflies began to appear in her stomach just as they were about to run onto the field. The music began and Zara was the first to run through the tunnel, on her own, and enter the wide-open space. Her specially chosen music began to play and she danced her solo piece. She stood tall and proud and performed the difficult movements with ease. Even Jane had to admit she was doing very well. A smile was fixed to her lips as everyone watched her perform. It was hard to believe, watching her now, that she was the same madwoman that had attacked her in her bedroom that one strange night.

The music died down. Zara stopped and held her position with arms high in the air. The music began again, which was the rest of the group's queue and they all ran onto the field to join Zara. They took on the same position that Zara still held. Jane looked around the stadium as their music began to play and she herself began to dance. The seats surrounding them were practically empty, but there were still some people sitting around the edges of the field watching. They felt so very far away. She did not have time to dwell on it, for as they had rehearsed, they split into three groups. The red dancing in their own group, as was the blue and the yellow. Finally, everyone came together again, in an array of sparkling colours and danced the final scene. Jane was only dimly aware of the lights changing and swirling around them on the ground, and as they danced off the field, a million white twinkle lights followed them back into the tunnel.

Zara remained were she was, alone on the field, holding her position as she had done before. When she was completely alone, the lights changed yet again and different music began to play. She began to move faster and faster, until she was dancing around the entire field, making a dramatic exit for her final scene. Her last moment of glory. As before, she danced well, using all the space offered to her. The lights were amazing too, swishing about her, in an array of colours. Finally she did her last leap and ran tiptoed back into the tunnel, a massive smile playing on her lips. She had loved every minute.

It took half the day to get through each group who had a part to play on the big night. There had been quite a few hiccups, as it was only the first time that everyone had practised together. Now, with the first rehearsal finished, all the organizers and instructors got together so they could discuss what had to be changed and where things could be improved. There was a lot that needed to be adjusted and perfected. The girls stayed in their changing room, talking among themselves excitedly.

It was some time later before Helen came back to them, talking on her radio in earnest. "Yes, the red lights. They need to be stronger. They look more like pink. I want red. Bright fire engine red." She stopped and nodded, as if the person she was speaking to was right there next to her. "No. The blue lights are fine. It's just the red. Yes. Okay." She switched off the radio and looked at the girls round her. Her attention now fixed onto them. "That was good. Very well done." Helen beamed. "Zara,

I noticed you were a little offsides at the beginning. Try to keep in the centre of the field when you dance your solo piece."

Zara nodded, smiling from ear to ear. She was still on a high from her solo pieces. She loved being the centre of attention.

"Tiffany, try and keep your leg straight when you kick. It's slightly out of line with everyone else and it's quite noticeable from where I was standing. And you, Sue, when you turn, you are not centred. Try and stay centre. You girls all must move together. You normally do this one-hundred percent, so it must be nerves. Try to stay calm and enjoy yourselves." Only when Helen had disposed of her advice, did she switch the radio back on. Almost immediately she was back to giving orders.

Chapter 42

All the girls were still in a state of wonder and excitement over the day's events. Things were turning out to be grander than any of them had imagined. This was not just a show, this was an international event to be broadcast to the entire world. When they arrived back at the hostel they were all still chatting away excitedly. No one was tired and no one wanted to disappear to the solace of their quiet and dull rooms. The buzz and excitement in the main hall was tangible.

Up until they had arrived back at the hostel, Zara had managed to enjoy the day. She had hardly had any time to think of the previous evening, not with everyone watching and praising her performance. Now though after it was all over, she cold not stop thinking of the dreadful evening with Matt and what he has said to her. The tears began to fall again and her spirits could not be raised. It seemed much worse with everyone else in such good moods and high spirits. Then, in her unhappy state she had thought of Pat. Some friend she turned out to be.

Zara was finding it hard to comprehend that she had lost to plain old Pat. It was a disgrace. What had Matt been thinking? And how could Pat betray her like that. And that was when Zara decided that she would have to get even. Pat would pay for what she had done to her.

Zara climbed the stairs and left the chatter of the other girls behind her. They were beginning to give her a headache. Unless they were talking about her performance today, she did not want to be included. Her spirits seemed to fall even further when she realized that she would have to stay in the hostel that evening. No exciting late night jaunts for her. She had no doubts that Helen would be watching her like a hawk. Zara hated knowing that someone was keeping tabs on everything she did. Normally, she would have done something about it, complain to Daddy maybe, or even try and get Helen fired, but that would have to wait for now. What she needed to concentrate on was winning Matt back.

Since she was first to arrive in their bedroom, she took her time in the bathroom, adding some of the bath salts to the water and enjoying the bubbles. She had not managed a decent, undisturbed bath for a long time as she was always getting interrupted by someone. With four girls sharing the same space, Zara found it difficult with only one bathroom. She was used to spending hours pampering herself and doing her makeup. Here, she had been forced to speed up, and although she could do her face quicker, she hated rushing. She preferred to take her time and get it perfect. As she enjoyed the rare silence, she mentally went through the events of the last few days. She would need another plan.

After she could stand it in the bath no longer, she dried herself and spent an age dressing. Normally she would have enjoyed every minute of the pampering, but what was the point now? There was nowhere for her to go. She felt at odds of what to do with all the time on her hands. It was too early to go down to dinner and she really did not want to join the nattering of the girls downstairs. Before, she would have rushed to get out of the hostel as soon as she could, eager to catch a cab to the Four Seasons. Just thinking of the hotel made her think once again of Matt and Pat. And dinner. And that led to her next major dilemma. Food. She knew that her meal that evening was not going to be enjoyable.

With nothing else to do, Zara finally took a slow walk to the excuse of a restaurant. She knew she was early, but she wanted to get an advance peek of what was being served. She hoped that she would be pleasantly surprised. She had no doubt that whatever was to be served would be horrible. She knew that, without a doubt, but still she hoped. Maybe, just maybe, there would be something edible.

Zara deliberately took the far staircase. She could still hear the natter of the other girls and sighed in relief that she could avoid them. She was not feeling in a good mood, and them being all jolly and excited just made her feel sick. She was miserable and wished that everyone was miserable with her. When she arrived at the restaurant, the lights were on, and the kitchen staff were laying the dishes in neat lines on the hot trays, ready for the hungry girls that would be appearing shortly. Zara went over and looked at the meals that the kitchen staff were working so hard on keeping warm. Sloppy pasta with even sloppier mushrooms, way past burnt. Zara tried to think if the dark shapes could be anything else, but failed. No, they were definitely burnt mushrooms. Then there was weak, runny curry with dry, white rice. Chicken roasted, past being juicy and dry and hard around the edges. Zara could not bring herself to look at what else they had lined up. Just the smell of it all made her want to retch. She closed her eyes and blinked. It could not get any worse. Prison food had to be better than this stuff.

"Not looking so good tonight, is it?"

Zara jumped. She had not heard anyone else come in. Sonia stood before her, also taking in the food spread before them, a look of displeasure on her face.

"The food here is normally good," she continued, "but, I could murder a hot, cheesy, pizza."

Zara closed her eyes and imagined it. Her mouth began to water, and she could almost taste the pizza. "Oh, yes, pizza would be good. Very, very good," she confirmed. Crusty pizza base with rich melted mozzarella cheese. Maybe some ham and pineapple. She shook her head. No such luck. There was nothing that delicious on the table before them. Then she had an idea. "Do you think we could order in?" Zara asked in desperation.

Sonia looked up eagerly. "I don't see why not." The idea seemed to take shape, rapidly. "All we need to do is get the number and place the order. They can deliver here. I'm sure Helen won't mind. We're not leaving the grounds or breaking any of her millions of rules."

"Where would we get a number from?" Zara asked. She had seen no pamphlets lying around.

Sonia thought for a minute. "We could try the telephone directory. There's one by the public phone box just outside the offices." Together, with a plan in motion, they made their way to the office and, as Sonia had predicted, they found a thick yellow book containing all the local telephone numbers. Together they scanned the pizza places. They chose the one with the biggest, brightest advert, and quickly dialled from Zara's mobile. Within minutes they had ordered a feast. Four giant pizzas with cans of cold cokes to wash it down with. Honey glazed ribs and fleshly fried onion rings were also on the menu. They also ordered a portion of fresh chips and four sticky toffee-banana puddings. Zara hung up and smiled. They were set for a good evening with some good food. "The others will be so excited. Our own little party," Sonia said.

"Okay, let's go and find them. But we must be back at the entrance in twenty minutes. We don't want anyone else picking up our delivery, now do we?"

"No, definitely not. This is our own little secret," confirmed Sonia, as they left to find the others.

Zara waited at the hostel entrance while the other three stood watch. No one must know what they had planned. They did not want to risk Helen finding out and putting a stop to any future feasts that might take place. Zara paid the deliveryman when he arrived and then, with the help of the others, took the food back up to their bedroom, careful not to be caught. It was a small wonder that they managed to get safely to their bedroom undetected with all the giggles and heavenly smells that drifted down the halls.

They closed their bedroom door as soon as they entered. Zara was pretty sure they had managed to get through without any of the others finding out what they were up to. It did not take long before all the food was unloaded and they were tucking into it while it was still hot.

"It's delicious," voiced Sonia as she took a bite into one of the spare-ribs. Zara took a huge sloppy slice of Pizza from one of the four boxes, and watched as the cheese fell from the base. She took her first mouthful and sighed with pleasure.

* * * * *

Helen was back at her table. As before, she was uneasy. Zara had not appeared for dinner, once again. She knew she must contain her anger and not jump to conclusions, even though her previous conclusions *had* been spot on. She knew that if Zara had disobeyed her again, she would have no choice but to call her parents and get them to come and collect her. She refused to be made a fool out of again. As before, she took a stroll around the grounds, keeping her eyes open lest she see the girl wandering around. She did not, so she made her way to Zara's bedroom. As Helen approached the bedroom door, she was faintly aware of giggles and lighthearted shrieks. As she got closer, the giggles and laugher got louder and louder. It sounded like the people inside were having a good time. She knocked lightly on the door first, before opening it. She had long since learnt that sometimes it paid to catch the girls first hand in whatever they were doing. The sight that greeted her was one she would not have expected. All four girls sat on the floor, big boxes of pizzas between them. Zara held a large slice and was just about to take a big bite when she had opened the door. Helen took in the smell, and could feel her own mouth begin to water. It smelt delicious, like the Pizza Hut she used to frequent when she was a girl. She took in the girls, sitting cross-legged, enjoying themselves, having fun together as a group. Helen nodded, and without a word, closed the door behind her. At least she could be assured that they were in their bedroom. Safe and sound. She could overlook that they had ordered pizza. There was no rule to say that was not allowed. Helen left feeling much better. She really did not know what she would have done if Zara had gone off on her own again. She knew she would have been forced to call her parents, but that would have only created another problem. Who would have taken her place as lead so late into the rehearsals? She was glad that Zara had obeyed her for once, because with everything going on, she really did not have time to deal with more unnecessary problems.

Chapter 43

With the Word Games drawing closer and closer with each passing day, it was decided that the weekends would be cut short. Helen had finally announced that they were to practice all seven days a week. Most of the girls knew it was coming, so for many the announcement was not a surprise.

They covered a full dress rehearsal every day. It took two hours to run through the entire show, and then the coordinators would meet to discuss and correct bits and pieces. They spent some of the time also arguing over things like the best lighting, the sound and many other small issues that arose. All in all, the girls managed to practice their piece only about four times a day.

Helen was right there among the thick of it all, her radio still her faithful friend. With all the free time allocated between practices, Jane and Sarah managed to get to know a few of the other performers. There was a group of gymnasts they got on particularly well with and would often sit with. Jane still kept a constant distance from Zara, who also had joined another group of girls that she had met. Although she should have been sufficiently distracted with her new group of followers, she still frequently threw Jane dark looks of undisguised hatred. Jane, as before, ignored them as best she could, but somehow it seemed to be getting more difficult. The field just did not seem to be big enough to cater for the both of them, with Zara strutting around like she owned the place. She had managed to keep away from Zara, but for how much longer?

The next morning they were up early and were due to catch the bus to the stadium. The weather had turned dramatically overnight and unlike the previous days, where it had been fine and hot, today it was cold and damp. It had been raining almost throughout the night, and although the rain had now ceased, big clouds still loomed dark and bold in the sky. Jane looked out the window just as they were about to head downstairs. It looked very windy.

"You think it's going to rain again?" Karen asked as she joined Jane at the window.

"I don't know," Jane answered. "There are still a lot of clouds, and they look about ready to break. We might be in for some more rain yet."

"Better take a coat then today, it will be cold and windy on that field."

"And an umbrella," added in Sue, "in case it rains. By the looks of things, it's going to."

The girls met at the front of the hostel as scheduled. They all had the same concerns about the weather and had come prepared. Some had worn warm duffel coats while others wore thick windbreakers. There were even those that wore brightly coloured gloves and hats to protect themselves against the icy wind that had developed. They knew that out on that field they would suffer all the harsh elements of nature and that there would be no protection from the wayward weather.

The weather continued to turn, and even as they stood and waited for the bus, the bite in the air deepened. It was unexpected after the lovely warm weather they had been having. The bus arrived a little later than usual, and as soon as it had stopped in front of them they began to board, glad to get out of the cold wind. The wind seemed to take unkindly to their desertion and developed an even stronger temper, howling nosily through the trees as it wiped their jackets and hair, without mercy. The strong force even whipped one of the girls hats clean off her head. Jane watched as the hat rolled and rolled in the strong wind, its owner scurrying unsuccessfully after it, until eventually, the wind let go of its prize and it landed in a huge, dirty puddle of mud. The owner managed to retrieve it, but it was caked in dirt and ruined.

They settled comfortably in their seats, aware of the heating as soon as they stepped onto the bus. It was warm and cozy and it was a relief to be out of the cold howling wind outside. The drive to the stadium was abnormally quiet. The wind had not let up, and through the windows they could see it howling furiously. The trees were taking great strain, blowing uncontrollably in all directions. Their leaves suffered too, and were being pulled off by the sheer strength of it. It continued blowing ruthlessly, showing no mercy. Not once during the drive did the incessant howling relent, and for the entire journey, the bus rocked from side to side from the vigor of it. The birds had also chosen not to take flight into the dubious looking sky and tried to remain sheltered in the wayward branches.

No one wanted to leave the warm confines of the bus when they finally made it to the stadium. Everything, including the gray building, looked cold, damp and uninviting. They left the bus reluctantly knowing that it was going to be an icy, uncomfortable day that lay ahead of them. Their dressing room was cold, and when they went onto the field, it was even worse. The ground was wet and soggy in some places and in others, very muddy. It seemed that it had rained very hard at the stadium the evening before, proven by the large puddles that lay in almost all corners of the field. Even in the damp and dreary conditions the organizers tried to remain as optimistic as possible, showing a false enthusiasm and eagerness to begin. One small consolation was that the wind blowing on the field was not as strong as it was outside, as it was slightly protected by the stadium's high fences. But, even without the harsher winds from outside the stadium, it was still blowing a small gale and extremely cold. Jane rubbed her fingers together again in a hope of trying to keep warm. The wind had managed to cut right down to the very core of her. Her fingers were slowly going blue and the tips prickling from the icy cold wind.

The procession began, and everyone tried to continue as normal. The first group ran onto the centre field. Mud could be seen sloshing on the ground as they ran, splattering their new costumes. Jane was instantly glad that they were in normal dancing attire. Their costumes had been collected the day before and taken to the seamstress for last minute mending and tightening of sequents that had loosened during the many practices. It had been a blessing in disguise. The first group continued as normal, but by the time they had finished their sequence, mud was splashed onto their costumes and some mud had even managed to splatter high onto their white, cold faces.

It was then that many of the other groups changed out of their costumes. It was a difficult morning as everyone had predicted. Jane huddled in her coat, trying to keep warm as she watched the second group proceed onto the field. You could see they were battling with the strong winds and many of the girls with loose hair were struggling with their wayward locks. Hair could be seeing flying wildly in all directions.

The gymnasts had an especially hard time trying to proceed with their routine flick flacks. By the time they had finished twirling around the fields, their hands and feet were wet, and caked in mud. Still the organizers would not stop, and continued on with the music. Next, the little boy with the hula-hoops appeared, only to have the first accident, by slipping in a muddy pool. All his hops went flying. Someone, Jane was not sure whom, maybe his instructor, had tried to come to his aid, but they too, had slipped and fell. It was a mess. After this accident, the organizers agreed that they would be forced to wait for the field to dry. They knew they could not risk anyone else slipping and maybe injuring themselves.

At first, everyone tried to remain outside under the coverings, eager to be as involved as possible, but as they hours wore on, and it appeared to get colder and colder, everyone slowly began to disappear, opting for sitting in the slightly warmer changing rooms. They were still cold and unwelcoming, but at least they were slightly warmer and drier than outside. Everyone was grateful for their designated areas, expect for Jane, who hated being cooped up. Being confined in a small space and in such close proximity to Zara put her on edge, but with the weather being as bad as it was she had been left with little choice in the matter. Zara however, Jane realized, must have known she was feeling uncomfortable so was going out her way to be irritating. Jane tried her best to ignore her, although the dry looks were hard not to miss. Zara was in full spirits, and together with her roommates seemed to be enjoying themselves. Their little group kept bursting into fits of laughter that no one else was privileged enough to join into.

All the girls waited inside for Helen. They were hoping for some sort of clue as to what the day would hold, but she never appeared. At around midday, almost everyone was bored. There was nothing much to do except sit and talk. It began to rain, light soft drops, but still Helen did not appear. The rain increased steadily and the downpour that had been threatening all day, finally gave way. Large drops fell heavily to the ground as the sky opened up with a vengeance. Everyone was banished inside. Until then, the music and lighting men had been working through the light drizzles, but now they too, had been forced to flee inside under cover. Everyone waited for the rain to cease, but after an hour of heavy downpour, there was little signs of it stopping. The men became irritated, watching and waiting. The drops if anything, seemed to be getting bigger and bigger, and still there was no signs of it relenting. They rain could be heard clearly in the dressing rooms, pelting hard against the roof in a deafening thud. The noise only seemed to increase as time passed.

Helen did not return even when the rain was at its most powerful. The wind outside could be heard howling and whining in accompaniment. It was quite frightening. It was soon after that the organizers had to admit that no further practices would take place that day. All the girls huddled together and waited, wishing that Helen would appear and give them leave to go back to the hostel. Velocity was in agreement and went in search of her. The little bit of talking that had been taking place, stopped completely as the rain pounded on the walls and roof, and got louder and louder. Even Zara's newfound clique remained silent, not breathing a word into the frightening noise. There was nothing else that could be done but wait it out. Another hour passed and still no signs appeared that the rain was even a little lighter. It was cold, dark and wet, the wind was blowing a gale and the rain was thundering down. Eventually, Helen reappeared. Her hair was wet. Plastered to her face. Helen did not seem to notice, but continued to talk as if she was in a rush. She was eager to leave as soon as possible and return back to the safety of the hostel. "Okay, practice is over for today. It looks like a bad storm is approaching. We are all going back to the hostel, immediately. Gather all your belongings and make your way back to the bus. Quick," she urged.

The girls did not have to be asked twice and seconds later were ready and waiting. Other instructors like Helen, who had also been absent, had now also reappeared and their groups were also gathering together ready to depart. There seemed to be a great rush to get out of the stadium and leave. The girls waited at the entrance of the stadium as Helen signalled for the bus to come closer. The wind was howling viciously. The bus came as close as it could get, but not close enough. They would have to run the last few yards. Helen signalled for Sam to open the bus door. He did so immediately, but once the door was open it began shaking uncontrollably from the pressure of the wind. Helen held a thumbs up sign. "Okay, girls, run!" It took great physical effort to run through the strong wind, which was determined to push them backwards. Heads bent forward, they pressed on as their clothes flapped wildly in the unrelenting wind. Coats and scarves whipping mercilessly at their legs as the icy rain continued to drum down like huge sheets of glass. Helen ran too and made her way to the front of the line of girls, helping them onto the shaking bus. Big puddles that had formed on the ground soaked and splashed them with mud and dirt as they ran. Jane ran along with all the others and could feel the icy drops as they hit her face and neck. They felt like a million tiny pins, pelting down, stinging her skin. She felt herself shiver. By the time they reached the safety of the bus, they were drenched from head to toe, the large drops of water seeping straight through their clothes, leaving them cold and shivering.

As Jane reached the bus door, she saw Sarah a few paces behind. One minute she was running toward the open bus door and the next she had slipped. Her legs flew up and over her head. Jane felt like she was watching the accident as if it was in slow motion. Sarah lay on the gravel covered ground in a large dirty puddle of water with the rain pummelling down. She did not move. Time seemed to stand still. Jane continued to watch, expecting Sarah to jump up at any minute, but she did not recover. She continued to lie unmoving. Ignoring the howling wind, Jane ran back toward her friend. "Sarah. Sarah!" she shouted above the noisy downpour. Helen turned at Jane's voice and saw her running away from the bus. Then she saw Sarah. Unmoving. Still on the ground. Helen also began to run. The rain was showing no mercy toward their plight and continued to pelt down hard. Jane reached Sarah just as she started to came to. She tried to sit up, but was badly disorientated. Helen and Jane worked together in lifting her up, and half-carried and half dragged her back to the confines of the bus and out of the cold wind and rain. Sam unaware of what had happened, saw the two of them dragging Sarah. He came immediately to their aid and took Sarah in his strong arms and carried her up the few steps, into the bus. He laid her gently onto the closest seat. Sarah was limp and in shock. She had taken a nasty fall and Helen was worried she may have hit her head as she slipped. Jane ignored her own soaking and dripping clothes as she wiped Sarah's wet and plastered hair out of her eyes. Sarah blinked, in half recognition.

"You okay, Sarah?" Jane asked quietly, worried at the answer.

Sarah half nodded. She was not only drenched, but covered in mud from the puddle she had slipped into. The back of her clothes and her hair caked in the dark sludge. Sarah was shivering and her lips began to turn blue from the icy cold water. "I'm cold," she mumbled.

"Sam, can you put the heater up please," asked Helen as she opened one of the upper cupboards on the bus. She took out a thick yellow blanket as Jane tried to ease Sarah out of her soaking jacket. They then wrapped her into the warm blanket, hoping that she would warm up quickly. Sarah sat shivering, her blue lips chattering against the cold. Sam found another dry towel and passed it onto Helen. She dried Sarah's face and hands, and dried her wet and muddy hair as best she could before wrapping her hair up in the towel. Through all this, while Jane was trying to help and warm Sarah, she could not help noticing Zara. Watching and enjoying every minute, a smile on her pink lips as she enjoyed the drama before her. Jane could see she was barely containing her glee.

Sam was worried about Sarah, but there was nothing much he could do, so he left her in the safe hands of Helen and Jane. His job was only just starting and that was to get the girls back to the hostel safe and sound. In all his years as a driver, he had never seen this kind of torrential rain before. Driving was going to be difficult. He knew that they could not stay where they were and wait it out. They had no idea how long this was going to last, it could be hours and hours. They had no food or water, and he knew that Helen wanted to get Sarah seen by a doctor. He had no choice but to get them back to the hostel.

Sam reversed out of the parking bay and the journey home began. No one spoke or even dared breath as the rain continued to pummel down onto the yellow bus.

The wind was howling fiercely outside and the bus was shaking and rattling from the force of it. It was dark, all the sun from that morning blocked out by the big, almost black, clouds dominating the heavens. A large streak of lightning struck the sky a few paces ahead. Its blue light piecing the dark sky fiercely. With the bright jolt of lightening came they deafening sounds of thunder as it rumbled in the distance. Someone on the bus screamed in fright. A high-pitched sound. Then there was silence as it all became dark again. Sam ignored it all and concentrated on his driving.

The drive normally only took about fifteen minutes but he knew that in these driving conditions, it was going to take much longer. He drove very slowly. The rain was coming down in huge sheets and was very dense, so he was only able to see a few yards in front of him. Jane saw him turn on his bright lights, but they made no difference. It was like a hug, thick blanket had settled down on the road, making visibility almost impossible. Sam continued driving at a slow and steady pace as the huge sheets of rain made the roads slippery. Another ray of blue lighting hit the sky, and there was sharp light again for those few minutes. Everything seemed illuminated and an eerie glow descended.

Everyone waited in silence for the thunder to follow. The bus was silent. Expecting. No one daring to even breath. When the thunder did strike, it was a loud booming noise. Even though everyone was expecting it, the sound still managed to frighten and a few girls jumped at the loud roar. The girls were nervous and remained silent as they continued onwards. It was with a great sigh of relief when the roof of the hostel finally come into view.

They struggled up the driveway. The mud would not allow the tires of the bus to grip a firm hold. The wheels spun and spun and mud flew up in all directions. Sam held the brake firmly in place and tried again. Mud continued to fly and in a battle of wills, the mud eventually gave way. The bus was moving forward again.

They began to make their way up the steep driveway. Sam drove slowly and carefully. The bus lost its grip for a second time, but this time, it felt like the vehicle was sliding backwards. There was an audible gasp from the girls behind him. Sam used all his expert skills as a driver and after the initial slide backwards soon had the bus easing forward again. Almost as soon as it had started, it was over. They were almost there. Sam knew that he was almost done. He would soon have the girls back at the hostel and to safety. When he pulled up alongside the entrance, he gave a huge sigh of relief.

Jane and a few of the other girls present helped Sarah off the bus. She had not spoken a single word the entire trip home. Not even the thunder and lighting seemed to have registered in her mind.

"I'll go and find Doctor Shane and bring him up to your bedroom," Helen said, clearly concerned.

Jane nodded as they all helped Sarah up the stairs to their bedroom. She was cooperative, although not by much.

Doctor Shane was only a few minutes behind them, with Helen in tow. He did a full examination on Sarah. After what seemed like hours to Jane, he came out of the room and confirmed that she was fine. In shock and cold, but she'd be fine after a hot bath, some warm food and goods night's rest. The girls left Jane alone to tend to her best friend. Jane sat Sarah on the bed and ran into the bathroom, running the hot water full blast. Then she helped her friend out of her wet clothes and assisted her into the hot bath. Jane noticed with alarm that her lips were still blue and shivering, and her hands still icy cold. She hoped that the hot bath would sort that out and warm her.

Jane cleaned the mud off Sarah's hair and washed it until it gleamed, then she helped her friend out of the bath and dressed her. When she was dressed, Jane then helped Sarah into her bed. "I'll go and get you something hot to drink. I won't be long."

Jane went downstairs to the restaurant. She was sure she would be able to get something for Sarah to eat, even though dinner was still hours away. The hostel was warm and cozy, although the rain was still incessant outside, and the wind could still be heard howling with a vengeance. All the others were downstairs too, showered and changed, and were warming up with mugs of hot chocolate. It was only then that Jane realized that she was still walking around in her wet and soggy clothes. Her body was also cold and shivering, although she had paid it no attention.

"How is Sarah doing?" asked Karen, worried.

"She's okay. She's had a hot bath now and I've put her in bed. She should be feeling better soon. I'm just taking her something to eat…"

"That was a nasty fall," Sonia added.

"Yes, it was," Jane answered. "This rain is awful. I wonder how long it's going to last?"

"I have no idea, but it's not eased at all," Sonia replied.

As if to confirm her answer another loud bang of lighting and thunder penetrated the sky. Jane managed to get some hot soup and some fresh rolls and took a tray up to Sarah. She looked much better after her bath, although she was still very cold, so Jane piled her bed high with blankets. An early night would do her good.

The next day, everyone woke in shock. It was as if the previous day's storm had never existed. Gone was the insistent rain and there was no trace of the howling winds and monstrous thunder that had ripped through the sky the day before. All was calm. The sun was shining and big soft, billowing clouds floated in the heavens. It was a complete contrast to the storm from the previous day. It was as if the day before had never existed.

Sarah had recovered after a good night's rest. She was back to her old self and the only reminder of the awful day was a large black bruise on the top of her right leg. It was the size of a tennis ball, but as long as she did not touch it, it did not give her too much trouble. She had a slight case of the sniffles too, but that she could live with. Everything returned back to normal. The girls dressed and went outside to wait for the bus. They had a rehearsal to get to.

The drive to the stadium was the same as it had always been, bar the day before. Everyone was in high spirits and there was much chatter and laughter. The stadium field had already began to dry out, which was amazing considering the huge puddles from the day before, and after much fussing by the organizers, they began the rehearsals at eleven o'clock.

Some of the lights had been knocked out of position, so workmen were going around checking and refitting them. The speakers were checked too and assessed for damage. No one dared to ask Helen anything. She was busy running around the field, and as usual, she had her little radio alongside her. She seemed to be extremely agitated over a number of things.

"What do you mean there are no lights?" Helen demanded. She was silent for a moment as she listened to the person on the other end reply. "How many are broken?" she asked quietly. Silence followed. "Can they be fixed?" More silence. "Okay, get as many as you can. Yes, red, blue and yellow." Helen nodded into the radio and sighed. "As soon as possible. Yes." She clicked off the radio and looked around. It was not too serious. The lights would be replaced and would be in position again the following day. It was just that she did not need this additional kind of hassle so close to the big day. Things had been so in control one minute and the next, completely out of control. She wished, just for once, that things could go smoothly. She felt like she was spinning and spinning and could not stop. First, there had been the storm, which had caused havoc with the lights and sound. All the previous day's work had to be redone. And with the big day so close ahead, almost everything needed her final approval. The seamstress who had delivered the costumes early that morning wanted her opinion on the beads and final finishing touches. The light coordinator had a better idea for the solo piece and what lights would be best for Zara. She knew she had to listen to his suggestions. But even the kitchen staff, wanted her confirmation on what dinner they were to serve the girls on their big night. It was all too much in a short space of time. Could the caterers not even plan one dinner without her consent? Helen enjoyed organizing these events usually. She was an expert, but she had to admit that she would be glad that it was almost over. Never in her life had it been so difficult to manage twenty-eight girls. She knew Zara had a big role to play in her negative feelings, and hoped that there would be no more incidents before the big day. Then, once the World Games was over, she could take herself off on holiday and relax. She needed it.

    The storm had been unwelcome, but they'd soon be back on schedule. With only a few more days left to go, the tension was beginning to build. Anxiety and apprehension had begun to infiltrate the performers.

Chapter 44

Zara sat on the bench and watched the other performers. She knew she would not be up for another half an hour at least. She let the warm sun soak into her skin. Who would have thought that the day before had held such a horrific storm? One of the worst ones she had ever seen? It had been very scary, but, in the long run, it had been worth it. She had seen Sarah slip and then fall, and it had been one of the funnies things she had ever seen. Zara firmly believed that Sarah had gotten what she deserved. It was such a pity though, that it had not been Jane.

She had to admit that the storm had been very bad and she had been quite relieved when Sam got them to the safekeeping of the hostel. She had never before seen lightning and thunder that dangerous before and she, who had never in her life been afraid of storms, had been nervous. She immediately though of Pat. Pat hated lightning. Had been petrified of it since she was a little girl. Zara wondered if she had been at the hotel when the storm had hit or if had she been out in the town. Zara hoped she had been out and had got caught in the thick of the thunder and lightning. She hoped that Pat had been scared to death. It would serve her right after her recent behaviour. All these thoughts soon had her thinking of Matt. Had Matt been with Pat? Had he comforted her? The thought had her fuming. Zara knew she had to see Matt again. She was sure if she saw him, then things would be fine between them once more. It was only a small, tiny misunderstanding. He had not meant what he had said. Everything would be fine if she could just see him. But how? Helen was still watching her like a hawk and it would be so much harder to sneak away now. There must be a way Zara debated. There must be!

She was not sure how it had happened, but a plan began to form with amazing speed. Maybe, it was seeing her roommates talking and laughing together as they made their way over to her. Something triggered.

Zara had made a deal with the other girls. It had been so much easier than she had originally thought. She had used the oldest trick in the book. She had bribed them. If they covered for her for one evening, she would order them a full Chinese meal. Hand delivered to the hostel. Anything they wanted. All the trimmings included. After weeks of hostel food, who could refuse a small feast? She had promised them anything and everything...all they had to do was cover for her, for one evening. It was so simple.

Zara was not sure if they would agree, but she knew she just had to see Matt. There was no way she was going to leave things the way they were and there was no other alternative but to go to the hotel after him. She was desperate to see him and hated knowing that Pat was there with him instead of her. "But what if you get caught again?" one of the girls asked.

"I won't, silly. If you stay in our bedroom, Helen will think we are all here, together, having another girls night in. She won't suspect a thing," Zara added, to reconfirm that her idea was brilliant.

"What if she comes in like the last time?" was the second objection.

Zara thought for a moment, "You can tell her I have gone to the drink machine for more cokes, or to the kitchen for napkins. Anything believable."

"Will that work?" one of the other girls asked.

"Yes, of course it will work. You must just remember to stay in our room. No one is allowed to leave. That's the most important thing." Zara stressed. Finally, after a little coaxing and fine tuning her idea, they had agreed. Zara had left them a large wad of cash and given them the name of the Chinese restaurant near by. It was all set. Tonight she would see Matt and clear this whole horrid thing up.

She debated whether or not to call Pat and let her know she was coming. Then, after some consideration, she changed her mind. No way. That would give Pat time to prepare herself and maybe, even get rid of Mark in the process. That would totally ruin her plan. No, it was best that she arrive unannounced. That way she would have the upper hand.

She had no idea what she was going to do or say. She needed to get Matt alone so she could apologize. No man could resist a teary apology and then everything would be fine. Everything would go back to normal. This little hiccup would be forgotten and they could get back to getting to know each other. Zara knew she really liked Matt, but she was sure there was a lot more to learn about the mysterious, handsome man.

Zara let herself daydream. Daddy would be thrilled when she introduced him to them. He was all the things a man should be. Smart, talented and handsome. And she knew he came from money. That much was obvious in the way he dressed and spoke. Probably from some expensive private school in the country somewhere. She would have to remember to ask more questions about his family and background. All her thoughts soon had her thinking of Raymond. It was odd. She had not thought of him in weeks. He still called her, but she had taken to ignoring his phone calls or letting the phone ring out. Sometimes he left a message, but most times he did not. She would have to sort their relationship out soon. Tell him, that his time was up. Thank you, but no thank you. After meeting a perfect man like Matt, Raymond did not come even close. Zara looked at him through different eyes now. He was hard and brash. Why had she not noticed it before? The answer eluded her. She shook her head. She did not want to be thinking of Raymond anyway. She had someone else on her mind. Someone tall, who smelled of masculine soap, and had a devilishly handsome grin.

After rehearsals they went back at the hostel. Zara dressed normally and headed for the restaurant. She had to make sure that Helen saw her that evening before she snuck out to see Matt. As an extension of her plan, Zara began to wander around the halls of the hostel, hoping she would deliberately bump into Helen. She walked around and around the corridors but could not locate Helen anywhere. She walked all over the grounds and back again. She had just about been ready to give up, when she eventually found Helen at the end of the hall, walking toward the library. She seemed happy and amused, talking to some of the other girls. Zara headed in their direction, as casually as she could. As she stopped in front of Helen, she deliberately dropped her cardigan on the floor, but as planned she continued to walk on, as if she had not noticed. Zara only had a few seconds to wait before she heard her name being called out. "Zara," Helen sang out.

Zara turned, knowing her practised look of surprise would fool anyone. "Yes, Helen?"

"You've dropped her cardigan, dear." Helen bent down and picked up the pink garment.

"Oh, thank you. I hadn't noticed that it slipped from my shoulders." With that, she took the cardigan, offered her biggest smile, and continued down the hall. She rounded the corner and stopped. She waited a few more moments and then took a peek behind the corner. She was unable to hide her satisfied smile, as she watched Helen turn the corner and head inside the library. It had worked exactly as she had planned. Helen had seen her. That was enough. After waiting a few more minutes, just for good measure, she ran as silently as possible the way she had come.

The cab had been waiting for some time now. She had given the driver strict instructions that he was to wait. No matter what, he was to wait. She would definitely be there. She even offered to pay him double the cab fare to ensure his presence.

Zara glanced at her watch as the cab made its way over to the familiar Four Seasons Hotel. It was much later than she normally went out, but it was still light. She knew that it was quite possible that Matt and Pat would have already sat down to dinner.

Once having arrived at the Four Seasons, Zara wasted no time. She paid the driver and headed straight for the dining room. Now that she was this close to Matt, she could not wait another minute. She had to see him. Without even stopping to give her name to the hostess, she went straight into the restaurant. She scanned the tables. At first glance she did not see him. Then, in the far off distance, she saw them together. Heads bent, quietly laughing. The sight of them made her feel physically sick. How dare Pat flirt so openly. Did she have no idea how she looked acting like that? Then she gazed and studied Matt unobserved. He was just so handsome. She took in his perfectly ironed shirt and his smooth hair. His sparkling eyes and his handsome smile. He was exactly the kind of man she was looking for. Again, Raymond came to her mind. He was way passed his sell by date. That was undeniable now. She was finished with him. Matt was her new man now.

She watched in numb fascination as Pat threw her head back and laughed at something Matt had said. Zara could not postpone it any longer. She had to make her way over to their table and make her presence known. Then she would have to get rid of Pat so she could apologies to Matt in private.

Matt must have sensed her presence as she began to walk over because he looked up then at that precise moment. His face froze in position as he watched Zara saunter over. She looked like a ghost in his mind. All sweet smiles and coy looks. It was impossible to believe that she would have the nerve to actually make an appearance after her outrageous behaviour the other night.

Pat was still laughing at what Matt had said when she saw the look on his face. "What is it?" she said, wiping the tears of laugher from her eyes. Matt tried to speak, but no words seemed to form. He was in a state of shock. Eventually Pat turned and followed his gaze. She, too was unable to hide her surprise as Zara reached their table. Zara grabbed her friend and hugged her fiercely as if there had never been any problem. Pat almost choked with the amount of perfume Zara had doused herself with. To anyone else, a male maybe, it would have been a pleasant smell, but to Pat, it just reconfirmed Zara's reason for being there. Zara was there to make trouble again.

"Hey there, you guys. I thought you had forgotten me," she purred. She bent over toward Matt, and gave him a playful kiss and a warm hug. Matt remained limp. The surprise he felt at seeing her, making him neither reject, nor encourage her hello. Zara either did not notice, or she chose to ignore Matt's indifference. Matt was sure it was the latter.

Zara took the seat between the two of them and sat down, smoothing her long blond hair as she did so. She was disappointed to notice that they had already finished with dinner and dessert, and were now drinking coffees. She had known she might miss the dinner, but she had hoped to at least make dessert. She tried not to let her irritation show.

Pat seemed to be the first to recover from the shock. "What are you doing here Zara?" she asked, as politely as she could.

"I came for dinner, silly. It's Wednesday."

Pat was unable to hide the dismay from her face. What did Wednesday have to do with anything? They had no set arrangement for dinner on Wednesday, or any other day for that matter. She had been having a nice dinner with Matt. Why did Zara always have to ruin things? Things had gone far enough.

She knew that the only reason Zara was there now with them, was because she had fallen for Matt. It had nothing to do with Zara being concerned for her, a faithful friend throughout childhood. If she had been, she would have called before and offered an apology. She had not. Pat remembered that evening clearly. It had been one of the most awful evenings of her life. A complete disaster. She had left the restaurant feeling betrayed by her best friend and convinced that Matt had been using her too. She was sure that the two of them were only using her as an excuse to see each other. It was only when Matt had reappeared at her hotel twenty minutes later that she realized that Matt had nothing to do with the monstrous evening and that the whole disaster had been completely Zara's fault. Matt had been innocent and not too happy about being used either. In fact, he had been furious with Zara.

Now she realized that it was silly of her to think that someone like Matt could actually fall for someone like Zara. She should have known that a man like him would see past her sweet smiles and fake friendliness, to the vicious, two-timing cat that she was. Pat had decided that she was not standing for it anymore. She was past overlooking Zara's many faults. Against all previous laws, Pat looked at Zara angrily. "We have no standing arrangement for Wednesdays, Zara," she said firmly.

Zara tried not to show her annoyance. No one ever contradicted her, least of all, Pat. "Yes, we do! Every Wednesday we meet. You know that, *silly*." She laughed looking at Matt, as if Pat had momentarily lost her wits.

"DON'T call me silly," Pat whispered in controlled words. "And NO, we do not meet every Wednesday!"

Zara, who had gone back to gazing up into Matt's eyes, stared shockingly at Pat. In all the years they had been friends,

Pat had always done exactly as Zara had told her. Never had she contradicted or disobeyed her, as she was doing now. It was just not done to Zara Maddox. Zara drew her eyes away from Matt angrily, and looked Pat square in the eye, daring her to contradict her again, one last time. There was no denying the challenging stare. "Yes, we do," she insisted.

Pat was unable to contain her own rage at the audacity of Zara. Did she not realize that the game was over. Unblinking she shouted back, "*NO— WE—DO—NOT!*"

Zara coughed, not quite sure how to discipline Pat. She really did not want a scene with Pat now, especially with Matt being there. She wanted Matt to see her all innocence and sweet and get him to like her, as much as she liked him. Pat however was intent on ruining her plan. She ignored her friend and changed the subject. She would deal with Pat later. "So, I see you guys have eaten. Thanks for waiting for me. Are you staying for another coffee? I'm dying to have one."

Matt spoke for the first time since she had sat down. "No, I don't think so. Pat and I are off for a walk along the river." It was quite obvious that he was trying to get rid of her, while at the same time trying to stay polite.

"Oh goodie. Well, let's get going then," Zara chirped happily as she turned and bent for her handbag as if she was leaving too. They had no choice. Zara jumped up elegantly from her seat and retrieved her coat. She was determined to come along. "Matt, would you be a doll and help me with my coat?" Matt coughed. He was uncomfortable, but he would not be rude. He lifted the heavy coat and held it in front of him as Zara slipped in first one arm and then the next. Matt threw Pat an apologetic look.

Pat was not angry with Matt, but she was furious with Zara. Of all the things, Zara had now outdone herself. Could she not see that she was unwelcome? Pat looked at her friend with newfound eyes. She had always known that Zara was spoilt and used to getting her own way, but never before had she acted like this. Zara was determined to get what she wanted. And now she wanted Matt. There was no denying that. The fact that her best friend was interested in him first made no difference to her. And with that realization came a strange feeling. It was as if she had been released from old chains that had been tying her down. She decided that there was no way that she was going to let Zara get the better of her—anymore. Now or ever again. Zara was finished with using her.

Chapter 45

Jane had spoken with her parents. They were due to leave the following day for Germany and she was finally going to see them again. It felt like months had passed since she had spent any time with them. She could not wait for their arrival.

As the big day grew closer, Jane grew more excited. Only four more days and that was it. She would have the opportunity to dance as she had never danced before. Her life would never be the same again. This event was going to impact the rest of her days.

Everyone was talking abut the press coverage they were due to expect. Jane knew that there would be many important people present that would be able to help her career as a professional dancer. They'd be on the lookout for girls to dance in Las Vegas. Others would be scouting for West End shows in London and New York. Others too would be there to assess for things—like music videos or even movie roles. This opportunity would make or break her career as a dancer.

Jane hoped that she would be noticed by one of the scouts present. The possibility that she might be made her feel like she could do anything, go anywhere. She just had to ensure she danced her absolute best and *was* noticed. Obviously, with Zara having the main solo dances, she would have access to the widest and most amazing opportunities. The scouts would see her first, so she would be first in line for the best opportunities available. Still, Jane refused to let this get her down. There would be many scouts present from all over the world, and she was determined to get noticed by one of them. She just had to make sure that when she was on that field, she shone like a star. That was her key and she was counting on it.

Jane let her mind wander. What would she do if no one contacted her for anything? It was a possibility, although one she hoped would not happen. She thought about what she would do then. It had always been her dream that she would one day open her own dance school. She had already decided that it would be somewhere close to home and near the opera house. She would use her school to ensure her dancers were in as many shows and productions as she could book. If nothing came of the World Games, well, at least she had enjoyed the experience. She'd open her dance school and she'd still be happy. And if she *was* picked by one of the scouts, she knew that she would still one day like to own her own dance studio anyway. So, either way, she was headed somewhere, and had a goal to reach. Still, even with this knowledge, she would love it if someone did approach her to take part in a West End show. Something big like "Cats" or "The Lion King." If that amazing opportunity presented itself, she would jump at the chance and grab the opportunity with both hands.

Her parents would arrive as planned, in less than an hour, and would be staying in a small hotel just outside the town. Surprisingly, she was able to meet them at the airport, as rehearsals were only taking place once a day. The intense training of the last few months was over. The organizers were now more concerned that all the performers remain rested so they'd be on top form for the big night. The intense training was complete and everyone and everything, was perfect. This left most of their remaining days free for them to enjoy.

Jane was excited to show her parents where she had been and what she had seen over the past few weeks. The fact that in the next four days she was to perform the most important event in her life, she tucked away at the back of her memory.

*****

Zara too was elated. Her parents were also arriving that day. They had booked and would soon be checked into the Grand Suite at the Four Seasons. She was elated for another reason too. She had managed to steal a few private moments with Matt, and she could firmly say that he had been kind and sweet to her. She had apologized for her behaviour and Matt had been wonderfully sympathetic, as she had predicted. That awful evening was now like a bad dream. When she first arrived, Pat had made it impossible for her to hold a conversation with Matt without being interrupted. Eventually though, through her persistence, she had won. She refused to let Pat get involved with her plan to make right with Matt. Zara supposed she must have realized that, for Pat soon became quiet and sulking. Zara did not care or pay her much attention. Why would she? She had Matt right at her side, being as charming as ever. They had so many things they had in common too, and the walk along the river had been a perfect end to the evening. Zara thought it was quite funny really. The more she thought about it, the more she was convinced that Matt was in fact using Pat to get to see her. It seemed a bold thing for him to do, being as sweet and kind as he was. Still, it was the only explanation she would accept.

Zara had enjoyed every minute of the walk and the easygoing conversation that followed between them. She found him to have a great sense of humour, too, and was unable to stop from laughing at his quick, witty comments. To her eyes and ears, he was perfect. In every way possible. So the big question was, when would Matt officially ask her out?

As she had planned, she asked many questions about his family and his background. She had been pleased with his answers. Pleased, but not surprised. She had known all along that he was from a good, strong background. And, as she had predicted, he came from a family with extreme wealth. He had not actually said so, not in so many words, but with conversation including time spent with his sister abroad on a family yacht and their house in the country, she could put two and two together. They had talked quite freely and openly all evening. Zara had been elated when she had finally made it back to the hostel. In only a few more days her parents would be meeting him too. Her father was going to be thrilled. Maybe he could even come on that holiday with her, now that Pat was firmly out of the picture and no longer invited. She could not very well go on her own. She could see it now. Them playing in the sea, then enjoying long relaxing walks on the beach. It would be very romantic and Matt would fall even deeper in love with her. It was going to be perfect.

They had arranged that they would all meet downstairs for dinner. Her parents had not yet tried the hotel restaurant and were eager to see what fine dining they had to offer. Besides, it was also known that they held one of the best wine selections available, and her father was eager to try these too, having developed a little wine collection himself over the years. Zara thought it was all perfect. She had already told her parents all about Matt. They had been surprised, but also pleased for their only daughter. Unfortunately, there was no getting away from excluding Pat from the dinner invitation. She would have to be joining them. Not only was she staying in the same hotel, but she had know her parents for years. It would be impossible *not* to invite her, although she had tried.

"So, what about Raymond?" her father asked over his red wine, while they sat at the bar that afternoon.

Zara remembered pouting. "I will have to tell him, I suppose."

"Yes, and soon," he agreed. "He is due to arrive here tomorrow at lunchtime."

Zara knew she could not put it off any longer. "Yes, I know. I'll tell him then." She agreed with her father. "But once you meet Matt, you'll understand."

Her father was intrigued as she knew he would be. "So what's this new guy like?" he asked, fascinated that his daughter was so excited and happy at meeting a young man. A gentlemen by the sounds of things. Zara proceeded to tell them everything, and it was evident to both her parents that she was totally taken by this new man in her life. They were surprised, too, at the glow of pride that took over on Zara's face. Never before had they seen her so happy and in love. Not even with Raymond.

Zara had already decided that she was going to introduce Matt to her parents as her boyfriend. She had deliberated over it long and hard, but in the end, she felt it was the best way to speed things up between them. She had already decided that she would say it casually in conversation. That way it would slide better. Until now it was unspoken between them that they were an item, and she wanted to make it official. Pat was still hanging around, and it was beginning to annoy her. She was due to go back home right after the World Games, so Zara knew she would just have to stick it out until then. But Pat's presence was now just so irritating. She wanted to be with Matt alone, and she had been unable to arrange it yet. She knew Matt was a decent guy and would not leave her out. After all, it was because of Pat that they had finally met. No, Matt was too nice to dump a friend, and as much as she hated to admit it, they were friends. Zara knew he would be as gentlemanly as he always was and Zara liked him even more for that.

It was strange, she had always thought Raymond was a perfect gentleman, but after meeting and observing Matt, she could definitely say that he was the furthest thing from it.

Now that all the dancers' families and friends had started arriving in Germany, the girls were given more freedom. Helen announced that they were welcome to stay out later during the evenings with their parents and could take advantage of having dinner with them. Zara was ecstatic, as it meant she could stop sneaking in and out of the hostel as before. Helen did stress though that they had to be present for their last remaining rehearsals each day and that no lateness would be tolerated.

Dressed in the best outfit she had bought with her, Zara looked at herself in the mirror. Her long blond hair was loose and freshly washed. Her makeup perfectly applied. She knew that it was going to be an excellent night. She was surprised at the tiny bubbles popping in her stomach. Was it nerves? She was not sure. All she knew was that she was excited. Excited at seeing Matt again, excited at introducing him to her parents and also excited that tonight, they would make their feelings official.

When she arrived at the hotel, her parents were already in the bar, enjoying their first drink of the evening. "Oh, darling, you look lovely," crooned her mother, approvingly.

"Thanks, Mum." She kissed first her mother, then her father on the cheek. Matt had not yet arrived.

"What would you like to drink, honey?" asked her father.

"I'll have a Perrier, please," replied Zara, looking around the room. Zara took in the restaurant before her. The candles had all been lit and there was a romantic feel about the place. Soft music could be heard from the speakers above them. Zara was not sure if it was the restaurant that was done up romantically or it was her own feelings. She could not wait for Matt to arrive and her parents to finally meet him.

Just as her drink arrived, Matt and Pat entered the room. Zara was slightly irritated that they had arrived together. Pat was just not accepting the inevitable and was holding on with every claw possible. Zara ignored the gesture and made her way over. Not even Pat was going to ruin this evening for her. She threw Pat a quick kiss on the cheek and then bent for Matt. She could smell his cologne. He smelled so nice and she was momentarily lost. It was a sharp masculine scent that she was unable to forget. She took in his appearance and as always, the sight of him seemed to take her breath away. The three of them walked over to her expecting parents. "Pat, honey, how have you been?" asked her mother eagerly.

Pat nodded, smiling at her parents. "Hi, Mrs. Maddox. Mr. Maddox. Very well, thank you."

"You been keeping our girl out of trouble?" asked her father, jokingly.

Pat nodded again, still smiling, "Trying to, sir. Trying to."

Zara waited until the reunion was over. Then stepping forward, she announced Matt. "Mum. Dad. This is Matt." Her father stood and shook his hand. "Nice to meet you, son."

Zara watched as he leaned toward her mother and kissed her politely on the cheek. The perfect move. Her mum would be impressed by that. She should have known that he would do things correctly. "Nice to meet you too." They had more drinks at the bar and then made their way to their waiting table.

Zara thought the evening was going splendidly. Matt and her parents seemed to have so much in common and they had been exploring all sorts of subjects since they sat down to dinner together. Matt seemed to have impressed them both with his knowledge and his unusual wit. Zara could not help beaming. How could they not find him anything but polite and easy to talk to? Pat too, was less irritating than she normally was, talking vividly with her mother. It was turning out to be a good evening. Everyone seemed to be relaxed and enjoying themselves. She had hoped to introduce Matt as her boyfriend, but the words had not seemed to come out. Still, she was not worried. There was plenty of time for them to make it official.

Dessert had been served. Everyone seemed to have gone for the chocolate torte and ice cream. The glass cart roaming around the restaurant had seen to that. There was just no denying that it was the best looking dessert on display, decorated with small shavings of white chocolate and filled with a soft dark, mouse.

"This dessert is delicious," her mother cooed as she took another spoon full. "You and I have always had an aversion to chocolate, haven't we, Zara?"

Zara nodded, agreeing happily. Everything was going so smoothly. Dinner had been perfect and Pat was her normal self. No sulking or grim looks. It was making for a much better evening for all of them. "You simply have to try Rose's strawberry cheesecake," stated her mother, looking at Matt. "She's the best dessert maker in the country."

Her father looked up and smiled, "I'm sure you will, now that you are going to be a more frequent visitor at our house."

Matt looked up from his ice cream, in confusion. "A more frequent visitor?"

"Yes, you know, now that you and Zara are seeing each other."

Matt placed his spoon silently on his plate. He then looked at Zara, as her father continued. "Zara has told us the wonderful news."

"Oh, has she now?" Matt replied evenly.

"Yes, and I myself have never seen her more happy. Our Zara is very much besotted with you."

Zara beamed happily from her parents to Matt. She was sure that he would take his cue and agree. Finally, things would be confirmed. Pat could move off and let her and Matt be.

"Well, you see, that's impossible, sir," Matt replied.

Zara dropped her fork, in shock. She must have misheard. Surely Matt was not disagreeing with her parents. Her parents looked from Zara to Matt and back to Zara again. A look of complete surprise on their faces.

"What do you mean?" asked her father.

"I cannot be dating, Zara, because I am dating and very much in love with Pat. We've been seeing each other for around three months now. I'm sorry, but you must be mistaken, or misunderstood."

Zara did not know what to say. She had been *so* sure that Matt's feelings toward her were returned. How could Matt possibly in his right mind choose Pat over her. It just was not imaginable. What could he see in Pat? There *must* be some mistake. She was the beautiful one. The rich one. Why he was not interested in her?

"Oh, there must have been some sort of confusion on our part," her father replied, obviously embarrassed.

"It's no problem. No problem at all!" Matt replied back.

"Actually," Pat continued, "we have some news of our own." She looked at everyone at the table. "Matt has asked me to marry him. And I have said yes. We're engaged," she announced smiling the words across to everyone.

Her mother jumped up, immediately, clearly ecstatic and hugged Pat. "Congratulations, Pat. Matt. That is wonderful news." Her mother beamed.

Her father stood and shook Matt's hand. "Congratulations to you both."

Only Zara sat rooted in her seat. Engaged? It was impossible. It was at that precise moment that Zara noticed the diamond ring glittering like mad on Pat's left finger. Zara jumped up quickly, as if her eyes were deceiving her, and grabbed Pat's finger. She took in the thin platinum band and the large diamond in the centre of the ring. Many other smaller diamonds were surrounding the larger, bright stone. It was sparkling and shiny. She stumbled back into her seat. Shocked. *It cannot be true,* she thought to herself. *Not my wonderful Matt. No. This could not be happening to me. To us. What's going on? I must be in a bad dream,* Zara told herself.

"Champagne." Her father cheered, "We need champagne."

Zara sat dazed. Her heart was hammering in her chest and her mouth had suddenly gone dry. She tried to speak, but her tongue would not move. She could not take it all in. Perfect Matt had actually chosen Pat. Had even proposed marriage. After just three months. Were they mad? You cannot get married after just three months? In her state of wonderment, Zara noticed the champagne being brought over to their table. Her father was soon filling the tiny flutes. The bubbles fizzing to the surface. Everyone laughing and joking, as well wishes were bestowed. Pat smiling from ear to ear, and Matt, holding her hand tightly. Zara was numb and barely remembered taking a sip of the sweet liquid. All she could see was the diamond ring on Pat's hand glittering wildly and impossible for anyone to ignore. Its radiant sparkle was blinding and was giving her a massive, dull headache.

Chapter 46

Helen was in a complete fluster. They were due to go onto the field in less than an hour and the lead of their show was missing. Helen was furious. She approached the rest of the waiting girls and asked, "Has *anyone* seen Zara?" Everyone shook their heads no. Helen tried to remain calm. Zara would show up. It was the second last rehearsal. Zara knew that. She would be here, she was just running a little late.

Another half an hour had passed and Helen was not so sure anymore. Zara had still not appeared. Helen knew that the chances of her appearing now were getting slimmer and slimmer as the minutes ticked passed. She knew she should not have been surprised. Both Zara's parents and boyfriend were in town and unlike the other girls, she would take full advantage of having her father around to bail her out of any unfortunate incidents, including skipping rehearsals with only two days to go. Helen could not believe that Zara could be so inconsiderate. They had all been specifically warned not to miss any of the last rehearsals. Did she have no loyalty? Not for the first time Helen wished that Zara had never been chosen for the lead, In fact, she wished that Zara had never been chosen for Germany at all. She was an ungrateful, inconsiderate, spoilt brat.

Helen went in search of Velocity and found her standing beside one of the pillars, doing some last minute checks on the sound. Helen told her their problem. They had to locate Zara as quickly as possible. "Call her mobile," she ordered. "We have to get her here ASAP. We're on in less than twenty minutes"

Velocity was annoyed and also angry. For Zara to not show up now, two days before rehearsal was unheard of and incredibly selfish. Everyone was working so hard. Did Zara care for no one else—except herself? Everyone knew her reputation, and Velocity wondered if this was yet another one of the tactics. Not only to worry everyone, but also to show her upper hand. She knew without a doubt that when she did find Zara, she'd be one of the first ones to have words with her. Helen rejoined the waiting girls. She was now desperate. "Does anyone have *any* idea where Zara could be? Any idea at all?" she asked again. There were no replies as everyone shook their head.

Zara was untraceable and their time for finding her was up. It was now their turn to take to the field. Helen was furious. She no other option but to continue with the show as planned, but without her lead present. She *had* to let the music run. It was not fair on any of the other groups for her to make them all wait, just because her main lead had disappeared.

At first, the producers thought there had been some sort of problem, but Helen just shook her head in response to their silent questions. They must have understood what she meant to say, so as bizarre was it was, they allowed the music to continue playing. Zara's cue began as usual, and as everyone knew, she was now due to run onto the field then begin her solo piece. Instead, her music began and where Zara should have been, was now just an empty space. Everyone waited. Was there a problem? People began looking around. Questions were being asked. Helen held her head down in embarrassment and disgust. How could Zara do this to them all?

Zara's piece came to an end, and the rest of the girls ran out onto the field. They danced as they had been taught and continued as if nothing was the matter. Then, as the music died down, they ran toward the exit and through the tunnel. Zara, if she had been present, would now be doing her final exit piece. Everyone was aware of the open field again, as her music continued to play.

Chapter 47

Zara had woken up late that morning and immediately knew something wasn't right. She could feel the knot in the pit of her stomach even before she got out of bed, but was not sure what it was from. Only once she had sat up and took a sip of water, did the previous evenings events come flooding back to her. And then she was thrown back into the worst nightmare of her life. The massive diamond ring that should have been hers and the golden wedding at some exotic location. Then she thought about Matt. Lost to her forever. She keeled over in pain. It was all too much. How could Matt do this to her? She grabbed for the little red rose that she had been treasuring and squashed it mercilessly.

An hour later, Zara was dressed, ready to go to the airport. Raymond was arriving shortly. She would meet him and he could offer her some much-needed diversion. He did not know what had happened the night before and how close he had come to being dumped. And now, there was no need to tell him. She would pick him up as normal and he would never have to know. Zara felt reckless. She wanted to do something exciting. Anything wild. She was determined that Raymond would offer her a diversion to the deep ache in her heart.

Zara met Raymond at the airport as planned. He had been thrilled to see her and she had been somewhat happy to see him. She wanted someone familiar to help her through this depression she was feeling and Raymond was as good as anyone. She went back with him to the hotel where he was staying, then after he had checked in, they hit the town and the sights. Anything to keep busy and not think of the awful thudding in her heart. Zara was especially glad that Raymond seemed to be even more charming than usual, and she was instantly glad that she had decided not to break up with him. He was not her wonderful Matt, but at least, for now, she was not alone.

As the day progressed, Zara found it increasingly difficult not to think of Matt. She knew she was in the depths of depression about all that had happened. As for Pat, well there were no doubts that they were no longer friends. Just thinking of Pat put her hairs on end. No friend of hers acted that way toward her. And to think her parents had been thrilled when they had announced the news. It was too much to bear. And there was no way that was she attending their wedding. No way. She'd rather kill herself first.

Zara was still brooding on her refusal to go to the wedding when, as she turned the corner, she saw them. Standing close together, on the corner of the street, holding hands. Pat was beaming from ear to ear, and Zara would never forget the look of love written on Matt's face. It was there for the whole world to see. And all reserved for Pat. She turned away in disgust. She did not want to see them. It was like rubbing salt into her open wounds.

Zara looked at her watch and knew she would have to leave soon. Rehearsals were at 11:00 a.m. They continued down the small street, Raymond oblivious to Zara's boiling anger. They passed a small chocolate shop, its rich warm smells wading down the street, then a florist, with all sorts of exotic arrangements in the window. Zara pretended great interest in them by looking through the shop windows. And then she saw it. A solution to her frustrations. Before them stood a place where they could hire motorbikes. Yes, yes, yes. This was exactly what she needed. She looked at her watch again and knew she did not have the time. Helen would be expecting her within half an hour. Suddenly, she did not care about rehearsals. She had had enough. It was time to do what she wanted. Helen could go to hell. "Want to do something exciting?" she asked Raymond mischievously.

"Always," he replied a glint in his eye. She pointed toward the motorbikes, a questioning look on her face. Raymond smiled back broadly. "Hell, yes," he replied.

Twenty minutes later they had their motorbike. It was a big silver Honda, newly shined with large curving handlebars. Zara strapped on her yellow helmet excitedly. Yes, this was perfect and exactly what she needed to help take her mind of things. All she cared for now was having the wind blowing in her hair and feeling as free as a bird in the sky. She'd deal with Helen later. In fact, she might even miss tomorrow's last rehearsal too. That would show her. No one told Zara Maddox what to do. She laughed aloud as she thought of Helen's face when she did not show. It would be priceless.

Raymond eased on his helmet, and then got onto the bike. "Hop on," he said.

Zara obliged without hesitation and held Raymond tightly around the waist. He switched on the engine, revved it for a second or two, and then they sped off. The power of the motorcycle was strong, and it reared them forward with a great mighty force. Zara could feel the rush of wind as it hit her face almost immediately, even with the helmet on. She laughed out loud again. This was perfect.

Raymond was an accomplished driver. He zoomed in and out of the traffic like an expert. Zara loved every second of it. It was brilliant. It was exactly what she wanted, to feel the wind against her skin. Soon her hair came loose and it was flying wildly behind her as they drove on down the streets.

They left the highway and were soon travelling through the little country lanes. Raymond got braver and braver on the bike, but Zara did not mind. She held on tighter and egged him on. The feeling was totally exhilarating. "Faster," she yelled into his ear. "Faster." The motorcycle, whipped forward and she laughed again. The speed was fantastic. Like she was flying through air. Her stomach was high in the sky and she felt like she was floating as they took corner after corner. Zara closed her eyes and enjoyed the air rushing into her face and the speed of the adrenalin in her veins.

They drove fast and hit a rock. The bike stumbled awkwardly, as Raymond fought to regain control. Then they skidded, and within seconds, they were thrown from the motorcycle and were flying through the air. Zara was catapulted high into the sky and thrown into the nearby bushes. Leaves and twigs whipped her soft arms and branches scratched her face. Eventually she came to a stop as she hit against something hard and solid.

Zara lay unmoving, winded by the sudden crash. She blinked hard but all she could see was tiny black dots. She closed her eyes and concentrated on breathing, then opened her eyes again. She turned her head, which took a great effort, and looked for Raymond. He was on his knees, his clothes ripped, crawling over toward her. She tried to sit up and crawl toward him too. And then, that is when she felt her ankle rip. The scream that tore through the calm fields was undeniably Zara's.

Chapter 48

Jane was in her bedroom and entirely amazed by Zara, who still had not surfaced. Where was the girl? Did she have no idea how lucky she was to have been chosen for such a prestigious role. She had been hand-picked as the lead. Chosen out of ALL of them. Jane could not understand how anyone could take that for granted. It was unbelievable. She'd been given the best opportunity possible and she was blowing it.

Helen had arrived back at the hostel and had locked herself in her office. No one had seen her since and everyone was aware that she was furious with Zara.

Jane was getting dressed for afternoon tea in town with her parents when her bedroom door burst open.

Helen stood in the doorway, hot and flustered. "Do you want the lead role?" she asked. Jane was not sure she had heard correctly. Helen walked in quickly and sat down on her bed, then continued, slower. "Zara has had an accident. She has taken a fall from a motorbike and broken her ankle and ripped the muscles in her leg." Jane remained motionless. "Jane? Do you understand what I am saying? What I am asking?" Helen asked her. Jane nodded her head. "Zara will not be able to perform. She is out and I need another lead dancer to take her place. Otherwise, we are finished. Do *you* want the role?" She asked the last sentence very slowly.

Jane could not take in Helen's words fast enough. Then it hit her all at once. Zara. Broken leg. Lead role. *HER* dancing that lead role. She must have found her voice, as before she even registered what she was saying she nodded, and shouted! "YES. YES. Yes, I want the lead role."

Helen visibly slumped with relief. "Okay. Good. Now come with me. We have two days. You will have to learn Zara's part in that time. Are you sure you're up for this kind of challenge?" Helen asked.

Jane nodded and smiled. Oh, yes, she was more than up for it. As they made their way to the training rooms, Jane tried to take in the news and what this meant for her. The endless possibilities this opened up. More unbelievable still, was Zara. Zara on a motorbike? Anyone involved in anything this important would know that you kept away from any and all dangerous sports. It was an unspoken rule. There was always a possibility of something dreadful like this happening and now it had. Zara's chance was gone. What on earth had she been thinking?

Jane stayed with Helen and danced throughout the afternoon, going right through into early evening. She had watched and envied Zara so many times and without realizing it, she had picked up many of the steps. She heard the familiar music and the movements just seemed to come naturally.

Jane managed to grasp the first solo piece without any problems. They continued to practice the steps, over and over again, until Jane felt her hair wet with sweat. Dinner approached quickly and she had to call her parents to cancel with them. At first they were disappointed, but once she had explained why, they had been thrilled at her good fortune. She herself had a quick bite to eat, then was back in the studio. Helen and Velicity took turns teaching her throughout the night. They did not stop until she had the second solo mastered down to perfection. It was well past two in the morning when she finally stumbled back into her bedroom, exhausted.

* * * * *

Helen's entire day had been a rollercoaster. She had been so embarrassed when Zara had failed to turn up for practices and then furious that she had been let down at the last minute. It was all especially bad, since Zara had not been her first choice in the first place. When she had arrived back at the hostel, there had been a message from Zara's parents and then things had really begun to crumble. Without a lead, she was unsure how they would proceed. It was only due to Jane that she had any sanity left.

Helen was once again amazed by that girl. She was totally dedicated and astounded that Jane had picked up so much from just watching Zara over the weeks. It proved that Jane was very talented indeed.

The next morning, Helen snuck into Jane's bedroom and woke her up grudgingly. It was very early, only five a.m. and still dark outside. Helen gave her a gentle shake, knowing Jane would still be tired since she had only managed a few hours sleep.

Jane woke immediately and slipped out of bed without complaint. She took a long overdue shower, then headed back to the training rooms for more practising.

Rehearsals for that day had been booked for late in the afternoon and this took on a new meaning for Jane. She was more nervous than she had ever been before. All the girls had found out about Zara and her "unfortunate" accident and there was a lot of speculating and worried glances. No one actually thought that it was possible for *anyone* to learn all the steps required in such a short time. Jane knew their doubts and understood them and it only made her more nervous. She was confident that she could do it, but at the same time she was apprehensive. This first practice would be her test.

That afternoon they ran through the entire procession as normal and before Jane knew it, it was their group's turn to take the field.

The music began, and Jane found herself running through the tunnel. It felt strange, running through on her own. She was used to having all the other girls with her and dancing as a group. She left the tunnel and took her place in the middle of the field as she had seen Zara do countless times before. She was very aware of the lighting crew following her with a large white light, that kept growing bigger and bigger, as it focussed on her in the centre. Jane concentrated hard and tried to block out everything else. Her piece began. She hesitated. It was only for a second, and then she was dancing. She danced the solo with all the energy she could muster, knowing everyone was watching and assessing her every move, comparing her to Zara. She finished, held her position and waited for the others to join her, then they all danced together.

She finished the final piece alone and ran back toward the tunnel delighted. She knew she had done it perfectly and she felt like she was on top of the world. It was the most amazing feeling she had ever felt.

Helen sat on the sidelines and watched in awe. Jane was magnificent. For the first time since she had heard the news, she knew that things were going to be all right. It had been a stressful two days. When it was confirmed that Zara had been in a motorcycle accident and had broken her leg, Helen had thought it was all over. Her lead gone. There was simply no time to find a replacement with only two days remaining. The thought almost made her faint. And then she thought of all the other girls. Working so hard all these weeks, to have the opportunity ripped out from under them at the very last minute. It was too unfair. This was all the result of Zara's reckless and uncaring nature.

And then she thought of Jane. Her name seemed to have been whispered to her, like a breath of fresh air entering the room. She was not quite sure why Jane had not come into her mind straight away. It must have been the shock she was feeling when she had received the unfortunate news. She knew that what she was asking of Jane was immense, but it was their only chance.

Helen had been nervous proposing her idea to Jane. It was an enormous responsibility, but she knew the girl could do it. Jane had proven to be everything Helen knew she was. Eager and dedicated.

Helen knew that she was pushing Jane. Pushing harder than she had ever pushed anyone in her life. It was imperative that Jane get the steps correct before the night was through. She was the perfect pupil. Willing and eager to learn, pushing herself beyond what she had ever seen before. For someone who had never danced these particular steps before, Helen knew she was doing brilliantly. They worked hard through the rest of the day and right into the night. Helen knew she must be tired, but not once did Jane utter a single word of complaint. She danced each step as it was her first. She did not stagger. Did not let her tiredness show. It was amazing, and Helen was glad that Jane was finally getting the opportunity she deserved.

Now, as she watched Jane, with only one day's practice behind her, she was mesmerized. She had never known anyone to pick up anything so quickly and work so hard to achieve something. As she danced on the field, alone for the first time, Helen was silent in wonderment. It looked as if the role had been made for her. No one could believe that she had only been practising for one day. Even Helen had not expected this kind of success. She had just hoped that Jane could do it, not expecting that Jane *would* do it, and do it extremely well. For the first time in her career, Helen was stunned into silence. Jane seemed to flow like liquid and moved well with the music. It was at that precise moment that Helen knew. Even without this lead role, Jane would have made it and become world famous. With only one day's proper practice behind her, she was already better than Zara had ever been. It was truly amazing.

Chapter 49

The big night had arrived. Jane checked her makeup in the large golden mirror again. She knew it was perfect, but checking it again gave her something to do. It had taken the makeup artists hours and hours to get through everyone that needed doing. Luckily though, she had been one of the last dancers to take the small chair and wait while the artists performed their magic. A small mercy. The thick makeup was renowned for making your skin itch. The later it was applied, the better.

The noise from outside seemed to get louder and louder as time progressed. Jane wished she could leave the dressing room and go outside and see the stadium. See all the people coming in and taking their seats. Unfortunately, none of the performers were permitted to do so and the entrance of the tunnel had been heavily guarded since early that morning. Security was tight. Unless you had the correct authorization, you were not allowed anywhere near any of the performers and any of the equipment. Not even her parents had been able to get in to see her. The organizers had gone to great lengths to enforce that everything ran smoothly and was tightly protected. Still, Jane wished she could at least take a small peek outside. She knew her family had arrived already and could imagine them sitting in their seats, taking in the lights and the excitement of the growing crowed. Again, she wished she was out there with them, experiencing every moment.

The time for the show to start soon approached and Jane had to admit that she felt oddly calm. She had thought she would be shivering with nervousness and that by now, the butterflies she always got would be fluttering like mad. Instead, she felt nothing. Normally before an exam, she also could not eat any food either and could just about manage a few small sips of water. Today, she had surprised herself with her appetite and had eaten quite a generous helping of lunch. That had never happened before. Her anticipation of being a nervous wreck dissolved into nothing.

She did not feel nervous, but her head was still reeling at the prospect of actually doing the prestigious entrance and exit solo pieces. What an honour. She was thrilled to bits. This really was her chance to shine. She knew she should not wish any ill on Zara, but of all the stupid things for anyone to do, this had to take the cake. Zara's loss had been her gain and she was determined to make the most of what was given to her. She knew she might never get another opportunity like this again.

"Can you apply some more hair spray to the back of my bun?" asked Susan, as she played with the can in her hands.

"Sure," replied Sue, "give it here." Jane watched in the mirror as Sue applied even more hair spray to Susan's hair. She was positive that nothing was going to move that bun on her head. It was so rock solid, held by more clips and hair spray, than an entire salon. Jane laughed. She understood their nervousness. She had been there many times before.

They had about an hour before the show actually started. Everyone seemed to be getting more and more nervous as the time drew closer and closer. They began fiddling with their hair, then their costumes. Jane knew she should be feeling the same nervousness, but for some bizarre reason, she still felt nothing. Just sheer excitement and a strange calmness, that was still very much evident. It was a nice feeling. Totally foreign, but nonetheless, still nice. As the time approached, there was nothing left to do except watch the clock on the wall and listen to the hum of people outside growing steadily louder and louder.

They all knew the time had arrived, but when the very first song began to play, it did not stop them from jumping with a frightened start. The first procession was about to enter. The roar of clapping from the expectant audience had all the girls on their feet. This was it. They stood and listened to what was happening outside, wishing they could see. Never before had they heard anything so loud or thunderous. The deafening noise seemed to vibrate throughout the entire changing room.

From that very first procession time seemed to fly rapidly for Jane. One minute she was listening to the roar of people clapping and the next she was concentrating on her breathing, about to enter the mighty field herself.

She had still thought the butterflies and weak knees would arrive, but the strange calmness that she had been feeling all afternoon was still with her. She was completely in control. In that moment she had known there would be no nervousness. No butterflies. Not this time. She was made for this moment.

Her music began to play, and on cue she ran. Through the tunnel, past the security guards and onto the centre of the field. The large light beamed down onto her as the crowd clapped in tune to her music. As she danced her first solo piece she noted all the people sitting in the stands around her. They looked like a haze of colourful, tiny dots, very far away. She kicked high and danced energetically and realized that she was enjoying herself immensely. Even now, on the field, in front of millions of people and dozens of cameras broadcasting to all corners of the earth, she felt no nervousness. None at all. Her piece came to an end and there was another deafening roar of clapping. She was unable to stop her brilliant wide smile, as she waited for the rest of the girls to join her so they could continue with their group piece.

She knew that from afar their sequined costumes would be dazzling the spectators and the lights would be catching them at every magnificent angle. The variety and complexity of the lighting, would be mesmerizing everyone present. She felt like she had never danced as well as she had before that night. All her movements felt easy and rhythmic. She was achieving everything she had ever hoped to achieve. Her kicks were high, well above her head, her arches almost touching the ground and still she felt like it was the easiest, most natural thing in the world.

And then, as if in slow motion, the girls ran toward the exit and she was alone again on the field. She took her practised position, waited for her cue with the music and continued to dance her solo piece as the lights changed again into a burst of sparkles in the night. Then all too soon, she found her solo piece also coming to an end. She did her last final leap high in the air and ran back inside the tunnel.

*****

A full week later, Jane found herself back at home. It was all over. When she thought of that night she knew, without a doubt, that she had been involved in something amazingly special. A once in a lifetime event. She had watched the video and was amazed at the total effect of the entire show. The lights were spectacular, the costumes dazzling and the music perfect for what they had all wanted to achieve. The gymnasts, the ponies, all the well-rehearsed shows had all blended together perfectly. Then, unexpectedly at the very end, there came a surprise for everyone, as fireworks took to the heavens. Big rockets that lit up the black velvet sky in a maze of colours. Pink splashes as far as the eye could see, followed by a fountain of blue, proceeded by blots of sparkling yellow and dazzling green dashes. The wonderful display had lasted a full half an hour. Everyone, even the organizers who had known about the fireworks display, had stood mesmerized by the total beauty of it all. And only after the very last fireworks hit the sky did the event finally come to an end.

When Jane watched the video taken, she had been very critical of her own performance, but even she had to admit she had done well. Very well. She looked like she had been born into the part. She walked over to the kitchen counter and fingered the two white letters. She already had two amazing offers. One for a West End show in London, and another for a weekend musical due to run for a full year. Jane beamed with excitement. If she played her cards right, she just might be able to accept both.

Jacqueline Bell was born in Port Elizabeth, South Africa, in 1978, before emigrating to London at the age of nineteen where she began a career in Futures and Options, a division of Investment Banking. *Fierce Rivals* was inspired by her background in dance and love for music.

Printed in the United States
66584LVS00003B/150